Places I've Never Been

A BELLAMY SISTERS ROMANCE

MELINDA VANLONE

Written House

Nothing lasts forever. Mattie Bellamy learned that lesson for the first time when she was eight years old, when she found out the hard way that parents weren't invincible. Her mom was dead, and life would never, ever be the same.

The happily-ever-after of fairy tales never actually existed.

So Mattie focused on the fleeting moments of life and tried to capture them in words that she turned into songs that she and her sisters sang. It was her way of making sense of the world.

When her first boyfriend broke her heart, she wrote about it.

When her family sang for the first time on stage, she wrote about it.

When her father died, she wrote about it.

She processed all of her life experiences in notebooks that she carried with her everywhere so that if inspiration struck like a butterfly in spring, she could capture it before it flitted away.

Years later, she and her sisters had taken those songs an'

turned them into a life filled with the things she loved most in the world: travel, family, and music.

Then one day, the now world-famous pop sensations Bellamy Sisters sang the last note of the last encore of their last tour, not that she knew it at the time. Mattie led the way off stage, like she always did, followed by her sisters Piper and Della, still so high on the music that she wanted to laugh and cry at the same time.

Lizzie waited for them backstage with a face full of pride and love and joy. "That last song was perfect. Fantastic job, all of you."

Mattie threw her arms around her sister and hugged her tight. "Thanks. You inspired it, so of course it is."

Lizzie rolled her eyes. "I inspired a song about a man magnet?"

Piper laughed. "Pretty sure you're the exact opposite of that."

Mattie shook her head. "No, no, it's her. Just because she's always behind the scenes doesn't mean she doesn't like attention. It just means she doesn't like certain *kinds* of attention."

Della bounced by. "Dibs on the shower!"

Mattie tugged at Lizzie's hand. "Come on. The wrap-up party is in an hour, and I can't go smelling like this."

It took thirty minutes to make it the short distance to the greenroom because people kept stopping them with high-fives, or questions about loading the trucks, or any number of small details.

Lizzie handled the logistics of focusing a small army of roadies the same way she'd handled everything for their family since their mother died. Lizzie was mother hen and cat herder, fixer of problems and cog in their family wheel. The Bellamy Sisters wouldn't be anything at all without her, because it was

Lizzie's suggestion for them to step onto that first stage when they were kids.

While Lizzie wrangled the end of the tour into shape, Piper met with backstage-pass fans, posed for photos with a long line of autograph hounds, and gave a quick interview to the media about the end of their tour. She felt the most important part of their job happened after the show, behind the scenes. Without Piper, The Bellamy Sisters might be popular, but their fans wouldn't feel like the extended family they were now.

Mattie and Della waved at the waiting fans and shook hands with roadies along the way to the greenroom. Mattie loved the music, but she found the one-on-one interactions exhausting. Della treated the backstage antics of fans and roadies just like she did everything else in her life—with enthusiasm. She found joy, on or off the stage, simply being around people, but she didn't feel the need to linger with them the way Piper did.

Della and Mattie managed to make it to the greenroom, shower, and get mostly dressed by the time Lizzie and Piper showed up.

Lizzie flopped down onto the couch with a loud sigh of relief. "Can't believe the tour is done. I'm going to sleep for a month. Two months maybe."

"No time for that," Piper said as she peeled off her sequined vest and tossed it aside. "We have a new album to work on."

Della bopped back and forth in front of them like an excited Chihuahua. "I have something to tell you."

Mattie sensed something more than normal post-show excitement in Della's tone. "What's going on?"

"Can it wait?" Piper said as she peeled off her skintight stage pants. "Some of us still need showers."

3

Mattie gave Lizzie a quizzical look. Lizzie looked as confused as Mattie felt.

"I need to tell you this before I explode." Della shook out her hands and bounced on her tiptoes. "Come on, it'll just take a second."

Piper flicked her hand in a hurry-up gesture.

Something flickered across Della's face. Doubt? Anxiety?

Mattie knew in that fraction of a second that she wasn't going to like what she was about to hear.

"I signed with Self Evident Records," Della blurted. "They're going to produce my first solo album."

White noise filled Mattie's ears. Time slipped sideways. The surreal moment stretched and twisted and bent around Della's shining face until she looked like a character in a cartoon.

Della continued to bounce and smile, as excited as she was the day they'd gotten their first puppy. "Finally, *finally*, I'll be taken seriously. I'll get to do stuff with more edge, more *adult*. I can't wait."

Mattie tried to process what she was hearing. Her youngest sister had always been the center of attention, both in their family and on stage. When people thought of The Bellamy Sisters, they pictured Della first. Mattie had always known that, and it didn't bother her. All that mattered was the music. But her thoughts raced ahead to the next logical step on this roller coaster her sister had just thrust them onto without consent: Della couldn't go solo and still be a Bellamy Sister.

With one stroke of a pen and a flippant announcement, Della had changed their careers forever, and she hadn't even talked to them before she'd done it.

Just like that, life as they knew it was over.

The future stretched out like an enormous blank wall that

Mattie couldn't climb, couldn't go around, couldn't see through.

If they weren't The Bellamy Sisters anymore, what were they?

Mattie exchanged looks with Piper and Lizzie.

Della's smile faltered. "Well? Aren't you going to congratulate me?"

Piper found her voice first. "You can't be serious."

Della stopped pacing next to one of the dressing tables and thrust out her chin in the defiant way she'd done ever since she was a toddler. "I signed the papers yesterday."

"Yesterday." Lizzie's voice was breathy and high pitched, not at all like her usual take-charge tone. "Renic signed you yesterday? How long has he been talking to you about this?"

"This is bullshit," Piper's voice rose, loud enough to make Mattie wince.

"Why?" Della glared at Piper. "Why is it bullshit, Piper? Because you didn't think of it first?"

"Because you didn't think *at all*." Piper squared off in front of Della. "You never think about anything but yourself, you spoiled, selfish brat."

"Let's just...everybody, calm down." Lizzie raised her hands in a placating manner. "Before someone says something they really regret."

Piper whirled to face Lizzie. "You *know* this is the most self-centered thing she's ever done, and that's saying something considering it's Della. She's just wrecked all our lives without even *asking* us. Without telling us anything. This is what happens when you treat someone like they're the baby. They act like one."

"Hey!" Della shoved Piper.

Lizzie stepped in between the two. "Back off. Both of you."

Mattie felt like she was moving through a molasses-filled

nightmare. One word kept circling around her brain until finally she found her own voice. "Why?"

Della swiveled in Mattie's direction. "Why? Because *finally* I'll be treated like an adult. I'm tired of always having to be what everyone else wants me to be. Renic says if we keep going the way we've been going, I'll be stuck as a pop princess forever. I'm more than this. *We* are."

"More than what?" Piper's voice rose. "More than us? You just kicked what we've built together to the curb with no more thought than you'd give to spitting out a used piece of gum. Did you think about how the fans will take this at all?"

"Piper...Della," Lizzie said in her soothing Mom tone that she used whenever they squabbled as kids. "We all need to calm down."

Piper and Della didn't even notice.

"And stop blaming Renic. This has your selfish fingerprints all over it." Piper's voice was rough and low, and her eyes flashed with dangerous light.

The tension was so thick Mattie found it hard to breathe. "Hey...you guys...can we just talk about this?"

She might as well have been invisible.

Piper and Della sparred like this every now and then over the years, but underneath the bickering was a firm foundation of love and support. Piper and Della weren't just sisters, they were best friends.

But now Mattie could feel that bedrock crumbling with every word. The pieces of it broke off and dragged her down, down, down with them.

Della lifted her chin in defiance, oblivious to the pain behind the anger in her sister's eyes. "You're just jealous that I have the guts to make a big change and you don't. You've always been jealous of me. You can't stand it that my voice is better than yours. I always get the spotlight, and it drives you crazy."

Mattie gasped. She covered her mouth with both hands, but it didn't stop the pressure that built in her chest.

"Della!" Lizzie's voice was sharp and stern. "You don't mean that. You know you don't. Both of you take a breath and back off."

"Yes, she does," Piper said. Her voice was rough and thick and nothing like her normal rich alto. "Look at her. She means every word. Hell, she's probably been planning that speech for years. I have news for you, *little* sister, I wouldn't have to fight for a spotlight if you knew how to share. And if your voice is so damn perfect, why do the fans always want to interview me instead of you? If you knew how to make a genuine connection, you wouldn't *need* to go solo."

"Please..." Mattie clutched her throat. It felt like someone was choking her from the inside out. "Please stop fighting."

Della breathed like she was in the middle of a difficult dance number. Piper's dig had struck a deep nerve. "Oh bite me. I don't *need* to go solo, I want to because I'm sick of you constantly dragging me back into the shadows just so you can steal the glory. I'm sick of having to twist into knots so you feel special too."

Piper's head jerked back as if she'd been slapped. From the look in her eyes, there would be no coming back from this fight.

"Screw you, Della," Piper snarled. "Someday you'll wake the hell up and realize what you did today, and you'll come crawling back to us, crying about how sorry you are. I'm telling you now. Don't bother. As far as I'm concerned, we aren't sisters anymore. I don't even know who you are. You're a goddamn stranger."

Piper snatched a pair of pants and a shirt off the rack and stalked out.

"Piper, wait!" Lizzie reached out, but she was too late. The door slammed shut behind Piper, leaving the three of them staring at it in silence.

Mattie shuddered and gasped, but the pain in her chest wouldn't let her breathe. Her family was broken, and she wasn't sure the pieces would ever be mended.

"Bitch." Della whirled away from the door. "She always has to have the last word. She'll get over it."

"You really don't know what you've done, do you?" Lizzie sounded incredibly sad, and the devastation etched lines on her face, making her look older.

Della bit her lip. "I know what I'm doing. I'm not an idiot, and I'm not as naive as you all seem to think I am. Renic has plans for all of us. If she hadn't been so pigheaded I would have explained the rest of it. This will work out great, you'll see."

Mattie couldn't tell if her sister really believed what she was saying, or if she was trying to convince herself. Something tense and desperate bubbled underneath all that bravado. Della wasn't as happy as she appeared to be and probably hadn't been for a long time. Maybe since Dad's funeral. That was when Della's sunny disposition had seemed to tarnish, but Mattie hadn't been able to offer her the support she needed because her own heart had been so devastatingly broken.

The last three years had been rough, but the music pulled them through. At least, she thought it had. Now she wasn't so sure. All the things they left unsaid had festered and spoiled all the good things.

"I don't give a crap about what Renic has planned. This thing that you two cooked up just split up our *family*." Lizzie's voice broke on the word family. "We became The Bellamy Sisters *together*. We made music, we toured the country, we grew up *together*. And now we won't be together anymore. Do you get that?"

Mattie covered her face. The silent tears converted to sobs she just couldn't stop. She couldn't take this. It was her father's death, all over again, only this time there was no car accident, and no drunk driver to blame. The only thing she could blame was her sister, and she didn't want to do that.

"This is stupid," Della said. Her voice was thick now, too. "We're still sisters. We can't change that, no matter what Piper says. It's genetics."

"If you really believed that, then why didn't you talk to us about this first?" Lizzie's arm shook as she put it around Mattie's shoulders. "I always knew you were a little too focused on yourself, Della. I just never realized you were so...so...cruel. It's not like you. You can't go through with this."

"I already did." Mattie heard Della move closer. "Mattie... you get it, don't you?"

Mattie lowered her hands and met Della's gaze through a haze of tears. "No."

Della huffed out a breath. Her face was blotchy, and there were tears in her eyes now, too. "Come on. You have loads of songs nobody will ever hear because Dream Works and Omega won't let us record them. They don't fit our brand." Della stretched out the words with the snotty undertone of a spoiled child. "Don't you think they deserve to be heard? You always say how sad it is, all those words going to waste."

"I didn't mean this." Mattie blinked, but the tears wouldn't stop. She wasn't sure they ever would. "I told you, the songs that really matter are the ones we sing together. Without us, they're just empty words."

Della pressed her lips together and wrapped her arms around herself. "Renic says this will open doors for all of us. You'll see."

"Renic." Lizzie gripped Mattie's shoulders so tight she thought they might break. "This is his fault. We're going over there and fixing this. Now."

No." Della dropped her gaze to the floor and sniffed. "There's nothing to fix. It's done."

"No it's not." Lizzie glanced at Mattie. "Do you want to come with me?"

Mattie shook her head. She was too numb to do much else.

Lizzie picked up her purse. "I'll see you guys at the party."

Mattie almost called her back. Nothing Lizzie did would fix what had just happened, and nothing would ever be the same again. But she knew Lizzie had to try, for her own sake. She was their problem solver and their rock. But it wasn't going to work this time.

Mattie sensed that as sure as she sensed when a song would hit big. It was just something she *knew*, deep down, in the pit of her stomach. Nothing Lizzie could say to Renic would change or fix what had just ripped apart.

She took a deep, shuddering breath. She felt so lost and alone that she thought she might drown.

Della touched her arm. Her eyes pleaded for understanding. "You get why I did it, don't you, Mattie?"

"No." Mattie struggled to make her voice come out steady. "But I guess I don't need to. As you said, it's done. The door is closed on what was. It's true, nothing gold can stay."

"What's that supposed to mean?" Della sat next to her to pull on white tennis shoes trimmed with sparkling laces.

"It's a poem by Robert Frost. It means things change, and all things end. Nothing stays the same forever." Mattie sighed, but the pain in her chest remained. "If this is what makes you happy, then clearly that's the only thing that matters."

A hint of uncertainty flashed through Della's eyes. Then it

vanished, replaced by a spark of determination. "I *am* happy. You will be too. You'll see."

"I guess we all will," Mattie said.

Her tears had slowed, and the deep, stabbing pain in her chest had dulled to an ache she had a feeling would be around for a long time. She picked up her purse, and walked out, leaving Della behind in the empty dressing room.

"I should have known," she told the air. "Nothing lasts forever. Not even us."

Chapter One

FOUR YEARS LATER

M attie Bellamy waited for her sisters in the hidden back patio of her favorite Los Angeles restaurant, The Flower Pot, with barely contained anticipation. This brunch was the first time she'd seen Lizzie and Piper at the same time in nearly four years. Four years was *way* too long to go between group hugs.

Mattie glanced at the three empty chairs. One of them would remain empty, which twisted her heart. Her youngest sister, Della, hadn't been invited to this family reunion.

Most people didn't know there were four Bellamy sisters, because her oldest sister, Lizzie, stayed backstage, organizing, planning, and making sure everything worked. Mattie, Piper, and Della had been the ones out in front, making the music and living the public life. At least, until Della split up their band four years ago.

"Mattie Cake!" Lizzie's voice carried from inside the house out to the patio, a triumphant happy sound. She hovered in the doorway, looking country-girl beautiful in faded jeans and a turquoise top with her rich brown hair pulled back in a wavy ponytail.

"Lizzie!" Mattie jumped up and ran to her sister. They met in a flurry of arms and smiles and fell into a tight, fierce hug. "Missed you!"

"Missed you more. I don't ever want to go a whole year without seeing you in person ever again. It's too long." Lizzie pulled back and looked Mattie over. "Oh my God, look at you. You got bangs! And I love that skirt. You look like an earth fairy. I had no idea you could get this tanned."

Mattie flounced her hair and lifted her face to the sky. "The sun worships me."

Lizzie laughed. "I don't blame it. You actually glow like a goddess."

"I'm just a girl who really loves her rooftop deck. You should come check it out while you're in LA." She grabbed her sister's hand and stared at the flashy new ring that adorned a very special finger. "Video chat doesn't do this thing justice. It's perfect."

Lizzie gazed at the ring with a secretive smile. "It really is."

"Have you and Renic set a date?"

Lizzie's eyes danced with amusement. "Four of them actually. Every time Renic picked a date, there was already an event planned, so I booked every weekend in June next year just in case. That gives me over a year to get it together. I'll have to let some of the days go eventually but I wanted to get everyone's schedules nailed down first."

"Sounds like a solid plan to me. I'll block the whole month too so I can come help you with all the fun prep stuff."

"I'll need all the help I can get." Lizzie offered her a grateful smile. "I swear other people's events have so much less pressure. The bride's never look as frazzled as I feel."

"That's because they have you to plan for them." Mattie let

her go and gestured to the table. "I ordered chips and guacamole while we wait, and they make a great screwdriver. Or they have this new red thing with an umbrella that you might like."

"Give me one of those," a voice called out from the doorway.

They both spun and called out in unison. "Piper!"

Piper strode in wearing dark jeans, a plain white t-shirt, a denim jacket studded with rhinestones, and a cute derby hat. She looked like she was on her way to a biker convention or a country bar.

They fell into a group hug, giggling like kids. Mattie didn't want to let them go, but eventually the server cleared his throat and they settled into chairs at the table. After drinks and more appetizers were ordered, Lizzie sat back with a look like she'd eaten a secret.

"What?" Mattie asked. "I know that face. What's going on?"

Piper glanced back and forth between them, then settled on Lizzie. "Are you pregnant?"

Lizzie's eyebrows rose a full inch, and the look of shock was so genuine that it made Mattie laugh. "What? No. No, I'm *not* pregnant. God no."

Piper smirked. "Why the hell not? You've been together almost a year, might as well get cracking. Besides, you'd have gorgeous, talented kids."

Lizzie shook her head. "No. We're not ready for that. Maybe...no."

Mattie studied her sister. She wouldn't meet her eyes and kept glancing over her shoulder at the door. Something was definitely up.

Mattie's stomach did another flip-flop. "Lizzie, is someone else joining us?"

The look of guilt that flashed over Lizzie's face told her everything she needed to know.

"Is Renic coming?" Piper said. "I thought you said just us girls, but that's fine. He can be one of the girls for a day."

Piper popped a chip in her mouth and chewed, looking relaxed and carefree until she finally noticed how stiff Lizzie sat in her chair. Her chewing slowed to a stop. "It's not Renic, is it."

Lizzie looked down at her drink, then back up. "Please just hear me out before you freak."

"Okay," Piper said, drawing the word out. "You're scaring me."

Mattie glanced at the door. Nobody was there, but she knew any second *someone* would be. They were one sister short. "I thought we decided..."

Lizzie flashed her a pleading look. "It's been a long time since we've all been together, and I miss you. All of you. I miss my family."

"Me too." Piper leaned forward with her elbows on the table. "We should do this more often. But that doesn't explain the guilty eyes. Whatever it is, just spill it."

Lizzie sat up a little straighter and tried to look casual. "I invited Della. She should be here any minute."

Mattie closed her eyes. She should have known Lizzie would do that. There'd been something in her voice the day she called to suggest going to brunch. It was the same tone she'd used to get them to eat vegetables when they were kids.

Lizzie took a long swig of her cocktail and avoided making eye contact.

Piper crossed her arms and scowled. "What the hell did you do that for?"

"Because she's our sister," Lizzie said firmly. "She's family. It's been four years, and life's too short to hold a grudge like this. Besides, were you expecting me to pick sides at my wedding? I want *all* my sisters there."

Mattie took a deep breath and opened her eyes. "You're right."

"I know you—" Lizzie stopped, looking a little stunned. "I'm right?"

Mattie nodded. "Yes. It's been too long. It's okay."

"No it's not," Piper said. "It's not ever going to be okay until she grows the hell up and apologizes for being a selfish bitch."

Lizzie turned a stony gaze on Piper. "Do you even answer the phone when she calls?"

Piper ground her teeth. "That's not fair."

"Hey..." Mattie held out a hand to stop them. "We haven't been together in a long time. Can we please just try to enjoy it?"

Lizzie's gaze softened. "I'm sorry, Mattie. You're right. We're here to have sister time, not to rehash old wounds."

"I don't see how we'll avoid the rehash, especially if you-know-who is coming," Piper said in a low, growly voice.

"Voldemort?" Mattie suggested brightly.

Piper stuck her tongue out at her. "Fine. Because I love you both and you asked me to, I'll sit here and pretend to play nice."

"That's mature." Mattie rolled her eyes.

Della bounced in wearing a flouncy yellow sundress and white flowers in her gold hair. She could have just stepped off stage or maybe a beauty pageant. She beamed at them all and held her arms out wide. "Sisters!"

Piper swore under her breath.

Mattie cringed. She could feel the air thicken with tension.

"Della!" Lizzie sprang up from her chair and wrapped Della in a warm hug.

Mattie heard them whispering but couldn't make out what they said. She looked at Piper. Her sister's face had turned into a thundercloud. Piper stared so hard at Della that Mattie wouldn't have been surprised if Della's head exploded.

Lizzie and Della finished their conversation and came back to the table. Lizzie sat and gestured to Della.

Della gripped the back of the last empty chair but didn't sit. Her smile remained sunny, but there were lines of strain in the middle of her forehead. She looked at Mattie first, then her gaze drifted to Piper, where it lingered. "I know this is awkward. I know you weren't expecting me to be here, and I know what you're probably thinking, and I just want you to know this isn't Lizzie's fault."

"Of course not," Piper muttered. "Lizzie actually cares about other people's feelings." She drummed her fingers on the table, then looked up to meet Della's gaze. "Why are you here? What do you want?"

Della's smile fizzled. "I'm here because I wanted to see you. All of you. I...I miss you."

Mattie's heart melted a little. Maybe the separation had been just as hard on Della as it had been on the rest of them. Maybe her little sister was growing up.

Piper threw one arm over the back of her chair like she was in a bar. "Oh really? Why? I hear your solo career is going gangbusters. That tour you're finishing up must have been a blast, what with all those strangers dancing around your every whim. Why would you need to see us?"

"Piper," Lizzie snapped. "Let her talk. Please."

Piper flicked a glance at Lizzie, then at Mattie. "You're okay with this? You interested in what she has to say?"

Mattie pressed her lips together. It was as if they were right back in the greenroom, and the fight that started so many years ago was still going. Except it wasn't years ago. It was today. She was four years older and wiser, and she *hated* fighting. She nodded.

"Fine. For you and Lizzie, I'll listen." Piper gestured with one lazy flick of her wrist. "Go ahead. Talk."

Della flashed her a look of annoyance. "Thanks for your permission, Pipsqueak."

Lizzie cleared her throat. "Della. Say what you came here to say."

Della traced the back of the chair. "I came to say the song I wrote, you know, the bonus single? It was for you. All of you. I was hoping...I thought maybe...I mean, did you listen to it?" She bit her lip, the way she used to do as a child when she'd done something wrong.

Piper countered the plea in her sister's voice with a cold retort. "Is this supposed to be an apology? Because if it is, it sucks."

Mattie thought about the song. The words that had stuck with her were simple, direct, and filled with raw emotion.

> *Would you listen, would you hear me*
> *If I said that I was sorry. I was wrong.*

Mattie would have known the song was for them even if Lizzie hadn't sent the backstage recording of Della performing it live. The meaning behind the words was clear to anyone who knew what was going on. It was part of what helped her push past the hurt she'd carried around for years. "It's a really good song, Della."

A grateful smile flittered across Della's lips and vanished. "It's okay. It would be better if you wrote it. You're better with words."

Mattie shook her head. "No, it wouldn't. The story was yours to tell, not mine. You did great."

Piper pushed her chair away from the table. "Oh please. You're really letting her off that easy? She writes one song and suddenly it's all better? Does she even know what she did wrong?"

Della turned to Piper. "I screwed up, okay? Is that what you want to hear? I thought I needed...wanted...I went the wrong direction. I *know* that."

"You still don't get it." Piper's voice rose. "All these years later you still haven't figured out that the part you got wrong has nothing to do with going solo and everything to do with you *not talking to us about it first.*"

Mattie's stomach twisted and churned. She was beginning to regret the Bloody Mary. The alcohol left a sour taste in her mouth, or maybe it was the family drama. Her own words came back to haunt her.

Nothing lasts forever, not even us.

She looked around the table, from Piper's stony anger to Della's desperate defensiveness to Lizzie's pained patience, and wondered if this rift in her family would be the one thing that *would* last forever. "This isn't getting us anywhere. Can we just calm down and talk like adults?"

"Let me finish. Please." Della said. "I just wanted to tell you all that I was wrong, and you were right. I talked with Renic and told him you win. I want The Bellamy Sisters back together."

Piper wrinkled her forehead. "I win? What the hell is that supposed to mean?"

"No. Not you." Della's nervous laugh sounded too high and sharp. She swept her arm from left to right as if including the whole patio. "All of you. Us. We all win, together. I want us together."

Lizzie moaned softly and rubbed her temples. "Della, that's not what we talked about."

"We...win." The words repeated over and over in Mattie's mind like a fire alarm rung by a crazed clown. "We win. We win?"

"Yeah, like we've all been playing a giant game of poker for the last four years, except all I remember is Della leaving us with a handful of crap." Piper narrowed her eyes. "What do you mean you want The Bellamy Sisters back together?"

Della rolled her eyes. "I mean I want us to be *us* again."

"We...win," Mattie repeated, still stuck on the concept that they'd all just been playing a game for the last four years. "We win what?"

Della continued as if Mattie hadn't said anything. "None of you wanted me to go solo and I've realized you were right. It was a bad call. So I told Renic I won't do any more solo albums, and I want to get our band back together. Even the crew. As many as we can anyway. It'll be great. We'll all be happy, just like we used to be."

Della's announcement landed in front of Mattie with a loud, blood-rushing-in-the-ears thud.

She was aware of Piper and Lizzie talking, or shouting, but their words blurred together and became noise. Time expanded like a balloon while Mattie processed the words "you win."

The day Della had announced she was going solo was one of the worst days of Mattie's life, topped only by the deaths of her mother and father. Now Della flounced back into their lives as if no time at all had passed and nothing had gone wrong and it all had been just fun and games.

Her sister hadn't grown up at all.

Something inside Mattie snapped.

She stood up so fast her chair tipped over. "No."

All eyes turned to her.

Lizzie had a hand on Della's arm as if she were trying to

keep her from speaking, or leaving, or doing whatever it was Della most felt like doing.

"What?" Della asked.

"No. You're not doing that to me—to us—again." Once the words started tumbling out she couldn't stop them, or the anger that bubbled out with them. Everything she'd thought that day, and every day since—everything she'd felt but hadn't told anyone—came spilling out. "You ripped our lives apart and now you're here trying to say, 'Sorry, my bad,' like that's all it takes? You turned my life upside down, and you didn't even ask me. Like my opinion didn't matter. Like *I* didn't matter. Do you have any idea what happened after that? Do you have any clue what I've faced since then? Do you even care?"

Della's eyes widened, and her lips parted, but Mattie rushed on.

"I spent a year wondering what the hell to do with myself, with no energy to even try to write a song. You get that? It took me a damn year to get past that little stunt of yours. It took a lot of effort to find my feet and get my voice back, only to find myself facing a wall of assholes who thought *the studio* wrote the songs instead of me. I've spent the last two years building my career songwriter. I've finally started to gain some sort of reputation, not just as a Bellamy Babe but an honest-to-God talent. But you don't know about any of that, do you, because you don't give a shit about anyone else's life. All you care about is yourself."

Hot tears spilled down her cheeks. She brushed them away, but more took their place.

"Mattie—" Della said.

"You don't get to waltz in here and demand we all jump like nothing happened. You wanted to live life on *your* terms. Well, guess what? When you dumped us, we all had to learn to live life on *our* own terms too, and I've learned that lesson really well. You think I'd hook my future to yours now and just hope you wouldn't change your mind again? No, Della. You don't get to un-ring that bell. For once in your spoiled life you have to live with the consequences of your decisions."

"Mattie—" Della said. Her voice cracked, and her eyes widened as if she saw an oncoming train and couldn't move out of the way.

"Save it." Mattie picked up her purse with shaking hands. She brushed the tears off her cheeks again. She'd done enough crying over the years, and she was done with all of it. "You have to be the most selfish person on the entire planet if you thought you could just simper and bat your eyelashes at us and it would all be okay. It's never, *ever* going to be okay that you ripped my heart out and didn't even notice. I just...I'm done."

Della's face crumpled. She looked devastatingly pretty in the middle of the beautiful flower-filled space, like the tragic heroine of an old movie.

Mattie felt the tug of her sister's distress, and for half a second concern replaced anger. Then anger came to her rescue and the urge to comfort Della vanished, replaced with bitter resolve.

Mattie stalked to the door, determined to get away from the pain, the hurt, and the sadness before they ripped yet another hole in her heart.

"Mattie," Lizzie called. "Wait. Please...don't leave."

She turned back. "I'm sorry, Lizzie. I can't do this."

Mattie caught Piper's eye. "See you later, okay?"

Piper looked stunned and a little proud. She touched her cap in salute and nodded.

Mattie brushed past the server and stormed out of the restaurant on a wave of fury, leaving absolute silence in her wake.

Chapter Two

Adam Brooks stood in the cramped lobby of his band's Los Angeles recording studio and stared at the text his dad had just sent with exasperation.

It won't work. It has a pool.

He'd been trying to buy his parents a new house for the past two years. The place they lived in now had been beaten up by years of kids, dogs, and general living. His dad was close to retirement, and his mother had always dreamed of traveling. Adam wanted to give them the easy retirement they deserved, and the first step to that was a house they didn't have to constantly update.

His mother was excited by the idea and had embraced the house hunting trips with relish. His dad, however, found an excuse to say no to every option they found. The yard was too big or too small, the plumbing too old or too new, the floors creaked, the walls were crooked, it smelled, the bedroom faced the wrong way—that one had totally thrown Adam—the list went on and on.

Adam shook his head and texted back. *What's wrong with a pool? Swimming is good for you.*

Dots indicated his dad was responding. He waited.

"Dude," His brother Brandon called. "We got the new track queued up. You coming?"

Brandon was three years younger and three inches taller, but they shared the same black hair and dark brown eyes they'd inherited from their mother, and the lopsided grin they got from their father. They also appeared to share terrible luck with women, since neither of them had kept a girlfriend more than a couple of months. Brandon had managed to get married once in Vegas, but it had been annulled the next day, so it didn't really count.

"Yeah," Adam shouted back. "In a sec."

Their band, Delusions of Glory, was in the studio trying to find yet another new writing partner to help them finish the last three songs for the new album. The process had been tedious, mind-numbing torture so far. Maybe they should just release what they had. Would anyone notice three fewer songs?

Finally, the reply text chimed. *More trouble than it's worth.*

"Seriously?" Adam rolled his eyes, shoved his phone in his back pocket, and went into the studio. "Who the hell doesn't like a pool?"

"Everybody likes pools." Cooper Peady, Adam's best friend since grade school and the cofounder of the band, looked up from the soundboard and grinned. He usually played lead guitar and provided backup vocals, but he also had a passion for technology and made an excellent wingman at parties. "Especially if there's ladies in bikinis around it."

"Don't need a pool when you got the ocean right there," Lucas Austerberry, their manager, said. He was almost fifty, with graying hair and the greedy smile of a used car salesman, but he'd been instrumental in taking Delusions of Glory from good local band to international sensation.

They now had four platinum albums and three Grammys on their resumes, along with merchandising, endorsement deals, and a video game, thanks in large part to the way Lucas helped them make the most of every opportunity. The man had found ways to turn one song from an unknown high school band into a franchise and he'd done it in under three years. If he seemed pushy and aggressive, well, it was helpful to have a shark on your side, especially in the music business, and Lucas had always done right by them.

Drummer Flynn Mackie, with spiked blond hair and arms covered with tattoos, tapped out a rhythm on the back of a chair. "Can we get on with this? I got a date later. Me and that girl I met at the bar are going to see the new Bond movie. She had a bit part as a maid or something."

Flynn had been Brandon's best friend since they were in diapers. Adam hadn't been so sure about including him in the band at the beginning, but he'd come to respect the man's skill with the sticks, and he'd grown fond of his wild and crazy ways over the years. Flynn always brought life to any party and reason to any argument, and he was always, *always*, on time. It was a quality Adam wished would rub off on Brandon.

Adam gestured at the soundboard. "Queue it up. I'm listening." He settled down on the couch next to LT Sullivan, their bassist.

LT grinned. "You ain't gonna like it, man. We should probably stop now."

Lucas held up a hand. "Hey, don't start dissing it before he even hears it."

Adam frowned. "What makes you say that?"

LT shrugged. "Just a feelin' I got. No reason."

"Hm." Adam grunted and closed his eyes. LT was enjoying

this a little too much, which meant he knew something. "I can't reject until I hear it, that's the rule."

"Uh-huh," LT said, amusement providing a million layers of subtext to the simple expression.

"Okay, gentlemen," Lucas said. "Keep in mind this is just an audition piece. If you like the style, I'll get Rachel in here to work on the real thing with you. She's available this week and next."

"Rachel?" Adam's chest tightened, and his eyes flew open. "Are you talking about Rachel Saunders? The blonde with big, er, assets?"

LT chuckled. "Told ya."

Lucas nodded. "She said she'd worked with you before, so I figured you'd at least listen to the whole song before you shot holes in it."

Adam groaned. "We should move on. Now."

Brandon snorted. "Dude, they didn't work together. They banged each other nonstop for three weeks and then ditched each other like yesterday's fish."

"Yeah," Cooper said. He wrinkled his nose as if the fish were in the trash next to him. "She's not our style."

Lucas gave them an incredulous look. "She worked with Carrie Underwood."

"She's better with women," Adam said. He had a brief flashback to their last encounter. It involved a mattress on the floor, a jar of honey, and a box of macaroni and cheese. It had taken three hot showers to get all the honey off his body. He shuddered. "Trust me. Let's move on."

"We can't," Lucas said. "There's nobody left to move on to."

"What do you mean there's nobody left? What about Rodriguez?" Cooper asked.

Lucas shook his head. "He was the second one Adam rejected."

"Oh yeah." Cooper nodded. "Right, he was the one who screwed Miranda while she was supposedly googly eyed for Adam."

"Is he still going out with her?" Brandon asked.

"No," Adam said. "He's with some model from Paris. Not that it matters. His stuff's too angry. We need someone more in line with where we are."

"Which is where, exactly?" LT poked him on the shoulder. "Besides still pissed off at Johnny J."

Adam swatted back at him but missed. "I'm not pissed off. He's doing the right thing. If my daughter had leukemia, I'd drop all of you in a hot second." His throat tightened. He, Johnny J, and Cooper had always been tight. The loss, even though it was totally understandable, still stung.

"Admit it, you were rip-roaring angry," Flynn said. "You stuck one of my sticks through the bass drum."

Adam winced. It hadn't been his proudest moment. "I wasn't pissed off. I was worried about Trisha, and disappointed. You know, for us."

"Your disappointment cost fifteen hundred dollars," Cooper muttered.

Adam flashed him a dirty look. "Johnny J's as much a brother to me as the rest of you. We've been writing songs together since we were ten years old, so of course I miss him. But his wife and daughter need him right now. He made the right call."

"Gentlemen, please, can we focus on the task at hand?" Lucas gestured at Cooper. "Let's hear the song before we start burning it in effigy, shall we?"

"Gotcha." Cooper spun around, pushed a button, then a few levers.

Adam knew from the first seven notes that he would hate the song, because he'd used those same notes for the first song he ever wrote. They belonged originally "Beat It" by Michael Jackson. He'd spoofed the song for a joke back in high school and told Rachel about it during one of their love-making sessions.

The fact that she'd used it for her audition meant she wasn't serious about working with him and the band. She was flipping him off from a distance.

"No," Adam said. "Cut it."

Lucas held up a finger. "You have to hear the entire first verse. That's the rule. And, Adam, if you turn this one down, there's not much left. Your reputation precedes you, my friend."

Adam scowled and turned his back on the room to stare at the floor-to-ceiling montage on the wall. A large poster of their first performance on a real stage was the focal point, surrounded by photos of Brandon's prom, LT's first motorcycle, Cooper arm in arm with his girlfriend from senior year, and Flynn buying his first real drum set.

Their entire life as a band was on that wall, good times and bad. It was both a scrapbook and a reminder to not take themselves too seriously.

A sultry voice snaked through the air to a melody that would have worked well for porn if it hadn't been for the ridiculous upbeat behind it.

Where did you go, why did you disappear?

Cooper hit the Pause button. "Think she has anyone specific in mind?"

Adam could hear the smirk in his voice. He glowered at the wall and did his best to ignore his now former best friend.

"Don't leave me, Adam!" Flynn wailed.

"Just play the damn song," Lucas growled.

"Fine, fine." Cooper hit Play.

DON'T WANT to face my life without you near.

COOPER HIT PAUSE AGAIN. "Didn't you break up two years ago?"

"Two and a half," Brandon supplied in a helpful tone.

"Right. Okay." Cooper hit Play.

THE FIRE'S in my heart and my blood is running clear.

FLYNN HIT the edge of the soundboard with a drumstick and shouted, "So beat it!"

I NEED YOU, I want you...oh

COOPER STOPPED THE SONG, and laughter filled the space where horrible music used to be.

"What the fuck?" Adam spun around to stare at Lucas. "Did you even listen to this crap before you brought it over here?"

"I thought it was charming." Lucas spread his hands in false apology. "I told you, son, we're scraping the bottom of the songwriter barrel out there."

"That's not even close to the barrel, Lucas. She's trolling us —and you."

"My blood is running clear?" LT said. "What's that even mean? She a vampire?"

"Yeah, she sucks blood, music, and Adam's...you know." Flynn beat a *ba-dum-bump* rhythm out on the back of a chair.

The guys all laughed harder.

"She's the only one in the last three weeks to even return my call," Lucas said with exaggerated patience.

Adam suppressed the surge of irritation. He could imagine the conversations Lucas was having on his behalf. He probably sounded like a snake oil salesman offering the latest potion. "Maybe you should stop leaving messages and actually go *see* people. Or hell, I'll go see them. Who haven't you tried?"

Lucas shook his head. "Won't do you any good. Most of the good ones are attached to projects, and the ones who aren't have the impression that you're difficult to work with. They don't want to waste their time."

"Neither do I." Adam scowled at his bandmates. "Knock it off."

Brandon laughed harder.

Flynn mocked him through fits of laughter. "I want you. I need you! Oh baby, oh baby, oh baby!"

Adam picked up a pillow and threw it at him. "Let's find someone new. Someone fresh."

"Yeah, someone who doesn't want to get in Adam's pants." LT chuckled. "Like a nun."

"I'd be more than happy to do that, if there was anyone left to find. Men, I need you to work with me here. Help me, help *you*." Lucas turned to Adam. "I've done all I can on my own. Give me a name,—any name—that you're willing to work with, and I'll do my best to get that person onboard."

Adam opened his mouth to protest that it wasn't his fault, but before he could launch into the same tired speech he'd given a dozen times before, everyone shouted out two words in perfect unison: "Mattie Bellamy."

Brandon nodded enthusiastically. "He's been beating it to her poster since high school."

Adam levelled his best glare at his soon-to-be-dead younger brother. "Shut the hell up, Brandon."

Lucas raised his eyebrows. "She's locked into an extremely lucrative project with Devon Morales right now. Not sure she'll even take calls, but I can check with her manager."

"She's done with him, according to Twitter and Instagram," Cooper said. He raised his phone and showed them the screen, then flipped it around to read, "'Truth is, I loved her, and she used me. Hashtag hurts when love dies.'"

"Ouch," LT said.

Adam frowned. He followed Mattie Bellamy on all social media platforms, but somehow he'd missed that one. "What a prick."

"You've had a thing for her forever," Flynn said. "Have you even tried to meet her?"

"No," Brandon supplied before Adam could speak. "He worships her from a distance."

"Why?" Flynn tapped the back of his chair. "You're hot. If I were a chick, I'd totally do you."

"I wouldn't," Brandon said.

"I wouldn't do either one of you." Adam glared at them. "Leave it. She's busy."

"No she's not," Cooper said. "That's what I'm trying to tell you. They broke up. Here, this one spells it out. 'She knows I wrote the words. I'm done letting her ride my coat tails. Just wish it didn't hurt so much. Hashtag Heartbreak Blues.'"

"That's complete and utter bullshit. There's no way he wrote that song." Adam hummed the first few notes, then sang the next line. "'I'll be there like the sun after the storm.' He might have had a hand in the melody, but the words are all hers."

"What makes you say that?" Lucas asked.

"Dude," Brandon said, "he knows every note of every Bellamy song. Don't test him. We'll be stuck listening to them the rest of the day."

Adam gestured at Cooper. "If you queue up 'Every Rainy Day' off the first album, the words mimic the second verse of that, but more important, listen to the bridge. It's basically a lead-up to the melody they used for Morales's shiny new hit, which wouldn't be a hit at all without Mattie Bellamy. The guy's a complete ass."

Lucas held up his hands. "No need to prove it. I believe you."

Adam paced to the door of the studio and back. If Mattie Bellamy was available, this could be a fantastic opportunity to meet her. Brandon wasn't wrong. He *had* followed her for a long time.

He remembered the first Bellamy song he'd ever heard. Every time "I Won't Let Go" came on the radio, he was instantly transported back to his bedroom in the same house his parents still owned. He'd been trolling YouTube when he came across someone's recording of The Bellamy Sisters in concert.

Whoever made the clip obviously had a thing for Della, but Adam's attention had been drawn by the honey blonde who stayed in the background, either on the keyboards or on backup vocals, until the part of the song that brought her to the front of the stage. Her face was radiant and filled with promises.

In his fantasies, she sang that song just for him.

. . .

exactly true, but now that they'd put the idea of Mattie into his head, he couldn't get it back out. Hell, he didn't *want* to get it back out. For the first time since Johnny J left, he felt a spark of hope that a great new song might be in his grasp, and he wasn't about to walk away without at least trying to meet her. "We need someone actually good with words. Johnny J was world class, but he's not an option. That leaves Mattie Bellamy. She's the best songwriter of our generation. So let's get her." He turned to Lucas. "Make it happen."

Lucas pulled out his phone. "I'll give it a try, but I can't promise anything."

"And Lucas?"

Lucas paused with his fingers over the screen.

"Make sure you tell Rachel the joke's on her," Adam said.

There was no way anything Rachel did would live up to even one line written by Mattie Bellamy.

Chapter Three

Mattie was so keyed up from the non-brunch fiasco that she didn't remember the drive home. She climbed to her rooftop deck in a daze and tried to write, but the outburst of anger she'd unleashed on Della left her feeling drained and empty.

Della sent text after text after text. *I'm sorry Mattie! This is all my fault. Please come back!*

Mattie deleted them.

Piper called, but Mattie didn't pick up. Piper left a voice mail she didn't listen to, followed by a text. *I'm proud of you. I'm here when you need me.*

Three hours later she'd come down off the initial wave of anger and was left wallowing in a pit of embarrassment. She never spoke like that to anyone, and the experience had been both liberating and exhausting.

She almost picked up the phone when Lizzie called. Almost. But what would she say? That she was sorry? She wasn't. Not in the slightest. It felt like a weight on one part of her soul had been lifted. She'd finally said everything she wished she'd said years ago.

Of course, now there was a hole that instantly filled with regret and sadness. She shouldn't have done it. Not like that.

Lizzie didn't leave a voice mail, but a few seconds later a text dinged. *I love you, Mattie Cake. We'll get through this. I promise.*

Her sister's kind concern came through the texts, which made her feel even worse. Mattie curled up in bed and cried until she ran out of tears.

Monday morning she once again sat on her deck, dry-eyed and soaked in LA's smoggy sunlight with a cup of coffee in her hand and nothing to do.

Maybe she should go on vacation. She could recharge somewhere pretty, far away from everything and everyone.

That sounded depressingly lonely.

Her phone buzzed and the song "Genie in a Bottle" by Christina Aguilera played. She'd picked that song for her manager, Kat Crawford, because she was so good at making things happen. If Mattie needed a project, Kat found it. If Mattie wanted a girls' night out, Kat arranged it. She was a shoulder to cry on and a business sounding board. She'd only known Kat about four years, but she trusted her almost as much as her own sisters.

Well, all but one.

Kat's face popped up on the screen. Her dark hair was in a high ponytail, her lips were a bright shade of purple, and her eyes danced with laughter.

Mattie sighed and picked up the phone. She accepted the video chat and tried to smile. "Hey, Kat."

Kat gave her a soft, soothing smile in return. "Hey, there. How you doing, sweetie?"

Mattie shrugged. "I'm fine. I'll get over it."

Kat raised an eyebrow. "Oh really? I thought you'd be over-the-top-pissy about this. I mean, it's a low blow. A *really* low blow. I'm looking into whether we can sue for libel or defamation. Something."

Mattie frowned. "What? I'm not suing my own sisters, no matter what they said. Besides, I'm the one who erupted this time."

Kat sat back in her deck chair. "What? You erupted? Wait... are we even talking about the same thing?"

"I'm not sure. What are *you* talking about?"

Kat shook her head. "No, no. You go first. What about your sisters?"

Mattie sighed and propped the phone against a notebook on the table next to her lounge chair. "Remember I told you Lizzie was in town?"

Kat nodded. "Yes. You were going to brunch at The Flower Pot. Totally jealous. Next time I want to come with."

Mattie grimaced. "I may never show my face there again. Lizzie invited Della."

Kat's mouth formed an *O*. "I thought you said you both talked about it and decided not to invite her."

"We did."

"So, what changed?"

"I think Lizzie hoped we would all talk it out and get past the whole breakup thing."

Kat took a hit off a cigarette and blew out the smoke. "I can guess what happened next. Piper saw Della, went ballistic, and dishes were thrown."

Mattie bit her lower lip to ward off the shimmer of shame. "Actually, Piper was pretty low key. I'm the one who went nuts. I didn't throw anything, but I said plenty."

"What brought this attack of voice on?" Kat tamped out her mostly unsmoked cigarette.

"She said she wants to get the group back together. Just flipped that right out there like it was no big thing. Drop what you're doing, be my beck-and-call girl." Heat crawled up the back of her neck as she thought about it.

Kat looked thoughtful. "What did you say to that?"

"I said no. A lot." Even three days later, the anger of that moment threatened to overwhelm her again. Leave it to her baby sister to push every button she had.

"Okay. That's...okay." Kat glanced down at something, probably her iPad, and frowned. The woman was the queen of multitasking. "How did Lizzie and Piper take it?"

"Piper didn't really get a chance to react. I started shouting and that stopped everything else." Why did she feel like she'd been caught doing something wrong? "Anyway, Piper didn't need to say anything. Everyone knows she's still mad at Della, though I think if Della would just apologize, Piper would get over it. She follows everything Della does in social media, and she tells us every time anything happens. She misses Della as much as me and Lizzie, she just won't admit it."

"And Lizzie? Did she break up the fight or what?"

"Oh, we didn't fight like that. Mostly Della just stared at me in horror. Nobody expects me to act like that. It's usually Piper." Mattie thought back to the day and tried to sort out what she'd seen. During her emotional outburst, she'd caught flashes of Lizzie's face. "I think Lizzie knew Della wanted to get back together, but I don't think she was supposed to ask us that day. Lizzie looked surprised, but not shocked."

They were silent for a moment. Kat gave her space to process, which was one of the things Mattie loved most about her friend and manager. "You know, if we could *really* talk, just once, I think we'd get past all this. But we never do, you know? Piper keeps herself too busy, Lizzie's preoccupied with Renic, and Della's oblivious."

Kat's look of understanding was so tender and sincere that Mattie felt like crying again. "That's family for you. Can't live with 'em, can't divorce 'em or sue for alimony. You should see how crazy mine gets around the holidays."

Mattie thought about the last holiday she'd had with all of her sisters. It was almost five years ago now. The thought made her incredibly sad.

"Hey." Kat tapped the phone. "Don't worry. Della's reaching out, which is a good start. You'll get through this. You all will."

"I hope so." Mattie sniffed and dragged her thoughts back to the subject. "What did you mean before? Who are you trying to sue? For what?"

Kat grimaced. "I guess you haven't seen it after all."

"What?"

"Devon Morales tweeted about you all weekend. You haven't checked?"

"No. Why? What'd he say?" Her creative partnership with Devon had started out pleasant enough. Devon was funny, and charming in a boy-next-door sort of way. They worked on the love song that was currently topping the charts for over six months, which was longer than she usually liked to spend on one project. They had a lot of laughs, and more than a few late nights in the studio.

Then one night he kissed her, which made everything awkward. He was a friend, but she wasn't attracted to him, and she hated when romance interfered with the music.

"For one thing, he says you broke his heart."

"Seriously? How?"

"He says you basically dumped him at the altar. Well, not quite, but you get the drift."

"That's ridiculous. We're just friends. We weren't in a relationship. I mean, sure we went to dinner a few times to work on the song, and we spent a lot of time together in the studio. But that was work, not a date. I didn't even know he liked me until he tried to kiss me. And I told him I didn't feel that way about him. We were never a thing."

"I'm sorry, sweetie." Kat's commiserating look didn't make her feel any better.

"What is it with men? Just because I wrote a love song doesn't mean I was in love with him."

"I know."

Frustration bubbled. "Mark Serano did the same thing, except he didn't wait for me to finish the song before he started pushing me for sex."

Kat held up a finger. "Don't forget Roger Cruise. And Bishop Keller. Oh, and Greg Nelson. I still get emails from all of them. Bishop called last week to ask if you were available for another project."

Mattie stiffened. She liked Bishop, but not that way. He was a nice guy, full of down-to-earth charm and honest to a fault, but too, well, boring for her tastes. "What did you say?"

"I told him you were already committed." Kat winked.

Mattie rolled her eyes and leaned back in the chair. "I'm done working with men. They can't separate the feelings in the song from actual feelings for a real live person."

Kat bit her lip. "Yeah. About that."

"What?" Mattie narrowed her eyes at her. "There's more, isn't there."

Kat flinched. "After he called you out a few times without an answer he went on to say other things."

"Should I go look?"

"No." Kat shook her head. "Definitely not. But here's the thing. He's claiming he wrote the songs, and you're trying to steal credit."

Mattie blinked. She couldn't have heard that right. "Say that again?"

Kat lit another cigarette. "It's complete bullshit, of course. We have a contract, and it stipulates that your name be on the jacket as cowriter. If he tries to bypass that we'll definitely sue."

Mattie picked up one of her notebooks and thumbed through it. All the scribbled verses, jumbled captions, and doodles were proof she'd written the lyrics on Devon's new hit. Except nobody ever saw these notebooks on Twitter, and it wasn't like they announced the songwriter on the radio. "Think I should call him out on his bullshit? Maybe post pictures of my notes?"

"No, sweetie. Don't take the bait." Kat held up her iPad. "Thing is, I got an email this morning that makes this a bigger deal than it should be. The song's been submitted for a Grammy. Best Pop Solo Performance."

"Not song?"

Kat tossed her iPad aside. "No, hun. Sorry."

Mattie sipped her tea while she absorbed the implications of that. "So not only did the label submit in a way that basically ignores me, but now Devon's on Twitter calling me a fake?"

Kat took a long drag of her cigarette. "They can't ignore you completely. Like I said, your name's on the jacket. But if it wins he doesn't have to acknowledge you and from the looks of things, he definitely won't."

Mattie swore. "I knew he was pissed off when I told him I wasn't interested in a relationship, but this is unbelievable. What a spiteful little weasel! This sucks."

"Yes, it does." Kat flicked ashes off the end of her cigarette.

Mattie shook her head in disbelief. "I've been writing songs since I was old enough to hold a crayon, but my name's nowhere."

"Plenty of people know what you mean to music, Mattie, and everyone knows he's full of shit."

"Do they really? I mean, when someone says Bellamy who do you think of first?"

"You, honey. Always." Kat puffed out smoke.

"You have to say that. I meant you in the collective sense. I was never the face. Never the one in front. So when you think of a Bellamy song, you think Della or Piper. Not me. I mean, we won a few awards as a group but never Song of the Year. The way things are going now, I'm never going to win anything, because I'm not performing them myself, and I'm not signed with a label. Of course they back their own artist, and not me. I'm basically invisible."

"Sweetie, you've never been invisible." Kat tamped out her cigarette and picked up a mug. "But I get your point. You do need some visibility, and an award would give you that. If you don't get back with your sisters, have you given any thought to going solo yourself?"

Her gut churned at the idea. "No. I'm done with that. I'm done with all of it."

"You don't mean that."

"Yes I do. The well's dry. I don't have any songs left in me. Maybe I'll pull a Della and go move in with Lizzie to help run the inn. It's really peaceful up there."

"I guess that means you wouldn't be interested in a new project." Kat looked far too coy, and her tone was carefully casual.

Mattie's first instinct was to end the call. "I haven't written anything at all in three days."

"That's quite a dry spell for you." Kat reached for another cigarette, glared at it, then put it down.

"I thought you were going to quit smoking," Mattie said in her most diplomatic voice.

"I am. I've been tapering by taking no more than three hits per cigarette. It's costing me a fortune. Anyway, I think what you really need is a chance to put all this other stuff behind you by focusing on something different."

"Hmm. I'm not sure I'm up for anything right now. Between Morales the Misguided and Della the Diva, I'm just... I'm done." The thought of writing another song right now made her sick. Her emotions were spinning like a load of laundry stuck on the high heat setting.

"It's Delusions of Glory." Kat's voice rose and her face lit up as she said the band name. "They're looking for someone to help them fill out their album, and Adam Brooks asked for you specifically."

"Really?" Mattie thought about that. She knew the band, of course. They were world famous. And unlike The Bellamy Sisters, nobody thought the studio wrote their songs. She didn't know if it was because they were men, or because they were older when they got started, but either way, she resented the unequal treatment. "Why?"

"Because Johnny J left, and from what I hear the fantastically gorgeous Mr. Brooks hasn't really meshed with anyone else."

"So why would I be any different?"

She didn't know much about Adam Brooks. She had a vague memory of him in the tabloids. Something about a model he was dating or dumping. She hadn't paid it much attention.

"Because you're you, and because according to his manager you're the only one he's asked for by name."

She remembered a couple of Delusions of Glory songs. Their two biggest hits, "You Got Something" and "Living in the Moment," were fun and catchy, with beats designed to drive up the blood pressure of any parent and solid-gold lyrics as far as angsty teens were concerned.

They were good songs, but rougher around the edges than she liked. If she was listening to music for fun, it usually featured softer melodies that suited her voice so she could belt it out in the shower.

"I don't see it working out, do you? I mean, we don't have the same style at all. He's edgy race car rock, and I'm dreamy romance and pop. They don't really go together."

"I wouldn't be so sure. They're looking for something new. Their manager told me this album is nothing like anything they've done before. They need a new perspective now that Johnny J is gone. That's where you come in. I think meshing your dreamy with their steamy would make excellent music. Plus, they're already planning on submitting one of these three for Song of the Year. If you want credit, this is the way to get it. They mentioned making one a duet."

Mattie's heart jerked like a fish on the line. Winning Song of the Year would mean more than just a writing credit. It would feel like the sun rising after a long, dark night, but it would also mean working with one of rock's playboys.

Mattie closed her eyes and pictured the last time she was in the studio with Devon. He'd kept staring at her and licking his lips, as if she were a juicy piece of steak. "If it's just me and Adam Brooks in the studio, it could get touchy-feely and awkward real quick."

"I doubt it'll be just him. There's five in the band, and I know his brother, Brandon, is listed as cowriter on a lot of the songs over the years. Plus, the duet doesn't have to be a love song."

"If it's the whole band, we might never get a song written at all. Writing by committee never really works out, you know?" She didn't need any more drama, and this gig sounded like it would be nothing *but* drama. It would have to be with so many people involved.

But "Song of the Year" revolved in her head like an old record.

"Take this job as a favor to me. Keep it strictly professional. No dinners. No alone time."

"I took the *last* job as a favor to you. Look how well that turned out." Mattie stuck her tongue out.

"Here's the thing, sweetie." Kat leaned in closer to the phone. "You need to get your name out there on something that's not sweet pop. Delusions has the edge you need. It's a great chance to show your range, get your name in lights, and stick it to Devon and everyone else. Especially if you keep things strictly professional."

"Hey, I'm *always* professional. He was the one who made up a fake relationship. How is that my fault?"

"It isn't. That's not what I'm saying." Kat picked up another cigarette and shoved it between her lips. It dipped up and down while she spoke. "What I'm saying is, you need this. *We* need this. If you win Song of the Year with no added drama, it'll make it obvious all the crap-talk from Devon was just that. Otherwise he's got the clout behind him since he's still riding high on a number one hit, and he's the one talking the loudest, and you know it's always guilty until proven innocent as far as public opinion is concerned."

Mattie sat back. On the plus side, if she took on this project, she wouldn't have to fight with Della over whether The Bellamy Sisters should get back together. She would be legitimately busy and unable to take phone calls. The lure of a possible Best Song dangled in front of her, shiny and tempting and just out of reach.

On the flip side, if she didn't take this project, eventually she would cave and talk to Della, who was extremely skilled at getting what she wanted out of just about everybody.

She took a deep breath to steady her nerves before she admitted she'd already caved to the inevitable. "I'll meet with them."

"Great! I'll set it up for Wednesday. Your studio or theirs?"

"Theirs. That way I can leave if I need to. And make sure they agree to no love songs." Mattie waved at the phone. "Thanks, Kat."

"Hang in there, girl." Kat waved and ended the call.

Mattie lifted her face to the morning sun and tried to push all the drama out of her mind. When that didn't work, she threw on a sundress and went for pastries.

Chapter Four

Adam arrived at the studio for his meeting with Mattie Bellamy an hour early and looked around, trying to see the place through the eyes of a stranger. From the outside, it looked like just another Los Angeles storefront on yet another tree-lined street not far from Griffith Park. The lobby was more entryway than proper waiting space, and as first impressions went, it was clean but plain. He'd insisted the cleaning crew come twice just to make sure it didn't smell like stale french fries. He sniffed. The scent of vanilla and spice hung in the air. Perfect.

A hallway led from the lobby into the control room, which contained two large, overstuffed sofas, a couple of club chairs, plus all the latest equipment for mixing, effects, and recording. The walls were covered in acoustic tiles that gave the place a cave-like vibe. It was comfortable and reminded him of the band's early days in his parents' garage. His dad had never taken the tiles down, and most of their setup was still there, even though he still grumbled about it from time to time.

On the other side of the glass, the studio was big enough

for the entire band, their equipment, plus a few extra micro-phones and odds and ends. Two large monitors hung in the corners to display lyrics or other notes about the song they were recording.

The spaces together were a little heavy on male influence, maybe, but overall he thought it would impress most people as a high-tech, professional place where serious music happened. They'd set it up years ago because renting someone else's studio in Los Angeles was expensive and had too many strings attached. Plus, the songs came out better when they were in a place that felt like home.

Flynn and Brandon were already setting up the equipment, but LT and Cooper were nowhere to be seen.

Adam took out his phone and tapped out a text to them. *Where R U?*

He opened the door to the studio and stepped inside.

"Hey," Brandon said without looking up. He played a few bars on the keyboards, tilted his head, then nodded. "Good to go here."

Flynn ran through a quick test of the drum kit and grinned. "I don't know. Think it's good enough for *her*? I mean, have we dusted every nook and cranny? Shined the metal bits? Do we have rose petals?"

Adam rolled his eyes. "Try to behave, okay? If we scare this one away, you're stuck with whatever I wrote in high school."

"We all know what that means," Brandon said. His fingers danced over the keys, playing the melody to "Every Breath You Take" by The Police.

"Would you cut that out?" Adam flashed an irritated look at his brother. "I've never been that kind of guy."

"Sure, bro. Sure." Brandon kept his gaze down, but the song changed to "I Want You to Want Me" by Cheap Trick.

Flynn tapped out a *ba-dum-bump* and hit the cymbals for good measure.

Adam's phone chimed. Cooper had responded. *Caffeine and Carbs.*

Hopefully, that meant LT was with him. He checked the time. Mattie would be here in thirty minutes.

He tapped out another quick message to Cooper and LT. *Bring some for Mattie.*

LT responded this time. *Like what? Coffee? Tea? Red Bull?*

Cooper responded, *Balloons that say I Love You?*

He shook his head. *Ass. Coffee, tea, muffins.*

Cooper sent, *Leave the gun.*

LT quickly responded, *Take the cannoli.*

Adam sent a flip-off emoji and went back out to the control room.

When the lobby doors opened he jumped to his feet, expecting to see Mattie. Instead, it was Cooper and LT with the provisions.

Cooper flashed him a knowing look and unloaded the bags of goodies onto the coffee table in front of the couch. "That's not happiness to see us, is it?"

LT smirked. "That was definite disappointment in those baby browns. But here, a shot of caffeine will fix that."

Adam took the offered cup. "Let's get set up, okay? I want to make a good impression."

Cooper took a sip from his own cup. "You sure you want to play 'I Promise You' for her? It's still rough, man. Not our best work."

"There's nothing wrong with that song." Adam checked his phone. Five minutes.

"Maybe we should just do a best hits album instead," LT suggested. "That way we don't have to write anything new."

"No, we need to move forward, not back." Adam set down his cup. "Coop, can you queue up the tracks, please?"

"Sure thing." Cooper sat down at the computer on the control board.

The lobby door opened.

They all swiveled to look down the hall.

Mattie Bellamy stood just inside the door, framed by the morning sun. Her gold hair was in loose waves that played with her bare shoulders. She wore a simple, flowing blue sundress made of material so thin the light silhouetted the soft curve of her breasts, the sensuous contours of her waist and hips, and the lean lines of her legs all the way down to sandals that were so flat she might as well have been barefoot. It left him with the impression that she was gloriously naked.

She was a radiant sun goddess who had obviously gotten lost on her way to the beach. The girl from his poster had turned into a woman so stunning it took his breath away.

"I get the obsession now," Cooper whispered.

LT whistled a single high-pitched note. "She sure grew up, didn't she?"

"Shut it, both of you. Get Brandon and Flynn out here, and pretend you're all actually adults," Adam told them in a low voice before he rushed to greet their guest of honor.

"Mattie," Adam called out, hoping like hell she couldn't hear the whispered comments that continued behind his back. His long strides couldn't get him down the hallway fast enough. "Glad you could make it."

Mattie held onto the strap of an enormous blue shoulder bag like it was filled with priceless artifacts.

He hadn't realized how nervous he was to meet her until this moment. It was strange to see his fantasy standing there in the lobby as if it were an everyday thing. He smiled, held out his hand, and hoped like hell he sounded like the rock star he was supposed to be and not a breathless fan boy.

"I'm Adam. Brooks." For crying out loud, he was stumbling over his own damn name. He took a deep breath. "Welcome to our studio."

She shook his hand. Her grip was steel wrapped in sunshine, firm but warm. "Nice to meet you."

He forced himself to let go of her hand and act cool. "Come on back, we're about set up. I have coffee, tea, and I think muffins of some sort if you're interested."

"No, thanks." She followed him down the short hallway into the control room. She stopped short when she saw the rest of the band huddled together casting furtive glances in their direction.

He wished he'd told them all to dress better. Cooper looked decent in a collared shirt and pressed jeans, but Flynn and Brandon wore board shorts, and LT might have just stepped out of a biker bar. All of them sported various tattoos and piercings. Flynn had full sleeves of ink. Hell, she probably thought they all looked like street thugs.

"Oh...everyone's here," Mattie said.

Adam caught a lot of Southern politeness in that short sentence. Mattie was poised and professional, and her face was carefully neutral while he made introductions. She might have just stepped into a board meeting instead of a creative session with musicians.

She was utterly at odds with the girl he'd imagined.

It unsettled him. It felt wrong, somehow. Like someone had caged a butterfly.

After the introductions, Mattie's gaze lingered on the textured dark gray walls. "That's cool. Very moody."

She touched one of the tiles with a delicate hand, and her face went a little dreamy. For a second, he caught a glimpse of the girl he thought she could be. Then she lowered her hand. "Why don't we skip all the small talk and jump right to it? Kat said you had a song you wanted me to hear?"

Small talk was exactly what he'd been hoping for, but Adam hid his disappointment behind commands. "Sure. Boys, let's do this."

Cooper handed a set of headphones to Mattie and pointed to the volume controls. She nodded and took a seat. Then they all filed into the studio, leaving Mattie watching them from behind the glass.

Adam stepped up to the microphone and waited for everyone to get into position.

Mattie's gaze settled on him, and for a long moment it felt like they were the only two people in the building. He pictured her picking up a microphone and singing alongside him, flipping her hair the way she used to, that dazzling light in her eyes making her larger than life.

After the song, he'd take her to dinner. He'd hold her hand as they walked along the beach. Then they'd go back to his place, and she'd lay naked in his bed, and that cloud of gold hair would spill out around her all messy and sexy and utterly irresistible.

Mattie narrowed her eyes as if she sensed exactly what was going through his head.

He smiled at her, trying his best to look innocent.

She tilted her head and tapped the headphones for emphasis.

"Right." He turned away to check on the guys. He had to get a grip. She obviously wasn't the girl he'd put on a pedestal as a teenager. She was a woman who left broken hearts everywhere she went. He couldn't reconcile what she seemed to be on stage with who she was here. It didn't make sense. How could she write the songs she wrote and be this detached?

Cooper watched him with a knowing look on his face. LT smirked at him, and Flynn outright laughed.

Adam huffed out an irritated breath. "Guys, count it down."

Flynn's grin broadened and he nodded. "Here we go in three...two...one..."

The intro started, and Adam drifted away from his thoughts and into the rhythm of the last song he'd written with Johnny J. It was different from their usual stuff. More introspective. They weren't the heavy-hitting teens anymore. They'd grown up, and the song reflected that.

Adam kept his back to Mattie until it was time to sing the first verse. He turned, picked up the mic, and the words took over.

YOU WERE JUST *a little sweet thing,*
so much smaller than you might seem,
When I heard the news that stopped me in my tracks.

HE LET himself sink into the song until the studio disappeared.

I SPENT *the next few hours swearing,*
at the gods above, the
News I wish I never heard
could not be right,
We had to fight.
This would not be the end.

. . .

MOVEMENT CAUGHT HIS EYE, and he saw Mattie waving at him.

He stopped singing. It took a few more bars for the guys to stop.

"What's wrong?" Brandon asked.

"Not sure," Adam said.

Mattie shook her head, removed the headphones, and opened the door.

"Adam, can I talk to you for a second?" She turned and walked back out.

Adam glanced at Cooper.

Cooper shrugged. "Told you it was rough, man."

"That's not it," Adam said. "I'll be right back. Try not to act like cavemen."

"That's just not fair," Flynn said. "This is the cave. We are men. That makes us…"

Adam followed Mattie out and shut the door on whatever he said next. "What's wrong?"

Mattie pressed her lips together, as if she were trying to keep words from slipping out. Finally, she huffed out a sigh and spoke. "The words are saying one thing, but the melody and, well *you*, are saying another. Did you write this song? What was the inspiration?"

Adam's jaw tightened. He didn't want to fight with her because he didn't want to chase her away. But at the same time, what was she trying to say? That he was a lousy songwriter?

"I cowrote it with Johnny J, but the inspiration was his. It's about his daughter, Trisha. She was diagnosed with leukemia last year."

"Oh." Mattie's hand flew to her chest, and the stiff, professional mask dissolved. It made her look instantly younger. More real. "I'm so sorry. I thought it must be something like that."

Adam gestured at the couch. "Why are you asking? You didn't like the lyrics?"

"No, no. It's not that." Mattie sat down and waited for him to join her. Then she turned her earnest, expressive eyes on him. "Okay, for this song to work you have to *feel* what he feels. You can't just sing it like it's about a breakup or fling or whatever, which is what it sounded like just then. The words are full of pain and fear, and you looked...I don't know. Happy isn't the right word. Determined, maybe. Anyway, it's disjointed. And the beat is a little too fast. Try softening it a little. Really put yourself into his mind, you know? I mean, think about it. How would you feel if it was one of you who was diagnosed with something like that?"

Adam glanced through the glass at his brother. The guys were all laughing, probably at him. He imagined one of them missing, not in the way Johnny J was, but in a final, never-coming-back, can't-email-or-call kind of way. He wasn't sure the band could continue if they lost someone like that. "I'd feel horrible."

Mattie nodded. "Right. So feel that. *Then* sing it. Here, let me show you what I mean."

She stood up and led the way into the studio.

He followed, curious. He thought he *had* been putting those feelings into the words. The song echoed the heartache and terror Johnny J had felt when he heard about his little girl. The two of them had spent a long night drinking, talking, and writing this song. A couple of days later, Johnny J walked out. It was impossible not to think about that night whenever he sang it. How could he possibly put more feeling into it?

Mattie smiled at everyone and stepped up to one of the backup mics. "If you don't mind, I'll take the first, you take the second, and then we'll hit the last bit together?"

"Sure." Adam pulled the song up on one of the studio

tablets and handed it to her, then nodded at Flynn. "Slower this time, okay?"

Flynn nodded and started them off again, about 3/4 time. The rest of them picked up the new pace, and the song took on a softer, more mellow undertone that hadn't been there before.

When Mattie sang in her rich, high alto, her face transformed into the ethereal vision he remembered. She sang the first two lines with such intensity that he could hear exactly what she'd meant. He hadn't allowed himself to sink that far into the song, because the truth was it brought him too close to tears. He didn't want to cry in front of everyone over a song. It wasn't his style.

When it was his turn, he tried to match her, but he could tell by the look on her face that he still wasn't doing it right as far as she was concerned.

Then the second line hit him like a sucker punch to the gut, and suddenly he was with Johnny J in the doctor's office, trying to comfort his little girl and his wife while feeling out of control himself.

He and Mattie sang the last two lines together, and it became a struggle to make it through. When they hit the end of the first verse, he stopped, expecting her to do the same, but she didn't. She followed along with the lyrics on the tablet and kept singing. Her face turned dreamy, her voice filled the room, and he was transported to a concert where he was the audience of one and she was the only person on stage.

Sweet thing, I promise you

You'll go running through the flowers

You'll go dance away the hours
You'll go out on dates, and get your first real kiss.

You'll slide down a pile of rainbows
You'll spend days in distant castles,
You'll spend nighttime snuggled up with your best friends

We will make it through this darkness and come out
Stronger than we ever could pretend
Girl, I hope you understand
I won't let it be the end.

MATTIE PUNCHED every line with hopeful optimism, and they followed along with her, pushing the song into a celebration of life that left Adam feeling triumphant. He'd never noticed that about the lyrics before. That spirit belonged to Johnny's little girl.

The fact that Mattie had picked up on it impressed him even more than her voice. The girl he'd crushed on was still there, and he was in the same room with her.

The song ended, and for a few seconds, everyone was silent.

"Wow." Cooper stared at Mattie. "That's...how'd you do that?"

"We've been working on this one for months." Brandon hit a few notes. "We never got the sound like that. I like it slower."

"It fits," Flynn said. "Think I'll change up some stuff. Go softer. It doesn't need a lot of help."

"Yeah, maybe we should take it the whole first verse with just the piano," LT suggested. "Then push it more through the chorus."

Adam turned to Mattie. "That was amazing."

"Sometimes all you need is an outside perspective, that's all. You almost had it there. I just added window dressing." She smiled, and this time her eyes sparkled. "It's a good song. It's not exactly your usual style, though. Is the rest of the album like this?"

"Not exactly," Adam said.

"We were trying to give this one an edge like the others, but it wasn't working." Brandon pounded out a few of the notes. "I think we're having an identity crisis."

"Speak for yourself," Cooper said. "Just because you haven't grown up yet doesn't mean we're in crisis."

"Just because you were old before you were born doesn't mean the rest of us have to act that way," Flynn said.

"Guys." Adam gave them his best settle-down-or-I'll-end-you look, then turned to Mattie. "That's the only soft one. The rest are more in line with our usual stuff. We can run through them for you."

Mattie's phone chimed. She tugged it out and checked a text. "Um, sure."

She drifted out the door.

Adam watched her go, then turned to the band. They all looked as confused as he felt.

"Hang tight. I'll be right back."

Chapter Five

Mattie glared at the phone and thought seriously about changing her number. That way Della couldn't text her at odd moments and stir up her emotions again.

I love you Mattie Cake. I miss you. Please talk to me.

What was she supposed to say to that? She thought about it, then tapped out a quick response. *In a meeting.*

She was about to go back into the studio when another text came through. This time from Piper. *When did this happen?*

Piper included a link to an article on the *LA POP* website. Mattie tapped the link and waited for it to load while dread danced in her stomach.

When the headline came up, she swore.

Mattie Bellamy Moves on to Next Victim?

Beneath it was a blurry image of her standing just inside the front door of the Delusions of Glory studio, shaking hands with Adam Brooks.

Mattie checked the hallway. She didn't think anyone could get a good shot all the way back here, but she instinctively stepped out of sight just in case.

She closed her eyes and tried not to panic. She wouldn't normally care what they said, but with everything Devon had posted over the past few days she was more than a little jumpy. A headline like this would make his lies sound true.

This couldn't be happening. It wasn't possible that gossip blogs had picked up the story so fast. They must have followed her from her house. Nobody knew she was coming here.

She thought about that. Kat knew. So did Adam's manager, because he'd made the call to Kat. The entire band and maybe their families knew, too, of course.

That left quite a few people who could unintentionally leak information.

She looked at the image again. Did it look like she was swooning over Adam?

He was maybe three or four inches taller than her, with dark hair shaved close and stubble along his jaw that gave him an edgy, street-wise vibe. He wore jeans, a plain black T-shirt, and combat boots.

He had an athletic body but didn't look like he spent a ton of time in the gym. He was good looking in a bad-boy, rough-around-the-edges sort of way.

Devon Morales, by contrast, was a pretty boy. He was so photogenic that it had given him the idea that every woman swooned the second she laid eyes on him. It was part of what went so very wrong on the last project.

She hadn't swooned.

After Kat had told her about Devon's tweets, she'd spent hours combing over all of his recent posts. He hadn't just complained about how she'd ruined his life by leading him on. He'd doubled down on the lie by posting some of the selfies they'd taken while working together.

Somehow he'd turned innocent friendly poses into suggestive intimacy with clever use of filters. She had to admit by the time he was done it really did look like they'd had a six-month romance, at least on the internet.

Now the gossips had this new photo to add fuel to the already raging fire. Maybe she should just pass on this project right now, before it went any further.

Another text from Della sang out. *When's the meeting over? I'll call you.*

Her first instinct was to send back a retort along the lines of "never talk to me again and lose my phone number," but she couldn't bring herself to do that.

Piper texted again. *If you're still there, stay till the sun sets. Do you need cover? I can pick you up.*

Mattie closed her eyes. Piper was offering to take the headlines off her back. If they saw Piper, they'd forget about boring Mattie.

The problem was cover only lasted so long. Once they got over their Piper Bellamy sighting, the gossip rags would focus on her again. The longer she was here, the more they'd have to sell. She could only imagine the next headline: *Mattie Bellamy Gangbanging Delusions of Glory.*

Dammit.

She was usually so careful to avoid prying eyes, but thanks to Devon she'd become front-page news in a way she'd never wanted to be.

She should leave.

She spun around to get her bag from the couch where she'd dropped it and bumped into Adam.

His hands immediately went to steady her. They were warm, solid, and entirely too comfortable.

"I'm sorry." She stepped away. Had he told the paparazzi she'd be here?

Adam lowered his hands. "What's going on? You look tense."

"Nothing, really." She studied his eyes. Concern and curiosity stared back at her. She relaxed and shook her head. "It's just Twitter drama."

"We can run through the other songs," Adam suggested. "Might take your mind off Twitter."

Mattie thought of several reasons why she should say no to that suggestion. The one song she'd heard nearly ripped her heart out, and she was too emotionally spent to deal with another one like it. Plus, cameras with long lenses were probably still waiting outside, counting the minutes she was spending in his company. The more minutes, the more sensational the gossip.

On the other hand, it felt safe in here. Nobody could see in. She liked the band. Adam seemed like he had a good head on his shoulders, and his second run-through on the song had been perfect. Bonus points for not giving her the puppy eyes afterward like Devon usually did.

Even better, the guys all seemed close, like a family. She'd had that once. Watching Delusions of Glory be the brothers they obviously were hurt in a way she couldn't define.

"Hey, we can take a break, if you want." Adam's concerned look had been replaced by a carefully neutral mask. "No pressure. Or we can do this another time. Your call."

He was being so nice, and here she was contemplating running out the door. It would be unprofessional to walk out now. She'd come here to prove a point, and to get the chance to write the Song of the Year, and there was no way a few paparazzi were going to scare her away from that goal.

"No, that's okay. Let's do it." She nodded and offered him a professional smile, just to prove she could put aside personal issues. "This time I promise I'll just sit and listen."

Adam's grin lit up his whole face. "Feel free to step in any time. We could use your voice in there."

"I know what I sound like. It's more important to hear what you all sound like. I'm a behind-the-scenes kind of girl now."

She sat in front of the board, put the headphones on, and tapped out a quick reply to Piper. *Still here. Will stay in hopes they get bored.*

Piper responded with a quick answer. *K.*

Adam tapped her shoulder. He'd obviously been talking to her, but she hadn't heard a word. She lifted the headphones. "Sorry, what did you say?"

"I said there's no way you're ever behind the scenes. Your words are out in front, all the time."

A hint of something flashed across his face. Admiration, maybe. It vanished so fast she thought—hoped—she imagined it.

Another text dragged her attention away from him. This time it was Kat. *Devon's posting again. You might think about responding.*

"Great," she told the screen, "that's what I need."

"Were you talking to me?" Adam sounded confused and uncertain.

"No." She looked up, embarrassed. Her thoughts were so fractured she couldn't even pay attention to the good-looking man standing next to her. "I...thanks. I think. Sorry, I'm a little distracted."

"I can see that." His lips lifted in a crooked smile that she found incredibly charming.

Her professional mask softened a little.

The phone chimed again. She winced.

His eyes sparkled. "You're very busy and important."

She scowled at the phone. "I should change my name and number, or maybe move to another country."

"Sounds drastic."

Piper sent another link, this time to a Twitter post. She wasn't sure she wanted to know what it said. "My sister likes to make sure I know about all the potential disasters on Twitter."

"Twitter is like watching a fire that's trying to take down a city," Adam said. "It demands an audience while it roars and eats everything in its path."

"Especially when the story is something like this. Did you know the paparazzi already got a shot of us together?" Mattie searched his face for any flicker of recognition.

Adam's eyes widened a little in genuine shock. "When? You've only been here thirty minutes."

She nodded at the hallway. "At the door, when we shook hands. I'm sorry. I should have known they'd follow me. Especially this week."

She pulled up the image.

"It's part of the game. No big deal." Adam peered at it, then shrugged. "Why this week?"

"My sisters are in town, for one. And my name has been trending lately, for another." There was nothing special about the photo. It was just a handshake, and a blurry one at that. But she knew it would mean so much more than that to one particular person. "And it *is* a big deal. At least, it could be. Dev—my previous project is...never mind."

Adam's eyebrows raised in recognition. "Ah, you mean Devon the Douche."

She stared at him in shock before giggles erupted. "That's so wrong. He's not like that, not really. You know Devon Morales?"

"Not personally, but I follow a lot of people in the music industry. He posts everywhere. It's hard to miss." He glanced at her phone. "What's the jackass saying now?"

"It doesn't matter."

The link Piper had sent taunted her, but she was afraid to

touch it. Maybe it would be better if she didn't know what he was saying.

Adam sat down next to her and leaned on the board. "It does matter. Whatever is going on is obviously causing you stress, and since songwriting would be a lot easier if you weren't feeling like that, what can I do to help?"

She sighed and pushed on the link. Devon's latest post filled the screen.

A faker is hooking up with a sellout who's only interested in money. #sad #AdamBrooksDelusionalGlory

She cringed. "I don't think there's anything you can do to help with this."

He leaned over to get a look at her phone. She almost hid it from him, then realized how ridiculous that was because he was tagged in the tweet, so he was bound to see it eventually.

"Delusional Glory? That's the best he's got? Hell, my own father came up with something more creative than that." Adam snorted and sat back in the chair.

"He did?" She tried to picture her own father saying something like that and couldn't.

"Oh yeah, he told me we'd forged new advances in noise pollution, and that we all demonstrated a complete and total absence of talent." Adam's eyes danced with amusement.

She laughed. She couldn't help herself. "He did not. He didn't tell you that."

"Ask him. He'd tell you that, and more. He's actually the one who came up with the Delusions of Glory name. Not that he knew he was doing it. Mostly he was trying to convince me how stupid the whole band thing was. Look how that turned out. Seriously, forget about that crap. If you don't react, they get bored and go away."

Her lighthearted amusement vanished in the face of harsh reality. "No, not always. The last time I ignored a post like that, the guy camped out on my doorstep. He brought a tent and everything. The video of him singing to my door went viral. The police finally hauled him away, but not before a horde of paparazzi had documented it from every angle. The look of betrayal on his face will haunt me for the rest of my life."

"He deserved worse than that." He pressed his lips together.

She raised an eyebrow at that. She didn't disagree. The incident had been creepy and made her feel unsafe, and she'd asked the guy to back off too many times to count. He just wouldn't take no for an answer.

"Well, anyway, that's why I try to stay off social media. It doesn't usually end well, for me."

He nodded. "I get that. But you shouldn't have to hide who you are just because some people can't get a grip on reality."

"Maybe not. But life's easier that way." Mattie looked back at the tweet. "I just wish some people could figure out that writing a song is not the same thing as having a relationship. They take the emotions around the project and turn them into forever, and nothing lasts forever. The project ends, and they're supposed to move on to something—or someone—else."

Mattie bit her lip to stop the babble. She'd said more than she meant to say, but Adam was surprisingly easy to talk to, and he seemed sincere in a way a lot of industry people weren't. It was probably because he had family around him. That firm foundation of love and support kept things real. A tiny flare of jealousy ran through her, followed by the cold realization that she was in trouble. Adam Brooks made her forget she was supposed to keep her distance.

"I don't think that's true," Adam said. "Sure, the project might end, but the song can last a really long time, right?

Might as well be forever. I still sing 'My Girl' in the shower, or 'Purple People Eater' while I'm driving."

She saw the goofy look on his face and couldn't stop the giggle. "Point. I still like to sing 'Over the Rainbow' when I'm in a bad mood."

"See? Some things do last forever." He looked smug.

She rolled her eyes. "You know what I mean. And those songs are only from the forties and fifties. That's hardly forever."

"Hey, they came out long before we were born, and they'll be going strong long after we're gone. That's as close as it gets, right?"

He sounded so sure of himself. He had no idea how quickly things could change.

"We should get to work." She turned off the sound on her phone and placed it upside down on the table. "Let's give the paparazzi something to talk about and run through the rest of the album."

Chapter Six

Adam stepped back into the studio determined to take Mattie's mind off everything that was bothering her. First, he sent a quick text to Lucas.

Buzzards camped outside. Need a ride.

The studio had a side entrance meant for deliveries that was hidden from the street. His manager happened to have a van with a cleaning company logo on it for just such an occasion.

When? How's Bellamy?

Adam glanced at Mattie. She was trying to hide it, but she was looking at her phone again.

He sent back: *Distracted. Give us a few hours.*

He tucked the phone away. Maybe once the music started, she'd settle into the creativity and forget the drama. "Let's start with 'Her Demons Beat My Angels and go down the list."

The guys all nodded their agreement.

"Let's party!" Flynn shouted and counted down.

After what Mattie had done earlier with Johnny J's song, Adam knew she was exactly what they needed. If she agreed to work with him, they'd not only be able to finish off the album, he'd be able to spend a lot of quality time with her.

Problem was, even though she looked up from time to time as they ran through each track, he could tell she was only half paying attention. He checked Twitter surreptitiously during instrumental sections. Devon Morales was certainly making an ass of himself, but it seemed mostly harmless. Just empty words from a blowhard drama queen.

He had to come up with a way to take her mind off the douchebag and get her undivided attention.

They started the fifth track, "Get Back," when the idea sparked. The song was about getting back to the simple things of life. They'd written it near the end of a tour three years ago. They'd been exhausted and running on fumes. Someone, he thought maybe Brandon, had mentioned how they should take a vacation after the last show, which started a round-robin on where they would go.

The ideas grew more and more outrageous as they'd unwound from the show high. Cooper had ended up researching the world's most expensive resorts and had found one they'd all agreed on. But life had interfered, and they'd never made it. As he watched Mattie's expression shift from worried to tired to sad and back, he had a feeling she now might be a great time to put that plan into action.

When they finished the tenth track, they all filed out of the studio and collapsed onto the couches and chairs in the control room.

Mattie put her phone in her lap and covered it with her hands. "That was really...that was great, guys. Thanks for running through all that."

LT picked up one of the donuts from earlier and took a big bite. "What'd you think of track five?"

Everyone had to have noticed how distracted Mattie was

while they were playing, but LT would have taken it the worst. He was the middle child of a large family and fought for scraps of attention as a survival sport. He was probably trying to get her to admit that she'd been ignoring them.

Adam jumped in. "We aren't really worried about track five. We need the help on the last three tracks."

Mattie flashed Adam an indignant look, then gave LT her full attention. "I think the title's wrong, and the chorus could use a little polish, but overall the melody is full of surprises and it's fun. I think it's a keeper."

Adam leaned against the side counter and crossed his arms in satisfaction. She *had* been listening.

"What's wrong with the title?" Flynn asked, sounding a little hurt. The title had been his idea.

Mattie turned a patient smile on him. "Have you really thought about how people who don't know you might interpret 'Pleasure Sticks'? It sounds like you're masturbating with dildos."

There was a moment of stunned silence, and then they all burst out laughing.

"I meant these," Flynn protested, twirling drumsticks.

She held her hands up in surrender. "I'm just saying maybe something like 'Stuck on Love' might work better."

"Dude, I *knew* we shouldn't let you pick the title," Brandon said. "Your mind is in the gutter most of the time."

"Glad Mattie pointed that out *before* we released," Adam said. "Although now that you mention it, maybe we should pass the song to a girl band."

"Don't do that." Mattie said. "It's perfect for you."

"Not sure what that means exactly," LT grinned, "but I like the direction you're going."

Adam was about to ask her take on the other songs, when

Mattie started and looked down at her phone. Again. Yet another text flashed on the screen.

Time to put his new plan into action. He pushed off from the counter and paced closer to Mattie to get her attention. She glanced up long enough for him to make eye contact.

"Now that you've heard most of the album, you can see what we need for the last three. I was hoping for a transition from 'This Is Not the End' to the more lively stuff, but so far nothing I've tried has felt right. That's where you come in."

"Yeah, since Johnny left his writing sucks," Brandon said.

"Not just mine," Adam pointed out. "The melody of that last try was more like something for a horror movie."

"What's wrong with it?" Brandon looked affronted.

"It was supposed to be about life and love, not death and destruction." Adam shook his head at his little brother. "Even if you had just broken up with what's-her-name."

Mattie gave them a look of understanding patience. "It's hard when something you depended on is suddenly gone. It takes time to adjust, I think."

Adam pushed forward before anybody else derailed the conversation. "So, Mattie, one of these three songs is going to be submitted for Song of the Year. When we're working on something like that, we usually do a writing retreat."

"We do?" LT asked.

Brandon looked at Flynn.

Flynn snickered and wiggled his sticks.

Adam shot them a dirty look. "You know, get away from everything so we can really focus on the music. Unplug. Go off the grid."

"Live out every cliche." Cooper rolled his eyes.

Mattie looked amused. "Writing retreat?"

Adam nodded with enthusiasm. "Yeah. We're going to do a month at Syer Island to finish up the album."

"A month?" Cooper choked on something.

LT helpfully pounded him on the back.

Mattie looked back and forth from Cooper to Adam. "Syer Island? Where's that?"

"Isn't that the place by Africa?" Brandon asked.

"The Seychelles," Cooper supplied. "It's really—"

"Beautiful," Adam finished for him. "Totally off the beaten path. They have these amazing villas that open right to the beach. It's a great place to get away from everything."

He saw the second he really caught Mattie's attention. Her phone buzzed as another text came in, but she didn't look down. She had a dreamy, faraway expression in her beautiful hazel eyes, and a small smile lifted her lips. She was already there.

"I'd like you to come with us." He leaned against the control panel next to her. "Our treat. Help us finish these last three songs. At the very least, think of it as a free vacation. We'll be unplugged, just us, a beach, lots of good food, and quality time away from the daily crap. What do you say?"

"Us?" Brandon said. He edged closer to Flynn. "Does he mean all of us?"

"I don't know," Flynn replied.

"I doubt it," Cooper said. "I'm sure he means just the two of them."

Mattie looked doubtful.

Adam jumped in before they could convince her *not* to go. "I meant everybody. I always mean everybody."

LT looked a lot more interested in the conversation. "All five of us?"

Cooper grimaced. "Is this coming out of the general budget, or are we all pitching in?"

Adam kicked his foot. "It's coming from me."

LT's eyes widened. Cooper gave an appraising look that shifted from Adam to Mattie and back.

Flynn hit Brandon's arm. "Told ya."

"Told him what?" Mattie asked.

"Nothing," Brandon said too quickly to be innocent.

Mattie narrowed her eyes at them. "You don't usually do this, do you?"

"Yes, we do," Adam said. "Once a year-ish."

He stood just behind Mattie, so she couldn't see his face, which allowed him to give his bandmates a challenging look. He mouthed, *Go with it.*

Brandon snickered. Adam flipped him off.

Mattie glanced up at him.

"I'm serious." Adam smiled at her. "I need a change of pace, and it sounds like you could use one too."

"Are you really submitting it for Song of the Year?"

Adam nodded. "Not me personally, but the label, yes. It'll be in the contract, with you as lyrics and the rest of us as music."

Mattie bit her lip. "A month."

He could see the glint in her eyes when he mentioned the award. His band already had a Best Song award. Surely, The Bellamy Sisters did too. He made a mental note to look that up.

"It's been awhile since we've won an award, so this means a lot to us. You don't have to decide right this second." Adam kept his tone casual and made sure to look around at everyone rather than pin his gaze on her.

He was just a guy, arranging a work session with colleagues.

No ulterior motives.

None at all.

"Maybe." She glanced at the door. "Not sure we'll be able to leave the studio, much less go away for a month."

"Not a problem," Adam replied. "I have a ride coming to

sneak us out of here. We can drop you at your place, and if you leave me the keys, we'll make sure your car makes it back to you by morning. That way the paparazzi will be off your trail. I'll send you all the details on the trip and you can let me know if you're in. Deal?"

She blinked up at him with hopeful, but guarded eyes. "I'll think about it."

They talked titles and music for another hour until Lucas finally showed up in the delivery van. Adam and Mattie were able to sneak out and take off with nobody noticing, thanks to the invisibility cloak of office supplies and the distraction of the rest of the band leaving out the front door.

Legendary LA traffic being what it was, it took over an hour for Lucas to drive them to Mattie's house, which gave Adam plenty of quality time to talk. At one point, he thought he had convinced her to go on the impromptu writing retreat, but by the time they arrived at her townhouse, he thought she'd changed her mind.

If Adam ever got his hands on Devon the Deranged, he'd throttle him. Between the tweets and two new gossip columns detailing every bit of their love life, it was no wonder she didn't want to take on a project with another man.

He walked her to the front door, racking his brain for something to say that might convince her.

"Look, I know you have a lot going on right now, but I also know the best way to stop being the flavor of the month is to get away from the people with nothing better to do than harass you. There's no paparazzi at Syer Island, and Dismal Devon won't be able to find you."

"I love the names you come up with for him." She smiled faintly. "I'll think about it. Thanks for the ride home."

He knew from the look in her eyes that she planned on saying no; she was just too polite to tell him to his face. He tried not to let the disappointment show. "Sure. Go on in. I want to make sure nobody camps on your doorstep."

She chuckled, and let herself in.

He waited until she'd locked the door and the lights went on inside before he got back in the van. He climbed into the front seat and shut the door.

Lucas lifted an eyebrow. "I think you made a great pitch. Seriously, well done. If I were her I'd jump on it in a heartbeat."

"I want her."

"Yeah, I got that." Lucas put the car in drive, then paused. "So what's the problem?"

"I don't think she wants *me*." It felt odd to put that into words. Like he'd somehow failed a test he didn't know he was taking. "I invited her to a writing retreat on an exclusive tropical island, and she told me she'd think about it. Pretty sure that's girl code for no."

"It's truly a first," Lucas muttered. "A woman turned *you* down."

Adam frowned at him. "It's not like that."

"It's *always* like that. She's a woman, you're a man. Laws of the jungle apply. Look at it this way, she didn't say no to your face. That means the door's open."

"I doubt that," Adam said. "She's just too nice to reject me outright."

Lucas glanced at him. "Let's find out. Computer, call Kat Marshall."

The phone autodialed as Lucas pulled out onto the freeway and immediately slowed to a near stop in rush hour traffic.

"Kat Marshall," a woman answered.

"Kat! This is Lucas. I hear things went very well today between your girl and my boy."

"Oh, Lucas. Hi. Um, I haven't heard from Mattie yet. Are

they done for the day?" Kat sounded surprised, like she'd expected a longer session.

"Vultures were parked out front so we gave her a ride home in my delivery van. Listen, Adam tells me the band is leaving for a writing retreat soon and he wants Mattie to go with. He's buying."

"Oh really? The whole band, or just him?" She sounded suspicious.

Adam made a whirling motion with his finger and mouthed, *All of us.*

"Uh," Lucas watched his finger, so confused he nearly ran into the car in front of them. "Oh, all of them. Of course. It's a nice place, very respectable. *Very* exclusive tropical island."

He gave Adam a sideways look. "She'll have her own room, and there'll be no unwanted bedroom creeping."

"I'll need to talk with her about that. She's having kind of a tough time right now," Kat said. She paused, then added, "What tropical island?"

Adam mouthed the name, but Lucas couldn't tell what he was saying. "I forget the name off the top of my head, but trust me, it's going to be fantastic. Thing is, Adam thinks Mattie's going to say no. Think you can change her mind? It would be a great way to wrap up those last three tracks without distractions, and it'll be a lucrative deal for everyone if these two kids work together on this. Especially if they take Best Song, which how could they not, right?"

"Right. Best Song. Would submission be in the contract?"

Adam nodded emphatically.

Lucas eyed him. "Uh, yes. Of course. All we need is a signature."

"Great." Kat sounded as distracted as Mattie had been. He wondered if she was texting Mattie right now. "Interesting. A tropical island retreat? For how long?"

Lucas glanced at Adam.

"A month," Adam said loud enough for her to hear.

"Is that Adam?" Kat asked.

"Yeah," Adam said. "Hi, Kat. We'll stay a month to really give the song the attention it needs, but of course Mattie can come and go whenever she'd like. No pressure. I know she's been through a lot of stress recently, and I just thought she might like a chance to get away from it."

"That's very thoughtful of you. *Very* thoughtful. What resort is this?"

"Syer Island, in the Seychelles," Adam said. "She'll have her own private villa that opens right onto the beach."

He stressed the word "private," hoping to drive home the idea that he wasn't a Devon Morales clone. Mattie deserved a lot better than that prick.

He could hear typing in the background. He glanced at Lucas, who shrugged and mouthed, *Wait*.

"Syer Island. I just looked it up. Wow. That's beautiful. You're staying a *month*? I'm not sure I'd ever come back if I stayed that long."

Adam laughed softly. "Think you can talk to her for me? I'd really like to work with her on this project, and I think she'd have fun."

"Let me see what I can do." She sounded a lot friendlier than she had at the beginning of the conversation.

"Thanks, Kat," Lucas said. He ended the call. "Well you got her vote. Now we wait. I got to say, I'm impressed. I didn't think you'd get Mattie Bellamy to come around."

"I don't think I did. I think the rest of her life might do that for me." Adam looked at the gridlock in front of them. "I think it would be faster if I walked back to the studio."

Adam texted Cooper while they crawled toward their destination. *Set up Syer. April. Book the whole month. My account. Exclusive access.*

"Trust me, if she goes along with this crazy idea it'll be because of your sultry eyes and dazzling smile."

Adam huffed a laugh. "I doubt she even noticed my eyes. She'll go because she really wants to escape from her life. Can't say I blame her. The last tweet from Devon said the love of his life stole his words. The dude is clingy as shit."

An incoming text from Cooper chimed. *You know how much that costs?*

Don't care, he sent back.

You do. It's 1.5 mil.

Adam stared at the number. *All inclusive?*

Yes.

Adam nodded. *Do it.*

Deposit not refundable. What if she says no?

He thought about it for at least a half second. *We're going anyway.*

This is messed up.

Adam huffed out a sigh. *Book it.*

"Yeah that photo of you two wasn't a great shot. Maybe we should have a photographer on the island to get some candids for the media." Lucas honked the horn. "Wake the fuck up, asshole! Think we got all day here?"

"No." Adam turned toward Lucas so he could make sure the man heard his message. "No cameras. No photographers of any kind. Got me?"

Lucas shrugged. "Stupid to turn down publicity. You got a new album coming out, and you need hype to win awards. Not to mention the tour after that. We got to think about drumming up interest now."

"No cameras. Got me?" Adam pictured what Mattie might

do if she saw someone taking a picture of them on the island. She'd never speak to him again, that was for sure.

Lucas eyed him, then slowly nodded. "Got it."

Adam sat back and stared out the window. He didn't see the traffic. He saw a beach and a girl with honey hair and hazel eyes.

His phone chimed. Cooper had sent one word. *Done.*

Now all he had to do was wait for Mattie Bellamy to say yes.

Chapter Seven

Mattie stared down with delight at sparkling ocean waves from the kind of helicopter used by people who had no idea that money was anything other than a way to keep score. She was headed to a tropical island so remote she'd had trouble finding it on a map, with five men she didn't know, to a place she'd never heard of, to live and breathe music and nature for an entire month. She'd never taken this kind of break before. They were supposed to be working, but there was a beach, and adult beverages, and songwriting had never felt like work. This might as well be a monthlong vacation from everything.

There was no way to drive to Syer Island. There were no bridges to connect it with any other island in Seychelles. It was the very definition of isolation.

She hadn't received a call, text, or notice of a tweet the entire twelve hours they'd been in the air. It felt strange and a little unsettling to be so out of touch.

"There it is." Adam pointed toward land in the distance.

"See the cliff? The main house is up there. The villas are below."

Adam's thigh touched hers as he leaned closer to the window. She felt the warmth of him through the thin material of her skirt, which stirred all the nerve endings along that side of her body. She dragged her mind back from the blossoming images of her lying somewhere beachy with Adam and focused it instead on the job she'd been hired to do.

She had a song to write. Three songs. This was a working relationship. Nothing more. Nothing less.

"It's beautiful," she said, just so Adam wouldn't wonder why she was so quiet.

Adam leaned closer. "Yes. Very."

Why did those two words send a little thrill down her spine? For heaven's sake, he was just talking about the view.

When they landed, she stepped out of the helicopter and into a fantasy. They were greeted by fresh sea breezes, rhythmic music, and a line of happy faces dressed in crisp white shirts and shorts.

The luggage, including the instruments and gear, traveled behind them by boat, so Mattie carried only the bag that contained her essential notebooks and pens.

A tall blond man in khaki pants and a white button-down shirt stepped forward and snapped photos with his heavy professional camera as they exited the helicopter.

"Welcome to Syer Island!" he called out. "Smile, you've just stepped into paradise!"

Mattie swore under her breath at the intrusion and instinctively shied away. It was a silly overreaction. He wasn't paparazzi. Not really. But she hadn't expected it. What if the photos of all of them together got out before she was ready? What if Devon saw them? How would he react?

Adam stepped in front of her with his hands outstretched. "Hey, man. No photos."

The photographer lowered his camera and smiled the broad smile used by con men everywhere. "Don't worry man. I'm not the press."

Adam remained in between her and the photographer in a protective wide stance.

"I don't give a shit who you are. You have a camera in our face, and we don't want it there." Adam's tone was low and dangerous, like he was her own personal attack dog.

It was ridiculous, but it made her feel safer than she had in a long time.

The photographer held his hand out in apparent apology. "My name is Don, and I'm the official Syer Island memory maker. At the end of the trip, you'll get a flash drive with all the images I take of your entire group, plus a video montage, and prints if you want."

Adam shook his head. "No. We don't want. We don't want any photography of any kind. No videos, no shots, no prints. Nothing. Got me?"

Don glanced around at the others, but they gave him cold stares in return. He shouldered the camera and nodded. "Your call. No problem. Have a great stay."

Don sauntered off down the path, whistling.

Mattie breathed a sigh of relief, though the encounter had left her feeling unsettled. She had a sudden urge to check her phone for Twitter updates.

At the edge of the landing area, they were greeted by a line of people who surged forward to greet them.

A man about her height, with high cheek bones, the deepest brown eyes she'd ever seen, and a small scar above his right eyebrow stepped up to her. "Welcome, welcome, Miss Bellamy. I am your personal butler. It is my pleasure to help you with your bag. I am Abayomi, which means bringer of great joy. Come with me, I will show you to your new home."

His attitude was infectious. She found herself smiling back at him. "Nice to meet you, Abayomi. Please, call me Mattie."

When he reached for her shoulder bag, she shook her head. "I'll take this."

"It is no trouble, Miss Mattie, no trouble at all. I have strong muscles, you see?" He held up one bicep and flexed it, which made her giggle. "If you like, I can take your things to your home while you explore?"

She glanced at the others. They were all being similarly accosted by helpful staff.

Adam gestured for his own butler, a short, spry woman with a little gray in her hair but a young-looking face, to lead the way. He caught Mattie looking waved. "Go get settled. We'll meet up for dinner at sunset."

"This way, Miss Mattie." Abayomi gestured for her to follow, then led the way down a weathered boardwalk to a pathway of smooth packed dirt to the south. It ran under a canopy of tropical trees and bushes on one side, open to the bright white sand and crystal-blue ocean on the other.

The only noise along the way was Abayomi's cheerful chatter and the soothing sounds of ocean waves.

"We are excited to have you stay with us. Anything you need, anything at all, you are to tell Abayomi immediately. I am all yours. I take care of your villa like it was my own home. Do you like a drink of coffee or tea in the mornings, Miss Mattie? I can make sure it is ready for you when you wake."

"Coffee, please. With cream." She felt a little overwhelmed by the attention. She lived casually simple most of the time. She didn't even have a cleaning crew. She cooked all her own meals and didn't go out much, and when she did it was to small, local places where nobody would know her.

Even when The Bellamy Sisters were at the height of their popularity, she hadn't really enjoyed the lavish lifestyle of the rich and famous. She'd avoided most of it, most of the time. She was always going to be the small-town girl from Tennessee. Even if she had lost most of the accent and roamed a long way from home, it was still a part of her.

Abayomi glanced over his shoulder and beamed at her. "Miss Mattie, we are in the villa near the turn far ahead. It is a long walk. Are you tired from your journey? We can take a car."

"A car?" She hadn't seen any sort of road, much less vehicle, until they reached a small clearing filled with several four-seater golf carts. Abayomi placed her suitcase on the back seat and ushered her into the passenger seat.

"I take you this way, so that you are not too tired. You relax now, Miss Mattie. I will get you home. See to the left? That is where we play the volleyball. If you go north from the landing, that is the path to the Big House on the cliff."

She nodded and let him rattle on about the many things there were to do on the island. After a short drive, they approached a clearing, which opened up to reveal a large, thatched-roof, open-air building on the right and a pit of comfortable chairs on the sand to the left.

Abayomi stopped the cart and waved at it. "This is the dining place. You come here when you are hungry, yes? Or you call me. Or you go to the Big House. This on the right we call Sunset Beach. You will come here tonight, yes? Yes, it is very nice. There will be music, and dancing, and stars, and waves. What more could anyone want, yes?"

"It's perfect," she assured him.

By the time they reached the first villa, Mattie was glad they'd taken the cart.

Abayomi zipped past what looked like a large, open-air hut,

with walls completely open to the elements and a living room that took full advantage of the view. Nobody was inside.

"How far down is my room?" Mattie asked.

"We are number nine, Miss Mattie. There are ten homes on this side of the island, not counting the Big House at the north end. It is very private. You will love this, it is an escape, no?"

"Yes, it is. There are ten of these? How many stay in each one?" She wondered if the band was all sharing one house. As they passed the second hut, she thought it looked more than big enough for seven people.

"It is your home, Miss Mattie. It is yours. None other will stay, unless of course you invite them." He grinned at her. "This island has a way with love, so who is to say how long you will wish to be alone."

She processed that information. "How big are these homes?"

"450 square meters."

Mattie tried to do the math in her head, but the number she came up with couldn't possibly be right. "These villas are five thousand square feet?"

Abayomi screwed up his nose in concentration, then brightened and nodded. "Yes, Miss Mattie. Each home has an indoor and outdoor shower, a pool, fully provided kitchen and bar, as well as space for massage and private exercise. Anything you want, you pick up the phone, Miss Mattie. I will make it happen. I am your, how they say, fairy godfather. I want to make your stay the best memory."

She gaped at the next one they passed. How many had it been? Seven? Eight? "Do we each have our own villa?"

"Yes. Yes, of course." Abayomi nodded emphatically. "Arrangements were made for each to have space to, what did they say, retreat. We are here, Miss Mattie."

He brought the cart to a stop in front of Villa 9, according to the hand-carved sign out front. She could just make out Adam's golf cart and Villa 10 through the trees ahead. He was right next door.

Why did she find the idea of that so disconcerting?

"This way, Miss Mattie. Just up these steps." Abayomi led the way across a deck filled with overstuffed lounge chairs and a plunge pool to the open-air living room of the villa.

"There's no wall?" Mattie stepped slowly over the threshold and glanced around, but there was nothing to stop the ocean breeze from flowing in and out the entire front of the villa along with the sound of the waves.

"The wall slides back to allow nature inside your heart, Miss Mattie." Abayomi gestured to a control panel discreetly hidden behind a plant in the corner. "If you wish the glass to close, you simply press the button."

The living room faced the ocean, with the kitchen and bar behind it also facing out. Everything from the furniture to the side walls was bamboo, tropical charm, and serenity. The overall effect was an invitation to escape into another reality, one where walls weren't required. "There's no front door? People just come in?"

It felt both too exposed and dangerously free.

Abayomi gave her an understanding smile. "This island is yours, Miss Mattie. None will bother you here. But the walls lock if you wish, as do the bedroom doors."

She blinked, non-plussed by the idea of leaving the entire front of the house open.

Her phone buzzed. She must have stepped into a Wi-Fi hotspot because when she fished it out of her purse at least a dozen text messages pinged one after the other.

"This way, Miss Mattie." Abayomi led her down a hall toward the bedrooms, pointing out the features of the villa along the way. "There are three bedrooms, each with a private bath, plus the master suite. The library is to the right of the kitchen and includes a game system and other activities for your amusement. I will be here in the morning and evening, to be sure all is as it should be. If you require anything, you have but to pick up the house phone and ask."

Mattie followed him, but her phone kept demanding her attention. Two texts from Della begged her to call back, three from Kat detailed possible new projects, and one from Lizzie asked if she made it okay.

Abayomi set her suitcase on a small stand at the foot of the bed and gestured to the door in the corner. His smile was kind enough to melt some of the tension from her shoulders. "There is a refreshing shower waiting for you, and food and drink in the kitchen."

"Thank you. This is amazing." Her phone dinged, and a text from Piper appeared with a link to another gossip blog, which showed Mattie arriving at the airport with the headline *Bellamy Babe Hunting for Next Victim?*

Piper sent along a helpful comment. *Make sure there's no cameras at that resort.*

"How am I supposed to do that?" she wondered out loud.

Abayomi gently took the phone away from her.

She started to protest, but he shook his head and with a kind expression laid it carefully in the nightstand drawer, then slid the drawer closed. The muffled ding of incoming texts sounded almost resentful.

Abayomi studied her with an understanding, almost fatherly gaze. "You must relax, Miss Mattie, and take in paradise. She will warm your soul, if you let her."

She smiled, feeling a little rueful. "It's easy to say, but not so easy to do."

"While you are here, leave the things that bring you stress

in the drawers, and only take with you the things that bring you joy."

He opened the closet door and waved his hand. "Remove the outside world from your shoulders, and be with us, in this moment. While you are here, *this* is all that matters. The rest of the world will be there when you have reclaimed yourself. It will wait, Miss Mattie."

"I'm not sure I want it to wait on me." If Devon found someone new to fixate on, that would be ideal. "But I understand what you're saying. I'll try to really *be* here, and not there. Thank you."

"My pleasure, Miss Mattie." He bowed his head, then left.

Mattie was tempted to take the phone back out of the drawer, but she resisted the urge. Maybe just one night, she would see how long she could go without the constant interruption. She pulled a change of clothes out of her suitcase, then went to explore the outdoor shower.

Ten minutes under the refreshing stream of water, surrounded by lush green plants and the sound of the ocean, and Mattie realized Kat had been right. This was the perfect place to get away from cameras and social media and gossip blogs and most of all, sisters.

She was glad she came.

Chapter Eight

Adam took the steps to Mattie's villa two at a time. He'd changed into island wear consisting of khaki shorts, a white untucked linen shirt, and docksiders. If Mattie hadn't been there, he probably wouldn't have bothered with the shirt or the shoes, but he was trying to impress her with how adult he was compared to Devon.

The glass walls were wide open, allowing him easy access to her living room. "Mattie? Ready for dinner?"

She appeared from the back of the villa wearing a dress that made him trip over the last step. The halter-style top revealed her shoulders and, when she turned to pick up something, her bare back all the way down to her waist. A slit up the side of the long skirt revealed a tantalizing amount of thigh.

He recovered his footing in time to lean against the couch in what he hoped was a cool, suave pose.

She crossed to the control panel. "I can't believe there's no wall. People live like this?"

"I think they like to leave it open to give you the feel of being one with nature. I'm sure we'll get used to it."

Mattie looked unsure, as if the idea of leaving all the doors and windows open was too much exposure, but she didn't push the button to slide the walls shut.

He hurried to reassure her. "There's a safe in the bedroom closet, and the bedroom door locks. You don't have to worry about thieves, or anything else here. You saw how hard it was to even get on this island. It's not open to the public."

She frowned. "What if it rains?"

He shrugged. "The butlers take care of all that. You're supposed to leave all cares and worries behind. Wasn't that in the brochure?"

She huffed a laugh. "I haven't lived somewhere with no locks since I was about eight. After mom died we moved from a little po-dunk town outside Nashville into an apartment in the city. With four girls you can imagine how paranoid my dad was about locks. This open-air thing feels a little strange. What if someone...I mean, that guy with the camera might..."

"He won't bother you again. I promise. Would you like a ride to dinner?" He gestured to the golf cart outside.

"I guess I can give it a try." She dropped her hand away from the control panel and crossed the living room to the sofa to pick up her bag. "Sure. Let's go."

He took the drive to dinner as slow as he could without looking obvious. It wasn't hard. The cart appeared to have only two speeds: slow and stop.

"There's something different about you."

She watched the ocean as they drove, seemingly entranced by the waves. "Oh?"

"It took me a few minutes to figure it out, but I got it now." He grinned. "No phone."

She gave him a rueful smile. "My butler told me I should leave the things that were causing me stress in the drawer. So I did. Just for tonight."

Adam nodded. "He sounds like a wise man."

"Did you bring yours?" She tilted her head. The blazing orange of the sunset brought out the gold in her hair.

"Guilty. But I have it on vibrate, and mine doesn't stress me out like yours seems to."

"That's because you don't have sisters." She returned her attention to the waves.

Even without the phone in her hands she didn't seem completely on the island. Not yet.

He'd planned for this moment all day, but now that he had alone time with her, he was coming up blank on what to say.

By the time they reached Sunset Beach, everyone else was already there. Flynn and Brandon were kicked back on a couch near the firepit with a bucket of beers between them. Cooper and his girlfriend, Tina, a stunning brunette model he'd picked up at the end of their last tour, occupied a love seat next to Flynn, and both held half-drunk cocktails. LT stood nearby chatting up a very attractive server. Judging by the way the girl giggled, he might not be sleeping alone tonight.

A fire blazed in the pit, and the setting sun played with the waves in the background. He couldn't have created a more romantic setting. It was perfect. He and Mattie crossed to an open love seat next to Brandon and sat down.

"This place is ten out of ten for style," Cooper raised his glass. "To tropical islands and making music."

"I'll drink to that," Flynn said.

"The French Polynesians have more amenities and less mosquitoes." Tina tossed her hair.

"Shame you didn't go there, then." Brandon smiled politely at her.

Adam shot his brother a hard look. The last thing he wanted their first night on the island was a fight with Tina.

She'd been upset about something the entire way here, and he could tell Cooper was embarrassed by her behavior already.

Mattie gave Tina an appraising look, then turned to Adam with a business-like expression. "Let's talk about the album. It feels like the theme you're going for is change. Changes in love, and life, that kind of thing. So the last three songs should carry that forward. What topic do you feel like you haven't covered yet?"

"We had a theme?" Brandon asked, his face wrinkled in confusion.

"Yeah, the same one we always have," LT said. He'd lost the server's attention and meandered closer to the firepit. "Make songs that don't suck."

"That's not a theme, that's a motto," Cooper said.

"The theme wasn't exactly change," Adam said. From the look on Tina's face, there was about to be an implosion if he didn't provide distraction. "This one was mostly playing around with minor keys. So, that slightly off-kilter feel. We'll want to keep that going."

"I noticed that, but that's not the theme," Mattie said. "That's the voice. The tone. If we're going to write a new song, I need to know what message you want to focus on."

Adam turned away from the group so he could focus entirely on Mattie. "Why limit ourselves? First we play with the melody, then we'll see what words pop out. Let them flow from the music."

"We can't just let them flow." Mattie drew the word out with a note of derision. "We won't end up with the story we need to tell if we do that. First we have to tell the story, *then* we craft the melody to match."

Adam blinked at her. "I always start with the melody. It's the foundation of the song."

"No, it isn't." Mattie's chin lifted a little. "Words are the foundation of every story."

"See," Flynn said, "this is the kind of thing people usually sort out *before* they partner with someone on a project."

"Yeah," Brandon said. "This is like watching a first date happen, without the fun sex stuff."

LT muttered something Adam couldn't quite hear, and Cooper's attention was focused on Tina.

"Without the melody, the words are useless." Adam shifted, a little uncomfortable with the direction of the conversation.

She frowned up at him. "Words don't need a melody to tell a story."

"A melody doesn't need words to tell a story." He started humming a random melody. He let it dip, then soar, and finally he sang out the last few bars. "Ba-ba-bum-bum-da-dum."

The guys cheered, and several servers clapped in polite appreciation.

Mattie rolled her eyes. "And what story was that little snippet trying to tell?"

"It's the story of a man who's hungry and needs a drink." Adam smiled victoriously at her. "The last bit was announcing that food is here at last."

"That's not the story I heard." Her expression turned crafty. "I heard the story of a man so filled with ego that he lives his entire life alone until finally he throws himself on the mercy of the ocean. The last bit was the ocean, telling him there is no mercy for a man who does not know love."

He stared at her, dumbfounded. "That wasn't what I had in mind when I sang it."

"But it's what came to my mind when I heard it. Without words, the listener will always make up their own meaning." She took a smug sip of her cocktail.

Her insistence on doing it backwards was going to cause problems. His mind didn't work that way. "The melody *has* to exist first, otherwise there's no vessel to hold the words. They'd just be poetry sitting on a page that nobody gets to hear. With the melody worked out first, we can be sure of having a catchy hook that people will hum to themselves in the shower or on the subway."

"Without the lyrics, there's no direction. The music has no point. It's just background noise. The lyrics are what they'll quote to their friends. Lyrics are what make the song truly memorable."

"We've done just fine making memorable songs so far." He couldn't believe how utterly and completely stubborn she was being.

Her smile challenged him. "If you want to work with me, we'll need to work on the lyrics first. Then the melody."

"You're not serious." He ran his hand through his hair. "I've always done the melody first."

"Well this will be a nice change for you, then." Mattie shrugged. "You hired me for words, so that's what you'll get. Words."

Brandon looked delighted. "This should be fun."

Adam shot his brother a dirty look. "Don't laugh. If we do the words first that means you'll have to figure out the melody that fits them instead of running off into the forest to frolic with whatever mood strikes."

Brandon shrugged. "Challenge accepted."

Mattie glanced around at the group. "Look, I'm not saying that melody isn't important. Of course it is. Inspiration comes from all kinds of places, including the little bits of chords you play on the piano or the guitar. I'm just saying that to make a cohesive whole, I—we—need to really focus on the words and how they join with the melody."

Adam wanted to keep the argument going. It was both fun and frustrating to get a real glimpse at how her mind worked.

Then he realized what she'd just said.

We.

He pictured the two of them, sitting side by side on one of the love seat like they were now. He could feel the warmth of her body next to his. Her hair might fall across his arm. His hand might accidentally-on-purpose brush against hers. The fantasy killed most of his frustration.

They could debate how they'd approach the songwriting later. For now, he'd heard the magic word, and that's all he really needed. "That's exactly what I'm saying. Together, we'll make magic."

Flynn groaned.

Brandon rolled his eyes.

Mattie's eyes sparkled with amusement. "Do you always give up an argument so easy?"

"No," Cooper said dryly. "Not normally."

Adam glared at Cooper. "I'm starving, let's eat."

AFTER DINNER, they sat around the fire drinking something green that was sour and sweet and burned all the way down. It was nice to unwind from the trip and sink into a little jet lag.

Eventually, LT pulled his acoustic guitar out of its case and began plucking random chords, tuning the strings, while Brandon hummed bits of songs.

Cooper stirred from where he sat with his arm around his girlfriend to lean forward with his drink held high in the air. "Gentlemen, let's show our respect to the classics."

Tina shifted away from his arm and settled back in her seat looking petulant. For a woman who appeared desperate to date a musician, she didn't seem to like music very much. He had no idea what Cooper saw in her. Great sex, probably.

Flynn grinned and beat his chest, then started a beat on the table next to him. They all bobbed their heads in time to it, and the energy started to build.

Mattie smiled in obvious delight. "What song is this?"

"Wait for it," Cooper said. He handed his drink to Tina and stood up.

Adam held up a hand and closed his eyes.

Flynn stopped the beat.

After a couple of seconds of relative silence, Adam took in a long breath and sang the first line of "Seven Bridges Road" by the Eagles. It was just his voice extending through the night, punctuated by the distant wash of the ocean.

He sang a cappella through the first four lines, then opened his eyes and smiled at Mattie.

Her answering smile made the stars seem dim.

LT started up with the guitar, then he, Adam, Brandon, and Cooper sang the next verse in harmony while Flynn picked up the beat. When it came to the bridge, Cooper's high tenor rang out strong and true and built to a crescendo. Then the beat stopped, the guitar drifted away, and it was Adam standing alone to finish the last notes of the song.

When he let the last note go, Adam bowed with flourish.

Mattie clapped. "That was wonderful! I love the Eagles."

The guys slapped palms and congratulated each other on a job well done. Several servers applauded and cheered.

"Hey, let's run through 'Big Dreams,'" Adam suggested. It was the eighth song on the new album, had a simple arrangement, and was well suited to just a guitar.

LT started up the song. Flynn joined in with the rhythm, and the rest of them fell into step, with Cooper providing air guitar support.

"Do you know where Adam is?"

"One moment, Miss Mattie. I will check for you." After a muffled exchange, Abayomi cleared his throat and continued. "It appears Mr. Adam is scheduled for deep sea fishing at ten a.m. Would you like to join him?"

She blinked. "He's leaving for the whole day?"

"Yes, Miss Mattie. The boat will return at sunset."

Adam was playing some kind of game, but she didn't know the rules. When they spoke *about* the songs he sounded sincere, but when she tried to actually work on them, he dodged or changed the subject. And there was always something in the way of getting the job done: a meal, a guided tour, a game of volleyball...something.

Every time he distracted her from the project, he had that manic, I'm-winning twinkle in his eyes.

The first couple of days had been amusing. She'd played along since she'd desperately needed to unwind, and she'd enjoyed getting to know the entire band better. But this was getting ridiculous.

"Yes," she said. "I would like to join him."

"I will bring the buggy to you right away."

"Thanks, Abayomi." She double-checked her bag to make sure she'd included the notebooks with her latest lyrics, several colored pens, and sticky notes. Perfect. She had everything she'd need for a day of battle with the uninspired and reluctant.

She climbed into the golf cart with a determined smile. "Thanks for the ride, Abayomi. Has Adam left yet?"

He pulled onto the path toward the docks. "No, Miss Mattie. The captain will not depart until you arrive."

"Good. I think."

A debate about whether she should be doing this or not raged in her head. On the one hand, at least Adam wouldn't be able to run off or distract her with anything while they were trapped on a boat. On the other, she'd be trapped on a boat. With Adam.

The more time she spent with him, the more comfortable she felt around him. She wanted to find out even more about him, like how his hands would feel if they massaged her shoulders, or how soft his lips would be if they touched hers.

She shouldn't be thinking things like that.

"You like fishing, Miss Mattie?" Abayomi asked.

"I won't be fishing." She patted her bag. "I'll be working."

"Work. Who needs that?" He waved a dismissive hand at her. "Be where you are. Enjoy the moments. The days spent here are not like any others."

There was something about his words that triggered a spark in her thoughts.

Be where you are. Enjoy the moment. These days are not like any others.

She fished a notebook out of her bag and wrote them down before she forgot them. "I could enjoy it more if Adam would focus on the project we came here to do."

"Oh, I think he *is* focused, Miss Mattie." He nodded and grinned. "He is focused like the sea at high tide."

"What do you mean?"

"The sea, it pushes, it pulls, but always it reaches to the same place." He winked at her. "This man you hunt, he does the same, yes?"

"The only thing I've seen him reach for is procrastination." She shook her head. "If we moved any slower on this project, we'd be going backwards. He just doesn't seem to understand how important this is."

Abayomi stopped next to the dock.

"Sometimes we have to go slow to go fast, Miss Mattie." He pointed to the largest boat at the dock and smiled. "The Imagination is waiting for you. Enjoy the day."

She'd come to really like the unassuming, happy man who brought her smiles and coffee every morning. She gave him a quick kiss on the cheek. "Thanks for the ride. And the advice."

"My pleasure, Miss Mattie. Always." He bobbed his head and took off down the path.

She walked up the dock to a white boat with rich wood accents and the name *Imagination* written in black on the side. It looked more like a yacht than a fishing boat. There was a main cabin with windows so tinted she couldn't see inside, and a deck big enough for twenty people at the rear of the boat. Steps provided access to the water for would-be swimmers or divers. Padded seats lined the edges of the deck, and fishing poles had been arranged neatly at the end of each bench.

She spotted Adam lounging in the captain's chair in the center of the deck. He held a drink in one hand and a book in the other. She stopped with one hand on the rail.

He wore white cargo shorts and a white linen shirt that lay open to expose his bare chest and the Delusions of Glory tattoo. The spiral artwork played with her eyes and confused her thoughts. How could such a simple design look so...*inviting*? Her gaze traced the lines of it around and down to where it ended in a flourish just above his belly button, then continued the remaining distance to where his shorts interrupted the view.

The pang of regret she felt at not being able to see more of him didn't make sense. Neither did the sudden itch she had to trace that tattoo with her finger.

This was her writing partner, not her date.

A deckhand cleared his throat. "Welcome aboard, Miss Mattie. Can I bring you anything?"

Mattie jumped. She hadn't even seen him approach. Her cheeks heated with embarrassment. "Um, just some water, thanks."

The young man gestured to the right. "Please have a seat. We will be underway in a moment."

Mattie nodded her acknowledgment but didn't move. She had to get a grip on herself before she talked to Adam.

She was here to write a song. If she let herself get carried away, she could end up with even worse headlines than she had already. She'd barely kissed Devon and it had turned into a fake Twitter breakup of epic proportions.

What would happen if she let herself be swept away by Adam and tropical island lust? It wasn't like they had any kind of future together. He was a rock star. She was a pop princess. In what real world would they mesh?

She didn't think Adam was remotely like Devon, but there were still a million ways things could go horribly wrong if she followed her sex drive instead of her head.

The boat shifted, reminding her they were trying to get the fishing expedition underway. She gave herself a mental shake, gathered her resolve, and stalked toward her prey with determination to get the project back on track and her thoughts under control. "You're avoiding me."

Adam peered at her over the top of the book. "No I'm not. I've been waiting for you for two hours."

"You are aware you didn't actually invite me, right?" She stared the way she used to do when she wanted her sisters to stop teasing.

"Are you sure? I could swear I mentioned going fishing."

She narrowed her eyes at him. "Yes, I'm sure you did. You went over a list of *every* activity available on the island. You didn't actually say you were going *today*, or that I should come along with you."

He shrugged and didn't look the least bit bothered by her frustration. "I woke up this morning thinking about how much easier it is to work while being rocked by ocean waves. I knew you'd find me sooner or later."

Her inner Southern girl politeness collided with the exasperation she increasingly felt around Adam. She wanted to tell him to stop being a jackass, but instead she summoned her syrupy sweet voice, the one she used with people being intentionally dense, in the hopes he'd get the message. "You could have knocked on my door or left a note."

"Where's the fun in that?" He tossed the book he'd been reading onto the nearest bench.

The boat shifted as they pulled away from the dock. She sat down so she wouldn't trip and fall into his lap. "We came here to get some work done."

"We have all day to ourselves." A hint of a twinkle lit his eyes. "We'll have to figure out some way to fill the time."

The teasing innuendo in his tone made her lose her train of thought for a second. For one brief, wild flash, she imagined a very different day than the one she had planned. Then she shook herself and clung to her need to be professional like a security blanket.

"Would you focus, please?" She opened her bag and pulled out the most recent notebook and a pen. "I've been working on the chorus. Do you want to hear what I have so far?"

Adam stretched and yawned. "Sure. But give me a minute?"

He ducked into the cabin before she could answer.

She followed him with the notebook, but he disappeared behind a door just inside the cabin.

"Adam!" She wiggled the knob, but it was locked. "Open this door."

Someone cleared their throat behind her. "Water, miss?"

Mattie glanced over her shoulder at the deckhand who held out a small silver tray with a frosted bottle of water.

She shook her head. "Do you have the key to this door?"

"It's the facilities, miss."

"Oh." Heat rose in her cheeks, until she remembered he was doing this on purpose. She pounded on the door again "You have to stop this."

Adam's response was too muffled to make out, but she thought she heard laughter.

"If we don't finish this song, it can't be submitted for the awards, which means there's no point to me even being here." She hit the door once more to vent her frustration. "It might not mean much to you, but it matters to me. If don't want me here, just say so and I'll get out of your life."

Adam said something else she couldn't understand but didn't open the door.

Mattie spun on her heels and stalked back to the deck. Maybe she should write the song by herself.

She double-checked the chorus she'd come up with last night during dinner.

Changing is hard
Changing is rough
But what if it changes minds, what if it helps us find
Something we once lost, somewhere along the way?
Isn't that worth the time?

THE LYRICS DIDN'T FEEL RIGHT for Delusions of Glory, or for Adam. They were too...something. Girly? Earnest?

She glanced behind her. Adam still hadn't emerged from the bathroom. The man was either avoiding her or he was having serious bowel trouble.

The island slipped by while she rearranged words. No matter what she did, they didn't fit together the way they needed to. Her gut told her to scrap the entire attempt and start over, but she really wanted some feedback before she did that.

Something about being around Adam scrambled her ability to put thoughts together, and it was getting more than a little aggravating. He wanted to play when she wanted to work. He pushed her to try new things when all she really wanted to do was curl up with her notes and make a beautiful song.

The last few days had been completely unproductive, even if they had more fun than she'd had in a long, long time. If she'd known tropical resorts could be like this, she would have visited one years ago.

The boat shifted course toward a jetty that emerged from a secluded cove. The beach was small and pristine. Something inside her yearned to let go and enjoy the sand, a book, and the ocean breezes.

What was she thinking? She didn't have time to read. She needed to make these songs better than anything she'd ever written. The more Adam distracted her, the further away from her goal she was.

Damn the man for bringing her somewhere so enticing.

She spotted a table for two nestled under an overhang on the right. It was perfectly romantic and entirely wrong for what they were supposed to be doing.

She looked back at the cabin.

Adam had finally emerged from the bathroom and now leaned against the doorway, watching her with that crooked smile of his. She'd learned over the past five days that this particular smile meant he was about to suggest they play hooky. Again.

"Welcome to Du Nord Beach," Adam said. "The only way to get here is by boat."

Mattie pushed herself out of the chair. She was so full of conflicting emotions she didn't know what to do with them. She wanted to demand he stop goofing around, but she longed to enjoy the day on that beach, so the words she should say came out all garbled. "Why...Is this...I thought we were going fishing."

"We can do that too." Adam gestured at the beach. "I just thought we might have lunch and do a little snorkeling first. But no pressure. We can spend hours embracing smelly fish instead. Your call."

She blinked at him. Everything about this day said romantic ambush, but his tone was casually considerate. The two things didn't go together. "We're not supposed to be doing either of those things. We're supposed to be working, remember?"

Adam shrugged. "So who's stopping you?"

"You. You're stopping me." She waved her notebook at him, and irritation pushed politeness aside enough for her to say what she was really thinking. "You've been doing everything you can to avoid work since we stepped foot on this island."

"I have not." His eyebrows rose as if he was offended, but his voice betrayed amusement.

She held up her index finger. "First, you called off a session so the guys could surf."

"The waves wait for no one. And it was the first day. We all needed to relax a bit to get in the groove." He pointed at her. "You had a good time body surfing, admit it."

She'd had a fantastic time body surfing, but she wasn't going to tell him that, not when he looked so smug.

"That's not the point." She held up two fingers. "You

completely forgot about the second session, and when I tracked you down you insisted we have lunch first."

"I was starving." He patted his abs. "You can't work on an empty stomach."

"Lunch turned into dinner and a two-hour horse ride along the beach."

"But you were relaxed at the end of it, right? All the better for writing."

"No. I wasn't relaxed. That's not what I was." She'd found the experience so exhilarating that she'd been completely transported back to childhood, which turned her around so completely she actually left her bag behind on the beach. She found it waiting for her on the couch when she woke up the next morning. She couldn't remember the last time she'd gone so long without opening one of her notebooks.

She gave herself a mental shake. The fact that she'd enjoyed herself didn't change the fact that it was another day of song writing lost.

Adam raised an eyebrow at her. "Is that it? You seemed like you were on a roll."

"No that's not it." She held up three fingers. "Yesterday you said you had a headache because the sun was too bright, and then insisted on an all-day spa treatment to recover."

"I thought all girls loved facials and massages." He looked genuinely perplexed.

She wasn't fooled. Adam was a first-rate performer. He could fake confusion. "I like them fine, but they're supposed to be a reward *after* I've written a song, not before."

He snorted. "Life's way too short to put off the things you enjoy like that. Eat dessert first, I say."

"I do *not* put things off."

Adam gestured at the notebook in her hand. "You live

inside your notes instead of out here, with us mere mortals. That's the ultimate putting things off, I'd say."

She gave him her best be-reasonable glare. "You invited me here to *work*. And you can stop pretending that you don't work just as hard as I do. I've read the blogs. You're driven and insanely goal oriented, which is one of the reasons I took a chance on coming here. I shouldn't have to chase you all over the island."

Adam's face contorted into a blend of thoughtful confusion and the beginnings of irritation. She'd finally struck a nerve. Which nerve she wasn't sure, but at least she'd found one. "You've been reading blogs about me? Which ones?"

A burst of irritation surged through her. She would *not* throw her notebook at him. She liked her notebook, and it deserved better than being turned into a projectile weapon.

"Stop deflecting." She wiggled four fingers at him. "You were supposed to meet me at the Big House this morning to go over the chorus, but instead you booked an all-day fishing expedition without me."

His jaw tightened. "*With* you. I waited until you showed up to leave, didn't I?"

She set the notebook on the captain's chair to remove the temptation to throw it at him. "If you're not serious about this, just say so. I'll quit right now."

A look of alarm crossed his face. "You can't quit. We have a contract."

"These songs aren't going to finish themselves, Mr. Rock Star. We can't just half-ass our way through this."

"I don't half-ass anything." His eyes flashed with irritation. "Really good songs come from a spontaneous, inspired place. You're so determined to spit out words there's no way they'd be any good. Admit it, if you had great lyrics in that notebook of yours, nothing would stop you from singing them at me."

He pushed past her toward the steps at the back of the boat. "Stop trying to force it. Come over here and look at this view. If this isn't inspiration, I don't know what is."

What he'd said was so unfair and at the same time so undeniably true. She thought back to the horrible chorus she'd just read and tried not to cringe. She joined him at the steps, embarrassment rising as his words hit home. "If I don't have great lyrics, it's because you haven't given me anything to work with."

"Oh please. I've given you an entire island to work with."

She clenched her fists. "I don't need tropical scenery, Adam. I need feedback from *you*. I need to know what matters to you and the rest of the band. What themes you want to explore. What messages you want to send." Her heart pounded and her voice rose as she went on. "I need to know what you want to sing *about*."

"Well maybe if you unclench and spend more time with us you would figure all that out." He stood at the top of the steps that led to the water with his shirt flapping in the breeze and his face lifted in smug satisfaction.

"Unclench?"

"Yes. Unclench. You know, the act of relaxation? Surely you've heard of it." He turned away from her to gesture at the beach. "You know, live a little. Maybe if you relaxed, you'd feel a little more inspired."

"You want me to feel inspired?" Something sweet and dangerous came into her voice as inspiration of pure evil struck.

"Yeah. I do."

"Spontaneous?" She raised an eyebrow.

He turned back to face her and looked far too excited. "Definitely."

"How's this for inspiration?"

111

She put her hands on the smooth muscles of his chest and shoved. She had a brief impression of taught muscles and hot skin, and then he toppled off the back of the boat.

His startled yelp of surprise was swallowed by the splash as he hit the water.

A wave of satisfaction rolled through her, followed by a flicker of guilt, which amplified into mortification.

What had gotten into her?

She'd just shoved Adam Brooks, a world-famous rock star and, more importantly, her *client*, off a boat.

She never acted like this. Piper did. Della, sometimes. But her? No. Not ever. She was the nice one.

She looked over the edge of the boat.

The deckhand joined her with a life preserver in one hand. "Mr. Adam?"

Adam sputtered to the surface and wiped his face.

"It's okay," she told the deckhand. "He's fine. I think he's fine."

The deckhand looked doubtfully at her.

Mattie stared down at the man bobbing in the water and cringed. "He's probably fine."

He sure had a way of pushing all her buttons. She usually hid her emotions well, but it was becoming painfully clear that she couldn't hide anything around Adam.

Chapter Ten

Adam coughed out salt water and squinted up at the woman who'd just thrown him off the boat. She looked horrified, like she couldn't believe what she'd done. He couldn't believe it either. Never in his wildest daydreams and fantasies had his dream girl pushed him off a boat, or called him on his bullshit.

He burst out laughing. "I did tell you to be spontaneous."

Her mouth dropped open, then snapped shut. She disappeared from view.

He'd pushed her too far, and he deserved what he got. All he'd wanted was to slow things down a little. At the rate she wanted to work, they'd finish all three songs in three days and there'd be no more excuses to hang out, which was unacceptable as far as he was concerned.

HE SWAM over to the ladder and climbed back onto the boat. The deckhand fluttered around him offering a towel and first aid, which he refused.

Mattie paced back and forth across the deck, clearly agitated.

"Mattie."

"Look what you made me do. I can't believe you. I can't work like this. This is insane." Mattie stopped long enough to flash him a look he couldn't interpret, then continued pacing.

"Mattie, I'm sorry."

She stopped. "Why'd you bring me out here today?"

He rubbed his neck and tried to look contrite. "I wanted to get to know the real you, not the one you're pretending to be."

A flicker of doubt flashed through her eyes. "I'm not pretending."

"Oh yes you are," he scoffed. "You put on that mask every time you look at me, and all you ever want to talk about is the damn song. You're all work, all the time, which I know isn't really you."

"How would you know who I really am? You don't know me. You don't know me at all." Her eyes flashed a challenge.

He didn't back down. "I've seen you on stage, and I've heard your songs. They're the reason I wanted to work with you, because the *real* you finds the joy and life in music. I wanted to have some of that in mine, and I was having a hard time finding it on my own after Johnny J left."

She blinked at him, as if what he'd just said had to be processed and examined.

"It's been years, but I'm still that kid in the garage who will do anything to get heard. I did a stupid thing to get your attention, and you called me on it. It won't happen again. I promise. Can we start over? Please?"

Mattie bit her lip and looked out at the water.

He kept his mouth shut and let her think. It was hard. He had to bite his tongue. Twice. But he managed to give her the space she seemed to need.

Finally, her face softened as she came to some sort of internal conclusion. "If you want to start over, answer a question for me."

"Shoot." He nodded. He was so glad she hadn't taken the first helicopter off the island that he'd have agreed to almost anything.

"Why did you start writing songs? Originally, I mean." She picked up her notebook and sat in the captain's chair.

He thought about it. "Just after I turned sixteen, my dad got me a job in the pressroom at the paper where he worked. Making up melodies was a way to pass the time while I mopped the floors. I knew I had something good when the press guys started humming the melody back at me. I took that home, and we worked out the rest."

She smiled. "Tell me about that. How'd you work it out?"

"By arguing, mostly." He admitted. "Lyrics didn't come natural, not at the beginning. Hell, I suppose they still don't. I remember sweating buckets in the garage day after day with the guys. We worked out melodies by trial and error, but the words were all over the place. We had next to no rhythm. That was before Flynn. Me and Johnny J would toss out different ideas, while Brandon and LT would shoot them down. It was noise, and really not fit for a dog to listen to, but it was a blast."

She looked thoughtful. "I can see that. I bet it felt like a secret clubhouse. I'm not surprised you formed a band."

"At first it was just something to do. Then Dad started in on me. He thought it was a stupid waste of time. So it became a mission. A way to show him his way wasn't the only way to be. Besides, I loved music. My mom used to sing to me as a kid, and my grandpa played for us every time we visited him. Why'd you start writing songs?"

She watched the waves with a wistful expression on her face. "They weren't songs, at first. They were poems. My mom died when I was eight, and writing was my outlet. It helped me get my feelings out, you know? Then Lizzie had the idea for us to put on little musical skits for Dad to cheer him up, and one thing led to another. Piper added the melodies, Della added the style."

He nodded. "And you added the heart."

She shook her head. "Not just me. All of us. Together."

He leaned forward. "I don't think you get it. You provide the inspiration. The Bellamy Sisters would have been less—a lot less—without you."

She shook her head. "I'm just the backup. If anything, Piper is the inspiration. She connects with the fans better than the rest of us."

"There's nothing backup about you. And you know what? This song we're writing is going to take us—you and Delusions of Glory—to the next phase. I can't wait for the world to hear it."

She gave him an impatient look. "How are they going to do that? We haven't even written it yet."

He sat on the nearest bench and kicked his feet out in front of him. "So let's get started. Tell me what you have so far."

"Really?" She eyed him with suspicion.

He held up his hands. "I told you, we're starting over. Show me what you have."

She shrugged and flipped open her notebook. "Snippets, really. Nothing solid. Remember when I asked you what you wanted to sing about? You never answered the question, which makes it a lot harder."

You, he almost said out loud. *I want to sing about you.*

Instead, he said, "Maybe since the last song talks about a sick little girl, we should focus on a happier kind of change. Making new friends? Meeting a stranger, getting to know them until they become something more?"

"Are you talking about me?" Exasperation colored her tone.

"Maybe." He blinked innocently at her.

"What about the old friends?"

He thought of Johnny J. They would always be friends, no matter how far apart they were, and no matter how much time passed. "Who says you can't keep the old friends while you make new ones?"

She got a funny, distant look in her eyes, and then dipped her head and wrote furiously in the notebook.

"What? Did I say something cool?" He leaned forward.

She covered the page with one hand so he couldn't see what she wrote. "Keeping old friends while making space for the new is a great idea for a song."

He thought about it, then hummed a few notes that had been circling around in his head. They could work. He sang them out loud just to try them out.

"Who says we can't keep old friends while we make a little space for someone new?"

She nodded. "Let's start with that and see where it goes."

Adam waved at the cabin. "Want to work over lunch? They can take us back while we eat."

Mattie glanced at the beach and the table that remained out there like a monument to stupid decisions everywhere.

She stood up. "I'd like that."

As they head into the cabin, he heard her hum the little tune he'd just composed on the fly and grinned.

Chapter Eleven

Several days later, Mattie had settled into a morning routine that included a refreshing outdoor shower, coffee, and a daily check-in with her phone. Dealing with everything at once and then shutting the phone away in the drawer left her feeling remarkably free. The days were peaceful, and the words came easier without the constant chatter from the real world.

She sat on the bed and scrolled through the texts waiting for her, then dealt with the ones she thought were the most urgent. She sent a quick note to Lizzie, reassuring her that all was well. Another to Piper, who kept a steady stream of updates coming whether Mattie wanted them or not, including the latest headline that read, *Bellamy Babe Bamboozles Boyfriend*. She had to admire the effort at alliteration, but it was old news now, and most of the blogs had moved on to fresher meat.

She tapped out a quick note to Kat. *Making progress.*

Coming home soon? Kat sent.

They weren't anywhere near done with the first song, much less the other two. This place was fantastic, and she felt more relaxed than she had in a long time. She wasn't so sure she wanted to finish fast anymore. Besides, they'd only been here nine days.

Finally, she replied, *Not that much progress. Still working on song 1.*

Kat sent back a wide-eyed emoji. *What's taking so long?*

She decided not to reply to that one, and instead forced herself to read the texts from Della.

I hate that I made you unhappy.
How can I fix this?
I love you.
Please let me fix this.

Mattie sighed and closed her eyes against the obvious pain embedded in that message. She hated this. She hated the hurt that Della had caused, but more than that she hated the rift between her sisters and the indignant anger that crawled back through her heart every time she thought of what Della had said at brunch.

Adam's band had suffered a loss, too, but they'd all seemed to take it in stride. Of course, most of them were still together, while The Bellamy Sisters weren't.

They were still sisters. Nothing would change that. They were all still making music in their own ways. They just weren't doing it together.

But we could be, a small voice whispered in the back of her mind.

For the first time since that awful brunch, she thought about what it might be like to get back together as a group.

She wasn't sure she missed the stage, exactly, but she did miss the near-constant travel. She loved going to new places. She loved meeting new people, as long as it wasn't a large crowd, and she really loved, deep down in her soul, sharing music with people. It filled her in a way nothing else ever had or would.

That's what had made her so angry. Della had taken all that away.

A tiny jolt of realization flicked at her. Della might have broken up the group, but she hadn't taken everything away. Not really. Mattie had continued to travel. Maybe not as often as before, but she still went somewhere new every few months. She still met new people, including Delusions of Glory. The only thing she hadn't done was share music with an audience or her family, but whose fault was that?

Della constantly tried to talk to her, even though Mattie ignored most of her texts. Piper lived minutes away from her, and they had lunch once a week when they were both in town. Lizzie did her best to keep them all in touch with one another like a mama duck with her ducklings.

The anger she'd been holding on to since that silly brunch —since the day Della had split up the group—thinned.

She tapped out a response to Della. *I love you too.* Then she put the phone back in the drawer, grabbed her bag of notebooks, and set out for the Big House at the north end of the island.

She was glad for the long walk, because it gave her time to think. She was nervous. So far on this trip, she'd played hooky with the rest of the band, but she'd only worked on lyrics with Adam.

Since she'd thrown him in the ocean, the hours had been filled with banter, discussions, arguments, and laughter while they took long walks down tropical trails or along the beach. Working with him didn't feel like work at all. He listened when she had ideas, he gave honest feedback, and he hadn't even tried to kiss her.

Why did she feel a pang of disappointment at that?

Now they had to bring the rest of the band in on the project, and the prospect filled her with anxiety. They had the beginnings of a working chorus, but she didn't feel good about it. A lot of the lyrics she'd jotted down felt disjointed and wrong, and it wouldn't get any better until she had input from the group.

It was almost lunchtime, and the guys were already in the living room by the time she got there.

Adam leaned against one of the floor-to-ceiling windows overlooking the beach and watched the room. He wore crisp white shorts, a rough beige linen shirt, and an expectant expression. The brilliant midday sun framed him with an entirely deceptive halo.

She couldn't stop the grin or the mischievous need to tease him. "Well that's false and misleading advertising."

He looked confused. "What is?"

"You, standing there with a halo around you like you're innocent."

The guys all laughed.

Adam glanced up at the imaginary halo, then shrugged. "I can't help it if the sun loves me."

"I don't think he's ever been *that* innocent," Cooper said. "Should have seen him in high school."

Adam pointed at LT. "Hey, he was sent to the principal's office a lot more than me."

"Yeah, but that don't mean you didn't *do* more than me," LT said. "You just didn't get in trouble. You'd bat eyes at Mrs. Dixon and she'd swoon and you'd end up in *private* study with her instead."

"It was detention," Adam said. "She made me write essays after school. It was *not* some kind of hot-for-teacher session."

"Sure it wasn't." LT nodded in mock agreement. "What was the subject of those essays? Kama Sutra positions?"

Adam scowled. "No."

Cooper looked up from his guitar. "I thought you said she made you write about the Civil War."

"It was poetry," Brandon said. He pulled a beer out of the refrigerator and twisted open the top. His clothes were mostly dry, but his hair looked damp and there was sand all over his shorts. "Very girly stuff."

Adam waved his hand. "Can we drop the trip down memory lane and get to work?"

Mattie giggled. "What were the poems about?"

Brandon opened his mouth to answer, then saw the look on Adam's face, and took a swig of beer instead.

"There's only one reason to write poetry." Flynn caught the angry look Adam tossed in his direction and shoved a chip in his mouth.

"What's that?" Mattie asked.

"To get the girl. Or guy. Whoever." Flynn carried a large plate of chips and other snacks from the kitchen to the living room, dodged past Adam like he was avoiding a land mine, and plopped down on a small chair next to the drum set. His bare feet were coated in sand.

"Hey, Mattie," LT said. "Think we'll be done by seven? I promised Malika I'd go horseback riding."

Cooper sat on one of the overstuffed couches tuning his guitar. "Who's Malika?"

"One of the tour guides," Brandon said. "She wants to show him *her* private beach."

"Show a little class, bro. There's a lady present," Adam said in a stern, older brother tone. He gestured at Mattie. "We're all set to go whenever you're ready. Food's on the counter, drinks in the fridge."

Mattie crossed to the kitchen to get a bottle of water, noticing along the way that they'd set up the keyboards, drums, and amplifiers for the guitars. All that was missing was a stage. She looked at Adam. "What's with all the gear? Are we having another Adam moment?"

Flynn pointed a drumstick at Adam. "You told her about Adam moments?"

"You threatened to dip us in acid if we told her," Brandon said.

"Does that mean we can tell her about the time—" LT said.

Adam cut him off firmly. "No."

Mattie got the distinct impression that there was a lot of subtext going on. There was something Adam didn't want her to know. He was embarrassed. She wanted to push a little more out of curiosity, but his cheeks were so red they made his tan glow.

She took pity on him with a change of subject. "Have you shared the idea we came up with?"

Adam strolled to the center of the room. "Not yet. It's all yours."

He perched on the arm of a chair and gave her a grateful look that was so cute she wanted to giggle. She adored the way they constantly teased each other, because underneath it all she sensed a bedrock of love and affection.

They all settled into chairs or couches except for Flynn, who remained next to the drum set. Mattie picked a bright blue, overstuffed love seat and curled up on it, then pulled the idea spark notebook out of her bag and flipped it open.

"I thought we'd start by keeping the theme of the album going."

"Which one?" Flynn asked.

"Life and death," Brandon said.

"Love and loss," Cooper said.

"I thought it was about corruption and chaos?" LT looked confused.

Adam muttered something under his breath and looked embarrassed.

Mattie suppressed a smile and held up her hand. "What I heard in the studio was a lot of songs about change. Big life changes."

Cooper looked impressed. "Yeah, I get that."

"I don't think we did that on purpose," Brandon said.

"It doesn't matter if it was on purpose," Adam said. "It's there and we're running with it."

"Right," Mattie said. "We came up with the idea of making new friends while keeping up with the old ones. Does that spark any ideas for you guys?"

LT chewed on chips with a distant look in his eyes. Cooper plucked a few notes on his guitar. Flynn stared blankly at her.

Adam shook his head.

"Change sucks," Brandon said. He looked around at the rest. "Right?"

LT nodded. "Sometimes. But not all the time."

Adam looked at Mattie. "Sometimes it's exactly what we need."

He looked at her like she was the only one in the room.

"Yeah, but even if it's something you think you want, it sucks," Brandon said as if he'd stated an obvious, universal truth.

"Why?" Mattie asked. Somewhere in this idea was a song, if they could get to it.

"Because...because..." Brandon rolled his eyes. "I don't know. Because it's hard. Because even if it's something you want, it means what you had is gone."

"Does it?" LT asked. "I mean, just because we came to this

island, a big change of place, doesn't mean we left everything behind."

"Well, except we did, kind of," Flynn said. "I mean, wasn't that the whole reason we came here? To leave all the crap behind?"

Mattie thought about that. He was right. That was exactly why she came.

"Yeah but the crap isn't gone. It's just hanging out, waiting for us to come back," Brandon said.

"What if it helps us face it, though?" Adam asked. "That's a good thing, right?"

Cooper made an impatient noise. "How is this therapy session going to get us a song?"

Mattie held up a hand. "Just a second, I have to write this down."

Adam started humming, which annoyed her at first, but the longer he went on, the more the words she was trying to write slid into place.

Once she had the words down, she sang them out to Adam's hummed tune.

Change is hard,
Change is tough
Change is not always enough
If you want it, if you need it, you can't let it pass you by
You have to try, you have to try

ADAM BOOSTED THE MELODY, adding in a little bit of harmony at the end.

"Hey, that's kinda cool," Brandon said. "Hang on a sec." He crossed to the keyboard and tapped out the basic melody as if it had been his all along. Then he added chords to it until the sound was full and real.

Mattie nodded along as Brandon added another verse with a bridge to join them together. It sounded a little high toned, not edgy enough. "Try it a third lower. This should sound rougher, I think."

Brandon nodded and shifted his hands.

"Let's do it again," she said. "Cooper, jump in when you think it fits."

Brandon started the opening he'd cooked up while they were talking.

Flynn found the beat.

Then Mattie started to sing, and Adam joined her. His harmony fit neatly beside her melody and gave it the desperate push that she'd been looking for. When they reached the end of the verse, Brandon and Cooper continued with the basic melody, adding flourishes until it spiraled out of control and ended up sounding like the theme song to *The Addams Family*.

"Okay, clowns, let's run it again." Adam made a wind-up motion with one hand. "Remember, LT has a date to get to."

Mattie giggled. Writing songs with these guys reminded her so much of writing sessions with her sisters that it made her want to laugh *and* cry. She hadn't had this much fun with music in a really long time.

Chapter Twelve

Adam realized a month wasn't going to be enough time with Mattie after their first jam session with the guys, but he wasn't sure what to do about it. Plans to sweep her off her feet seemed too rushed and pushy, but if he didn't let her know how he felt soon he thought he might explode.

When she suggested they take a day off to do something as a group, he'd enthusiastically agreed, even though he'd rather have her to himself. He didn't want to make her uncomfortable when she was finally starting to relax. They all settled on a tour of the island by Jet Ski, which he thought at least gave him a chance to experience something with her besides music, even if they did it while surrounded by the rest of the guys.

He walked up to the personal watercraft station with Brandon and Flynn with a growing sense of suspicion. A white storage shed with paddles, vests, and various equipment leaning against it sat on the dock. Down below, Jet Skis with racing stripes and flames bobbed up and down with the waves.

He counted six, but there would be seven, possibly eight,

people riding, not including the guides. The math didn't add up.

One of the dock workers, a woman in her late forties named Bayo, approached him with a friendly smile. "Good morning, Mr. Adam, Mr. Flynn, Mr. Brandon. The weather is perfect for a day on the water. Nassor and myself will be with you as guides for the day. That is him, with the white cap."

She indicated a twenty-something with braids, a face like Denzel, and arms built by heavy lifting. Nassor waved at them in acknowledgment.

Adam shook Bayo's hand. "We're looking forward to it. Are there more Jet Skis? I think we have eight."

She glanced at Brandon, then back at Adam with a knowing look. "Ah, it will be fine, I think. Some ride two by two, yes?"

Adam pictured himself sharing a Jet Ski with Mattie and realized exactly what his friends had planned. He didn't know how Mattie would feel about being so close to him, and he wasn't sure he wanted to find out. She finally trusted him to not treat her like the last guy. He didn't want to ruin it.

He glanced at Brandon. "What are you up to?"

"Me?" Brandon blinked with feigned innocence.

Flynn bumped into Adam's shoulder on his way to talk to Bayo. "What's the speed limit on these things?"

The two of them walked toward the end of the dock, out of earshot.

Adam watched them, then studied his brother's expression. "Seriously. What did you do?"

"I worked hard on a new song, that's what. We all did. We deserve a day off. And we deserve to spend it on Jet Skis." Brandon pointed at the first one, a one-seater with bright red flames along the sleek black body. "And I deserve that one right there."

Adam took in a breath of patience. "Brandon. This isn't helping."

Brandon raised an eyebrow. "Helping what? Your sudden obsessive need to pretend you don't like your high school crush? Please. It's absolutely helping. Did you see her face when I suggested we go Jet Skiing today? I've never seen that shade of pale."

"So?"

"So, that means she's scared and she needs a big, strong man to cling to. It's like taking a girl to a horror movie, only it's three dimensional and with actual sharks. She'll stick to you like a barnacle." Brandon patted him on the back. "You're welcome."

Adam clenched his jaw to rein in his frustration. "Dammit, you guys have to stop this. I told you, I have to keep it hands off around her."

Brandon scoffed. "Group dating is a really bad strategy. How are you going to get her naked if you're never alone?"

"Get every thought of her naked out of your head." Adam narrowed his eyes. "She's not an idiot, Brandon. She notices when all of you get up and leave at the same time when we're not done with dinner, and she sure as hell noticed that you were all an hour late to the session yesterday. What did you do, tie Flynn to a chair? He hates being late. When you finally showed up I thought he was going to break the drum."

"I didn't tie him to anything." Brandon beamed. "I switched the time zone on his phone. Can't do it again, though. When he figured it out, he changed the passcode."

Adam stepped closer. "This. Stops. Now." He poked Brandon in the chest for emphasis. "She's going to think I'm some kind of stalker if you keep this up."

"Hey! Knock it off." Brandon slapped Adam's hand away and rubbed his chest. "If you'd just get out of your own way, she'd see you for the overly assertive, clueless-around-women man with a fantastic circle of friends that you are."

"I'm not clueless. I'm a professional performing artist in need of new material."

"Uh-huh. Because it's so professional to whisk your crush away to a tropical island so she can't be distracted by the men she left behind. Right." Brandon glanced over Adam's shoulder. "Someone's coming. Seriously, if you don't make a move soon we'll leave this sideshow before you even get to third base. We've all decided to take pity on your barren love life and give you a hand."

"I'm trying to—" He registered what his brother just said. "Give me a hand how?"

Brandon rocked back and forth on his feet and looked so smug that Adam felt a knot tighten in his stomach. The last time he'd looked like that, he'd taken Dad's car without permission, dented the fender, then blamed it on Adam.

"Brandon..." He put as much warning into his voice as he could without shouting.

Flynn rejoined them looking satisfied. "It's all set."

"What's all set?" Adam narrowed his eyes at Flynn. "Whatever you have cooking, knock it off."

Flynn and Brandon exchanged looks. "Bayo says she'll make sure it works."

The golf cart driving up the path carried a single rider with long, honey-gold hair.

Anticipation and nervous energy surged through his gut. "Make sure what works?"

"Operation Help a Brother Out is on." Flynn leaned in and spoke in low undertones like he was in a spy novel. "Bayo will offer us two activities. All we have to do is let Mattie choose what she wants first. Whatever she picks, the rest of us do the opposite. Got it?"

"Perfect," Brandon said. "Then we all get lost for the rest of the day and they can have some quality alone time."

"No." Adam saw exactly where this was headed. He and Mattie would wind up alone on a beach somewhere just like he'd tried to do before. Every bit of trust he'd built with her would be gone. "We can't do that. She'll be so pissed! Just stick together."

"At least this time you can't be thrown into the ocean. Not if you're driving." Brandon chuckled. "Though I'd pay a million to see it. I wonder if we can get her to do it again just so we all can watch?"

"If you bring that up to her, I'll break your arm." Adam bared his teeth.

Brandon grinned back without a hint of shame. "You'd have to catch me first."

Flynn's eyes widened, and he waved at someone behind Adam. "Hey, Mattie."

Adam turned to see Mattie coming up the walkway. She wore a long-sleeved rash guard covered in pink flowers and black shorts. Without the usual flowy fabric covering her body, she looked athletic and strong.

He could imagine those legs wrapped around his waist—

No. He could not think like that right now.

Mattie waved back at Flynn, and a soft smile curved her lips, but something about her walk was less buoyant than usual.

"She looks nervous," Adam said in a low voice.

"Yes!" Brandon pumped his fist in triumph. "Remember, make sure you're driving so she can hold on tight."

"This plan is ridiculous." Adam wanted to pace back and forth like a caged animal, but it would make Mattie even more nervous if he did that. "She'll see right through it, and I'll look like an asshole."

131

"Not if you play your cards right." Flynn grinned. "I mean every other girl seems to want to bang you so I don't see why this should be so hard."

"Hard," Brandon repeated, then turned away, shaking with laughter.

"You two are forever stuck at fifteen, aren't you," Adam muttered.

"It's a fantastic age," Flynn said. "You should try it sometime. I think you missed yours."

"Good morning," Mattie said when she got closer. She bit her lip as she looked at the Jet Skis. "I'm not so sure I should be doing this. I'm not a strong swimmer."

"Don't worry," Brandon said, with only a hint of giggle. "We'll have two guides and life jackets, and you'll have a big, strong—"

Adam jumped in before his brother could finish that sentence. "You seem to be missing something."

Mattie cocked her head. Her eyes sparked with amusement, as if she knew exactly what Brandon had been about to say. "What? Sunscreen? I put it on before I left."

"The bag," Brandon said.

"Yeah," Flynn chimed in. "I thought it was permanently attached."

Mattie laughed and patted her side like the bag was still there. "I know, I feel naked without it. But I thought it might be a bad idea to bring my notebooks along for the ride. Paper doesn't do so well around water."

A golf cart carrying Cooper and Tina pulled up. They hopped out, and their driver backed the cart off the dock. Cooper smiled brightly at them as they reached the group. He'd dressed down for a change and wore swim trunks, a white T-shirt, and sandals. Tina, on the other hand, wore a frown and a string bikini that didn't hide much of anything. She looked at the Jet Skis and wrinkled her nose.

"Hey, Coop," Adam said. It was obvious Tina wasn't happy. The sooner they got going the better, but they were still missing someone. "Where's LT?"

"LT isn't coming," Cooper said. "He's busy following his island sweetie around. Apparently they aren't allowed to go on activities with the guests unless they're one of the guides."

"Coopie." Tina hugged Cooper's arm in a way that made her breasts push up and out. "Aren't there any boats? Jet Skis are so loud and rough."

"This will be fun." Cooper put on his patient face, the one he used with overly demanding girlfriends or small children. "And afterwards we have a picnic at Lanmou Bay, just you and me."

Tina sniffed. "I really shouldn't be out in the sun this much. I have a photoshoot the week we get back."

"I have another rash guard, if you'd like to borrow it," Mattie said. She smiled politely at Tina.

"Those things chafe." Her tone made it obvious that she thought Mattie was low class and stupid for offering.

Adam started to object, but Mattie responded before he could.

"So do wet seats." Mattie gestured at the Jet Skis. "Maybe you should put on something to cover your, um, thighs?"

Adam snorted a laugh. Tina would never wear something that covered that much skin,

Tina tossed her hair back. "I have to avoid lines for the camera. That's why I shouldn't be out all day in the sun."

"It's not going to be all day," Cooper said. "And you bathed in sunscreen this morning. You'll be fine."

Adam exchanged looks with Cooper. "You don't have to go with us. You could hang out on the beach or something."

Cooper's expression hardened. "We've had enough hanging out."

Adam glanced at Tina. The look on her face said she'd had enough of just about everything, but she didn't make any other comment, so he let it go.

Flynn tapped Cooper on the shoulder. "Hey, man, come help me with the vests."

"Sure." Cooper and Flynn sauntered toward the tour guides, talking in low whispers. Flynn must be filling Cooper in on the throw-Mattie-at-Adam plan.

Adam turned away before his impulse to stop them made him do something foolish.

"Adam," Mattie said, "have you thought about where you want to go with the second song? I have some snippets and thoughts written down from our sessions..." She patted her hip and grimaced. "In my notebook. Which is in my bag. In my room."

"I thought there would be no work today," Tina said with a petulant pout. "Coopie promised me it would be fun."

"It's going to be fun all right," Brandon said. He wiggled his eyebrows for emphasis.

"Right, no work." Adam winked at Mattie.

Mattie smiled, and a calculating look crossed her face. "You know, when you love what you do, work is a reward, not a punishment. Maybe that could be the subject of the next song."

Adam scratched his chin. "Says the girl who ripped half the pages out of her notebook yesterday because they weren't cooperating."

"I didn't say it wasn't annoying sometimes," Mattie flashed a pointed glance in his direction, "just that it's worthwhile."

Tina made a tsk sound with her tongue. "I'm here to play, *not* work. I do plenty of work at home."

"Lucky you aren't in a band, then," Brandon said with heavy sarcasm. "You know us musicians. It's work, work, work all the time."

Adam pictured Tina on stage. She was at home under spotlights, as every model would be, but she didn't seem to like music very much, and she couldn't sing any note on key.

Mattie, on the other hand, was a natural on stage. She didn't need a spotlight. The crowd could find her in the dark.

He turned away to hide the grin and saw Bayo, Nassor, Flynn, and Cooper striding back toward them carrying life vests.

"We are all here, yes?" Bayo asked.

"Yes," Cooper said. "All set."

"Good, good, then we will have a quick demonstration of safety before we set off on our adventure." Bayo gestured at Nassor.

Before Nassor could speak, the staff photographer they'd met on the tarmac days ago stepped out from behind the storage building with a fake smile on his face and a camera in his hands.

"Good morning everybody," Don said. He wore the same bright white as all the other staff, but he'd turned up the collar on the shirt like he thought he was Elvis.

Mattie stiffened beside him and drew in a quick breath.

Adam instinctively took a step toward the guy and put himself in between the camera and Mattie.

Don held up a hand in surrender. "I know, I know. You said no photography."

"Right, we did," Adam said.

"I just thought I'd check in with you, since I doubt any of you brought your phones for this outing," Don said. "Wouldn't want them to get wet, right? Sure you don't want a

She slipped onto the seat and grabbed Adam's life vest with both hands. "I'd feel better if it didn't rock so much."

"Just hold on tight." He glanced back at her. "Don't worry. I won't bite. Yet."

She huffed out a nervous laugh, then wrapped her arms around his neck and squeezed.

"Ack. Can't. Breathe," he teased.

She let go with a giggle. "Sorry!"

"Around my waist." He guided her hands until they rested below the vest, where she could squeeze without cutting off his oxygen. "There. Think of it as a horse on water. Roll with the motion."

"There's no chance of drowning if you fall off a horse," Mattie grumbled.

"No chance of being eaten by a shark either," Flynn called out in an overly cheerful tone.

Adam glared at him. "That's not helping."

Flynn glanced at Mattie and winked.

"Don't listen to him," Adam told her. "He's an idiot who won't be alive much longer."

Mattie tightened her grip.

Bayo waved her hand to get their attention. "Ready?"

Everyone nodded and shouted, "Yes."

"Here we go," she called out, then pulled away from the dock and out onto the open water.

One by one, they all took off. Brandon and Flynn got an early lead as they raced each other in the general direction Bayo indicated.

Adam stayed behind their guide for a little while to let Mattie get used to the bouncing movement of the waves. Cooper and Tina trailed behind them, and Nassor brought up the rear.

At first, Mattie's grasp on him was so tight it was hard to

breathe. She shrieked when they hit a rough patch of water, then giggled when she got splashed.

"This is terrifying!" Mattie screamed in his ear. "Go faster!"

Adam laughed and sped up.

Mattie snuggled in closer, her arms tight but no longer constricting across his stomach. She was warm and soft against his back, and it made him want to turn around and kiss her. He leaned into her a little and grinned like an idiot as the sea spray slapped his face.

They went from one tip of the island to the other before Bayo stopped and gathered them all in a circle.

"Now is the time for decision. There are two sites to see. One is Aldabra Bay, around the south tip of the island. It is a breeding ground for the giant tortoise that grace our waters."

Mattie made a little squeal sound, like a little girl in a candy store. "I would love to see them!"

Adam squeezed her hand. "Then that's for us."

"The other site is a short ride to the island you see over there." She pointed to a bit of land in the distance. "It is the home of a beautiful underwater sea cave. We will split into two groups. Nassor will lead those who wish it to the cavern, and I will take the rest to see the Aldabra. Now who would like to go to the cave?"

Cooper turned to speak to Tina. Brandon and Flynn looked at each other, then at Adam. "What are you two doing?"

"Turtles," Adam said.

Flynn's hand shot up. "Caves."

Brandon raised his hand. "Sign me up for caves too. Coop?"

Cooper appeared to be arguing with Tina. Adam exchanged glances with Brandon and Flynn.

Mattie leaned in close and whispered, "Why didn't she stay home?"

Adam snorted a laugh. "An all-expense paid trip to a tropical paradise? Who would pass that up?"

"Good point," Mattie said.

"Hey, Coop," Flynn shouted. "Which way you going, man?"

Tina glared at him.

Cooper stared off in the distance as if he were counting to ten, or maybe twenty. "Caves."

Tina hit Cooper's arm. "I want to see the turtles."

Brandon and Flynn exchanged glances.

A few seconds ticked by, and tension mounted with every wave that rocked the skis. They couldn't keep staring at each other like this. Mattie would wonder what was going on. But he couldn't exactly say, "Don't worry about ruining our carefully manufactured alone time. The more the merrier."

"Oh good," Mattie said brightly. "I thought I'd be the only one wanting to see cute animals. We'll have a great time."

"I do not think...," Bayo said at the same time, then stopped before she finished the sentence.

"Hey, Coop," Flynn said. "Man, the caves sound fantastic. And you love scuba diving."

"Yeah, come with us," Brandon said. "You could always do the turtles later."

The innuendo Brandon managed to put into that sentence made Adam cringe.

Bayo and Nassor looked at each other.

Adam cleared his throat, relieved that the plan had been thwarted. "So we have our split then. Coop, Tina, Mattie, and me to the turtles, Brandon and Flynn to the caves. Have fun, guys."

"Okay. We are decided," Bayo said. She looked at Nassor. "We meet back home, yes?"

Nassor agreed with a happy nod. He raised his hand. "All seeking underwater adventure, follow me."

Brandon cast an irritated glance at Cooper, then saluted Adam. "See ya, bro."

He sped off after Nassor.

Flynn followed Brandon, shouting, "Later!"

Bayo smiled. "Please follow me. This way."

Adam gave Cooper a quick look of sympathy before taking off after Bayo. Cooper's expression was carved from stone. Tina, however, seemed satisfied with the outcome.

Bayo led them along the southern tip of the island to a large cove similar to the one he'd taken Mattic to before, except this beach was dotted with several giant sea turtles.

Bayo led them to a small dock located on the far end of the cove, around the tip of an outcropping that blocked the turtles from view.

She cut off the engine and climbed up onto the dock. "We stop here, so that we do not disturb the nesting mothers. Follow this path to the right for facilities, food and drink, and resting places. When you are ready, I will show you the turtles."

After a quick break, the four of them fell in line behind Bayo as she led them to the protected breeding ground. Mattie rounded the corner first.

Before Adam caught up with her, Cooper tapped his shoulder. He paused to glance back at his friend.

Cooper looked apologetic. "Sorry, man. I tried."

"Don't sweat it," Adam whispered. "Stupid plan anyway."

"Still." Cooper studiously avoided looking at Tina.

"Boys, you're blocking the way," Tina said.

Adam patted Cooper's shoulder to show him it wasn't a big deal and kept walking down the path.

141

While he might wish he were alone with Mattie, the last thing he wanted was for her to think he'd planned this on purpose. Though he had to admit, if he'd thought of it himself, he would have done it; he just wouldn't want her to know that.

Bayo and Mattie stopped in a clear portion of sand several feet ahead.

"This is so cool," Mattie breathed. "I've never seen anything like it."

"Look at that one, she has a huge gash on her shell." Cooper pointed to one only a few feet away.

Bayo nodded. "Yes. Procreation for these mamas is quite rough. The males will nip and tug, seeking permission to climb aboard, and once they are there, they latch on, while the other males fight for her attention. She is forced to swim with the male attached to her, sometimes twenty-four hours. After he is done, another will take his place until all her eggs are fertilized. Then it is *her* turn to bite, yes?"

Bayo winked at Mattie. "Enough is enough?"

"If I had to go through all that to make a baby I'd bite back too." Mattie laughed.

"Where's that one going?" Tina pointed to an enormous turtle nearly at the water.

Bayo nodded. "That is our most famous lady. She is called Amani. She returns to this beach every year, for almost twenty years now. She is returning to the sea, her work done. See? The section over there, near the trees? That was hers. She dug the hole and put her eggs safely away to grow during the night. She has one other clutch, over by the rock, there. See?"

Bayo pointed to a group of large stones across the cove. "She is a good mama. She will come back next season. But for now, she rests."

All of the turtles looked exhausted to Adam. Some still

worked to bury eggs, while others appeared to be sleeping. "They don't stay with the eggs?"

Bayo shook her head. "No, they do not. The babies are on their own. Though we will look out for them, yes?"

"They go through all that pain," Mattie said. "All that work, just to leave it behind. I wish I had my notebook right now."

She settled down cross-legged on the sand and stared with wide eyed introspection at the turtles.

Bayo smiled. "I leave you to watch as long as you like. When you are ready, lunch will be served at the rest area."

Bayo walked quietly back the way they'd come.

Adam leaned against the rock wall behind Mattie, but he was more interested in watching her than the parade of prehistoric creatures in front of her.

Tina glanced around. "Is this it? I thought we could pet them or something."

"No, don't," Mattie cried out. "If you touch them, they'll feel threatened and they won't finish laying their eggs."

"How do you know?" Tina looked at Cooper. "She can't know that."

"I watched a documentary," Mattie said wryly.

"I'm hungry," Cooper said. "I'm going for something to eat." He turned to leave, then looked at Tina. "Coming?"

"I guess." Tina clicked her tongue. "I told you we should have a spa day instead."

"We should have gone to the caves," Cooper said.

Tina snapped something in response, but Adam couldn't make it out.

He waited until he couldn't hear their voices over the sound of the surf, then settled onto the ground near Mattie with his back against the rocks.

They sat in easy silence for a few minutes. The turtles

basked in the sun, reaching a level of relaxation he only dreamed of experiencing. He was hyperaware of the woman sitting next to him. The shirt she wore hugged her body like a second skin. He wanted to trace her curves with his hands and discover the real woman underneath. His fingers twitched, but he forced himself to stay put.

"I don't think they're going to last much longer," Mattie said in a voice so low the wind almost swept it away. "Cooper and Tina, I mean. She seems unhappy."

"I'll be shocked if she lasts two more days."

Mattie looked at him with troubled eyes. "Poor Cooper."

He shrugged. "It won't be the first time one of Coop's relationships tanked while on vacation. One girl ditched him during dinner the first night to go off with some actor from Australia. She had the hotel move her stuff out before he got back. On the plus side, at least she didn't trash the room. He has bad luck with women most of the time."

"Maybe he just hasn't found the right one." Mattie scooted back until she leaned against the rock next to him, pulled off her shoes, and dug her toes in the sand.

"Maybe he should stop taking his girlfriends on vacation." Adam shook his head. "They just don't get it. I think they all expect to be the center of attention on trips like this, but with a guy like Cooper..."

"The music comes first," Mattie filled in.

He smiled and bobbed his head. "Yeah."

"I get that." She watched the turtles with a faraway look in her eyes. "It's hard, when you love something so much to pay attention to anything else sometimes."

"Yes," he agreed. He studied the curve of her face, the slight flush in her cheeks, and the smooth line of her neck, memorizing every detail. "Yes, it definitely is."

Chapter Thirteen

Mattie could feel Adam's stare, hot and intense, along the side of her face, and his words sent a little thrill through her chest. They barely knew each other, but they'd spent a lot of quality time together over the past couple of weeks, and she liked him. A lot.

There was more to know about Adam Brooks. She should find out all she could.

For the song.

It was only professional.

She let the thought roll around in her head.

There's more to know.

Something about it felt good. It was a start, anyway. Her fingers itched for her notebook.

"Darn it."

"What?" Adam asked.

"I just thought of a line I'd like to write down. But I can't, because I didn't bring my notebooks. I never should have left them behind."

"What's the line? I'll help you remember it."

"There's more to know."

He raised an eyebrow. "That's it?"

"Yes. Why?"

He nodded. "Okay. There's more to know. Got it."

"I know, it doesn't seem like anything. Yet." She returned her gaze to the turtles. "It's sad, don't you think? The babies will never know their mother. They'll pop out of those holes and have to make their way in the world alone."

"Except for hundreds of brothers and sisters." Adam scuffed the sand with his foot. "Your sisters make a huge difference, don't they? You aren't alone."

"It's not that simple. But I guess nothing ever is."

"Family," Adam said, as if that explained everything. "They can punch your buttons and trip your triggers. That's for sure."

She eyed him. "It's just you and Brandon, right?"

"Yeah. Mom and Dad wanted a big family, but it didn't work out."

"I'm sorry." She could feel the pain in that statement, even though it wasn't his own.

He shrugged. "It is what it is. I try to compensate for the lack of siblings by making things a little easier for them. Not that Dad is all that willing to let me. I've been trying to buy them a new house, one that doesn't need so much work. But every time Mom and I pick one out Dad finds something wrong with it."

She thought about that. "Maybe your dad doesn't want to move. Maybe he likes the house he has."

Adam snorted. "The damn thing's falling down around their ears. Mom's anxious to move on to something new, but he's a stubborn old fool."

She suppressed a chuckle. Adam's father wasn't the only stubborn one in the family. "Maybe you should ask him about it. What if you just helped him fix up the house he has?"

Adam smiled. "Brandon said the same thing. He thinks we should renovate the house, then send them on yearly vacations. But Dad won't go. He hasn't retired yet. Not sure he ever will."

"Why not? What does he do?"

"He works in the pressroom of the *Los Angeles Daily Post*. He's been there almost thirty years, and I think he's afraid of what comes next. You work your whole life, you know? You are what you do. Then suddenly you don't do anything. Then what are you? You're somebody who used to be someone who did something."

His words sparked a torrent of ideas rushing through her thoughts. "Oh...oh dammit *why* didn't I bring a notebook?"

The only thing she could use to write down any of it was the sand and her finger. She wrote keywords in the sand in sloppy scrawl.

What am I?
Afraid
Work
What's next?

The words were soft and hard to read, and the wind pushed at the edges. This wasn't going to work for long. "Do me a favor? Go see if Bayo has anything to write on?"

"On it." Adam jogged away.

"Toilet paper and a pencil would work," she called after him.

It took him a lot longer than she thought it should. By the time he came back, the sand all around her was covered in graffiti that she could barely read. If she didn't get it all down soon, she'd lose it forever.

She looked up with expectation, but Adam's hands were empty, and his expression was apologetic.

"Sorry, Mattie. There's nothing to write with and the toilet paper is way too thin to write on."

She swore under her breath, unable to hide the frustration. The song that bubbled somewhere in the sand slipped through her fingers every time the wind blew.

Adam took a step forward, but she waved him away. "Don't move! You'll erase it."

He stopped with one foot in the air. "Erase what?"

She stared around at the scribbles in the sand. "I swear I'm never leaving my notebooks behind again. Do they make water-proof ones?"

"Not sure about waterproof paper, but I have an idea." Adam shifted his feet away from the outer edges of her notes. "Let's work it out right now."

She stared up at him. "Now? Without writing it down?"

"If we put words to melody it will be easy to remember."

"I've been taking notes my entire life. I don't think I've ever tried to work on lyrics without writing them down."

He grinned. "Take a walk on the wild side."

It felt dangerous, but also oddly freeing. "Okay. Where do we start?"

Adam's gaze traveled the sand divots all around her. "You tell me. I can't read any of that."

The wind kicked up and smoothed some of the edges of the words. If they didn't act fast, it would all be gone. "Maybe the hook? The idea I had for it is all on this side." She pointed right.

Adam narrowed his eyes at the area, then shook his head. "Tell me."

"It's circling around change, like the rest of the album. In this case, I was thinking about your dad. How you said he was afraid of what comes next. The idea of letting go of the past, or the past crumpling down around you. Being anxious to move on to something new, but unable to let go of the past. Something like that."

Adam tapped his hand against his thigh, making a soft rhythm. "The past it haunts you, the future it taunts you."

She grimaced. It wasn't what she'd meant. She searched her mind for a way to make her intentions clearer. "Think about the turtles. They go through all that pain, all that work, just to leave it all behind. Your dad's change is a lot like graduating high school, right? Except he feels like things are ending instead of beginning. It's a perception shift."

Adam looked thoughtful. "Yeah. He thinks if he quits work, he quits life. But he put life on hold, just to hold onto that job. It's messed up."

She looked down at all of her sandy notes. "So now we have to translate all this—going through all the pain of work, of life, only to leave it all behind to start again—into song number two. And we have to do it without writing it down."

"No problem. We got this." Adam nudged her shoulder with his. "Just tell me what you think Dad needs to hear."

An ah-ha lightbulb went off in her head, sparking a surge of excitement. "That's it! The last song was about change and how hard it is. This song should be about how it's worth it to reach for that change. To take the next step. To...to...it's...what would *you* tell him?"

She pointed to the section of notes she thought was relevant. "He's been working hard his whole life. It's who he is, and what he is. Then suddenly what he does is gone. Then what? What would you tell him?"

Adam tilted his head, frowned at the words she indicated, then shook his head. "I don't know. I guess I'd tell him it's not over. Life, I mean. It's just a job. The job's done, but life's not. He can do what he wants, just like I did."

Her heart filled with excitement and adrenaline. "Yes!

That's it. It's not over. Life's not done. Just because the job is finished doesn't mean your life is meaningless. The next step's waiting. All you have to do is take it and you'll make it more than you had before."

She repeated some of it, whittling down the words to their essence, visualizing the piano in front of her and the beat underneath.

Hey
I know that it's been rough
Things change around you
and man it's tough
Your whole life you are what you do
Then comes the day your job is through
And all you have is what used to be.
But
There's more...to...life.

ADAM NODDED along as she spoke. When she finished, he grinned. "Again. Over and over. Don't stop."

She started again. Halfway through, Adam started to hum a melody. At first, it was just notes here or there, but soon it was a complete tune that supported the words with an upbeat, victorious finish.

They sang together, repeating the lines dozens of times, adding in harmony to complement his melody. Adam beat his chest and the rock behind him to keep the rhythm, and by the end they were well on their way to song number two.

Mattie leapt to her feet and whirled around on top of the notes she'd made in the sand. She didn't need them anymore, and it felt so *good*. "It's perfect! Well, not perfect, not yet. But it will be, I can feel it."

She flung her arms around Adam's neck, so caught up in the euphoria of a song coming together that she acted without thinking. Her lips brushed his in an expression of the happiness the song inspired.

Adam went completely still.

She should move away. Kissing him was exactly what she was supposed to avoid doing. But she didn't. She leaned into him and kissed him again.

Adam groaned, and his arms wrapped around her. His body was hot from sitting in the sun, and he smelled like sunscreen and coconut. He pulled her close and pressed his lips into hers, and she opened to him, exploring his tongue with delicate touches of her own.

It felt like waking up.

Her body came alive. Tremors shot through her stomach and sparked between her legs. She melted into him. She wanted more than just this kiss, she wanted *all* of him. She hadn't realized how much until this moment.

"Adam," a high-pitched voice full of irritation called out. "Mattie."

Startled, Mattie pulled away. He let go of her immediately and turned toward the path the others had taken.

Mattie scrambled back and stumbled over her sandals. She managed to catch herself on the rock, skinning her palm in the process.

"Lunch is ready," Tina said.

"Thanks." Adam's scowl was obvious to Mattie, but Tina seemed oblivious.

"Cooper says we can't leave until you eat, so can we get going? The sooner we get this over with, the sooner we can get back—" Tina narrowed her eyes and glanced from Adam to

Mattie and back again. "Did I interrupt something? You weren't...*ew*, in the sand? It gets *everywhere*."

Mattie's cheeks burned. It felt like the time Dad had opened the door when Jimmy What's-His-Name kissed her goodnight after her first date. She shouldn't have kissed Adam. He was her client. They had a project to focus on, she didn't want another Devon situation, and she'd promised Kat she'd be professional.

And he felt so good she wanted more.

Dammit.

"We'll be right there," Adam told Tina.

"Tina, what do you want to drink?" Cooper called out from somewhere behind his girlfriend.

"Whatever. One of those umbrella drinks. It doesn't matter." Tina rolled her eyes. "It's not like they taste like much of anything but sugar."

Cooper stepped into view and took Tina's hand with his. "Come on, the food's ready."

"I'm not having anything now if we're doing dinner later," Tina said. "And those two are too busy getting down in the sand to eat."

The amount of innuendo laced with sarcasm she managed to fit into that sentence was worthy of a five-star gossip columnist.

Cooper looked at Adam, and an entire unspoken conversation passed between them.

Mattie scrambled to get her sandals on and her. "I'm starving."

"Right." Cooper tugged on Tina's hand. She fell into step beside him.

"I don't know why anyone would want to do it in a sandpit full of turtles anyway." Tina's voice trailed off until they were blocked from view by the rocks.

Adam turned back to Mattie. His face was full of apology and passion, longing and regret.

Mattie closed her eyes. "I shouldn't have done that. I'm sorry."

"I'm not," he said. "Mattie, look at me."

She heard him move closer and put a hand up to stop him before anything else happened. "It's not fair. To you, I mean. We can't do this. Please. We have to stay focused on work."

"Why?" Adam's intimate tone would unravel her resolve if she let it. "What's so wrong about one little kiss?"

She opened her eyes and looked up at him.

How could she make him see what had to be, when all she really wanted was another kiss, and then another, then more? She wanted what she shouldn't have. It was island magic, nothing more than that.

It was the same thing Devon had done to her, only now she was the one doing it to Adam.

"It's just the song, Adam. Nothing more. It's not real."

Chapter Fourteen

Adam blinked at her, momentarily stunned by her announcement. "What do you mean it's not real?"

"I was excited. By the song, I mean. That's all. I shouldn't have done it. I'm sorry."

"Are you trying to say you didn't like it? Or that you don't like me." He wanted her in a way that sucked the ability to reason out of his brain. That had to be why her words made no sense.

"I need to keep things professional. You understand, don't you?"

"Sounds like a swear word."

The kiss had been unexpected, mind numbing, and glorious. He could still feel the press of her lips on his, and he wanted more. A lot more.

Dammit, she did too. He could see it in her eyes.

"Please, can we just go to lunch?"

"Mattie..."

She looked away. "If we don't leave soon, Tina might actually get snotty."

"Mattie, look at me."

She looked up and locked that sparkling gaze on his.

"I'll never be sorry you kissed me."

An adorable flush crawled up her cheeks. "Me either."

"Good."

He hummed the new song all the way down the path to the clearing where a picnic table had been set up in the shade of two large trees. A nearby grass hut housed a fully stocked bar and a counter filled with platters of sandwiches, skewers of meat, fruits, and other local snacks.

The rest of the afternoon passed in a haze filled with memories of Mattie's kiss and the new song they'd started together on turtle beach.

"That's bad ass," Cooper said. "I like it...I can hear a riff going right there in the middle, building to a climax just before that end. Maybe a solo after?"

Mattie nodded. "It definitely needs something like that, and I can't wait to hear Flynn's take on it. He always adds energy, and I think it needs that. We want people to shout this one, you know? It's a defiant, I'm-not-done-yet anthem."

Tina took a long sip of the red drink she held in her hands. "To me it sounds like the person can't accept that something is over. People should let go, you know? Move on."

Adam stood up. "Speaking of, let's get out of here. Bayo?"

Bayo hurried over from where she'd been sitting behind the bar. "All are ready, yes? We can make our way back when you like, Mr. Adam."

"Finally," Tina muttered. She stood up and walked to the dock without a backward glance at any of them.

Cooper followed her.

"She's not right for him," Mattie muttered.

"Don't worry. I bet she leaves the island first thing in the morning, if not tonight. He'll be able to relax then."

She frowned. "Not sure it's relaxation he's looking for."

When they reached the Jet Ski, Mattie stepped back to let him go first. He shook his head. "This time, you drive."

Her eyes widened, and her hand did the little fluttering motion it did when she was nervous. "I can't drive that."

"Sure you can. It's just like a motorcycle, only on water."

She raised an eyebrow. "I've never driven one of those, either."

"Bicycle?"

She nodded. "When I was a kid."

"Well this is easier. Go on, I'll be right behind you. If you get in trouble I'll be there to help."

"You mean you'll fish me out of the water when I go over? Is this to get back at me for pushing you off the boat?"

He grinned. "Only one way to find out."

She hesitated, then squared her shoulders and stepped onto the Jet Ski. Once she was in position, Adam lowered himself onto the seat and slipped his arms around her. "Okay, all set."

Mattie started the machine. He coached her on how to throttle, and then they pulled away from the dock.

Mattie's body was tense, but he didn't think it was from nerves. When he was sure she had a handle on it, he settled in behind her and debated with himself on which was better, her pressed against his back or her wiggling in front of him as she navigated the waves.

When they reached the dock and climbed off the skis, she was flush with excitement and a little too much sun. "We have to do that again."

"Not in this lifetime," Tina said as she swept past them.

The strip of white masquerading as a swimsuit flossed Tina's now slightly pink butt cheeks as she stormed down the pier.

Cooper swore under his breath and took off after her. "Tina, wait!"

Mattie pulled her life vest off and handed it to Bayo. "Thank you so much, Bayo. I had a fantastic time."

"My pleasure, Miss Mattie. Any time you want to ride, please stop by. There will always be a ski waiting for you."

Mattie beamed at their guide. "I'll do that."

They started walking slowly down the pier to where the rest of the band waited for them, giving Cooper and Tina space by unspoken agreement. From the wild arm gestures and the way Tina stomped as she walked, their conversation wasn't going well.

"He's such a sweet man," Mattie said. "Why does he go out with women like that?"

Adam shrugged. "He loves strong women, but he gets confused on where strength ends and bitchiness starts."

"What's the big freaking deal, they were making out *anyway*," Tina shouted. "I want to go back to the room, Cooper. Now."

Adam cringed at Tina's use of the word "anyway." If Mattie caught the meaning behind that, he was toast.

Tina spun on her heels and stomped toward one of the golf carts.

"Oh my God, she did *not* just do that." Mattie spun around and started walking the other way as if she were going back out on the Jet Skis. "She told them we...we...oh my God."

Mattie was more worried about the news of their kiss getting to the guys than she was about the implication that the entire day had been staged to get the two of them to do exactly what they did. Relief washed through him.

"Mattie, wait. Ignore her." He ran to get in front of Mattie before she made it all the way to the skis and took off.

"What a spiteful, selfish *bitch*!" Mattie glared at the retreating golf cart.

"Total, complete bitch," he agreed. "We should take her out on the boat so we can shove her off it."

Mattie's lips twitched. "No we shouldn't."

"She'd deserve it. She needs to cool off. Come on, let's go."

He slowed down as they reached the waiting group of guys so that Mattie got there first. From over her shoulder, he glared at them and dragged his index finger across his throat to indicate exactly what he'd do to each and every one of them if they mentioned the kiss.

LT pressed his lips together and blinked innocently at them.

"Hi, you guys. How was the cave?" Mattie asked.

Brandon grinned. "It's really cool. You guys should go see it. Loads of coral, and a little hidden den inside to, uh, hide in."

"How were the turtles?" Flynn's smile was so wide it would crack his face if he didn't rein it in.

"They are so amazing," Mattie said. "You all really should have come with us. And we made a good start on the second song. We can go over it now if you want."

Behind her, Adam shook his head.

"Uh, I'm supposed to meet Malika in a few minutes for a horse ride. How about tomorrow?" LT said.

"Yeah, it was a long day, and I need a shower," Brandon said.

"Yeah, you do." Flynn pushed Brandon away from him. "I'm surprised the sharks didn't come after you on the way back."

"A shower sounds great. Tomorrow, then." Mattie said. She turned to the golf carts and hesitated.

There were only two left, but each would seat four people including the driver.

Brandon hit Flynn in the arm. "You drive."

"See you all later." LT saluted them with a half wave and took off walking toward the Big House.

"Have a *good* time," Flynn said with a wide grin.

"Dude, you look creepy when you do that," Brandon said.

"Whatever. At least somebody's getting laid. Let's go."

The two of them hopped into the cart on the right.

Flynn waved at them. "Later."

Adam gestured to the one on the left. "I'll drop you off."

Flynn drove in front of them like a drunk at a NASCAR rally until he reached the turnoff for Brandon's villa. They shouted something rude that he hoped Mattie didn't understand and followed the cutoff to the right.

Adam kept going, grateful for the sudden absence of anyone who could say anything incriminating.

He pulled up outside of Mattie's villa and stopped. He wanted to kiss her again. Did he see desire in her eyes, or was it something else. "See you for dinner?"

"Sure." Mattie seemed on the verge of saying something, then appeared to think better of it. She gave an almost imperceptible shake of her head and got out. "I had a...it was a nice day."

"Very."

She hesitated, then gave him a little wave. "Thanks for the ride."

"Anytime." He waited until she disappeared through the living room into the bedroom, then went on to his own place.

He took a long shower and lost himself in a replay of their kiss in vivid detail. He could still smell the scent of her coconut sunscreen mixed with fresh sea breezes, and the taste of her, honey and spice and intoxication, still lingered on his tongue.

That one kiss opened a floodgate of desire that he absolutely could not show her. Not yet. He had to keep it together.

The way she'd looked at him after Tina had outed them had been full of promise but hidden by embarrassment and something else. He refused to believe it was regret.

The whole situation left him frustrated. He wanted to sweep her off her feet and tell her how fascinating and beautiful she was, but he didn't want her to reject him again. It was a freaking tightrope he was walking between showing his interest but not overwhelming her, and if it went on much longer, he was going to lose his mind.

He spent so long fantasizing about what might have happened after the kiss that he had to take another shower. This time, it was ice cold.

"Get a grip, man." He shook his head at his reflection in the mirror and finished getting ready for dinner.

When he stepped out of his bedroom into the living room, he found the band—minus Cooper—lounging in his living room with beers in their hands and smug grins on their faces.

He narrowed his eyes at LT. "I thought you were riding horses with what's-her-name."

"Nah." LT looked proud of himself. "I was just getting out of the way so you two could have alone time in the buggy."

Flynn leapt up and held a hand out for Adam to slap. "Dude, well played! We thought it got messed up when Tina pulled her little stunt, but Cooper told us lip-lock was achieved."

LT clapped his hands together in slow applause. "It's not a roll in the hammock, but it's a start."

Brandon put his beer down and high-fived Flynn. "We are masters of *looove*."

"How was it?" LT asked.

"Yeah, sweet and sassy, or hot and dirty?" Flynn wiggled his eyebrows. "I bet it was dirty. I mean, Tina said you were rolling in the sand."

Adam held up both hands in surrender at the onslaught. "We were *not* rolling in the sand."

Brandon and Flynn peered at him with suspicion.

"But you did kiss her, right?" Flynn asked. "Tongue was involved?"

Adam closed his eyes and counted to five. Then he went to the fridge to get himself a beer. "Tina practically told her about your little matchmaking attempt. I don't think Mattie caught on, but still. No more stunts like that. "

"I thought the idea was to get more hands on," Flynn said, sounding confused.

"We talked about this." Adam flashed a dirty look at his drummer. "I have to be more subtle."

"Yeah, but then you kissed," Brandon said, looking just as confused as Flynn. "That changes things, right?"

LT rolled his eyes. "If you don't act faster, man, you're not getting this girl. We only have two weeks left. If you don't make it happen here, it ain't happening at all. It's not like she's always in your orbit."

Adam took a sip of his beer. "The thing is, there's times when I think she wants me as much as I want her. Like, we have a real connection. Then bam, she slams on the brakes. I mean, I know why she's gun-shy. I get it. The last guy was a douche, but still. I'm not that guy."

"Why don't you just ask her out?" Brandon asked. He sounded practical and entirely too reasonable.

"Because the first time I tried to rush things I made an ass of myself and she pushed me off the boat." Adam took another swig of beer. "Pretty sure she'll take the next helicopter off this island if I do that again."

"Look, man, it's time to put up or shut up," LT said. "Either you like this girl and you want to make it happen or you don't and we might as well pack up now. You kissed. The door's wide open for you to tell her how you feel."

"Maybe you're right." Adam peeled off part of the label on his beer. Should he risk it? He'd only get one shot at this. If he pushed too hard a second time, that would be the end. She'd leave and he'd never see her again.

"I know I'm right," LT said. He finished off his beer and set the empty bottle down on the coffee table. "Pretty sure I'm right."

"How many relationships have you had again?" Adam eyed him. "Two?"

"Three," LT said, sounding indignant.

"Oh no," Adam said. "You can't count that girl in middle school."

"We dated all the way to freshman year." LT pushed off the couch and crossed to the kitchen. "That's over two years, which is longer than any fling *you've* ever had."

Adam snorted. "Sharing homeroom and lunch with her is not the same as dating."

LT pulled a beer out of the fridge and popped it open. "We kissed. That counts."

"Was there tongue?" Flynn asked, looking from LT to Adam.

"A good man don't kiss and tell." LT plopped back down on the couch.

Adam laughed. "She kissed him on the cheek during the yearbook signing at the end of eighth grade."

Brandon and Flynn both cracked up.

"That's true love right there," LT said. "I still think about that girl. She's the one that got away."

Footsteps on the deck outside announced Cooper's arrival. He'd changed into pressed khaki shorts and a white collared shirt so clean and stiff that it gleamed against his dark skin, and he'd shaved the vacation stubble off his chin. He looked ready for a date, except he walked in alone and wore the stoic expression of a man who'd been on the losing side of too many girlfriend conflicts.

Adam looked behind him, but the ever-present thorn wasn't there. "Where's Tina?"

Cooper grimaced and stalked toward the fridge. "She's packing." He dragged a bottle out then twisted the top off with enough force to fling it across the room.

There was momentary silence as everyone absorbed that information.

"Finally," Brandon muttered.

"Ding-dong the bitch has fled," Flynn sang out.

"Guys, have a little compassion." LT said. "The man's been under the ball and chain for a year. Let him decompress first."

"She wasn't a ball and chain." Cooper glowered. "She was cool at first."

"Sorry, man." Adam held up his beer bottle.

Cooper clinked it with his own then took a long pull. "Me too. She was out of line today. How'd Mattie take it?" He stretched out on the lounge chair next to the couch and laid his head back on the cushion.

"She was worried about you, actually," Adam said. "She said you're a good man, and you don't deserve that crap."

Cooper raised his eyebrows. "That's nice. She's a good egg. So what's the plan now?"

"You have to at least ask her out, man," Flynn said. "That's how it usually works."

"Actually, he should have done that before the kiss," Brandon pointed out. "He's having an Adam moment. Totally backwards."

"I did ask her out. This entire trip is one giant date." Adam stared at the dense line of trees that separated his villa from

Mattie's. She was probably taking a shower. The very idea that she might be naked right now sent a shiver through his body.

"Not if you don't tell *her* it's a date," Cooper said. "She thinks she's on a work trip. It's time for you to make a real move, bud."

"That's what I said," LT muttered.

"Okay, so why don't we arrange one of those sunset dinner cruises for them?" Brandon suggested. "We could say we're all going, and then back out or just not show up."

"Let me do the planning this time, okay?" Adam had to deflect the well-intentioned meddling in his love life before it really got out of hand.

"Okay, genius, what's the plan?" Flynn asked. "So far all I've heard is you dodging the question."

"You should take her on the picnic," Cooper said.

"Hey, yeah!" Brandon said, excited. "Now that Coop's ditched Tina, he doesn't need his dreamy dinner for two. He can hang with us."

"Thanks," Cooper said with heavy sarcasm. "That's exactly what I want to do now that my relationship has fallen apart."

"A little bro time is perfect after a breakup," Flynn said. "Everybody knows that."

"It's not a bad idea," LT said. "I mean, you both need to eat, right? She can't find fault with that."

"She could," Adam said, "since we've been doing the group thing for two weeks now. It'll be a pretty obvious move in exactly the direction she said she didn't want."

"I think her feelings on that might have changed." LT leaned forward to give Adam an intense look. "You said you wanted to handle this, so handle it. Ask her out."

Flynn grabbed the house phone and handed it to Adam. "It's a solid plan, dude."

Adam thought about it. Cooper had planned that dinner

with romance in mind, and since he'd done it to appease Tina it would be like something out of a movie set. Cooper always went all out where his women were concerned. It would be classy, sultry, and designed to create a lasting memory.

The guys were right. Time to put up or stop pretending he could ever get anywhere with the elusive woman.

"Okay. I'll call her." Adam took the phone out to the deck and dialed Mattie's extension.

Chapter Fifteen

Mattie returned to her villa flushed from the sun, the kiss, and the ride with Adam. No matter how many times she told herself it was a mistake, her thoughts kept circling back to how right it felt to be in his arms.

Someone needed to talk sense to her, because her promise to behave was about to be broken. She went immediately into the bedroom, dug her cell phone out of purgatory, then did the time zone math. It was almost seven here in paradise, which made it eleven a.m. in New York. Perfect.

She dialed the first person she always turned to for advice.

The phone rang six times and went to voice mail.

"Hi. You've reached Lizzie Bellamy at Belhurst Castle. Please leave—"

Mattie hung up. "Dammit."

She hit Piper's number. It was eight in the morning in Los Angeles, so she half expected the call to go directly to voice mail.

Instead, her sister picked up on the second ring, looking far too awake for the hour in a black studded cap and a white tank top. There was a microphone behind her, which probably meant she was in a studio session.

"Hey, Mattie Cake. How's the beach?"

"It's fine. Good, actually." She squinted at the background. "What are you doing up and functional this early?"

Piper glanced behind her and waved at someone. "Give me a few, okay?"

She turned back to the camera. "I'm practicing some of the voice-overs for the animated thing."

"I thought that didn't go into production until next year?"

"The animation doesn't, but the rest of it is already in the works. They're using me as a model for the character animation so the voice work gets done first. I'm going to be an actual princess." Piper wiggled her eyebrows.

"Tell me something I don't know," Mattie teased.

Piper stuck her tongue out at her. "Anyway, it's a fascinating process. I kind of pushed my way in at the beginning so I could see how it's done."

"Of course you did," Mattie said with a laugh. She felt sorry for the poor animator who tried to stand in Piper's way. "And they couldn't say no to Piper Bellamy now could they?"

"No." Piper bared her teeth. "I might bite. Besides, I just want to make sure I get it exactly right, which I think they appreciate. So what's up?"

Mattie took a deep breath. "I think I screwed up."

Piper's happy expression morphed into concern. "What's the rock hound done? Are you okay? Should I send in a team to get you out?"

"No." Her lips twitched at the idea of a SWAT rescue team being deployed on her behalf. "I'm okay. It's not him. It's me. It's all me."

"Oh, good. So what's going on?" Piper relaxed and leaned back against the wall.

It was such a long story Mattie didn't know where to start. Finally, she blurted out the main thing that kept invading her thoughts. "I kissed him."

Piper's eyes widened, and a slow smile crept onto her face. "I see."

Mattie groaned. "I shouldn't have done it." She propped the phone up against the lamp and picked up a pillow to hug.

"Why the hell not? He's hot. I'd kiss him too if I was there."

"I'm supposed to be a professional, that's why not, and now I've gone and made it all complicated."

Piper rolled her eyes. "Mattie Cake, there's nothing complicated about this. He likes you. You like him. You kissed him and he kissed you back. Um, he did kiss you back, right?"

"Yes." She buried her face in the pillow.

"Well there you go. So what's he like?"

Mattie lifted her head and smiled. "He's really into the music on a wholistic level. His voice is perfect. It's rich and a little growly, and right in that sweet spot between bass and tenor."

"Leave it to you to assess his music skills first," Piper said looking amused. "He's behaving better than Devon, right?"

"He started out being a little aggressively intense, but after I dumped him in the ocean he evened out."

"You pushed him." Piper blinked. "Okay, I'm going to need the whole story. Start with when you got to the island and finish with the kiss. Leave nothing out."

Her sister listened without interrupting until Mattie reached the boat incident. Piper howled with laughter, loud enough for someone in the background to ask if something was wrong.

"I wish I'd been there to see his face." Piper waved away whoever it was and wiped tears out of her eyes. "You know, he must really like you. Most men would have run after you did that."

"I still can't believe I did that. I can't believe I kissed him like that either, but I have to admit it was nice. *Really* nice."

Piper wiggled her eyebrows. "Nice as in superhot, or nice as in further exploration is needed before you decide?"

"Piper. You're supposed to be talking me out of his bed, not into it." She checked the time on her phone. "I have to go soon. I'm still covered in ocean and dinner is usually in about an hour."

"You want *me* to talk you out of having fun with a scorching hot rock star? What have you been smoking? If you wanted someone to be sensible with you, you should have called Lizzie."

"I did. She didn't answer." Mattie looked out the window at the trees that separated her villa from Adam's. He was probably over there right now, getting ready for dinner. She had a feeling he'd be washing off the salt and sand in the outdoor shower. She pictured his bare chest, wet and glistening in the sunlight. It sent a little thrill through her. She remembered how his lips had felt on hers, and suddenly it was too warm in the room.

"Interesting." Piper drew the word out in a know-it-all sisterly tone. "I haven't seen that look on your face in years. You really like this guy. Okay, if you want sense talked at you, here it is. I know you've been avoiding any real relationship for a while now. You run every time a man gets close."

"I do not," Mattie interrupted. "I don't run. The project ends and I move on. That's a completely different thing."

"You. Run," Piper said with emphasis. "You flit away like a bee in search of a new flower. You've been doing that ever since Della broke us up, and while I get how damaging that was for you, I say maybe it's time to work past that."

Mattie frowned and waved away her sister's concern. "I'm doing just fine."

"Yeah, we all saw how fine you're *not* doing at brunch. You ditch guys before they have a chance to ditch you because you think they'll behave just like Della, and I don't think living that way for the past four years has made you happy." Piper looked entirely too smug and satisfied with her assessment.

Mattie glared at her. "I suppose you ignoring men altogether and pretending Della doesn't exist for the past four years makes *you* happy, does it?"

"This isn't about me," Piper said through gritted teeth. "And because I assume you didn't call me to pick a fight I'm going to ignore that."

Mattie winced as the worms of guilt burrowed into her heart and squeezed. Why did guilt always, *always* follow after she lashed out with her unvarnished thoughts? Piper clearly didn't suffer that sort of reaction. Neither did Della. It wasn't fair. "I'm sorry."

"It's okay." Piper's face softened. "It's hard to keep feelings bottled up the way you do. You've been under a microscope lately, and you never liked standing in the spotlight to begin with. You were bound to pop your top eventually. To be honest, I'm proud of you. You finally told Della what you should have told her four years ago. That had to feel good."

Mattie shook her head. "No. Not really."

"Don't worry, it gets better with practice."

"Does it really?" Mattie had a feeling that brave face Piper wore was just that. Underneath, her sister was a pile of marshmallows.

"Well, it gets more satisfying anyway." Piper looked a little distant, as if remembering something. "The more you let it out, the less traumatic it will be, that's for sure."

Mattie squeezed the pillow in her arms. "So you think I should go out with Adam?"

"No." Piper gave her a wicked little smile. "I think you should have a fling with a sexy man on a tropical island and realize that not every relationship leads to a PR disaster, and not everyone out there is as selfish as Della."

"I tried that with Brian, remember?" Mattie said. "I did that weekend in Vegas with him to celebrate the end of the project last year and now he's using the photos as promo material for his new album."

"Brian's a tool, but what he's doing actually boosted your visibility, which isn't a bad thing. It's not like you were naked."

"I might as well have been. That was a sheer nightgown, and it was a private moment. He wasn't supposed to share it with the entire world on Instagram."

"Has Adam tried to get photos with you in a string bikini?"

"I don't wear those, and no. He sent the staff photographer away when we first got here. The only photo that's been taken this entire trip was today, when we got on the Jet Skis. The staff photographer, Don Something-or-Other, took a group shot since nobody had their phones with them."

"See?" Piper leaned back. "You're sequestered halfway around the world, away from prying eyes. Take advantage of it and live a little."

The thought was so tempting it made her want to run straight over to Adam's place and...what? She told Kat she wouldn't do anything like that, for good reason. "You don't get it. If I do that and word gets out, there'll be tabloid headlines for the next six months, and everyone will think I did it to get credit for another song I didn't write. They already don't take me seriously as it is, especially after Devon's Twitter rampage."

"Anybody who knows you and your work takes you seriously, Mattie. Haven't you seen how many people defend you every time he posts?"

She hadn't looked. She'd been too afraid of what fans would say. She got up and fished in the closet for something to wear to dinner. "Sure they defend me now, but what happens when the next juicy photo hits? So far all they have is a shot of us shaking hands. I don't want to put any more fuel on that fire. Devon would go absolutely nuts. I can just see the post now. Run, Brooks, run, before she spins her web on you too."

"That asshole doesn't get to police your love life. If anybody's going to do that it's me, and I say forget the jerks who came before and have some fun."

"I have to be careful, and professional. At least until I win that award." Mattie carried two dresses back to the bed. One was very short and fire-engine red with a sweetheart neckline and thin straps. The other was long and white, with a halter-style top that dipped low in the back. "Which one?"

"The red one. Definitely. And you're not being profes-sional, you're being a scaredy cat," Piper said. "Trust me, if the rest of the song is anything like the lines you sent me, this song will definitely win awards. People who matter will know the truth. So will your fans, which is the most important thing."

"If a photo of us goes viral the fans will forget all about the song." Mattie put the white dress on the bed and held the red one up in front of her. It barely reached her thighs, but she loved the color. "I don't know if I should wear this to dinner with the guys. It's not really a dress. It's supposed to go over a bathing suit."

"You'll never find out if Adam has other skills if you keep going to dinner with the entire band," Piper said with an exas-perated sigh. "You'll look hot in red. Put a bathing suit under it and stop worrying about what might or might not wind up on Twitter. Seize the moment. March your pretty little behind over to Adam's place and find out if he's good at something else besides singing and kissing."

Mattie gave her sister an exasperated smile. "I have to go."

"Promise you'll at least get another kiss," Piper demanded.

Mattie picked up the phone and hovered her finger over the End Call button. "Love you."

"Love you more." Piper waved half-heartedly. "Call me later. I want details."

Mattie ended the call and stashed the phone back in the drawer without looking at the waiting text messages or emails. She'd been on the phone so long she didn't have much time to get changed.

The house phone rang just as she stepped into the bathroom. Abayomi probably wanted to know what she'd like for an evening snack or breakfast the next day. She trudged back to the bedroom to answer it.

"Hello?"

"Hey, Mattie," Adam said. "I was wondering...would you like to go on a picnic with me? Cooper had it planned for him and Tina tonight, but she's backed out. It'll all go to waste if someone doesn't go, so he offered it to us."

"Oh," Mattie said.

Piper's advice rang through her head. *Live a little. Have some fun. Seize the moment. Find out if Adam is good at something besides kissing.*

"Mattie?" Adam sounded confused. "Are you there? Is this thing working?"

"I...um..."

A picnic. Probably on a beach. Under the stars.

She couldn't think of anything more romantic than that. Why would any woman turn that down?

What was she thinking? She really shouldn't do this. All the reasons she should say no lined up in her head like planes on a runway. What if something went wrong? What if it didn't? What if photos leaked to the tabloids? What would Kat say?

"Mattie?"

She started. "I'm here. Sorry, I'm just getting ready."

"Oh," Adam said. He paused, and it was her turn to wonder what was going on. She thought she could hear the guys in the background laughing, but maybe she was imagining it. "Um, yeah. Me too. So, anyway. About the picnic. No pressure. We can do the usual dinner around the bonfire with the guys if you want."

She pictured the two scenes and heard Piper's voice in her head. *You'll never find out if Adam has other skills if you keep doing dinner with the entire band.*

Her sister was right, and the realization that she very much wanted to know if Adam had other skills besides kissing made her open her mouth and say the words she probably shouldn't say.

"Okay. A picnic sounds like fun."

"Great. The driver will pick us up in about thirty minutes. That work okay?"

She glanced down at the white powdery dust covering most of her legs and arms, then over at the two dresses waiting for her on the bed. It was a good thing she'd never been one of those girls who needed two hours to do her hair. She could dash through the shower and spend the rest of the time deciding whether to be a seductress in red or an innocent in white.

"Okay. See you then."

They hung up, and she padded back to the shower feeling lighter than she'd felt in a long time.

Chapter Sixteen

Adam grinned at the waiting faces in his living room.

"Well?" Brandon asked.

"That's a yes," Flynn said. He pointed a drumstick at Adam. "That's the face of a man about to get laid."

"Shut it," Adam told him.

"It's about time." LT held up a beer in salute. "Well done, man."

Brandon high-fived Flynn. "Just call us the love doctors."

"Okay." Adam gestured toward the deck. "All of you get out. We're leaving in thirty minutes and I don't want you crowding around making her nervous."

Brandon stood up and set his empty beer bottle on the counter. "See ya. Come on, Flynn, they said there'd be a dance tonight."

Flynn waved a lazy salute at Adam, then stage-whispered, "Let's hide out in the bushes and watch."

"Out." Adam gave them his best I'm-going-to-kill you look.

"No fun at all," Flynn muttered as he and Brandon stepped out of the living room onto the deck.

"Later." LT grinned and joined the other two.

Adam sighed in relief.

Cooper stared after the rest of the crew. "One of these days we need to get Flynn laid."

Adam snorted a laugh. For all his bluster, Flynn had only had one serious relationship and very few casual flings. He had a girl who was a friend, but it hadn't gone any further than that, as far as he knew. "Yeah. Hey, man, I'm sorry about Tina."

Cooper shrugged. "I'm not. It's been coming for a while. I should have known, right? Vacation is my relationship kryptonite."

Adam drained the last of his beer. "Maybe next time you should try hooking up with someone who's never heard of the band."

Cooper snorted. "Where am I going to find that? Man, in case you haven't heard, Delusions of Glory is an international sensation. Sen-*sa*-tion."

Adam laughed. "True, but I bet you anything there's a woman out there who would care more about you than she does herself."

"Maybe." Cooper set his bottle down. "Enjoy the picnic."

Cooper walked out onto the deck.

Adam couldn't see any of the others lingering out there, but it didn't mean Flynn and Brandon weren't planning some sort of prank to "help" the budding relationship along.

"Hey, Coop?" Adam called.

Cooper looked back.

"Don't tell them where the picnic is."

Cooper laughed. "I'm your wingman, not your cock-blocker. I got you. Relax and enjoy each other. You two have a real connection. Don't waste it."

Cooper faded into the tree line and disappeared from view.

Adam spun around and headed for the bedroom. If he was having a romantic picnic with Mattie, he needed to wear something better than the T-shirt and shorts he'd thrown on after his two showers.

It took him a lot longer to change clothes than he thought it should. He usually didn't spend a lot of time second-guessing his appearance, but tonight he wanted to get it right. Problem was, they were in the tropics and his usual go-to date outfit of rocker leather and denim not only wouldn't work, he hadn't even brought it with him.

They'd be swimming, he hoped. The thought of doing that naked with her sent a flare of interest through his nether regions, but he shoved that thought aside and reached for bright aqua swim trunks and a white button-down shirt. He left the top three buttons strategically undone so the Delusions of Glory tattoo peeked out.

He shoved his feet into sandals and checked his hair. Not bad.

Adam heard the tiny beep of a golf cart horn from the front and strode out before he could rethink his outfit.

He hummed the song they'd been working on as he made his way to the cart until he saw Mattie and the song died in his throat.

She was radiant in a vibrant red dress that hugged her curves, then flared a little just at the thigh and stopped, leaving her luscious legs bare all the way down. She usually favored flowy skirts or long dresses, and the change turbocharged his adrenaline.

"Mattie. You look...damn."

Mattie greeted him with a warm, amused smile. She shifted her beach bag from one shoulder to the other. "Thanks. It sounds really good. The song, I mean. You put a new run in there. I like it."

"Thanks," he managed to say without stuttering like a fool.

He'd been on hundreds of dates with women ranging from models to musicians, but none of them had prepared him for Mattie Bellamy in a little red dress.

Mattie climbed into the back seat of the cart. "Hi, Abayomi. Thanks for picking us up."

"My pleasure, Miss Mattie. Always."

Adam slid onto the back seat next to Mattie. The hem of her dress had ridden up an inch or two, maybe three. It made his heart race even more.

"Everyone ready?" Abayomi drove down the path to the right. "I take you tonight to Lanmou Bay. It will be a beautiful night. All the stars will be on display for you."

Mattie looked up. "The stars shine just for us?"

"Always for the lovers at Lanmou Bay. You tell me tomorrow if you did not see more than you ever seen before."

Mattie dipped her head at the word "lovers," but Adam wasn't sure if she rejected the idea or felt embarrassed, or maybe, just maybe, excited.

Abayomi turned down a path Adam hadn't seen before and commented on all the plants and birds they saw along the way, as well as the beach they were headed toward.

"There is a small waterfall, but do not try to climb the cliff. The rocks are very wet and slippery, yes? The bay is protected, but do not go beyond the large boulder. There is a phone inside the hut if you need assistance. A buggy is waiting for you so that you may leave whenever you wish."

Abayomi stopped in a small clearing between two enormous rocks. Next to them sat an empty golf cart. A footpath led through the rocks to a small u-shaped beach. Water splashed somewhere to the left, and the ocean washed the shore in front of them.

Two beach chairs and a small table with a bowl of flowers sat in the middle of the pristine beach, with two giant white umbrellas providing shade. The sun was low in the horizon, and the golden color turned the sand and trees into a surreal painting.

He silently thanked Cooper, the resort, and the stars themselves that Mattie had said yes to coming with him.

He expected Abayomi to lead them down the path, but the driver stepped back. "Here is where I leave you. No one will disturb you here, Miss Mattie, Mr. Adam. This time and this place is yours to discover."

"Thank you," Mattie said.

Abayomi grinned broadly and climbed back into the golf cart. "Enjoy."

They watched him drive away, then Adam held out his hand to her. "Shall we?"

Mattie looked at his hand, and for half a second he thought she'd refuse. His chest tightened in anticipation. Then she linked her strong, slender fingers with his and smiled, and the tension vanished.

"Yes." She nodded. "Let's see what we see."

They walked down the short stone path that ended in sand. Once they passed the two large rocks that formed a cliff face, the rest of the bay came into view.

To the left, water spilled off the top of the short cliff, smacked the sand, and rushed into the sea. The saturated rocks glittered in the afternoon sun. Many of them looked like tempting footholds. He could see why they'd been told not to climb.

A thatched-roof hut nestled against the cliff to the right of the path. Next to that, a white curtained cabana covered a wood deck that stepped up from the sand.

"Oh look, an outdoor shower." Mattie laughed and whirled around with her arms stretched out wide. "I've never seen anything like this. Feel that air. This is pure magic. Who would ever want to give this up? Tina's missing out."

She looked so carefree and vibrant it was all he could do to keep his hands to himself instead of sweeping up and kissing her until they both ran out of breath.

There was magic in the air, all right, but he thought it came from the girl, not the place.

"Well, Coop's the master of romance, so I'm not surprised he found this spot."

"Shame he didn't find the right person to share it with." Mattie pointed at the hut. "What's in there?"

"Not sure. Let's check it out."

They trudged through the sand and pushed the door open. A shelving unit along the back wall held stacks of towels, games, books, and supplies like bug spray and sunscreen. A battery-operated refrigerator was stocked with everything from water to a pitcher of something red. A door at the back led to a bathroom and shower.

"Look, they left paper and pens." Mattie pointed at a writing desk in the corner, where someone had left a hand-bound notebook and several pens next to a hurricane oil lamp, a lighter, and one of the walkie-talkie island phones. "How sweet is that?"

"How did they even know to do that?" Adam stared around the small hut. Anything they could possibly want for a fun time at the beach was in here, along with other, more intimate things, like bottles of massage oil and several unopened boxes of condoms.

"I sang the second song to Abayomi. He likes what we have

so far." She flashed him a smile. "He told me to remember that every ending is a new beginning, which I think we should work in somehow."

"Maybe." He didn't want to think about the song right now. He didn't want Mattie slipping back into work mode. "Let's check out the cabana."

Mattie slipped her sandals off and dug her toes in the sand as they walked. Her honey hair glowed in the setting sun, her tanned skin glinted from the heat, and his eyes followed the sway of her hips.

The cabana provided an oasis from the sea and sun. A long white cushioned sofa looked out at the ocean. A polished teak coffee table, carved with vines and flowers, stood in front of it holding an enormous picnic basket. A small cooler that probably held drinks sat under the table.

Underneath the canopy behind the sofa was a queen-sized daybed made up with white linens and covered with pink and white flower petals. Tiki lamps provided light in the corners, while ocean breezes invited them to linger.

He glanced at Mattie, trying to gauge her reaction.

Mattie ran her hand over the top of the picnic basket. "I bet there's chocolate-covered strawberries in here."

Her expression was thoughtful and a little distant. He wasn't sure how to interpret that look.

"You're probably right. Bet there's champagne and tiny sandwiches. Tina loved stuff like that."

"Well I can't fault her for that." Mattie tapped the top of the basket and glanced at the ocean. "Want to go for a swim before the sun sets?"

He seized on that suggestion with a sense of relief. "That's a great idea."

Mattie set her bag and shoes down next to the sofa and reached for the hem of her dress. She lifted it up and over her head, revealing the colorful sports bikini underneath. Pink, blue, and yellow swirls burst like fireworks on a black background. It was bright and cheerful and perfectly Mattie.

Most of the women he'd dated wore the scraps-of-fabric variety that Tina favored. Instead of bits of string and goodwill holding it together, Mattie's suit looked like something a professional surfer would wear.

Mattie dropped the dress onto the sofa, then caught him staring and laughed.

"Come on. The water's waiting." She took off running toward the water.

Adam ripped his shirt off so fast he thought he popped one of the buttons. He tossed it onto her dress and chased after her.

Chapter Seventeen

Mattie kicked into the water feeling so full of happy energy she wanted to sing. Something about the ocean stripped away all her concerns and inhibitions and left her full of joy.

She pushed into the waves until they swept past her knees, then turned to find Adam only a few feet behind her. He'd stripped off his shirt, revealing the tattoo on his tanned, very well-defined chest.

He looked every inch a rock star standing in the surf, wet from the spray. She wanted to touch him. She wanted to trace the edges of that tattoo and then run her hands over his chest.

From the hungry look in his eyes, he knew exactly what she was thinking. Their gazes locked. Tingles of awareness shot between her legs. She could feel the anticipation building.

Was she really doing this?

She stepped back into the next wave and gasped as the water rushed over her stomach and between her thighs. "This is great. I'm sorry Cooper and Tina didn't get to see it."

"I'm not. If they were here, we wouldn't be, and I wouldn't want to miss this."

Her breath caught in her throat. Desire welled up inside, hard to ignore.

A wave hit Mattie in the back and shoved her forward. She shrieked and splashed to catch her footing.

Adam laughed. "Got a little distracted, did you?"

He flexed his chest muscles, obviously proud of his effect on her.

"Think you're funny, do you?" On impulse she scooped up water with both hands and flung it at him.

"Oh, it's like that?" Adam laughed, then picked her up in his arms and fell backward into the water with her, dunking them both.

They tangled arms and legs, each trying to get the upper hand. Adam had the advantage of height and found his footing first. He hauled Mattie up out of the water and steadied her. She clung to his arms for support while the salt water stung her eyes and drained out of her nose.

"Not fair!" Mattie sputtered.

"I got you." Adam's hands were firm and secure on her upper arms. He looked concerned, as if he thought he'd gone too far.

He had a brother. Surely, he knew better than that.

As a woman with three sisters, she'd had plenty of practice dunking people. She jumped up with the next wave and used it as leverage to kick Adam's legs out from under him.

"Whoa!" Adam shouted.

They both went under and tumbled toward the shore. Mattie found her footing, dragged her hair out of her eyes and smirked at Adam. "Bet you didn't see that coming."

"Nice moves." It was Adam's turn to sputter. "Thanks for that gallon of seawater that just went up my nose."

They both laughed. Spending time with Adam over the past weeks made her feel so happy she never wanted to leave this pocket of paradise.

She glanced at the large boulder that marked the edge of the bay. "Race you."

"What do I get if I win?" Sexual suggestion laced the question.

Not yet.

Too soon.

She wanted this joy to linger just a little longer before anything else intruded. "Bragging rights."

A flash of disappointment flickered through his eyes, but it was replaced by a glint of determination. "You're on."

Adam dove, his powerful arms moving him forward before she even managed to get turned in the right direction.

"Cheater!" she shouted, then swam after him.

Adam beat her to the boulder. He grinned at her with smug satisfaction when her palm finally slapped the stone.

"You cheated." She struggled to catch her breath. It had been a long time since she'd gone swimming.

Adam blinked at her with mock innocence. "You said race. I raced."

Mattie clung to the boulder and looked back at the beach. Between the dark, craggy rocks, the lush, green line of trees above, and the white cabana below, it was a postcard-perfect scene. The sun was low in the horizon now, and the golden light had shifted to darker blues and purples. The last rays glinted off the top of the cliff to the right.

She pointed at it. "What's that? Is there something up there?"

Adam looked where she indicated. "What?"

"There was something shiny." She squinted at the spot, but it was all trees and rock. "Never mind. It's gone."

"It might be minerals in the rock. They reflect sometimes."

"Maybe."

None of the other rocks had done that. What else could make that kind of shine? Something metal? Was someone up there? Unease flickered through her, but she brushed it aside. It had been a long, long day. First, the Jet Skis, then the song, and that kiss. She shivered as the memory of his lips on hers heated her insides.

Adam smiled down at her, a little wrinkle of confusion between his eyes. "Are you okay?"

She looked up at him. His face was close enough she could kiss him again if she wanted.

"I'm fine."

He looked doubtful. "What's going through your mind?"

Her thoughts sifted through a dozen versions of the kiss. Salt water dripped from her hair into her mouth, and she grimaced. "I was just thinking it's getting dark, and I'm hungry. Race you back?"

His smile was wicked. "Last one back gets a massage."

He pushed off from the boulder, and the waves carried him faster than he could have managed alone. He was at the shore before she even gotten started.

There was no way she could catch him, so she took her time and floated back.

Adam stood on the sand and tapped his foot. "Slow poke. You didn't even try."

"Nope." Mattie ducked her head under the water then flung her hair back off her face. "It's been a long day, and I'm too tired to chase after you. Plus, I could use a massage."

She stepped the rest of the way out of the surf.

Adam did a double take. "I was teasing. You don't have to... I can book you time at the spa. Just say when."

She frowned. He'd been acting funny ever since they'd kissed. No, before that. Ever since she'd dumped him off the boat. He hadn't made a move on her since that day, and it was starting to feel strange. Adam was a man who rushed toward what he wanted like a train with jets. She wouldn't have thought a little dunk in the ocean would slow him down this long.

"We should rinse off before we eat."

"Yeah, okay." Adam turned and started toward the grass hut.

"Hey, silly. Not there." Mattie pointed at the waterfall. "There."

Adam's gaze flicked from her to the plunging water and back again. "It'll be cold."

It was a narrow stream of water, so they'd have to get close to each other. Maybe that hint would be enough to get him to kiss her. "Good."

As they got closer, the sand turned from dry to wet and squelched between her toes. The waterfall had created a divot in the sand that was about five feet across and filled with water. Mattie stepped carefully into it and squealed as the cold water plummeted down on her.

Adam flinched away from the spray. "Told you."

She gasped and turned her head to the side. The cascade of water washed her back, not quite hard enough to sting but enough to not linger too long.

"Come here, you."

He shook his head. "Not enough room. You finish first."

"Don't be ridiculous." Mattie gestured with one finger.

Did he not *want* to kiss her? From the look in his eyes she thought he probably did. Why was he still holding back? Didn't he realize when she'd agreed to the picnic that she was saying yes to so much more?

He shook his head. "I think I'll go use the shower in the hut. It probably has hot water."

He took a step back but didn't look away.

Mattie put her hands on her hips. "You know, I thought for sure you'd make a move by now but you've barely touched me since we got here. What's up with that? Why haven't you kissed me again?"

"You told me not to. Have you changed your mind?" He looked cautiously optimistic.

She *had* told him that.

He'd tried hard to do exactly as she'd asked, and it warmed her heart so much that all the reasons why she shouldn't give in to temptation evaporated.

"Yes." Mattie grabbed his hand and pulled him into the waterfall.

Adam yelped as the cold water splashed down on his head, then laughed. "That's really cold!"

"Maybe I can warm you up." Mattie wrapped her arms around his neck and pulled his head down to hers. There was nothing timid or hesitant about the kiss. She wanted him to know that she *wanted* him.

Adam's lips softened against hers, then his arms went around her and he pulled her even tighter against him. Cold water buffeted her back while his body warmed her front. She shivered and opened her mouth to deepen the kiss. He tasted of sea and salt and sun.

Their bodies melted into each other. Her hands drifted to his shoulders, arms, then back up to his neck. His hand tangled in her hair and gripped it, while the other hand pushed the small of her back until there was no space between them. His heat wrapped around her, delicious and hungry. She lost herself in the sensation of wanting and being wanted in return.

When they finally broke the connection, Adam pressed his

forehead to hers. "Are you sure, Mattie? I don't want to pressure you. We can go back now. Your call."

Mattie tilted her head as if considering his suggestion. "We can't do that. You're covered in salt."

She spun him around until the water slapped him in the face.

"Oh you little—" He tugged her under the stream with him and held her there until they were both shivering but salt free.

They stumbled away from the waterfall laughing. Adam grabbed her hand and spun her around to face him.

The look of concern on his face made her stop. "What's wrong?"

Adam pulled her closer, but not so close she couldn't step away if she wanted. "I'm serious. I know what this looks like. Cooper obviously had something in mind when he set this picnic up, but that doesn't mean we have to run with it. We can go back right now. No pressure."

His gaze was steady and resolute. His grip on her arms was gentle, and easily broken. They stood near the path through the rocks that led to the golf cart that waited to carry them back to the villas.

She could go. She *should* go.

She lifted her face to his, and he kissed her, long and slow, until she was forced to come up for air. The ghost of his touch lingered on her lips.

She didn't *want* to go.

"Are you sure?" he asked again.

"You owe me a massage." She touched the Delusions of Glory tattoo with her fingertips. His chest muscles flinched.

Adam groaned as she traced the tattoo. "Mattie..." He put his hand on hers and pressed down. "If you keep this up I won't be able to stop touching you. It's damn near impossible to keep my hands to myself as it is."

She shifted her hand, laced her fingers with his, and led him toward the cabana. "Good. We aren't leaving until you pay up."

He said something under his breath, but she couldn't hear it over the crash of the waves.

When they reached the cabana, Adam gestured to the bed. "Have a seat. I'll be right back."

"Where are you going?" Mattie called after him.

He flashed her a wicked grin and left.

"I was kidding!"

Surely, he wasn't serious. Demanding the massage he'd offered up as a reward was just an excuse to move to the bed, not something to follow through on. She wanted a lot more than just a massage.

Adam came back a minute later with a bottle of massage oil in one hand. "I always pay my bets. Flip over and get comfortable."

She gaped at him. "Seriously? Now?"

"Now." He wiggled his index finger in a circle to indicate she should roll over.

Mattie stared at him. What kind of man refused to follow through the second a woman offered?

A frustratingly good man. The kind of man who cared about *her* more than he cared about himself. It figured. Just when she was ready to throw caution to the wind, the man she chose wanted to take it slow.

Then she caught the glint in his eye.

He wasn't taking it slow to be nice. He was teasing.

Two could play this game.

She shifted until she could get a good grip on her bikini top.

Adam's eyes widened.

The fabric was still wet, and it clung with the suction power of an octopus. She kept her gaze focused on him as she tugged, wiggled, and jiggled her way out of the top. She tossed it to the side, and it landed in a wet heap somewhere near one of the tiki torches.

She smiled suggestively at Adam. "A massage isn't as good with the bathing suit on."

Satisfaction surged through her when his mouth dropped open.

Mattie slithered to the edge of the bed and stood up, then slowly peeled the suit bottoms down. She kicked them over toward the tiki torch.

Adam made a strangled sound. He gripped the massage oil so tight in one fist that she thought it might pop like a champagne bottle.

She smiled in triumph, then slid back onto the bed and crawled toward the center, where she leaned back on her hands, stretched her legs out in front of her, and slowly kicked one leg over the other. The evening breeze played with her nipples until they stood at attention.

Adam stared at her like a starving man in front of a juicy steak. The muscles on his chest flexed as his breath quickened. Judging by the fullness in his swim trunks her invitation had been well received.

She arched an eyebrow at him. "Done playing games now?"

His eyes flashed with the challenge. He flipped the top open on the massage bottle with his thumb. "Roll over."

She waited long enough to be sure he knew what he was missing, then uncrossed her legs in a slow, deliberate way that revealed everything she had to offer.

Adam made a low, rumbling sound, but he didn't move any closer to her. He wiggled his finger again. "Keep going."

She groaned in protest and rolled over. "You know, it's not that I don't like massages. I just thought we might do something else instead."

Adam crawled onto the daybed with her and straddled her legs just below her butt. "We'll get to that."

He brushed his hand across her lower back. "I didn't know you had a tattoo."

She glanced at him over her shoulder. "We got them at the same time to celebrate after we won Best Pop Group Performance. Four bells, one for each of us, with the infinity symbol."

He traced the symbol with his index finger. "Bellamy Babes forever?"

She smiled at the memory. "Always."

"Nice." His wet shorts brushed against her legs. The cold sent a shiver of heat racing up her thighs and into her groin.

Something cold rained down on her back, and she wiggled away from it.

Adam chuckled. "Lay still, now. You don't want to miss this."

His touch was firm as his hands glided over her body in long, smooth strokes. Every time his fingers brushed the top of her bottom or the sides of her breasts, heat pooled between her legs. The anticipation that he might touch more sensitive body parts stoked tension higher and higher until she ached.

Adam's fingers pushed under her breasts, over her nipples, then away again. It was a small, quick touch, but it sent a shiver racing through her.

His hands traced her back, her butt, and teased her inner thigh.

She moaned, so ready for more she could hardly stand it.

Adam moved his hands up her back, then along her shoulders. He leaned forward, his body pushing her into the cushion, and blew on the back of her neck.

"Like it so far?" he whispered.

"Tease," she said. She wiggled her hips and felt his response against her back.

"I'm the tease?"

She glanced over her shoulder. "Yes. If you weren't you'd be naked right now."

Adam lowered his head and kissed her. Though their mouths barely touched, the movement brought his chest into full contact with her back, and his hips shifted until she could tell just how ready he was.

"Adam."

He moved his lips to her ear. "Roll over."

Adam shifted his weight to the side, freeing her so she could finally face him.

She lay on her back and reached for him.

He clicked his tongue. "Relax, Bellamy Babe, the bet's not been paid yet. This is a *full* body massage."

"Come on." Mattie groaned. She ached so much that if he didn't move on to more interesting body parts soon, she was going to have to take care of the need herself.

Adam lifted himself over her, his swim trunks still frustratingly in place, then lowered his mouth to hers and lightly brushed her lips. "I want you, Mattie Bellamy. I want to know every inch of you."

He settled over her, his thighs pressed against hers. He held the massage oil high over her stomach, and with a wicked grin crawling across his lips, he poured the oil, slow and steady, onto her breasts. Liquid cascaded over her nipples, drizzled across her stomach, pooled into her belly button, and dripped down her sides.

She sucked in a breath.

He put down the bottle and put his hands on her stomach, smoothing the oil in a circular motion.

His hands moved up, up, up until they covered her breasts. His fingers teased her nipples, then moved down her sides, to her stomach, then back up in long, slow, elongated circles. With each pass, his hands explored a little lower.

She moaned his name, low in her throat.

He leaned forward and ran his tongue over her left nipple, then blew on it. His breath felt cool against her heated skin. Goosebumps prickled. She arched up, and her hands found his arms. She tugged, wanting him closer, but he resisted.

"Oh. Sweet. Jesus." She was going to explode. Her body was going to break apart from the tension his hands evoked. "Adam. Please…"

"Shh."

Adam kissed her, his tongue erasing every thought from her mind as he plunged and explored, slow and deliberate.

His thumbs flicked past her most sensitive area and played with the soft flesh that was now so swollen that the brush of his fingers made her body twitch. Jolts of electricity raced through her as his fingers moved in slow, circular motions, over and around, in and out, steady, persistent, relentless, insistent.

She raised her hips, inviting more, more, more.

Adam moved his hands away in a slow caress of her thighs before they disappeared.

Mattie groaned and opened her eyes. "You're stopping?"

Adam looked at her with the intensity of a hundred suns. "I won't stop until you tell me to."

She gripped the covers with both hands. Every nerve in her body was a live wire. "Keep going. Oh God…don't stop. Keep going."

He made a feral sound and lowered his head. His tongue

PLACES I'VE NEVER BEEN

reached and licked until her body vibrated. Pleasure rose hard and fast. Mattie screamed as climax slammed into her and spilled over into wave after wave of spasms that made her buck against him.

He rode the waves with her, his face buried in her until her climax faded away. He gently licked and teased at the still-vibrating center of her until she put her hands on the side of his head and pulled.

Adam looked up. "Should I keep going?"

She huffed out a harsh, impatient breath. "Yes. But not like that."

"Like what, then?" He sat back on his knees, his legs still straddling hers.

"You know what I want." She pointed at his swim trunks. "And you can't do it like that."

He grinned but didn't move. "I don't think I finished the massage. I haven't done your feet yet, and I never welch on a bet."

"I don't want you to finish the damn massage."

"What *do* you want?" His voice was low enough to send a shiver up her spine.

Mattie sat up and grabbed his shoulders for leverage to haul herself closer to him. "I want you naked."

He chuckled, husky and low, and kissed her before he backed away and stood up.

Adam turned his back on her and lowered his trunks, revealing his toned, untanned behind. The tiki torches didn't provide nearly enough light, so half of his body was in shadow, but the parts she could see made her want to jump him. His bottom was round and firm, with a dimple on both sides that she wanted to squeeze.

"You have an award-winning ass, you know that? You should enter contests."

He glanced over his shoulder at her. "I do, and I have. I took second."

She pictured him on a stage at some beach with other men in a Speedo and shook her head. "They were blind."

Adam fumbled with the fabric of his trunks, then tossed them to the side. A package ripped open.

"Safety first?" she asked.

"Always." Adam turned around and held out his hands. "Now that you have me naked, what would you like me to do next?"

"I...uh..." Mattie sucked in a breath, then blew it out in a low whistle. He stood totally, gloriously, unashamedly naked, and he was offering to do whatever she wanted.

She'd never had a man ask what she wanted during sex. Ever. Usually, the guy fell into bed with her, romped a bit, and, pop, it was over. Sometimes she came, but more often she didn't. None of those men looked anywhere near as good as Adam did in this moment. The gold light of the torches played with his tan, accentuated all the angles of his torso and the muscles in his chest, and highlighted just how interested and excited he was to be here with her.

Adam smirked. "Tongue tied, word girl? Want me to get your notebook out for inspiration?"

She growled with frustration. "Get over here."

He crawled on top of her, not quite touching, until his face was even with hers. He was so close she could feel his heat on her breasts, stomach, and lower down.

He held himself that way, in a pushup position, and waited.

If he was going to tease, so was she. She traced along his most sensitive parts with the tips of her fingers.

He sucked in a breath, and his stomach twitched, which made the rest of him spasm. "Oh, that's not fair."

She smiled sweetly up at him. "How long can you hold that position?"

He groaned.

Mattie wrapped her legs around his hips and pressed down. "I want you inside me," she whispered.

"I thought you'd never ask." Adam shifted, then he was inside her, filling her up, igniting a wave of desire that was deeper than before.

He rocked forward and backward, slow and deliberate, maddeningly patient, driving her insane.

"Faster."

Adam did as she asked. She pushed her hips up to meet his, driving him deeper inside.

They rocked together, building the pressure until her muscles contracted around him and she pushed up, up, up and over the edge of another climax, this one more intense, a tremor buried inside of her that raced to shake the rest of her body like an earthquake. She shouted her release and clung to him as she rode the waves.

Chapter Eighteen

Adam's arms shook from the aftermath of climax and the effort of keeping his weight off Mattie so she could catch her breath. He started to roll away to give her air, but she kept her feet clamped tightly around his ass, so he stayed right where he was. He flexed a muscle, which made him wiggle inside her.

She sucked in a breath. "You're not ready so soon, are you?"

The tiki lights turned her gold hair into a halo belonging to a not-so-innocent angel, and her body glowed from all the activity. She wasn't a fantasy anymore. She was breathtakingly real and so much more than any dream he ever conjured.

"My God...you have no idea how perfect you are, do you."

She rested her hands on his biceps and squeezed gently. "I'm not perfect. Not even close."

He smiled at her. "You are to me."

He down to his elbows so that he could kiss her. He couldn't get enough of her.

Mattie squeezed her thighs, hugging him with her legs. "This trip was exactly what I needed. Thanks for suggesting it."

There was something in her tone that made him pause. She sounded a little far away, as if her thoughts were focused somewhere else. He pressed a light kiss to the corner of her mouth then slowly disentangled himself.

He rolled to the side and lay next to her with one arm holding his head up so he could look at her. The other gently rested on her stomach.

Her smile seemed a little wistful, or sad, or maybe just distracted. He had no idea which, and wished for the hundredth, maybe the thousandth, time that he could read her mind.

Mattie absentmindedly traced her fingers over the back of his hand. "How long can we stay here?"

He started to say forever. He'd buy the island just so they never had to leave if that was what she wanted. He reined in that thought before it had a chance to slip out.

"Until morning, I think."

"Mmm." She turned until her back was pressed up against his stomach and her head was cradled on a pillow. "Good."

They lay like that for a while in silence, just listening to the rush of the waves as they licked the shore and tasted the rocks. He'd never felt so relaxed in his entire life. As long as he could remember, he'd felt pushed to do the next thing, always afraid if he didn't seize every single opportunity that he'd miss something vital, something so important that his life would never be the same without it.

He rarely took the time to just sit and listen, like this. He drank in the dark night, the woosh of the waves, and the easy presence of the woman in his arms.

"He was right," Mattie whispered.

It had been so long since she'd said anything, it startled him out of his thoughts. "Who?"

"Abayomi. He said we'd see more stars than we'd ever seen before. Look at them. It looks like we're on another planet."

Adam squeezed her gently and looked out at the black water, the night, and the pinpricks of light above. "No moon, though."

"I think it's behind us." Mattie sucked in a breath. "Oh... yes. Yes! The moon is behind us...the stars set to guide us...that could fit in the bridge, don't you think?"

He frowned. "For the second song?"

She craned her neck to look at him. "Yes. Or it could be part of the chorus. Not sure we have that nailed yet, though I like where it's headed. I loved that little run you put in. It could work with this phrase, I think."

He stilled his expression. The last thing he wanted to do while he had Mattie Bellamy naked in his arms was work on the damn song. "Maybe. We can check it out—" He was going to say later, but he didn't get the chance.

Mattie slipped away from him toward the edge of the bed. "I have to write that down."

She couldn't quite reach her bag from the bed, so she stood up to get it. She was so focused on getting her notebook and pens and writing down the snippet of a phrase that she didn't even seem to notice she was naked.

Her process fascinated him, and when they were in a work session he loved watching the way her mind worked. She made connections he never saw, then easily shifted when he added melody that didn't quite work with the words. She took suggestions from the band well and made the whole process easy.

Writing a song with her was like playing a game or putting together a puzzle, and she experienced every emotion they were trying to convey in the song. He could tell by the look on her face as she sang. Now that he'd worked with her, he could see how her partnership with Devon Morales had gone wrong. Devon clearly wasn't smart enough to realize that it was her love for music he saw in her eyes, not her love for him.

"Mattie?"

"Mhmm." She stood with the notebook balanced on one hand and scribbled something. "Just have to get this down before I forget."

He lay back on the pillows with a frustrated sigh. The moment had slipped away, just like that. She was exactly like the waves, always in motion and impossible to capture for more than a second. Most of the time he found her dreamy approach to life completely captivating.

This was not one of those times.

"Do you ever go a day without writing in a notebook?"

"Hmm?" Mattie sat on the edge of the daybed and murmured under her breath, but she wasn't talking to him. He caught words here or there as she worked out the lyric. She made frantic marks on a page already filled with them, held up a finger, and bobbed it up and down to her own internal rhythm. Then she shook her head, scratched something out, and wrote something else.

She was a world away. He wanted her back.

How could he make that happen? If he stole the notebook, she'd probably scream. Not the reaction he really wanted, unless he was causing it in a more intimate, body-rocking kind of way.

He scooted over to her and massaged her shoulders while peered over her shoulder at the notebook. She'd written the phrase *the moon is behind us...the stars set to guide us* below two more lines.

It's not over, life's not done.
When one thing ends, another's begun.

"I like that line."

"Hmm?" Mattie put the pen in her mouth. "You like what?"

"You." He squeezed her shoulders. "And that phrase. 'When one thing ends, another's begun.' That's what I wanted to tell my dad."

She nodded. "I remember. I wrote it down, see?"

Mattie flipped back a couple of pages and there it was: *It's not over, life's not done.* She'd drawn circles and a star around it.

He hummed a few bars of the melody that kept haunting his mind.

Mattie nodded her head in time to the beat. "That works. That really works. What if we added a bit here"—she tapped her pen on a blank spot— "then we'd have a solid hook, I think. It should be right up top."

Adam traced his fingers down her arm. "Sounds good."

Mattie shivered. "Focus, please. I think we're almost there."

Adam kissed her shoulder, then he shifted her hair aside to kiss the back of her neck.

She stopped writing and sat very still. The pen hovered over the paper, but she didn't tell him to stop.

He worked his way around to the other side of her neck, while his hands wandered down her back, then around to her stomach and back up to her breasts.

Mattie dropped the pen. "Adam..."

"Yes?" he whispered. "Go ahead. I'm listening."

"You are...very...distracting." Mattie groaned and half turned toward him. "We..."

Adam swallowed whatever she was about to say by covering her mouth with his own. They lingered in it for a long time before Mattie moved away.

She stood up, the notebook held in front of her like a shield, but it wasn't big enough to cover anything. A slow smile lit her eyes with a mischievous glint. "You really don't want to work on this song right now, do you."

"No." He shook his head. "I want to work on you."

"Adam," she said in the patient tone, "we only have two weeks left, and we have another song after this one."

"They'll get done. We only have one night on this beach, under these stars."

He didn't mention he would book exclusive access to this beach as soon as they got back. Now that Tina was gone, Coop would have no need to come here, and the rest of the guys could find their own hideaways. As far as he was concerned, this place belonged to Mattie.

She laughed and pointed the pen at him. "I see what you're doing."

"Oh really?" He grabbed the pen out of her hand.

"Hey, give me that."

Adam threw it out of the cabana. It landed somewhere in the sand.

Mattie gaped at him. "I can't believe you just did that. That's littering."

"We'll find it in the morning." He pulled her closer to him. She resisted at first, a pretend frown on her face, but then the frown melted in a rueful smile. "You know I have more pens, right?"

She climbed onto his lap, the notebook pressed between them. He tugged at it, but she tightened her grip.

She narrowed her eyes at him. "You throw this notebook and you'll never see me naked again."

"Oh really?" He raised his eyes at her use of the word "again." It implied she already saw a next time in their future. He smirked at her. "It's a deal."

She looked confused. "What's a deal?"

"I get to see you naked again if I don't throw the notebook. Seems fair. How about tomorrow night?"

"We'll see."

The way she sat on his lap, her legs spread wide to straddle him, left her open to all sorts of things his body was interested in pursuing. He squeezed her ass and grunted. "Damn you feel good."

She kissed him, her soft lips barely brushing his, then leaned away. "Aren't you hungry?"

"Oh yeah." He nodded and moved in for another kiss.

Mattie put a finger on his lips to stop him. "Let's eat first, okay? I'm starving."

"Hmm." He pretended to think about it, but his stomach chose that moment to growl.

They both laughed.

"Okay, yes, I need food."

Mattie gently pulled away from him. "Can we rinse off first? I'm all oily and sweaty."

She put the notebook on the bed and took his hand to lead him out of the cabana.

They stopped by the hut to pick up towels, then walked naked across the sand to the waterfall. Solar-powered lights lined the edges of the rocks, transforming the simple cascade of water into a glowing, otherworldly realm filled with magic.

They splashed, laughed, and kissed under the cold, never-ending stream. She appeared as reluctant to leave it as he was, but eventually she started to shiver, so they stepped out to towel off.

He tucked the towel around his waist, then kissed her shoulder. "Ready for dinner?"

She smiled. "Yes, please."

They dove into the picnic basket that had been left for them.

Mattie pulled two LED candles out of the hamper and flicked them on while she continued to hum.

"No work, remember?" he teased. He was half afraid she'd dart off to snatch up the notebook again.

Maybe he should hide it.

"It's not work. Music is my happy place." Her smile lifted her eyes. "And it's not my fault the tune is catchy. You did that all by yourself."

He had to change the subject, or they'd *both* be hovered over that damn notebook. He picked up a tray of chocolate-covered strawberries, the cheese and fruit plate, and the wine.

"Let's take this back to bed. I'll feed you."

"Will you peel the grapes?"

"No need. They're already peeled. This place is posh like that."

She followed him with two glasses. "Something tells me you aren't all that interested in the food."

"I'm very, *very* interested in eating." He set the food down on one side of the bed, then took the glasses from her and gestured to the pile of pillows. "My lady, please make yourself comfortable. Mr. Adam will see to your every need."

She crawled on hands and knees to the spot he'd indicated. "My *every* need?"

"Oh yes. Every. Single. Need." He punctuated each word with a kiss placed strategically along her collarbone.

Then he kissed her until she made the low moan that let him know he had her full attention.

Then he fed her.

It wasn't long before the food lay abandoned, and the towels came off. This time, he didn't mess around with massage oil.

Chapter Nineteen

The next afternoon, Mattie walked hand in hand with Adam to the Big House for the songwriting session that should have taken place that morning.

"What are you smiling at?" Adam asked. He squeezed her hand.

"This." She gestured at the scene in front of them. The ocean kept them company on the right, while the jungle of trees stood guard on the left. In front of them, Sunset Beach waited, empty, and above that the Big House kept watch. "This place is surreal. It's such a shame this all has to end."

"It doesn't."

Adam said it so matter-of-factly, it set off an alarm bell in her head. He had a way of taking random things she said and making them come true. His Adam moments became more elaborate the longer she knew him, so she could imagine how far he might take her innocent, off-handed comment.

She shook her head. "Be serious. This place must be over-the-top expensive. We can't stay here forever."

Adam glanced sideways at her. "Why not? What's money

for if not to spend it? What if we bought our own island that we never had to leave?"

She stopped walking to force him to really look at her. "You always have to leave, Adam. That's the way life works. Nothing lasts forever. Especially paradise."

He took both of her hands in his. "Paradise is always here. All we have to do is *be* there."

He sounded so sure of himself. His gaze was full of promise and possibility, and the thought of it was so enticing that she let herself get lost in the idea that maybe this relaxed, happy feeling might last. It was like taking that first step off a cliff into a deep pool of water.

She lifted her face to his in open invitation.

His arms went around her and his lips found hers and she kissed him with all the wild feeling of joy that the island inspired every time she stepped outside her villa in the morning.

Two weeks. They had two more weeks of this utopia. The idea of it made giggles bubble up from her belly. She grinned against his lips.

"What are you laughing at?" He looked confused. "Did I tickle something?"

"Yes." She beamed at him. "You tickle me. All the time. There are no barriers for you, are there? You really would buy an island just so you could romance a woman there any time you wanted."

The look in his eyes told her he absolutely would, but before he could say it out loud the familiar hum of an electric motor sounded behind them.

They both turned.

LT pulled up next to them with a big grin on his face. "Good morning, oh wait, *afternoon*, you two. Want a ride?"

"Yes, please." Mattie slid onto the back seat and patted it.

Adam took the hint and joined her in the back seat.

"So, how was the picnic?" LT drove up the path as fast as the little cart would go.

They could have walked faster, but she couldn't bring herself to hurry, so she sat back and leaned against Adam. "It was really, *really* nice."

Adam put his arm around her and squeezed. "We should go back there tonight."

Mattie rolled her eyes. "Tonight we should get some actual sleep. We came here to write songs, remember?"

"Work, work, all the time." LT threw his hands in the air. "What about love?"

A little thrill rushed through Mattie's stomach as the word "love" reverberated around her head like one of those crazy choruses in a children's song.

"No reason we can't have both," Adam said.

He squeezed her shoulders and kissed the side of her head. *Love.*

They couldn't possibly be in love. Not yet. They didn't know each other at all, really. This was just a summer thing. It didn't mean anything. She didn't *want* it to mean anything.

Her heart fluttered. She took in a deep breath and tried to ignore it.

They caught up with Brandon and Flynn at the bottom of the stairs to the Big House.

"We should start at noon every day," Brandon said. "I'd be much more creative."

Flynn snorted. "You'd be much more awake, you mean."

Mattie smiled fondly at them. "You two are clowns, you know that?"

"Yes," Brandon said.

"Absolutely." Flynn nodded. "It's imperative that someone keep the crowd entertained. Adam's way too serious for that."

Mattie laughed. "You aren't fooling me, boys. I've seen you work, and I know you both have real passion for the music. We can start at noon if you don't mind staying in session until midnight."

Flynn wrinkled his nose. "No way. Nights are sacred."

"Besides, seems to me you'll be too busy..." Brandon trailed off when LT hit him on the shoulder.

"Shut it, you. Bro code. Sex talk is off limits." LT took the stairs two at a time.

Mattie winked at Brandon. "It would be a shame to miss the stars. Maybe we could do an outdoor session. That would be fun."

"Only if it's private," Adam muttered.

"We can be private later," she whispered.

He flashed her a hungry look. "How much later?"

She shook her head. "Work first."

Adam growled in a playful way as they climbed the stairs to the Big House.

When they reached the open living room, the boys headed straight for the kitchen. Cooper had arrived before the rest of them and was already sitting on one of the sofas, tuning his guitar.

"Slackers." Cooper strummed a few chords, tilted his head, and hit one note over and over. "This string's toast."

Mattie crossed the room to give Cooper a kiss on the cheek. "Lanmou Bay was amazing. Thank you, Cooper."

Adam leaned against the sofa. "Yeah, man. Thanks. It was cool."

"I'm glad you two had a good time."

Mattie sat down next to Cooper. "I'm sorry about Tina."

Cooper nudged her shoulder with his. "Don't be."

"To be honest, what I meant was I'm sorry you had to put up with her. You deserve better."

Adam chuckled. "You really do. She was high maintenance, man. You need to get a better picker."

Cooper gave them a wry smile. "Thanks. If you can let me know where to find that something better, that'd be great. Hey, Mattie, you have sisters. Any of them single?"

She shook her head in sympathy. "Lizzie's taken. Piper's single, but she's too wrapped up in work to notice any man right now."

"What about the dizzy one?" Cooper asked. "She seems like fun."

"Della?" Mattie's smile faltered. Della might be a good match for Cooper in a lot of ways. "I'm not sure. She probably has someone hanging around. She always does."

Adam snorted. "Not sure you need another dizzy blonde anyway. Remember how Lana turned out?"

Cooper nodded. "Truth. Well, if you find your clone, Mattie, I'm all in."

"I'll keep my eyes open."

She hated dating. All the awkward silences, the time spent eating with someone you didn't know or like, the failed dates replayed on Twitter like some sort of reality show.

"So, we doing this or are we dissecting Cooper's love life?" Flynn asked. "'Cause I'm happy to do either."

Brandon took a seat on the stool behind the keyboards and played the *Jeopardy!* theme.

"That's not helping," Adam said. He crossed to the center of the room. "Mattie's got a few new lines, but we need a filler, and then we need to cross to the verse. LT, you get anywhere last night?"

LT grimaced. "Nah. Malika had to go back to the main island. She slings drinks at a bar there every other week."

"He meant with the bass line, jackass." Brandon kicked LT's foot.

"Oh...yeah. I was bored." LT grinned and shrugged. "Think it's pretty solid up to the break, but let's play it through."

"Okay, let me show you what we came up with last night," Mattie said. She joined Adam in the middle of the room. "Brandon, can you play the opening for me?"

"Sure." Brandon played the part of the song they'd already worked out.

It was the intro and lead-in to what normally would have been the first verse, but she wanted to play a little with it.

"Let's try something new," she said when he finished. "Let's flip it and hit the hook first."

She sang out the hook with the new lines she'd been inspired to write the night before.

It's not over, life's not done.
When one thing ends, another's begun.
The future's still...an open door.

SHE TURNED to face Adam so she could look into his eyes while she sang the new lines.

The moon is behind us, the stars set to guide us
So take the next step, and make what comes next
Better than before.

There's more...to...life.

THE MUSIC STOPPED after she sang the last word. Mattie smiled at Adam. He stared back, his crooked grin lighting his eyes in a way that made her blood rush a little faster. For a heartbeat or two, they were the only people in the room.

Flynn coughed. LT strummed a chord.

"Hey, Mattie, can you two stop doing that?" Brandon asked. "You're looking at him like he's a juicy piece of steak, and I don't need that image of my brother in my head."

Adam glared at Brandon.

Cooper picked up the melody on his guitar. "So you're saying hook first, like this."

Flynn bobbed his head up and down, then brought the beat in. Brandon added the keyboards, and by the time they'd run through it three times, LT had the backup instrumentals fleshed out.

Mattie kicked in harmony and let Adam take over the melody. He made it his own, adding runs and thrills that sent a shiver down her spine. When he sank into a song, he really put his whole soul into it.

The concentration on his face and the softness in his eyes pinched her heart. She knew he was picturing his dad in front of him as he sang the words. From what Adam had said, they had a complicated relationship, but he clearly loved his dad very much. There was a desperation behind the message she didn't quite understand. She'd have to ask him about it sometime.

She rejected that idea almost immediately. Two weeks from now, they'd go their separate ways, and whatever his relationship with his father was wouldn't be any of her business.

That thought made her a little sad, but she brushed it away to focus on the work in front of her.

When Adam finished the last line, the melody trailed off, leaving only the beat, which Flynn ended with a crash of cymbals.

"I like it. It's got flash," Flynn said. "We should speed it up."

"Yeah, it's a victory dance," Brandon said. He played a few of the notes with a peppy bop.

"This reminds me of when we graduated," LT said. "That whole what-are-we-going-to-do-next vibe."

Cooper snorted. "We knew what we were doing next."

Mattie pointed at them. "Yes, that's exactly what we're trying to say. That feeling of excitement, or anticipation. But it's not just high school graduation."

"It's everything," Adam said. "Every change. Every next step."

"Like marriage?" Brandon asked. He stared at Adam when he said it.

"Not exactly," Mattie brushed past the obvious hint. "Marriage isn't an end like graduation is. It's a beginning."

"Sure it is," Flynn said. "It's the end of single life. Bachelorhood. Stagville."

"It's not a wedding song," Adam said. He sounded a little abrupt. "It's about retirement."

"I agree, it's not something people will play at weddings. At least, I don't think they will," Mattie said. "This isn't a love song. It's a rage against the dying of the light song."

"Rage?" Flynn frowned. "You want an angry beat on this?"

Cooper laughed. "No, you savage. She's talking about the Dylan Thomas poem. 'Do Not Go Gentle into that Good Night'? Something like that? Remember?"

Brandon tossed a chip at Flynn. "Fifth period English. We had to recite the damn thing. You acted it out by using the board as a drum."

Flynn shrugged. "I do that a lot."

"Guys," Adam said. "The point is this song is about life, not love."

"Well, not exactly. It's about loving life." Mattie grinned. "All the phases of it."

LT nodded. "I get it. It's like when Johnny J left. Learning to move on. Embracing the new."

Mattie beamed at him. "That's it exactly."

"Okay, so what's the bridge?" LT asked.

She glanced at Adam. "I don't know yet. Any ideas?"

They tossed words around all afternoon. Mattie finished one notebook and started another, but after a few hours trying to force it all to come together, she had to admit defeat for the day.

Adam took her hand as the session broke up. "We'll try again tomorrow."

"We're running out of tomorrows," Mattie said. A tiny dagger of pressure poked at her, like it always did when she was on deadline.

"Hey, that's not what you've been saying all afternoon," Brandon said.

"Yeah," Flynn chimed in. "You said life's not over. Don't let those negative voices in your head tell you different now."

"Truth." LT nodded.

Mattie stilled. "Don't let those voices…"

"I know that face," Adam said. "Quick, hide her notebook."

Mattie stuck her tongue out at him as she fished her notebook and pen out of her bag. "Let me get this down."

"I know, before you forget," Adam finished. He sounded patiently exasperated. "This could take a while, guys."

Mattie sat on the sofa and wrote the line down, then studied it.

Don't let those negative voices in your head tell you different now.

It wasn't quite right, but there was something there. She scratched out words she thought were extra.

Those negative voices in your head

"Hmmm." She chewed on the end of the pen, lost in that idea. That negative voice drummed along in her head all the time, especially if she was tired. But a new project usually made it fade to the background, at least for a little while. Everyone had that voice, didn't they?

"I only have one voice in my head, and it sounds like my dad," Adam murmured.

Mattie started and looked up from the notebook. Adam had joined her on the sofa at some point. Everyone else was gone, and they had the room to themselves. She hadn't even heard them leave.

"Your dad?"

"Oh yeah. His voice is what drives me most of the time. 'You can't pay the bills living a dream, son.' 'Music don't pay the rent.' 'Your hobby won't get you nowhere.'" Adam spread his arms along the back of the sofa. "He was wrong. I've spent my life proving that. Still, he's in my head."

"You went after your dream, even though he was against it." Mattie doodled squiggly ivy around the phrase she'd written. "What about your mom? Was she a fan of a steady paycheck too?"

Adam put a hand on her back and rubbed. It was so soothing she leaned into his touch, enjoying the way he felt through the thin fabric of her dress.

"My mom gave me my first guitar *and* my first microphone. She's much more of a free spirit."

"So you get the love of music from your mother."

"And my grandfather. He played every Saturday night at a small club in Memphis. Blues and rockabilly." Adam's hand traveled farther down her back, sending a little thrill up her spine. "He had a really cool vibe. Laid back, but not sleepy, you know?"

"You have some of that too. But with more edge. Maybe because you're younger."

He massaged her neck and her insides melted. "Oh that feels so good."

"I can think of something else that would feel even better."

Her smile deepened, and nerves tingled in all the most interesting places in anticipation. "Show me."

Chapter Twenty

Several days later, Adam watched the most beautiful woman he'd ever met sleep beside him, happier than he could ever remember being.

Last night had been a glimpse into what their future would hold. They finished dinner with the guys, made love, then passed out in each other's arms.

Mattie's hair covered the pillow, the sheets were tangled around her body, not quite covering one of her bare breasts, and every other breath she let out a soft snore. It was mind numbingly captivating.

In between one breath and the next, he saw the future. He pictured their kids running into the room on Saturday morning to watch cartoons with them in bed. He saw her in the studio with him and the guys, working out new songs, or joining him on stage for a duet.

A new melody sparked in his thoughts, and he hummed it softly while he waited for her to wake up.

A bird call interrupted his song. It was the sound Mattie's phone made when it received a text. He'd heard it often enough it had imprinted on his brain like an ugly tattoo.

He stilled, hoping Mattie was too asleep to notice.

She stirred, groaned, and stretched. "What time is it?"

"Don't know. It doesn't matter, go back to sleep." He stroked her hair.

"Mmm." She wiggled toward the nightstand. "It might be Kat."

"It's late for her, isn't it?" The world had to intrude at some point, but he wished she'd just turn off the damn phone while they were on the island.

Mattie opened the drawer. "Not if she had a show. She's a night owl..." Her back stiffened.

"What?" Adam sat up, but he couldn't quite see her phone.

Mattie swore as she scrolled through messages. "She just can't let me have these few days, can she?"

"What's wrong?" Adam rested his chin on her shoulder to peer at the screen, but Mattie clicked it off before he could read any of the messages.

"Nothing." Mattie threw the phone back in the drawer and shoved it closed. "I'm going to take a shower. You should go get a change of clothes."

She launched out of the bed like she'd been poked in the butt with something hot.

Adam blinked. One moment they were having a sleepy late morning in bed, the next Mattie was wide awake and pissed off. He had whiplash from the sudden change, and he wanted to know what the hell had set her off.

"Mattie. Hang on a second. What's wrong?"

"What's wrong?" She rounded on him. "We only have ten days left, and we *still* haven't finished the second song. You won't talk about the third one at all. This trip is going to end, and it'll be the first time in three years that I haven't finished a project, and my stupid sister wants to turn my life upside down again and won't leave me alone until she manages to do it. And I'm just tired. I'm done." Mattie ended on a shout so loud it scared a bird outside the window.

Adam got out of bed.

She turned toward the bathroom. "Go get changed, Adam. We're late."

"They'll wait." He tugged gently on her shoulder until she turned around. Her hazel eyes had intensified until they were a deep green, with gold flecks of fire in them. She wouldn't meet his gaze. "Which sister?"

"Della." Mattie huffed out an irritated sigh. "It's always Della."

He nodded, encouraging her to go on.

She didn't.

He knew everything public there was to know about her sisters, but he'd learned from his own experience that public information was a skewed version of the real story.

"You don't talk about her much." He tried to keep his tone light. "I thought you all were really close."

Mattie snorted. "'Were' being the key word."

He considered her. He'd never seen this much fury in her eyes. "Right. So if you aren't close, why are you so angry?"

"It really doesn't matter. It's just something I need to deal with when I get back."

He raised an eyebrow at her. He didn't believe that for a second.

Mattie huffed out an impatient breath and shrugged her shoulders as if that would somehow ease the tension. "She *always* does this. She knows I'm on a project, but once she decides she wants something she can't leave it alone. Piper's right. Della's a spoiled brat with no sense of boundaries."

"What does she want?"

Mattie pressed her lips together and looked away. "I need a shower."

She left the room before he could stop her. He followed the irritated woman into the bathroom.

Mattie was already in the shower. Her back was to him, and the water flowed down from her hair to trace the muscular curve of her ass before dripping to the ground.

"Mattie." He kept his voice soft, trying not to startle her.

She didn't turn around. "I'll be out in a minute."

He stepped in behind her and picked up the washcloth. "It's okay to be pissed off, you know. Especially at family. The world won't fall apart."

She sniffed. "She *really* knows how to push my buttons. And the shitty thing about it is I don't think she even knows she's doing it."

He worked the washcloth over her back, careful to take his time to leave room for her to say what was on her mind.

Mattie stayed silent.

"I don't know about Della," he said, "but I know my brother absolutely knows when he's pushing my buttons and he always does it on purpose, the little shit. But these days I can make him back off if I want. Then there's my dad. He may not know he's doing it, but he's really, *really* good at it. I swear he refuses to move just to piss me off."

"I doubt that's why." Mattie sniffed. "You said you used to practice in the garage. The memories you both share are there, in that house. Maybe he doesn't want to lose them."

He'd never looked at it that way. They'd fought so much over the music Adam thought the garage was more of a sore spot than a memory to hold on to, but he had to admit, he'd never asked *why* Dad didn't want to move. Adam squeezed her shoulder, then went back to work with the washcloth.

"Maybe."

Mattie rolled her shoulders and lifted her chin to let the water run down her face. "You said you could make your brother back off. How?"

He grinned. "I know all his secrets. He knows mine. We're a mutual destruction society. And if that threat doesn't work, we end up wrestling for dominance. I'm bigger than him, so I usually win."

Mattie giggled, which was exactly the reaction he'd been hoping for. "Girls don't do that. We fill the air with silence. It cuts deeper."

He ran the washcloth down her back and hovered at the little dip just above the curve of her bottom. "What did Della say to upset you?"

Mattie sighed and leaned into his hand. "You know The Bellamy Sisters broke up. You know she went solo. I mean, there's all kinds of gossip about it in the tabloids, right?"

"Yeah." He kissed her shoulder, then shifted the cloth to his other hand and went back to work. "I figured you were all tired of the circus. You'd been at it since she you were, what, twelve?"

Mattie nodded. "What's *not* in the tabloids is that Della did that without asking the rest of us."

"Seriously?" Adam stopped moving, momentarily stunned.

Mattie wrapped her arms around her stomach. "It was one of the worst days of my life. On top of Dad dying it was ...never mind."

"She just popped up at dinner and said, 'Hey everybody, I'm going solo?'"

"Not dinner. Worse than that. It was right after the last show of that big world tour. We were in the greenroom getting ready for the after-party. She was so excited to tell us she couldn't stand still, like it was Christmas morning and Santa was there with presents. She tore our family apart without a second's thought for how it might affect the rest of us."

"What a bitch." He probably shouldn't have said it quite that way, but the words burst out of him before he could stop them.

To his relief, there was a grin on her face when she turned toward him. "That's exactly what Piper said."

"Well, it's true. That was a shitty move. Kind of like when Johnny J quit. He had a good reason, but it was a gut kick all the same." His gaze followed the water now running between her breasts, over her nipples, and down the rest of her. "I will never, ever get tired of this view."

She took the washcloth from him and rolled her eyes. "No, no, no, we are *not* doing that now. We're already late."

He pulled her closer. "I swear, when we get back I'm having an outdoor shower installed just like this one."

He'd seen the faraway look that flashed through her eyes before. He just wished he knew what it meant. He kissed her long and slow to help ease her out of the bad mood her sister had inspired and bring her back to the here and now, with him.

The shower took a lot longer than it probably should have.

When they were both washed and satisfied, Adam handed a towel to Mattie.

She wrapped the towel around her body and picked up a hairbrush. "Sorry about before. I didn't mean to be so snotty. It's not me."

"You don't ever have to be sorry for saying how you feel. And everybody needs to lash out every now and then. It lets off steam."

"It doesn't make me feel any better." She sighed and worked at a knot in her hair. "There are at least twenty texts from her and every one of them makes me feel guilty. She thinks if she pounds in her idea enough times I'll just do what she wants. I guess I'm still processing that stupid brunch."

"Brunch?" He saw her grimace at herself in the mirror.

She caught his gaze. "Shouldn't you be getting dressed?"

He waved his hand. "It'll take me two seconds. Tell me about brunch. When was this?"

She walked past him to the closet and thrust clothes back and forth. The towel inched down her back with every move. "Just before this trip. It was just supposed to be Piper, Lizzie, and me, but Della showed up and announced that she wants us all back together, and something inside me just snapped. It was like the room turned upside down and inside out and all the things I should have said years ago came spilling out. It wasn't my finest moment."

"I doubt that's true." To distract himself from the flesh she slowly revealed, he picked up the swim trunks he'd discarded next to the bed last night and pulled them on. "It sounds to me like it was about time you told her what's what."

Mattie tugged a light blue sundress out and frowned at it. "I don't do that, you know? Like, ever. Lizzie calls me the peacekeeper of the family. That's why I'm the backup Bellamy. I sing backup on stage. I'm always there in the background. Whenever Piper and Della fight, I'm the one who steps in between them. At least, until we split up."

She tossed the dress onto the bed and dove back into the closet.

Adam retrieved the crumpled linen shirt he'd tossed aside last night from underneath a chair. "That's a long time to hold a grudge."

Mattie emerged from the closet with a white top and bright blue skirt. "I'm *not* holding a grudge. It's not that."

She dumped the clothes onto the bed, dropped the towel, then pulled on underwear.

It was a striptease in reverse that made his body tingle in anticipation. "I'm not saying it's a bad thing. You deserve to hold a grudge after what she did."

He pulled his shirt on and tried not to notice how her top and skirt didn't quite meet in the middle so that a tantalizing strip of bare skin winked at him.

Mattie slipped on sandals and picked up her bag. "I just wish we really could go back to before. I was happy then. It was fun. Me and my sisters, taking on the world. Traveling everywhere. Meeting new people. I loved it. I loved being with them. Then it was just gone."

"Yeah, but now you're here in a tropical paradise, with a rock star." He pulled her close for a quick kiss. "So obviously that's better, right?"

"You are remarkably self-assured, you know that?" She smiled and wrapped her arms around his neck. Her lips found his, and they let the conversation drop for a few minutes.

Mattie pulled away from him just as his hands began to wander. "We should go. We have a song to finish, remember?"

He stifled his inner protest and followed her out of the villa and into the waiting golf cart.

Chapter Twenty-One

With just eight days left in paradise, Mattie woke up alone and disappointed. She'd sent Adam home the night before because when he stayed neither one of them got any sleep. They had to be fresh for the work session today, a fact she'd told him several times before he reluctantly agreed.

Now she felt the pang of regret as she pushed herself out of the empty bed.

Mattie pulled her phone out of the drawer for the daily check-in.

Della had sent a flurry of texts during the night, or rather happy hour, if Mattie was doing the time zone calculation right. Assuming, of course, that Della was in New York now, and not LA. It was a big assumption. Della wasn't on tour anymore. She could be anywhere.

Mattie tensed in anticipation of what her little sister had to say.

Talk to me.

Please?

That guy's a pickle headed donkey wipe.

Mattie giggled at the phrase Della had come up with when they were kids. It was the worst possible insult her six-year-old brain had been able to come up with.

THAT SONG IS ALL YOU. Anybody can tell.
He wouldn't have a hit without you.
Want me to set the Bell Babes on him?

MATTIE SHOOK HER HEAD. It wouldn't do any good to have a horde of enraged Bellamy fans attack Devon on Twitter. Better if he just faded away into obscurity.

It was ironic her own work guaranteed that wouldn't happen. The song she'd written with Devon was still number one on the charts.

Della's texts continued.

I'M SO, so, so sorry. About everything.
I was wrong.
I should have talked about it with all of you first.
I should have done a lot of things.
I was a selfish bitch.
If I could take it back I would.
How can I make it up to you?
Please tell me how to fix this.
I miss you. So much.

SHE STARED AT THE TEXTS, absorbing the pain and admission of guilt from her little sister. Tears filled her eyes and spilled down her cheeks.

She tapped out a response. *Miss you too Dell Bell.*

Three dots appeared to indicate Della was responding.

Are we okay?

Can we talk?

Mattie sighed and tapped out a reply. *Not now. Heading to work.*

Mattie pictured the three of them back on stage together. It was easy to do. She'd spent a good portion of her life living that way, and she knew the sounds, the smells, and the emotions that bounced from the crowd, to them, and back again.

Most of all, she knew the way music caressed the souls of everyone in the room. The way it lifted hearts and minds. The way it connected them all so tightly that the buzz lasted for hours after.

Longing for what used to be poked at her, hard.

The problem was, she knew even if they did get back together, it wouldn't be the same. They were different now. Older. They'd navigated years apart. They weren't the tight unit they used to be, and she didn't think they ever would be again, even if they tried.

Della sent, *Mattie? Still there?*

Some conversations needed to happen face-to-face, and this was one of them. *Will talk later. Promise.*

She flicked to Piper's message and read it. *Hey, have you seen this?*

The link Piper sent directed Mattie to *LA POP*, one of the seedier celebrity gossip websites. A knot formed in the pit of her stomach when she saw the grainy photo of her shaking hands with Adam at the band's studio.

The headline read, *Bellamy Babe Banished?*

Mattie quickly scrolled past the photo to read the article.

Adam Brooks was last seen in the company of Mattie Bellamy, well known for her ability to snare men in her web, and now both have vanished without a trace. Are they together? Perhaps on some island retreat where anything goes? Or has she ensnared him somewhere closer to home? You'll know when we do!

Her gaze fixated on the words "island retreat." *LA POP* would say anything to get clicks, but the fact that it was true left her feeling cold and unsure.

"Assholes," she muttered out loud, then texted the same to Piper for good measure.

Seconds later, a video call from Piper chimed. She accepted it, then propped the phone on the lamp. Piper was in bed but didn't look like she'd been sleeping.

"Hey, Pipsqueak." Mattie frowned. "What time is it there?"

"Ten at night." Piper set the phone down on something, then lay back against her pillows. "I was about to call you. Wanted to make sure you saw the text."

Mattie bit her lip. "It's just speculation. Right?"

"I'm not so sure. It seemed a little too on point. They mentioned island retreat like they saw you land or something. Are you sure there's no paparazzi there?"

Mattie looked out the window. All she could see were trees, but trees provided excellent cover for long-range lenses. She knew that all too well.

"I'm pretty sure. It's a private island with no roads. How would they even get in without being noticed?"

Piper snorted. "They crawl through cracks like roaches. Trust me, they can get in anywhere. How many other groups are at the resort? Has anyone recognized you or the band?"

"We have the place to ourselves, and the staff photographer's the only one I've seen with a camera."

"Staff photographer. Right, you mentioned him before." Piper leaned forward. "What's his name?"

"Dan something?" Mattie furrowed her brow trying to remember. "Or Don. That's it. Don."

Piper picked up the phone and the screen blanked out with the word "Paused" in the center. "Don from Syer Island resort. Has he taken any other shots?"

Mattie thought of the night she spent with Adam on the beach. "I don't think so. We haven't done anything that would need photos."

Piper's face came back on screen.

"What about the other night? You wore the red dress, right? Are you telling me no photo-worthy moments happened?"

"Well, actually, Adam called right after we hung up to invite me on a picnic." She kept her voice casual.

Piper's eyes widened. "Nice. Did you say yes? Where was the picnic?"

"Yes, and yes, I wore the red dress." Mattie did her best to look innocent. "We went to Lanmou Bay. It's beautiful. There's a waterfall and a small private beach."

"Lanmou Bay. I saw that on the website. That's what they call their lover's hideaway." Piper grinned. "You actually did it. You did the naughty tango with Adam Brooks."

She rolled her eyes at her sister. "We had a picnic."

"Is that what the cool kids are calling it these days?" Piper's voice was filled with amusement.

"You did say I should relax and have a fling."

"Yeah but I didn't think you'd actually do it. I'm impressed." Piper golf clapped her approval.

Mattie checked the time. "I should go. We start session in fifteen minutes."

"Wait." Piper pushed herself up higher on the pillows. "You have to give me some details before you run away. How was it?"

"It was nice."

"Nice. That's how you'd describe wallpaper. Surely he was better than nice."

"I'm not going to give you a play-by-play if that's what you're hunting for." Mattie lifted her chin and looked away, pretending disdain.

"Just rate him on the scale of your last five. Was he better than Devon?"

"Bitch." Mattie glared at the phone. "I never slept with Devon. You know we only kissed once and *that* was the worst kiss in the history of all kisses. His nose was literally wet, like a dog."

Piper flashed an unashamed grin. "So Adam's nose was toasty warm, was it?"

"I'm not playing this game with you." Mattie flung the pillow aside. "I have to go."

"What about Hank the Tank? He was a lot of fun, if I remember right. You said he could hold you with one hand while he—"

"Adam's better than that," Mattie interrupted. "Hank was rough and in too much of a hurry. Besides, that was years ago."

"Tim the Tool?"

"He isn't a tool, he's a tailor." She glanced at the closet. One of her favorite dresses had Tim's label on it. "He makes great clothes."

"Yeah but did he make you scream more than Adam?" Piper wiggled her eyebrows.

Mattie huffed in exasperation. "Your mind is always in the gutter, you know that?"

"Just answer the question. Was Adam better than your last five hook-ups?"

Mattie thought about the massage Adam had given her and couldn't stop the sly smile. "Not just better. Best. Ever."

"Oh really?" Piper's wicked grin was half hidden behind the pillow. "Do you like him, or is he just good for a romp or two?

Happiness wrapped around her as she thought of him. "He's really sweet. A little too enthusiastic sometimes, but yes. I like him."

"Enthusiastic?" Piper looked confused. "Like a puppy?"

Mattie laughed. "No. I mean, he jumps into things with his whole being, you know? Like this room."

She picked up the phone and showed all the vases filled with pink and white hibiscus. "The whole villa is filled with these because I said I liked the petals on the cabana bed."

Piper whistled. "Nice touch, Romeo. He really goes all out when he wants someone, doesn't he?"

"I don't think he had to pay for these flowers. He just had to ask the butler to bring them over."

"Not the flowers, silly." Piper flicked her hand out in an isn't-it-obvious gesture. "He rented the whole damn island just to have some place to be alone with you."

"No he didn't. He didn't even know me when they planned this trip. He told me they do these writing retreats all the time."

"Uh-huh. Sure they do." Piper's voice and face dripped with sarcasm. "Do you have any idea how much those villas cost per night?"

"I didn't ask."

"Take a guess."

Mattie glanced around at the room. White marble, rich wood, and fine sheets gave the impression of understated tropical elegance, but she knew that kind of look cost a lot of money to achieve. She'd experienced a taste of that expense when she renovated her bathroom.

The villa wasn't small. Hers had three bedrooms, three

bathrooms, plus the living spaces. She assumed the others were the same. The band could have shared one villa and had plenty of room to spare, but they each had their own. She hadn't thought about how much it cost to take over that kind of space at a resort until Piper mentioned it. "A thousand?"

"Try five. Each."

Mattie gaped at her. "Five thousand for a week?"

"A night. There are eleven or twelve of them, do the math." Piper nodded knowingly. "I looked it up when you said you were going there. Not to mention what it must cost to keep the main house empty. Plus all the staff. *And* you said you have exclusive access to the entire island for a month."

"Oh my God." Mattie ran through the numbers as Piper spelled them out.

"My best guess is this little work retreat is costing somewhere around one and a half million. That's a lot of money even for a band as successful as Delusions of Glory. If they did this every time they put out an album, they'd be flat broke."

"What are you trying to say?" She felt a little sick.

Piper propped her chin on the pillow in her arms. "I'm saying there's a possibility Adam might have planned this little vacay as an excuse to get to know you."

Mattie stared out the window, thinking through every conversation she'd had with Adam. "He's careless with money but surely he wouldn't spend that much just to get me alone."

"Why not? You're worth it." Piper tilted her head. "You're a Bellamy Babe. We were famous before Adam and his glory boys had their first hit."

Piper's seed of doubt took root in Mattie's stomach and grew tendrils of uncertainty. "I told him if I came it would be just about the songs. He agreed."

"Of course he did. He wanted you to say yes. Out of curiosity, in a strictly scientific experiment, ask them about their other writing retreats. If they do this kind of thing all the time, they'll have stories, right?"

The phone buzzed, and a text from Adam popped up on the screen. *Ready to go?*

He was probably waiting for her outside her bedroom door. "I have to go. Adam's waiting."

"Okay. I'll let you know what I find out about the camera guy. Love you." Piper waved.

"Love you more." Mattie ended the call, picked up her bag, and hurried out to meet Adam.

After a morning spent hashing over the same four lines until Mattie thought her ears might bleed, even she had to admit it was time for a break.

She didn't understand why that break had to involve wind-surfing. She clung to the boom with both hands while the board wobbled in what felt like ten-foot waves and wished she were anywhere, *anywhere*, other than here.

"Turn into the wind," Adam shouted as he zipped past her for the fourth time.

"I *am* turning into the stupid wind," Mattie muttered.

She pulled on the boom. It moved a few inches, and the wind caught. The sail billowed, and her feet shifted and slid. The sail tilted toward the water in slow, horrifying motion. She squealed as it dumped her into the ocean for the fifth time.

"Ten out of ten for style, Mattie!" Cooper shouted from the top of a wave. He rode it almost back to the shore before he caught the wind and zipped off in the opposite direction.

Sputtering salt water and swear words, Mattie draped her upper body across the board and let the waves push her wherever they wanted. She'd never understand why they found swallowing gallons of salt water and getting beat up by fabric so exciting.

Adam splashed into the water nearby and swam over to her. "Are you okay?"

"I'm fine." Why did he look so exhilarated when she felt so exhausted? "My arms are going to fall off and I can't feel my legs, but that's okay. I don't need them."

"Ouch," Adam said with a hint of laughter. He patted her back in what he probably thought was a reassuring manner but came off as mostly condescending. "You'll get the hang of it. You've already mastered getting up on your feet."

"That's not mastery. That's panic." She clung to the scrap of wood harder as a gentle wave rocked past. "My whole body is shaking. I need a break from this break."

"Come on, I'll tow you back to shore."

"No, no, no. You're having fun. I can get myself back."

"Hey, brother!" Brandon called out. "Race you to the buoy over there."

Adam gave Mattie a questioning look. "You sure?"

She waved him off. "Go kick his ass. I'll be camped out on a lounge chair with an enormous adult beverage when you're done."

"Save me one." He gave her a quick kiss on the cheek and pushed away from her. "Loser buys the first round at O'Brians when we get back."

Brandon whooped and promptly fell into the water.

It took a second for Mattie to realize he'd done it on purpose. Adam, Brandon, and Cooper all lined up in a row in the water next to their boards.

Flynn sat on his board in front of them with his hand high in the air. "Okay, men, keep it clean and wet. On your marks. Get set. Go!"

The three racers lifted their sails up out of the water. Brandon was the first one to get his sail up over his head and into the wind. He stepped out of the water and onto the board with casual ease and shot out ahead of the other two.

"Eat my wake!" Brandon shouted, already a good distance out in front.

Adam was the next one to right himself and take off, with Cooper close behind him.

Mattie would have cheered them on, but she was too tired to lift her arms. She watched for a few seconds, then paddled her way to shore. LT waved encouragingly at her from the shore, then disappeared into the tree line with Malika.

Flynn was close behind her when she rolled onto the sand and stood up. She splashed water at the sand on her legs while she waited for Flynn.

"You looked like a pro out there." Flynn winked at her.

She snorted at that. "A pro what?"

"Hey, every pro starts learning how to windsurf with their ass up. The only difference between Brandon and you is he kept getting back on the board."

They walked back up the beach together. She was glad it wasn't far to the lounge chairs that surrounded the bonfire pit. Her body shook with overexertion. She wanted to sit and not move for the next three hours.

A cooler filled with bottles of beer and other beverages waited for them next to a table holding snacks.

Flynn grabbed a beer, while Mattie ordered a fruity cocktail called Exotic Passion from one of the servers. Then she collapsed onto one of the lounge chairs facing the ocean.

Adam, Brandon, and Cooper looked like ants riding kites on the vast expanse of waves. She couldn't tell who'd won the original race because they zipped in and around each other on their way to some other destination.

"They make it look so easy."

Flynn flopped down into the chair next to her with his beer

in one hand and a sandwich in the other. "They should. They been doing it their whole lives. Brandon learned to surf before he could walk, practically. He won the Junior Windsurfing Championship two years in a row."

Mattie squinted out at the three now racing toward the dock on the far left. "I guess that makes sense, growing up in California."

A server arrived with her cocktail, which Mattie took a grateful smile. Two long sips and her entire relaxed into the chair. "Oh, that's better. I'll be sad when we leave this place. It's been a lot of fun."

"Me too." Flynn took a swig of beer. "This is definitely the jam on my bread. Ten out of ten, would do again. Hey, maybe you can convince Adam to come back next year."

The comment hit Mattie like cold water on a bad tooth. Some of the lazy haze slopped away as she remembered the conversation with Piper earlier.

Adam planned this little vacay after he met you, so he could have a chance to get to know you. Ask them about their other writing retreats. If they do this kind of thing all the time, they'll have stories.

Mattie glanced at Flynn. He'd finished his sandwich and was sprawled on the lounge chair with his head back against the pillow. His sunglasses made it impossible to tell if his eyes were open or closed. Either way, he was relaxed, and it was just the two of them. She was never going to get a better chance to get answers.

"Flynn...where else have you gone for writing retreats?"

"Huh?" Flynn lifted his sunglasses to squint at her.

"Writing retreats." She offered him a dripping-with-Southern-charm smile. "You know, like the one we're on now. Where else have you gone?"

"Hell we've never gone anywhere like this." Flynn barked a

laugh. "Usually Johnny J and Adam go to some dive bar and bang it out over cheap beer and stale peanuts. Sometimes Coop and Brandon go with 'em, but most times not. Me and LT never come in until it's ready for spit 'n polish in the studio. I could sure get used to this, though."

Could Piper be right? Had Adam engineered this entire trip as some sort of seduction?

No. Her heart rejected the idea. Adam wasn't like that. He wasn't.

But what if he did?

She told herself it wouldn't matter, because she was just having a fling, but that was a lie. It was more than that now. It was the start of something—or at least the possibility of something—more.

The thought that he might have manufactured an elaborate scenario to spend time with her didn't feel sweet. It felt like something Devon Morales would do. It felt like a trap.

She needed to talk to Adam to figure out what was real and what was just paparazzi-induced paranoia.

She watched Adam chase Brandon across the waves while her thoughts bubbled.

Chapter Twenty-Two

Adam knew something was up when he stepped onto the beach. Even though Mattie smiled at Brandon and congratulated him for winning all four races, there was something off about the way she did it. Her smile wasn't quite as warm, and she spoke with the cool, professional tone she'd used when they first met instead of the laid-back Southern sweetness he'd come to know.

He hadn't been away from her that long. What possibly could have happened?

Adam sat on the loveseat with Mattie. "I really liked what you came up with for the last verse."

It was a lame start to conversation.

"Thank you." She sounded so distant he barely heard her.

Brandon walked up balancing two plates of food and a bottle of beer. "Hey, Mattie, want me to give you a few lessons on the board? Adam's a lousy teacher."

"No, thanks," Mattie said. "I think I'll stick to the beach. That really wore me out."

"I promise it gets better," Brandon said. He lowered

himself onto the love seat next to them and arranged his plates around him like a buffet.

Adam tried again to get her attention. "I think we'll finish the second song tomorrow, don't you?"

Mattie nodded.

The knot of tension in his stomach tightened. She wasn't frowning, but she wasn't smiling, either. She looked like she had a stone in her shoe that she just couldn't shake.

He shifted his chair closer to her until they sat face-to-face with their knees almost touching. "Okay, what's going on?"

"What do you mean?" Mattie took a long sip from her cocktail.

"Did something happen while we were out on the water?"

Mattie's gaze shifted to the left, then back. "Not really."

Adam looked to see who'd caught her attention. Flynn lay on the lounge chair beside them, snoring. "Did Flynn do something? He's an immature brat sometimes."

"Flynn was actually quite helpful," she said with a dangerous lilt.

It sounded like he'd just tripped over something important. "Really? How?"

Mattie pressed her lips together in a gesture he'd come to interpret as Southern politeness at war with the words she wanted to say.

He leaned toward her. "Come on. Just tell me."

She sighed, then nodded as if she'd just agreed to some internal debate. "Remember the photo they took of us the day we met?"

He thought about it. "Us shaking hands at the studio. Right, so what about it?"

"Piper sent me a link. *LA POP* has picked it up, so we've gone national. It's next to a headline that reads, 'Bellamy Babe Banished.' They think you and I escaped to a tropical island."

He could see how upset she was, but he didn't see any issues with what she'd shared. "So?"

She gave him a look that told him he'd missed something blindingly obvious. "How'd they know we're on a tropical island?"

"It's just a lucky guess." He shrugged. "It happens. Nobody actually knows we're here except us."

Mattie wiped the condensation on her glass. "My sisters know. So does Kat."

"You think your manager leaked the info?" That would explain why she looked so preoccupied.

"No." Mattie's voice was firm. "Kat wouldn't do that."

"Okay. Who?" He glanced around at the group. Brandon tossed popcorn at Flynn's open mouth with maniacal glee. Cooper avoided looking at them and ate his sandwich with the delicate touch of a world-class guitarist. LT was nowhere to be seen. "No way any of us would post anything about our location to anyone. They all know how important this trip is."

To me, he added silently.

"Maybe not on purpose." Mattie's gaze flicked back to Flynn.

"Flynn's not like that." Adam shook his head.

Brandon paused in his assault on Flynn. "Tina might have told someone after she bolted. She can be pretty spiteful."

Mattie frowned. "Maybe."

"Is that what's bothering you?" Adam asked.

"Not exactly." Mattie clutched her cocktail with both hands. "When we met, you said you did writing retreats all the time. But the way I hear it, you do most of your writing in dive bars."

Brandon winced. "Ouch."

Adam tried to keep his expression neutral. "Who'd you hear that from?"

"It doesn't matter. Is it true?"

He thought about it. Mattie had gone back to the beach with Flynn while the rest of them played in the water. "Flynn."

"Is it true?"

He sighed. The secret was out. He might as well come clean. "They aren't dive bars. Exactly."

"It's a karaoke bar down by the bridge," Cooper supplied. "Kinda sticky, but not seedy."

She arched an eyebrow at Adam. "How many writing retreats have there actually been?"

He thought about denying it, but he didn't see the point.

"None." He glared at his brother and Flynn, then flicked one at Cooper for good measure. "This is the first time we've done something like this."

"Okay." Mattie nodded. "Then why did you lie to me about it?"

He cringed at the way she said the word "lie," like it was the worst kind of curse. "I didn't mean to. I blurted it out without thinking. Then I decided to make it true."

Her expression shifted from suspicious to uncertain. "Why?"

"He does that a lot," Brandon said. "He's impulsive."

"Yeah," Cooper said. "He was having an Adam moment. Like the time his mother wanted a new dishwasher, so he bought them a whole new house. Then his dad turned it down. Adam had to turn around and sell it. His parents still don't have a new dishwasher."

"Or the time that his favorite ice cream place down the street from the studio was going out of business," Brandon said. "So he bought the building and leased it back to them for $1 a year."

Cooper grunted a laugh. "Or the time—"

"Stop helping." Adam waved a finger salute at the pair of them.

Brandon laughed so hard he snorted. Cooper grinned and tipped his glass.

Mattie's lips twitched with amusement, and the sparkle was back in her eyes. He took her hand in his and she didn't pull away. "Truth. You seemed distracted and overwhelmed. I wanted to help, and I wanted to get to know you. The idea popped into my head and out of my mouth and I didn't see any need to call it back. I scheduled the trip right after I dropped you off that night. Even if you'd said no, we still would have come here."

"For a month?" Cooper raised an eyebrow.

"Maybe. I don't know." He stared at his feet. "Trisha's been our unofficial mascot ever since she was born, and the diagnosis was a huge blow. Losing Johnny J left a hole we won't ever be able to fill. It's a lot to bounce back from. We all needed a break."

Mattie studied his face. "That's all this is? A break?"

"All?" Brandon snorted. "This is the best vacation *ever*."

"Not sure how we'll top this," Cooper said, "but I'm willing to try."

"Maybe next year we go skiing?" Brandon suggested.

"No way," Cooper said. "Too cold. I want sun and bikini babes."

"You need a girl to treat you right," Mattie said, "not another babe."

"Can't I have both?" Cooper grinned.

"Next trip," Adam promised. Just like that, he'd agreed to future vacations. "But next time you jackasses are paying your own way."

"Definitely somewhere cheaper then," Cooper said.

"Yo, Adam," LT shouted from the hut behind them.

Everyone but Flynn turned their heads in his direction.

LT waved his cell phone at them. "You see this?"

Mattie stiffened. "See what?"

LT jogged across the sand to Adam and Mattie and held his phone out. Brandon and Cooper crowded around so they could see the screen.

The group shot the photographer had taken before they went Jet Skiing was displayed in vivid detail, but it was zoomed in so that he and Mattie were centered, while only half of Cooper's face showed. Tina and Brandon were cut out entirely.

Mattie stood up and took the phone from LT. "Where did you find this?"

"*Buzz 9*. It posted about an hour ago." LT kicked Flynn's foot. "Dude. Did you send this shot to the vultures?"

Flynn snorted and jerked awake. "Hey! Watch it."

"No way Flynn did that," Brandon said. "Like, literally. Flynn didn't bring his phone, and besides that photographer never sent us the image. Not to me, anyway."

"Me either," Cooper said. "And he should have, since my name's on the account."

"He didn't send it to me either, and I'm paying the bill." Adam looked over Mattie's shoulder while she scrolled through the blog post. Tension rolled off her in waves.

Cooper pulled out his phone and tapped to bring up the website.

"What?" Flynn rubbed his face with both hands. "What'd I miss?"

"*Buzz 9* posted that group shot of you guys, that's what," LT said. "The story's the usual crap. Not a big deal, but some-one's definitely sold out."

"What's it say?" Brandon asked. "Read it."

Cooper cleared his throat. "'*Bellamy and Brooks in Paradise. Look who isn't wasting any time! It turns out the rumors might be true. Mattie Bellamy and Adam Brooks, along with the entire Delusions of Glory band, are in a tropical sweet spot and it looks like things are heating up. We think they look pretty cozy. Is it just us, or has this Bellamy Babe forgotten all about poor Devon Morales? No word on whether Devon is devastated over this latest development.'"*

Mattie groaned. "Perfect. Just perfect."

Adam watched the tension creep over her face to crinkle her forehead. Gossip like this was a daily fixture in his life. Most of the time, he made fun of it or shrugged it off. His friends and family knew the truth, and that was all that mattered.

But he didn't like that worried look in Mattie's eyes. He wanted to punch the asshole who put it there. He flexed his fists in anticipation. "Who the hell sent them that shot?"

Brandon snatched Cooper's phone out of his hand. "They post anything else?"

Adam looked at Cooper. "Would Tina do this?"

Cooper's face clouded over. "I don't know, man. A few days ago I'd say no way, but she was pretty pissed off when she left. She could have done it out of spite."

Mattie handed LT's phone back to him. "It doesn't really matter now. It's out there."

LT studied the screen. "You know it's none of us. Someone got paid, and none of us need the cash."

"Who had access?" Brandon asked.

"Any of the staff on the island could have done it," LT said, "but the best bet is the photographer. He had the shot."

Adam squeezed Mattie's shoulders. "I'll be right back."

Adam stalked toward the hut where he saw several resort staff huddled together. Halfway there Mattie joined him, matching him stride for stride. The rest of the band followed close behind.

The clustered group of employees watched them approach

with wide eyed shock. One peeled off from the rest to run through the doors at the back of the hut where Adam assumed the manager was hiding.

A short, thin woman with speckled gray hair and a freckled face stepped forward as they entered the hut. Her hands were outstretched in the universal please-don't-kill-the-messenger gesture. "Mr. Adam, I am Sonji, the day supervisor. I have just been informed that there may have been a...a..."

"I think 'leak' is the word you're searching for." Adam took the phone from LT and held it out to Sonji. "I want to know who sold us out."

"Mr. Adam, no one here would do such a thing. No one. I am so sorry this happened."

"Not as sorry as you're going to be," Adam said. He would do whatever it took to make this go away for Mattie.

"Where's the photographer?" Cooper asked in the calm, neutral voice he used whenever he thought Adam needed to be handled.

Sonji spread her hands out wide. "I do not know, Mr. Cooper. He has gone. I do not know where he went. I am so sorry."

The door banged open, and several resort staff rushed through, led by Mattie's butler, Abayomi, and a tall woman dressed in a crisp linen suit and air of authority.

"Mr. Brooks, Miss Bellamy." The woman held out her hand for them to shake. "My name is Veronique Labrosse, and I am the general manager for the Syer Island Resort. I apologize for taking so long to greet you. I wanted to check our records to be sure I could provide answers."

"Where's the photographer?" He tried to keep his tone polite, but anger made his voice shake.

"Mr. Donnelly has left the island, Mr. Brooks. My apologies, but he is no longer an employee."

"When?" Cooper asked.

"Where the hell did he go?" Adam demanded.

Veronique looked apologetic. "He left two days ago on the supply shuttle. He requested a day pass to take care of some business on the main island and did not return. His number has been disconnected, and the address on file is a post office box in Los Angeles, California."

"Bingo," Brandon said. "We have a winner."

"Why are we so worried about this?" Flynn asked. "The shot's not that exciting."

Adam gritted his teeth. "We're worried about it because we came here to avoid this kind of crap."

"I thought you vetted all the staff here," LT said. "How'd this douche slip through?"

The manager clutched her hands in front of her. She looked professional and polite, but not nearly concerned enough for Adam's liking right now.

"Mr. Donnelly was a temporary employee, hired from a very reputable agency to fill in for our regular photographer who was called away at the last minute. The agency performs rigorous background checks and sent him with the highest recommendations. We will, of course, be looking into this matter further with the agency." Veronique spread her hands in a gesture of apology. "We pride ourselves on our discretion and service and I assure you this will not happen again. To make up for our lapse I will be providing a substantial discount on the final total of your stay. I hope this in some way alleviates the pain this has caused."

"I don't need a damn discount," Adam snarled. "I need to know where this asshole went and what other shots he sold and where."

"How much of a discount?" Cooper stopped in front of Adam and held out a placating hand to shut him up.

Veronique smiled. "I am happy to negotiate the exact number when you have time, Mr. Cooper."

"I need someone to find this jerk." Adam turned to LT. "Isn't your cousin a detective or something?"

LT shook his head. "He's a state trooper in New York. Won't do you any good, man."

"There's bound to be somebody we can hire."

Mattie put a hand on Adam's arm. "There's no point. There's nothing we can do about it now."

Her voice sounded hollow and empty, and it ramped up his anger several more notches until the back of his neck felt prickly.

"I'll fix this," Adam told her. "I swear I will."

"How? You can't go back in time. You can't rewrite history. Nobody can." Mattie squeezed his arm then turned to her butler. "Abayomi, is there a golf cart I can use?"

"I will take you home, Miss Mattie." Abayomi stepped forward. "Come with me."

"Wait," Adam held out a hand to stop her, "I'll take you."

"No." She flashed a quick smile, but it was quickly replaced by a look of utter exhaustion. "I need to get some rest, and you need to stay and deal with this."

He wanted to protest, but she waved at the rest of the group and followed Abayomi out of the hut before he could stop her.

He watched her go, hoping like hell this stupid stunt didn't push her away from the island, and him. After the way she'd reacted when they'd first arrived, and the shit Devon the Douche had pulled, he had a feeling he might find her packing her bags when he got back to the villa.

He hoped he was wrong. He'd never hoped for anything more in his entire life.

Chapter Twenty-Three

The sun was setting when Mattie returned to her villa. Abayomi assured her she was safe, and that nobody would bother her, but she locked her bedroom door and pulled the drapes closed anyway. Then she dragged her suitcase out of the closet. It was past time to go. Staying in one place too long made it easier for cameras to lock in on her location.

She should never have agreed to a project like this. One song. That was the limit from now on.

The realization struck that the first song she'd been contracted to write was finished, and the second mostly there, but they hadn't even started the third song. Tears welled up at the thought of leaving the project unfinished. What kind of professional was she? She'd slept with her client, starred in yet another headline, and now she was running away before the job was done.

A tear spilled out and ran down her cheek. She wiped it away, angry with herself. This was nothing to cry over, and she wasn't running. She was making a strategic exit. Staying here would only make things worse for all of them.

She opened the drawer and took out her cell phone with the intention of telling her sisters that she was going home, but several texts from Piper distracted her.

Can you get Don's last name?

There are hundreds of them, five in the LA area.

There's no Don working at Syer Island. You sure that's his name?

Is it Hudson? Fernsby? Donnelly?

Shit. Hope it's not Donnelly.

He's called The Sniper.

Call me.

Mattie stared at the name Donnelly. The manager had called the photographer Donnelly. He'd introduced himself as Don. Don Donnelly? Was it the same as Piper's Donnelly?

She pictured the friendly face of the photographer and couldn't see how such a seemingly harmless man could have a nickname like The Sniper.

Mattie checked the time. It was seven in the morning in LA. Piper was a complete grouch when she woke up, but she *had* said to call. She opened a video chat and dialed.

It took Piper five rings to answer with a yawn. "Finally. Took you long enough. Did you get his name?"

"Yes, but it doesn't matter. *Buzz 9* posted that group photo I told you about."

"Shit, really? I was watching *LA POP*. Hang on." Piper sat up, now wide awake, then the screen blanked out with Paused in the middle. Her sister swore several choice words, then came back into view. "Assholes. You think Don did it?"

"He's the only one who had the image, as far as we could

find out." Mattie crossed to the closet and tossed a few dresses at the suitcase.

"What's his full name? Was it any of the ones I sent?" Piper asked.

"The manager called him Mr. Donnelly. He introduced himself as Don so I guess it's Don Donnelly? Seems mean of his parents."

Piper made a guttural sound, then cleared her throat. "Dammit. That's him. The Sniper."

Mattie tugged another armful of clothes out of the closet and dropped them on the bed. "Why do they call him that?"

"Because he specializes in long-range shots. Remember that naked pool shot of Kate Pierce last year? That was him. So was the one of Alec and Janice Duggar in bed with that prostitute. He's known for squirming his way into places and getting the shot from so far away nobody knows he's even there. How the hell did this guy get a job on staff at a resort like that?"

"He came through an agency. Supposedly vetted and background checked." Mattie added handfuls of underwear to the growing pile on her bed.

"He has a rap sheet in twelve states and three open lawsuits against him for trespassing. There's no way he passed a background check."

Mattie made a noncommittal sound and folded a pair of underwear, then placed it neatly in the suitcase.

"What are you doing?" Piper said suspiciously.

"Packing. Thanks for looking into it, but you can drop the search now. I'm coming home."

"Wait a second. Why are you packing? It's just one photo, and the shot's nothing exciting."

"It's only one shot right now. That could change any second."

"Mattie, I can't see anything but a pile of clothes."

Mattie shoved the pile to the side, then balanced her phone on top of the lamp so Piper could have a better view. "There could be other photos waiting to go live, and I don't want to be flying commercial when they hit. You know what that's like."

"Did you finish all three songs?"

Mattie folded her sunny yellow dress and shoved it into the suitcase. "No. We would have wrapped up the second in the morning. Probably. But we haven't started the third." The thought made her head hurt.

"Wait, you're leaving before the job's done?" Piper sounded incredulous.

Mattie didn't want to know what expression was on Piper's face, so she busied herself with sorting through clothes. "It's not like I can stay here forever. This place is expensive, and now it's been violated."

"Mattie..."

Mattie gestured with a pair of underwear to the covered window. "There's no walls anywhere, you know? The whole front of the house is wide open. Which at first I thought was creepy, but then it turned into something exotic and romantic. Now that stupid post is out there and everyone knows where we are, and it's just too exposed. Even if Donnelly is gone, there are plenty of others with cell phones and cameras to take his place."

"What about the band? What about Adam?"

She shoved the next dress into the suitcase without folding it first. Tears prickled her eyes again. "What about him? This was just a fling. No big deal."

"Really?" Piper didn't sound convinced. "You're ready to let it all go just like that?"

"Yes." She nodded for emphasis, then stuffed a handful of underwear into a corner of the suitcase. "I only called to let you know you can stop looking for Don, and that I'm coming home."

"Mattie..." Her sister's pleading voice made her want to cry.

"I should go. Abayomi said there's a shuttle in two hours to take me to the main island."

"Martha Lee Bellamy," Piper snapped. "Stop packing and listen to me."

Mattie expected to see Piper's stop-being-so-stupid face, but her sister's forehead was filled with wrinkles of concern and worry.

Piper never worried about anything.

Mattie sat on the edge of the bed and clung to her favorite tie-dye sundress.

"Have you even talked to Adam about this? Does he know you're packing?"

"No." A reflexive wave of guilt tightened her chest.

"You're going to sneak out without saying anything to him?"

"I'm not sneaking out. I'm leaving. There's a difference." She folded the dress in her hands and tucked it in the suitcase.

"Give me a break. You're ghosting him."

"No I'm not."

"Yes, you are. You do this all the time. You disappear any time there's conflict. I think brunch with Della was the first time I've ever heard you actually say what you wanted to say, *when* you wanted to say it."

Mattie flushed with remembered anger and embarrassment. "I shouldn't have."

Piper leaned closer to the phone so her face filled the whole screen. "Yes, you should have. It was perfect. You should do it more often. I just wish you'd stuck around to see the shock on Della's face. I think for once she really *heard* what you said. It was glorious."

A half-hearted giggle escaped Mattie's throat.

"You deserve to be heard, Mattie. And this guy you like deserves better than to have you disappear without an explanation. I'm not saying you stay if you don't want to. I'm saying ask yourself if you really want to leave. If you don't, then put on your big girl panties and talk to the man."

"There's no point. We only have a few days left anyway." Mattie swallowed at the lump now lodged in her throat.

"Life exists outside of paradise, you know. You have as many days as you want." Piper stood up with the phone and moved it somewhere higher.

"What would I even say to him?"

Her sister pulled clothes out of the dresser. "Start by telling him how vulnerable you feel right now staying in a house with no walls. Then maybe move on to how much you like spending time with him. See where that takes you. Hopefully somewhere that needs less clothes."

Mattie rubbed her forehead. "I don't know. Where are you going so early?"

"We're working on the opening song and it's not going great. The words are crap, and the first guy they cast couldn't sing on key if it was inserted up his rear. Hey, mind if we conference you in later? Only if we need it, of course."

"Sure, no problem."

Piper gave her a kind look. "Go get him, Mattie Cake. And don't worry about that stupid post. It'll get shoved to the side in twenty-four hours, tops."

"Love you." Mattie ended the call, then tucked her phone into the outside pocket of her suitcase.

Her clothes covered the bed. If she was going to make the shuttle, she had to get busy packing. Her temples throbbed, it was hot, and all she felt like doing was curling into a ball in a dark corner somewhere.

She peeked out from behind the curtains at the small patio behind the main bedroom. It was surrounded by a thick wall of trees and shrubbery that used to feel secluded and private. Now she felt like someone watched her from behind every tree. Her relaxed retreat had been destroyed with one post of a photo from someone a world away.

"Mattie?" Adam called. He rattled the bedroom door, then knocked on it. "Mattie, are you in there?"

She put the drape back in place and crossed to the door. "I'm here."

His eyes brightened as if he hadn't expected her to answer, then his face fell as he looked past her into the room.

"You're leaving." His voice sounded as flat as she felt.

"Yes." She moved closer to the bed but couldn't bring herself to fold anything. The pile of clothes mocked her.

"Why?" Adam came up behind her and put his arms around her.

"Why do you think?" She sighed and leaned back into him. It felt safe in his arms, but she knew it was a false sense of security. Their privacy had already been violated.

"That photo doesn't matter. So they have a group shot of us having a good time? So what?" Adam kissed the top of her head. "It's not a big deal."

"Maybe not for you." Mattie pulled away from him and picked up a skirt to fold. "But for me it's another headline and another reason why nobody will ever take me seriously. They'll say I slept with you to get credit for something else I didn't write."

She threw the skirt into her suitcase and picked up a cardigan she hadn't even worn. "And you know what? This time it'll be true. I did sleep with you. That's all anybody will see. *Mattie Bellamy Bagged Brooks.*' You'll get a gold star and a pat on the back, or maybe a line of sympathetic women at your door willing to help you forget all about how horribly mistreated you are, and of course they'll all buy your new album, and your new song will top the charts for months, but nobody will think I had anything to do with that, because the only way anybody will ever believe I wrote a song at all is if I... I...I don't know what I'll have to do. Tattoo it on my ass maybe."

She was breathing hard, and tears were building up in her eyes, but dammit she was tired of crying over crap like this. Maybe she should change careers.

"Wait just a damn minute." Adam snatched the sweater out of her hands and threw it on the bed. "I'm not Devon Morales. I'm not Mark what's-his-name. I'm not any of those assholes who've used you for free PR."

"No. You're not. But don't you get it?" She met his angry gaze with one of her own. "Reality doesn't matter. What matters is the next photo and the next caption. That's all anybody will believe. I'll never win Best Song or any other award because nobody—*nobody*—will ever sing my songs again. Nobody will want to work with me. I'm—"

"Yes, they will, because *I'm* going to sing your songs." He poked himself in the chest to emphasize the point. "Me. You're not getting out of that. I'm going to rock these songs you wrote on stage, and millions are going to sing along with me, and every goddamn one of them will know that Mattie Bellamy wrote them."

He shouted the last few words loud enough to startle her out of the doom spiral she'd locked herself into during her rant.

They stared at each other. Ocean waves pounded the shore in the background, and she thought she heard thunder, but maybe it was just the blood rushing through her ears.

She licked her lips, but her mouth was so dry it didn't help.

"Today's headline is just the start. It's no telling what other photos are going to pop up now. He can't have only one."

He scowled. "I don't give a damn what the headlines say. Not yours, or mine, or anybody else's. The only thing that matters is what *we* say. And anybody who doesn't want to work with you is a moron, because you're the best songwriter anywhere out there. There's no one better."

She sniffed. "You have to say that. It's in the contract."

He snorted. "No it's not, but it should be. Doesn't matter. I don't need a contract to tell me I'm working with the best songwriter in the world. I've known how good you are from the first Bellamy song I heard on the radio. So fuck them. You're better than all of them. It doesn't matter what they say. I got your back."

"How, Adam? How can you have my back for something like this?"

She sat on the bed and pulled a dress into her hands. It was turquoise and white, made of light cotton. Perfect for the island, but she hadn't worn it yet, either. The missed opportunity made her want to cry.

Adam knelt in front of her and put his hands on her knees. His gaze locked on hers, sincere and intense. "My manager is hunting for that asshole Donnelly right now. He's going to buy every single photo that guy has, and make him sign a non-disclosure. Even if Donnelly has another shot, nobody but us will ever see it. If they do, I'll hunt him down myself."

The way he said it made her believe something dire would happen to Don Donnelly. She bit her lip at the thought. "Are you having an Adam moment?"

"No. If I were having an Adam moment, I'd hire a hitman." He bared his teeth.

She shouldn't smile at that, but she couldn't help herself.

"Don't go." Adam gently pulled the dress out of her hands and tossed it behind her on the bed.

"It's the smart thing to do. You know it is. They can't take photos of us if we're not together."

He took her hands in his. "Stay with me tonight. Give my manager time to find that guy. I promise, nobody will bother us here. No more photos. No more headlines. Just us and the music. If you still want to leave in the morning, the helicopter will be waiting for us."

"Us?" She kissed him softly on the lips.

"A gentleman always sees his lady home safely. Besides, it's not paradise without you." He took her in his arms, and several long kisses later she forgot about leaving.

* * *

MATTIE STARTED awake to the ring of the house phone. She fumbled for the receiver with her eyes closed. "Yes?"

"Miss Mattie," Abayomi spoke softly, but there was a note of urgency to his voice, "I am so sorry to disturb you but there is a call for you in the office. You must come. I will be outside in the buggy to bring you when you are ready."

She rubbed her forehead, confused. "Call? From who?"

"Your sister, Miss Piper. She says to tell you she tried to call your cell phone but you did not answer."

"Can't she call this line?" She was cozy and too tired to get up, and she didn't want to wake Adam by turning on the light.

"She says she must speak with you alone. It is urgent. She is waiting now on the office line. I will be there in five minutes. Please come."

His voice was soft but insistent, and it set every nerve on edge. Exhaustion fell away, replaced by anxiety. "Okay. I'll be ready."

She hung up. She had to find something to wear, but it was so dark in the room she couldn't see the nightstand, much less her clothes or the door. She fumbled for the lamp and switched it on, then flinched as the light blinded her. Adam murmured something incoherent.

She opened the nightstand drawer, but her phone wasn't there. Where had she left it? No time to look for it now. Something horrible must have happened for Piper to call her like this. She couldn't get to the phone fast enough.

She pulled a sundress off the chair and threw it on, then looked around for shoes. She found flip-flops by the bedroom door and slipped her feet into them.

"Mattie?" Adam asked. He propped himself up on one arm and squinted at her. "What's going on?"

"Piper needs to talk to me, but my phone's missing. I'm going to the office to talk to her. I'll be back." She opened the bedroom door.

"I'll go with you." He blinked and yawned. "Just let me find my shorts."

"No, don't. I'm sure she's just forgotten the time difference." She climbed onto the bed to give him a quick kiss. "Go back to sleep. I'll be back in a few minutes."

She flicked off the light, slipped out of the room, and shut the door. It was pouring outside, and lightning temporarily lit her way through the living room and down the steps toward the waiting golf cart. Abayomi tried to cover her with an umbrella, but she was still soaked by the time she climbed in.

Abayomi took off as soon as she was settled. "I am truly sorry, Miss Mattie, about the intrusion on your privacy. It is not right."

She stared at the path in front of them and wished the cart could go faster. "It's not your fault."

"He represented all of Syer Island and he betrayed you. He failed us, and he failed you. It is unforgivable."

Abayomi pulled up to the side entrance of the main building where the door stood open and the general manager, Veronique, waited for her.

"This way, Miss Mattie." Veronique ushered her into a small office and gestured to the phone lying on the bamboo desk. "Your sister is still on the line, and the computer is ready for you. Take as long as you need."

Mattie snatched up the phone as the door closed behind her. "What's wrong?"

"Are you alone?" Piper asked. She sounded tense and worried, which shot stabs of adrenaline through her heart.

She collapsed onto the chair. "Oh my God, what happened? Are you okay? Of course you're okay, you're on the phone. Is it Lizzie? Della?"

"It's okay, we're all fine. I'm sorry, Mattie. I didn't mean to scare you, but this couldn't wait. I called and called. Why didn't you answer your phone?"

Mattie closed her eyes as the aftershocks of panic raced through her. The last time she'd had a middle-of-the-night phone call, it had been Lizzie calling to tell her Dad had been in an accident.

"I didn't hear it ring. I put it somewhere...oh, in the suitcase. Shoot. I forgot to charge it. It's probably dead."

"Was Adam with you?"

"Yes. Why?" She didn't like where this was going. Whatever had happened, it couldn't be good.

"But he's not there now, right?"

She wished they were on a video call so she could see Piper's expression. "No. He's back in my room. What's going on?"

"There's a computer on the desk, right? They told me there was one."

Mattie glanced at it. A multicolored screen saver bounced around to indicate it was on. "Yes."

"Go to the *LA POP* website."

Anxiety rushed up the back of her neck. "Piper, you're scaring me."

"Just take a look. I'm right here with you, and we're going to get through this together, okay? I promise." Piper's voice was calm and overly soothing, like she was talking someone off a ledge. That, more than anything, made Mattie want to run screaming from the room.

Beneath the *LA POP* banner, a larger-than-life photo filled the screen.

Mattie froze.

It was a shot of her and Adam under the waterfall at Lanmou Bay. It had been taken at night, from a high angle. The edges were grainy, but because the waterfall was surrounded by safety lights, the central image was more than clear enough to make out their faces and the fact that they were naked.

Her breath caught in her chest, and everything went a bit fuzzy.

She stared at the image. She could still feel Adam's hands on her back and the water cascading over her shoulders. The shadows played with her breasts, while her naked back glowed in the moonlight.

Adam was mostly in shadow, but the curve of his face was quite visible, as were the lean muscles along his thigh. They looked like two people deeply in love. It was a magical moment, perfectly captured.

Some detached part of her told her it would make a fantastic album cover.

She gripped the phone so tight it creaked in protest.

"Mattie? Are you still there?"

"Yes," she breathed.

If the photo was on *LA POP*, it would be everywhere.

Viral.

She was naked on computer screens and cell phones all over the world, and there was nothing she could do about it.

Everyone on the island had to have seen this photo by now. That was why Abayomi had groveled all the way to the office. He hadn't been talking about the group shot. He'd been talking about this. They'd all seen. They all knew.

She had to get out of here. She tried to stand up, but her legs wouldn't support her, so she hugged them instead.

"I'm so sorry, Mattie. I'm so sorry. I can't believe that asshole did this."

"So he...he had more photos...after all," Mattie stammered.

She was having an out-of-body experience. This was a bad dream. It had to be. Wasn't that what people always did in nightmares? Stand naked in front of crowd? Any second now she'd wake up. Adam would be lying beside her, and they'd laugh about how silly she was.

Piper cleared her throat. "That's not the only reason I woke you up."

"Sweet Jesus. What else could there possibly be?"

Maybe the Big One had finally hit California, and Los Angeles had slid into the ocean. Maybe a meteor was about to crash on Syer Island. Maybe a sinkhole would open up and swallow her right here, right now.

"I don't know how to...hell. I'm just going to straight-up tell you. Adam's manager, Lucas Austerberry, hired The Sniper to take shots of you, so they could leak them for publicity."

She blinked, not sure she heard right. "Adam's manager... how do you know?"

"A girl I know over at the studio. She's dating a guy whose sister works as his receptionist. Donnelly was placed at Syer Island just two days before you arrived, and he knows Austerberry from way back. They've worked together before."

"Is she...are you...sure?" Mattie curled in her knees and hugged them.

"I'm sure. She had details, including how much he was paid because she processed the payment."

"But...why?" Mattie closed her eyes and tried to pretend she was somewhere else.

"Publicity. Austerberry's known for being a pit bull. Once he sinks his teeth into an act, he doesn't stop until he makes them a worldwide phenomenon, and he's been with Delusions of Glory since he found them at a high school dance. He probably set up that handshake shot at the studio, too. Makes perfect sense, since they have a new album about to drop."

"Does...does Adam know?" Why did it hurt so much to say that out loud?

"I..." Piper blew out a breath. "I honestly don't know, sweetie. Donnelly was on staff, so he probably had access to schedules, right? Who else knew you were going to Lanmou Bay?"

It was hard to focus her thoughts. "The picnic was last minute. It was supposed to be Cooper, not...Adam asked me right before we left. The guys probably all knew. Abayomi too. He drove us. I'm not sure...I don't know. I don't know who else. You think...Adam?" She sucked in a breath, but it didn't help. Her thoughts refused to form the rest of the sentence. She pictured that night at the beach. The swim. The massage. "Oh...Jesus..."

"I don't know for sure. There's a lot of staff on that island, and Donnelly is a snake. He could have wrangled the information from someone. But if it was something Adam planned last minute, it doesn't look good."

Were there shots of them having sex too? When would they show up? Her body shook as time stretched around her. "I can't believe he'd do this."

"I'm sorry, Mattie. I can't believe I told you to stay. Adam seemed like a stand-up guy, and you were so happy. I can't believe he'd set you up like that either, but it seems unlikely that he didn't know. I can't believe I didn't see it coming."

"It's not your fault. It's my fault." She should have known. Adam's over-the-top antics could have been a smokescreen.

She scrolled down to read the caption under the photo out loud.

It's looking hot, hot, hot in the tropics tonight as Mattie Bellamy bags her man. Seen here in an LA POP *exclusive, Adam Brooks cools down, or should we say heats up, with a midnight dip in the waterfall with his high school crush. Will we be hearing wedding bells in the near future? It's too soon to tell, but one thing's for certain, Adam Brooks' teenage dreams have come true, because this Bellamy Babe has forgotten all about Devon Morales. Check back for updates, this story is sure to keep your blood pressure up!*

The words "high school crush" stood out to Mattie like an enormous, pulsating stop sign.

Adam had known about her, had followed her career, and then when he saw her struggling with Devon, he'd seen his chance to lure her to this sanctuary where he could have her all to himself by promising her what she wanted most: recognition.

"I'm such a—how could I be so blind?"

"Mattie. It's not your fault, okay? None of this is your fault. If he did this—and we don't know if he did—it's Adam's fault. Him and that asshat manager."

Mattie closed her eyes. Adam had been so intense when he'd said he had her back. He'd seemed genuinely surprised by the original photo leak, but he could have been faking it. Doubt slithered into her heart.

"I have to go. I have to get out of here. Jesus, how do I get out of here? There's no roads."

"I'm taking care of that. The helicopter will be there at dawn to take you to the main island, and a private charter will bring you home. Don't go back to the room. The manager will pack up your things and get them to you. Okay?"

Mattie bit her lip and nodded.

"Mattie? I can't see you. Are you okay?"

"I...I'm—" Mattie choked on the word "fine." If there were any less appropriate word, she didn't know what it would be. She wasn't on the same planet as fine. Hurt, confusion, regret, and betrayal cascaded against her heart, making it hard to breathe, much less think.

"I'm so sorry." Piper's voice cracked. "I know this hurts. I have giant bear hugs waiting for you. Just come home. We'll sort this all out when you get here. Okay?"

"Okay."

"Love you."

"Love you back." Mattie hugged her knees a little tighter. "Piper?"

"Yeah?"

"Thanks." A sob pushed at her throat. "For everything."

"It's the least I can do, sis. If I was there, I'd beat him senseless for you. Bellamy Babes stick together, right?"

A ghost of a smile tugged at Mattie's lips, but it quickly faded. "Right."

She hung up and stared at the photo for a long, long time, and when the tears came, she didn't try to stop them.

Chapter Twenty-Four

"Adam!" LT banged on the bedroom door. "Wake the hell up!"

It was dark, but a small amount of light leaked in around the edges of the curtains. "What time is it?"

"Get up," Cooper slammed open the door.

Adam looked for Mattie, but she wasn't there. She'd left to take a call from her sister. When? He must have fallen back asleep..

"What the hell is going on?" He scrubbed his face with both hands and pushed out of bed.

The entire band shuffled into the bedroom. All of them looked anxious and serious, but it was Brandon's wide-eyed, frantic stare that made Adam's blood run cold. "What's wrong? Where's Mattie?"

LT held out his phone for Adam to see.

He instantly recognized the waterfall at Lanmou Bay, and Mattie's beautiful backside. He snatched the phone out of LT's hand and checked the *LA POP* website.

Mattie's worst fear had just gone viral.

A snarling beast of anger prowled through his chest as the implications hit home. If the photographer had this shot, he probably had others. Piper had woken Mattie in the middle of the night. Piper had to have seen this and called to tell her sister.

Mattie hadn't come back.

"Where is she? What time is it?"

"She's not with you?" Cooper looked around as if he expected Mattie to pop up.

"Dammit!" He pushed past Cooper and LT. Brandon and Flynn leapt out of his way. "I promised her this wouldn't happen. I told her I had her back."

"You're in your underwear," Brandon said.

"Who gives a fuck?" He didn't have his shoes either, but he wasn't about to let that stop him. He ran down the steps into the early dawn, spotted a golf cart, and rushed to it. Gravel and sand bit his feet, but he didn't care. He had to get to Mattie.

Cooper jumped into the cart just as Adam took off. "Where we headed?"

Adam shoved the accelerator to the floor. The cart puttered along at the same speed. "The office. She went to take a call from Piper. Not sure when. Doesn't this damn thing go any faster?"

"Maybe if we get out and push." Cooper pointed at something on the horizon. "Is that what I think it is?"

Adam almost ran off the path trying to get a look. Sunlight glinted off metal, and the sound of whirring blades, faint but growing louder, wafted over the waves toward them.

"Shit, shit, shit." Adam reached the crossroads that split the path in two and went right toward the docks and landing pad instead of left toward the Big House and the office. "She's leaving."

The helicopter landed before they even reached the docks. "This thing is too damn slow!"

"Run for it. You can cross through the beach." Cooper said.

Adam stopped in the middle of the path and jumped out. "Find that fucking photographer!"

"On it!" Cooper called after him.

Adam took off running across the path to the beach, then sprinted toward the landing pad.

Mattie led a small group of people that included Veronique and Abayomi toward the helicopter. Her hair and sundress billowed out behind her.

"Mattie!" he shouted.

She didn't hear him.

He stumbled over something, caught himself, and kept going.

The pilot opened the helicopter door as the blades came to a stop, and a small step unfolded to allow Mattie access. A few more steps and she'd be whisked out of his life.

"Mattie!" he bellowed.

She glanced over her shoulder, and stopped. Her face was a mask he couldn't decipher.

Abayomi and Veronique both turned. Veronique glanced at Mattie, spoke to Abayomi, then waited next to Mattie with passive patience.

Abayomi moved to intercept him. "Please, Mr. Adam. You should not be here."

Adam ignored the man. "Mattie! Wait."

Mattie blinked. "Why are you here?"

Her voice sounded cold and detached. Almost clinical. She must be in shock.

"I'm coming with you."

"Mr. Adam, the helicopter is about to depart. It is not safe near the blades. Please. Step back." Abayomi gestured to the side of the pad.

Mattie stared at him with a blank expression. "Why would you do that?"

"I saw the photo." Adam sidestepped the butler and rushed across the remaining space to Mattie. "You shouldn't be alone right now, and there's no way I'm letting that asshole get away with this."

"Why not?"

He reached out to take her into his arms, but she flinched away. "What's wrong?"

"Get away from me, Adam. Leave me alone."

"Let me fix this. I have to fix this."

"How would you do that?" A spark of emotion flashed through her eyes. "Set up another photo shoot? Maybe create a new hashtag? You can do that without me now, can't you? Devon does."

She turned toward the helicopter.

"Wait a second." He tried to catch her arm, but Abayomi got in his way.

"Mr. Adam, we must step away. Now." the man said with firm authority.

Mattie whirled to face him. "Did you really think I wouldn't find out?"

Adam side-stepped Abayomi. "Find out what?"

"Stop the act, Adam." She sounded bitter and so unlike herself that he couldn't believe it was the same sunny girl he knew. "I know this whole trip was nothing but a PR stunt. Did you think you could use me for publicity and keep fucking me too?"

What she'd said was so unfair and so wrong that he almost choked. "What the hell are you talking about?"

She looked at him like he was the shit on the bottom of her

shoe. "Donnelly works for Lucas Austerberry. He arrived here two days before we did. Nice move, telling him to back off when we first got here. It really made me feel safe."

The word "safe" cracked like a whip. He took a step back, caught off guard by the accusation and the contempt in her voice. "Lucas? You can't really think—"

"How stupid do you think I am? Never mind." She looked away. "I already know the answer."

His jaw tensed. "Lucas might be an aggressive ass, but he knows where the line is. He wouldn't do something that low."

Even as he said it, doubt rushed through him. Lucas could be savage at times. His tactics pushed the edges of convention, but they made things happen. He was the reason Delusions of Glory hit the map so hard and fast. Adam hadn't questioned how he made it happen. He hadn't cared. Until now.

She huffed out a breath. "You really expect me to believe that?"

Heat rose along the back of his neck. "I didn't know anything about it until the photo dropped on the damn internet, same as you."

"Yeah, right." She narrowed her eyes. "How long did it take to cook up this little scheme of yours? Did the whole band help?"

"It wasn't a scheme. I don't know that damn photographer and I had nothing to do with that photo." His voice rose with frustration.

"Why should I believe you? You've lied to me about everything from before we even met."

"I haven't lied to you."

She so clearly didn't believe him that a growl of frustration rumbled in his throat.

"Did you take the time to read the post that went along with the photo, or were you too busy staring at me naked?"

"I barely glanced at it." He glared at her. "Then I ran to find you because I knew what it meant. I knew how devastated you'd be. I wanted to—"

"They congratulate you on finally landing the woman you've had a crush on for years. *Years*. It must have been exciting to finally screw your high school crush. Was it everything you fantasized about? I really hope it was worth it. It'd be a shame if all this went to waste."

He stilled as the venom in her words struck him. "Yes, I liked you in high school. So did a lot of guys. What's wrong with that?"

"You used me." Her voice was low and dangerous. "You tricked me into coming here. You found the thing I wanted most and you dangled it in front of me like bait, and like a sucker I took it." She shook her head. "No wonder you never wanted to work. The songs were just an excuse to get me in the sack and make a few headlines."

"I did *not* trick you." Her words were gasoline on the angry fire building inside him. "I'm *not* Devon Morales!"

"You sent the photographer away so I'd let my guard down."

"That's not why I—"

"You took me to that beach. You...we..." A tear rolled down her cheek, and she brushed it angrily away. "How hard was it to set up that money shot? The angle of it only works if we're under the waterfall, and the backlighting didn't hurt. It really shows our faces. I've been thinking about it for hours. It's a fantastic shot. A hint of boob and leg, just enough to be sexy but not quite sleazy. I have to admit it would make a great album cover. Devon will be jealous."

"You think I'm the kind of man who would treat you like that? That's really messed up."

"Would you even have thought of working with me if you hadn't fantasized about me in high school?"

"You're the best lyricist in the business, of course I would have." He glared at her. "What about you? Would you have worked with me if I hadn't offered a free vacation?"

"Yes! We would have worked in the damn studio or that stupid karaoke bar you usually go to, or some other neutral place like I always do. I would have gone home at the end of the day. I never would have been here, and there sure as hell wouldn't be any naked photos of me on the internet." She flashed him a look that ripped a hole right through his chest. "You know, I thought you were different. I really thought I could trust you."

She turned away.

"Yes, I had a crush on you," he shouted at her back.

She stopped but didn't turn around.

"From the second I saw you on stage. From the first note I heard you sing. And yes, when life threw the chance to meet you my way I seized it because I was never going to get another one."

She glanced over her shoulder. "So you admit it."

"I admit that I've wanted to get to know you for most of my life. And since you asked the question, yes, it was worth it."

Mattie sucked in a breath, but he went on before she could interrupt.

"Even if we did get screwed by that photographer. That makes me so angry I can't even process it. I want to find that guy and shove his camera right up his ass. I want to beat him senseless with it. I want to make sure he never, *ever* gets to do that to you or anyone else ever again."

She made a choked sound and turned away.

"I had nothing to do with that shot." He lowered his voice. "I'm sorry it happened, but I'm not sorry I met you. I'm not sorry I got the chance to work with you. I'm not sorry I got to know you, and I'm sure as fuck not sorry I got the chance to love you."

Her shoulders shook. "That makes one of us."

"Mattie..."

"Go away, Adam. Whatever we had...whatever it might have been...it's over."

She climbed into the helicopter. The pilot shut the door.

Abayomi took Adam's arm. "We must back away, Mr. Adam. We can't stay here. It's not safe."

He allowed himself to be led to the side of the landing pad, where he watched Mattie fly away.

Chapter Twenty-Five

Tears streamed down Mattie's face as she watched Adam turn into a tiny dot that vanished on the horizon. So much had been left unsaid, and undone. When she'd arrived on the island everything was exciting and new. The potential of songs not yet written hung in the air, and Adam had stirred her thoughts and imagination in enticing new directions.

It made everything hurt so much worse. Devon never had the power to hurt her like this. She'd never let him get close enough.

Adam, though, had wormed his way past all her defenses and doubts. He was intense, driven, and passionate about music and life, and he *saw* her in a way nobody else ever had, not even her sisters.

But it wasn't real. All of it had been a lie, and they'd never even started the third song.

A sob bubbled in her throat. She swallowed it down.

By the time she reached the hotel suite the resort had arranged for her to wait in on the main island she was so exhausted she could hardly put one foot in front of the other.

She barely noticed the well-meaning staff who ushered her through the lobby and up to her room, or the tray of fresh fruit, cheese, and coffee on the table in front of the sofa. She collapsed onto the bed, curled into a ball, and waited for oblivion to find her.

It didn't.

Her brain was too wired to let her sleep. She pictured Adam watching her leave. That twisted, angry, confused look on his face burned her heart.

How could she have been so stupid? After everything she'd gone through with past mistakes, he'd made her believe for a fantastic couple of weeks that she would finally be taken seriously. On the surface, he'd treated her with respect. He'd listened to what she had to say, worked with her as they struggled to find the right words, and he'd made her feel wanted and special.

Then he'd taken her on that romantic picnic and made her nightmares come true.

The image of them under the waterfall taunted her. She'd been happy. She'd felt cherished, and sexy, and alive.

"Nothing lasts forever," she whispered to herself. Her heart broke into a thousand tiny pieces.

Mattie lay there for hours, until she'd run out of tears and there was nothing left but the numb awareness that the charter would arrive to take her home soon and she still wore the sundress she'd thrown on when Piper had called in the middle of the night. She'd left everything behind. Her bag, her clothes, even her phone. She realized with a start that she'd also left her notebooks. She choked back a sob at the loss.

She was alone with self-recrimination and a broken heart.

A timid knock on the door, followed by a muffled "Mattie?" poked through her consciousness.

She wanted nothing more than to ignore the intrusion, but

it was probably hotel staff telling her it was time to leave, and she desperately wanted to go home.

She sat up and rubbed her eyes. The room they'd put her in was beautiful. Fine wood furnishings set off soothing cool white curtains and a lush white carpet.

"Mattie?" The voice was a little stronger now, and familiar. "The charter's here. Please open the door."

"Della?" She trudged to the door and opened it. Her sister stood on the other side with Mattie's suitcase and bag, looking anxious.

"Della!" Raw, shuddering sobs wrenched out of her despite her efforts to hold them in.

"Mattie!" Della dropped the bag and threw her arms around Mattie in a hug so tight she almost couldn't breathe.

Mattie melted. All of the anger she'd felt about her sister's behavior vanished in the familiar comfort of her sister's arms. "You're here. You came."

"Of course I'm here. Where else would I be when my sister needs me?" Della whispered.

Della let her go to drag the luggage, and Mattie, inside. Her little sister ushered her to the couch and rocked her back and forth just like Lizzie used to do whenever Mattie was sad or hurt, but she kept up a running commentary in a way that was uniquely Della.

"It's okay, Mattie Cake," Della soothed. "It's going to be okay. We'll fix this. I swear we'll fix this. Renic's legal team is already working on getting the photo pulled down. I'm so sorry this happened. I'm sorry your rock star turned out to be such a jerk."

"I thought he was different." Mattie hiccupped. "I thought...I liked him. I really liked him."

"I know. I know. Piper told me everything."

"Piper?" Mattie sat back and wiped her eyes. "You talked to Piper?"

Della wiped the tears off her own cheeks. "She called everybody as soon as she saw the photo drop. We all agreed you shouldn't fly back alone. That's a lot of time to beat yourself up, and you don't deserve that."

"Did you draw the short straw?" Mattie sniffed.

Della gave her a be-serious look. "I volunteered. Piper started pounding heads and contacted you while Lizzie and Renic woke up the lawyers and I took care of the transportation."

Mattie considered her sister. "You chartered a plane, and flew all this way, just to give me a ride home?"

"Yes. I did." Della took her by the shoulders. "Look, I know I make shitty choices sometimes, and I can be a selfish, self-centered, spoiled, you can stop me anytime now..."

Mattie giggled despite herself.

"I swear from now on I will have your back the way you, Piper, and Lizzie have always had mine. I'll be here whenever and wherever you need me. No matter what."

Mattie sniffed and smiled. "Bellamy Babes forever?"

Della lifted her hair to reveal the bell tattoo at the nape of her neck. "Always. Now go take a shower and change your clothes. The charter will be ready to leave by the time we get to the airport."

Mattie slept in fits and starts during the flight home. Every time she woke, tears would start, and Della would soothe her back to sleep. When they arrived, it was the middle of the night, and she had a throbbing headache and stuffy nose from too much crying. The airport was blissfully deserted. Della's rental car was a discreet SUV that blended into the night, but Mattie hesitated before climbing in.

"There's probably cameras camped out at my door, and Piper's. Adam knows where I live. So does his manager."

"We're not going there." Della gestured for her to climb in. "Trust me, nobody knows where you're going, and nobody's going to bother you tonight, except maybe me. Get in."

They stowed her bags, and then Della followed chirping GPS directions to a tree-lined street in Bel Air Estates. She pulled up to intimidating iron gates that broke up a long brick privacy fence and pressed a button in an app on her phone. The gates swung open, and Della drove through.

Mattie glanced behind them to make sure the gates closed. "Where are we?"

Della grinned. "Hideaway House."

Mattie rolled her eyes. "You can't be serious."

Della laughed. "No, but that's what I've been calling it. It used to belong to Nicolas Cage, but then it was foreclosed on, sold, resold, and spiffed up. Now it's owned by a company who leases it out to visiting dignitaries, scandalized actors, and girls in need of some quality alone time. They're extremely discreet, and they have no idea who we are. I leased it under a fake name."

Mattie gave her sister an appraising look. "That's very cloak and dagger. Have you been watching *Mission Impossible* again?"

"Hey, those are great movies." Della looked smug.

Mattie did a double take as the house came into view. She wasn't sure what she expected, but nothing she imagined could have come close to the enormous ivy-covered cottage nestled among stately old trees. It looked like they'd driven through some portal into the English countryside. It was too dark to see much of the landscape, but quaint Victorian streetlamps lit the way down the drive to the front door.

"Have we somehow stumbled onto a movie set?" Mattie asked.

"Nope." Della pulled up to the front door and parked. "We're home. For now anyway. Safe and mostly sound. I'm totally jet lagged and wired. Come on, let's get some tea."

Mattie grabbed her bag while Della took her suitcase. Della opened the door and stepped back for Mattie to walk through first.

"Mattie!" several voices shouted.

She was bombarded with hugs, tears, and a tangle of words from Lizzie, Piper, and Renic. It showed more than anything how horrible everything was that everyone she loved had traveled all this way to rally around her. Her sisters were here, in the same room, and they weren't fighting. They were united in their concern for her, and it was too much to process.

Mattie lost her battle with self-control and burst into tears again.

Lizzie wrapped her arm around Mattie's shoulders and escorted her through the kitchen into a cozy den filled with comfortable chairs and a fireplace big enough to stand in.

"It's okay, Mattie. Cry as much as you need. Let it all out." Lizzie stroked her hair.

"I loved him," Mattie burbled. She hadn't meant to say it. She hadn't realized that was why she felt so miserable until this moment, but it was true.

"I know," Lizzie whispered. "I know. That's why it hurts so much."

"I can kick his ass," Piper offered. "I've been taking lessons."

"So have I," Della said. "We can tag team."

Mattie caught a conspiratorial grin shared between the two, and suddenly her heart felt a lot lighter. "No thanks. I just want...I just wish...I wish I'd never met him. How am I going to finish that third song?"

"You aren't," Renic said. "Kat and my lawyers are working on getting you out of that contract. The work you've already done will remain, but there won't need to be any future contact, if that's what you want."

The way he said it made her look up.

He knelt beside the couch and put a comforting hand on her arm. "Is that what you want, Mattie?"

She thought she'd run out of tears, but she was wrong.

"Leave it for now," Lizzie said softly. "She's exhausted. Let's get her some tea, then bed. This will all look better in the morning."

Mattie didn't want to go to bed. She'd spent the past week sharing a bed with Adam, and now she had a sinking feeling the bed would feel too big without him in it.

Adam had lied to her. He'd used her. He'd tricked his way into her heart, and he was still in there. The sick thing was that even though she knew better, a part of her still wanted him.

Della handed her a cup of tea. "There's six bedrooms. You get first pick."

Mattie held the warm cup in her hands. "That's okay. I like this room. I think I'll just stay here for now, if that's okay. Y'all go on."

Renic squeezed her arm. "Whatever you need, kiddo. We're all staying right here with you." He stood up. "The lawyers should be awake by now. I'll be in the den if you need me."

"Thanks, hon," Lizzie said with a fond smile for her future husband.

Renic had been a fixture in their lives for a long time, but this past year he'd become more than just a family friend. Lizzie and Renic were going to get married, and on any other day it would have made Mattie happy to know that they'd found each other, but today, all it made her feel was sad. They had what Mattie hadn't known she wanted.

Della plopped down on the couch next to Mattie, while Piper sat on the floor in front of them and leaned against the coffee table.

"No way we're leaving you down here to stew all by yourself," Della announced.

"Yeah, we're not going to bed if you don't," Piper said.

Lizzie curled up on the couch next to her. "Want to tell us about the trip?"

"Not really." Mattie tucked her feet up under her and took a sip of tea. She was so tired. "Can we talk about anything else?"

Della waved a hand at the fireplace. "Did you know Dean Martin used to party here with Frank Sinatra? I hear they used to drink all night and pass out by that fireplace."

"Want to try that?" Piper asked with a sly smile.

Mattie smiled back at her. "No, thanks. Tell me about your project. How's that song coming along?"

She leaned into Lizzie, and Della leaned against her, and they all listened as Piper chatted about how cool the animation process was, and how the song needed some spark, and about all the potential male leads they were schmoozing. "They've targeted three new guys who can't sing, and one who's just meh. At the rate they're going, it'll be a decade before they find the male lead."

"How hard is it to do the voice-over?" Della asked.

Mattie pretended to listen while her sisters provided soothing noise. It had been a long day, and she was ready for all of it to just be over. But she couldn't bring herself to close her eyes. Every time she tried, she saw Adam's crooked smile and Delusions of Glory tattoo, and it made her want to cry all over again.

Chapter Twenty-Six

Adam strode into Austerberry Management, Inc., offices in one of the main LA Center Studios buildings like a man ready to storm the castle and murder the king. He'd spent hours in the air stewing over everything Mattie had said. All he had were questions that he couldn't answer: Did Lucas hire the photographer? If he did, why? Were more photos going to drop?

It was the last one that made his jaw hurt and put him in an extremely foul mood. Mattie already thought he was the worst kind of slime. What would she think if another photo, one of something far more intimate, was posted? He'd do anything to stop that from happening.

He ignored the receptionist, who took one look at him and the gang of jet-lagged rock stars who followed him and picked up the phone.

LT held up his index finger. "Don't."

They stalked to the largest office at the end of the hall. Adam was slightly disappointed that the door was open. He'd had visions of kicking it in.

Lucas looked up from whatever had his attention on the computer, and his eyes widened. "Adam..."

"Did you hire Don Donnelly?" Adam demanded.

Lucas glanced at the rest of the band. "You're back early. Everybody have a good time?"

"Answer the damn question," Cooper said in a tone that promised dark, painful things. He stood on Adam's right, while LT stepped up on the left.

"Yeah," Brandon said as he sat on the edge of the desk. "What they said."

Flynn crossed his arms and leaned against the wall. "Enquiring minds definitely want to know."

Lucas frowned. "What's with the hostility so early in the morning? I thought tropical vacations were supposed to be relaxing."

Adam leaned on the desk and rapped it with his knuckles. "Did you hire Don Donnelly?"

"Sure. I've hired him many times over the years. Why?"

"Dude, answer the question," LT said.

"Let me spell this out plain and simple," Cooper said. "Did you hire that asshole to take potshots of Adam and Mattie and sell them to the tabloids?"

Lucas leaned back in his chair and steepled his fingers. "Obviously."

He sat there with smug satisfaction all over his face like he'd just won the lottery with a fake ticket.

Brandon swore. LT muttered something incoherent.

"Unbelievable," Cooper said.

Adam stared at the man he had considered a friend. He'd known Lucas since he was seventeen years old. He'd found them raw and green at a high school dance and seen them through their first real gig, their first world tour, and three Grammys. He was a father figure, a mentor, and the one they called when they'd had too much to drink or needed a quick getaway from the paparazzi.

Lucas was also the one who had ripped Adam's world apart. Mattie was right. His manager had orchestrated her worst nightmare. Lucas hadn't just crossed a line, he'd obliterated it.

"You son of a bitch." Adam's voice shook with suppressed rage.

Lucas's forehead wrinkled in confusion. "What's the problem?"

"You *knew* what she meant to me. You used me, and her. How *dare* you?"

"How dare me what? Seize an opportunity?" Lucas spread his hands wide. "It's what you pay me to do, gentlemen."

Adam shook his head. "We don't pay you to invade our privacy."

"Yes, you do. You pay me to organize and foster your careers. You pay me to make sure the money and awards keep rolling in, and you pay me to keep your names on the tip of everybody's tongue. All that doesn't happen by accident, and besides, I wasn't the one who planned or executed this little escapade." Lucas pointed at Adam. "You did that all on your own."

Adam shook his head. "I did *not* do this."

"Yes, you did." Lucas leaned forward and put on his earnest it-wasn't-me face. "You told me to get Mattie Bellamy, remember? You took over an entire island so you could have her all to yourself. Everything that happened on that island was all you. Nobody pushed her into your arms, Adam. You did that. The only thing I did was send Donnelly to get some spontaneous publicity shots." Lucas shrugged. "He got a great shot."

"Yeah, and then you sold it," Flynn pointed at Lucas with a drumstick. "That's messed up."

"That's publicity," Lucas countered. "And it cost a pretty penny to orchestrate, believe you me. The Sniper doesn't come cheap, especially when he has to camp out all day. He's worth it, though. You boys are solid gold tickets, and the return is exponential."

Mattie's words haunted him. *You tricked me into coming here.*

Adam had wanted her to come with him. He hadn't meant for her trust to be abused the way it had been, but he couldn't deny that he did trick her into going. Bile rose in the back of his throat. "I thought we were friends, Lucas. I've counted on you since I was seventeen. How could you betray me like this?"

"This isn't betrayal. This is business." Lucas glared at him. "Who do you think made sure the last album went triple platinum? How do you think that happened? It sure as hell wasn't the songs. It was the marketing."

Lucas pointed at a framed poster on the wall from their last tour. Cooper and Tina were in the center making googly eyes at each other while the rest of the band catcalled from the edges.

"Are you saying that Tina was a setup?" Cooper asked.

"Come on, Coop," Lucas said with exasperation. "You had to know. You met her at *my* party. Marketing is all about strategy, and that album was full of love songs."

"You saying you *paid* Tina to screw him over?" Flynn shoved off the wall and stalked over the desk. "All his women were scams?"

Lucas scoffed. "Of course not. I just documented the inevitable outcome of Cooper's bad choices. His exploits are all on him."

"Where's the rest of the shots?" Adam couldn't remember ever being this angry, not even when Dad took his guitar to keep him from playing at the prom.

Lucas shrugged. "Donnelly has them. I only buy the ones worth paying for. The rest are his to do with as he sees fit, same as always."

Adam snarled. "You fucking son of a bitch."

Cooper put a restraining hand on his arm. "Let's get out of here, man. He ain't worth it, and we need to track down Donnelly."

"Look at these numbers," Lucas said. He tapped something on the keyboard, then turned the screen toward them. "Your sales are up across the board, and the preorders of that song you haven't even recorded are through the roof all thanks to the excellent publicity I arranged on your behalf. A little gratitude is in order."

"Gratitude?" Adam almost choked on the word. "You think we should be grateful for you meddling in our lives like this?"

"Yes. My tactics never bothered you before. You were just fine as long as the money rolled in. So what's the problem?" Lucas asked.

"The problem is I love her," Adam roared. "The problem is you just ruined any chance I had to be with her, for the sake of a little fucking publicity."

Lucas snorted. "Love. Love is nothing but a distraction. Keep your head in the game, son. This is what you said you wanted. I'm handing it to you on a platinum platter. Go back to being the playboy and let me make the sausage."

Having Lucas dismiss the worst moment of his life with a casual wave of his hand flipped a switch somewhere in Adam's head. "Don't bother. You're fired."

"You can't do that." Lucas spread his hands out in pseudo-apology. "We have a contract."

"Actually, he can," Cooper said. "There's an out clause

that's pretty damn clear. All it takes is all five of us to agree. Boys, what say you?"

"Fired," LT said.

"Toast." Flynn tapped out a quick rhythm on a nearby lamp for emphasis.

Brandon shook his head. "You're a real piece of work. You have no idea how much of an ass you really are, do you?"

"Yes or no, Brandon?" Adam asked.

"Oh definitely fired." Brandon wrinkled his nose and stared pointedly at Lucas. "It stinks in here."

Adam exchanged glances with Cooper, and they all turned and stalked out.

"You'll be back," Lucas called after them. "When the numbers tank, you'll be back in the high school gym, begging me to take you on. I'm the rainmaker."

"Delusional," Brandon said.

LT stabbed the elevator call button. "Arrogant bastard. We don't need him. We never did."

Adam's thoughts raced ahead to next steps. "I want The Sniper, and I have to talk to Mattie."

The elevator doors opened, and they all stepped in.

"We got you, man," Cooper said. "We'll hunt down the rest of those photos. Go get your girl."

ADAM SAT in a rented generic black SUV in the parking lot and dialed the first person he thought would have the information he wanted. When Kat Marshall answered the phone, she skipped all the pleasantries.

"Asshole."

Adam blinked. He should have expected this kind of reception. "I'm looking for Mattie. She's not home. I was hoping you knew where she was."

"Yeah, I know where she is. But I'm sure as hell not telling you."

Frustration bubbled up in his chest. "Please. I need to talk to her. If you won't tell me where she is, at least give me a way to reach her."

"I talked her into this project with you. Shows what a fool I am. You and Lucas make my ex-husband look like a decent human being."

"Dammit, my manager hired that asshole, not me."

"Look, the only reason I took your call was to tell you I'm sending over termination of contract paperwork for you to sign this afternoon. It lets you split the work already done but drops the third song. Get them back to me by tomorrow, or we'll sue for full rights of the two songs Mattie worked on."

"I'm not signing that." It was his last link to Mattie. If he signed it, he'd never see her again, and he desperately wanted to see her.

"Yes, you are," she snapped. "The lawyers assure me if you force this into court we'll win, and it'll cost a hell of a lot more money. Plus, it'll become my personal mission in life to make yours miserable."

"Can you act human for a couple of seconds? I need to talk to her. Please." He wanted to reach through the phone and strangle the information out of her.

"Eat. Shit." Kat hung up.

"Dammit!" Adam pounded the steering wheel with his fist.

If Mattie's manager wouldn't help him, he'd have to hope one of her sisters would. Della and Piper were both all over social media, but he couldn't find a phone number for either one of them.

He sent a quick text to LT and Cooper. *Mattie's hiding. Need phone numbers for Della, Piper, and Lizzie Bellamy.*

He received a quick response from Cooper. *Struck out with Kat?*

Adam huffed out a frustrated laugh. *Told me to eat shit.*

LT responded, *Give me a few...I know a girl.*

Cooper shot back, *Understatement.*

Adam waited for a few seconds, but nothing happened. He couldn't just sit there. He didn't want to be in the parking lot when Lucas came out.

LA Center Studios was a twenty-acre campus that served as a hub for the recording industry. There were sound stages, recording studios, and offices handling everything from voice-overs to location filming. The longer he sat here, the more likely it was he'd see someone he knew. That would lead to a lot of questions he wasn't in the mood to answer. The only person he wanted to see right now was Mattie.

How could he apologize for everything that had happened if she wouldn't even talk to him? He hadn't meant to lie to her. He'd just wanted to get to know her.

Hell, he'd wanted more than that. No sense lying to himself anymore.

A spark of a song tickled his brain. The melody had a country-rock vibe, very different from his usual stuff. Words tumbled into his brain as he hummed.

I didn't mean to deceive you,
I just wanted to make you mine.

THE PHONE RANG. He hit Accept.

"Hey," LT said. "You still at the Center?"

"Yeah, why?"

"You have no idea how lucky you are, man. I mean, stars have aligned and shit like that."

"You got a number?"

"I got better than that." LT sounded extremely satisfied with himself. "Piper's working on that animated gig today. She's thirty minutes away, and in session until three. If you leave now, you'll be there when she gets out."

Adam started the car. "Thanks, man. Text me the address?"

"Sure thing. Uh, according to my girl, Piper's not in a good mood today. She might just blow your head off. You got a strategy?"

"I'll come up with something." Adam shifted into gear and sped out of the parking lot.

He pulled up to Day Dreams Productions with fifteen minutes to spare. He parked in the visitor lot, then checked the directions LT sent. He needed Building 2. He raced across the lush central garden, past the fountain, and down a path he hoped led to the building he wanted.

He caught sight of Piper exiting the next building over and changed direction.

"Piper!" he shouted. "Wait!"

Piper saw him and kept walking. "Fuck off, asshole."

He was getting that a lot today, and he was starting to feel like he deserved it. What Lucas said had stuck with him. He'd never questioned how Lucas had managed their careers. All he'd cared about was that Lucas was as driven as Adam was to make it work. He'd never asked about the photos of Cooper that had leaked to the tabloids or about the headlines that had popped up about his own escapades. He'd never cared. Not until Mattie.

He was a little out of breath when he reached her. "Please, just hear me out."

Piper stopped and rounded on him. "Why should I? I can't believe I stood up for you. She didn't want to go out with you. Did you know that? I'm the one who talked her into it. Me."

Piper started walking again. "It's a real slick move. Offer up pretty vacations and the chance to work on a meaningful project. You really had all her buttons pushed, didn't you? She's always felt like the backup to Della and me. She's always felt overlooked, then you come along and make her feel wanted, and valuable. Except it wasn't real, right? It was a ploy to trick her into a little sack time on camera just to push your own career."

Adam chased after her, feeling like the last lifeline he had was slipping through his fingers. "I didn't hire that photographer. My manager did. I didn't know."

Piper gave him a one-finger salute. "Get lost, dickwipe."

"Dammit, listen to me. I love her!"

Piper stopped walking. She turned slowly around and gave him an appraising look.

He rushed to finish before she walked out of his life forever.

"Mattie's not a backup anything. She's...dammit she's *everything*."

Piper raised an eyebrow.

"I can't stand that she thinks I was only with her for a PR stunt. I just wanted to get to know her. That's all. Even if she never speaks to me again, she needs to know that."

He couldn't quite read the expression in her eyes. He hoped it was understanding, or at least not hatred. "Please, can you tell her that I fired Lucas. The guys are making sure there won't be any more photos. She doesn't have to worry about anything else dropping."

Piper looked surprised. "You fired your manager?"

"He crossed the line a long time ago, I just didn't know. Or maybe I didn't want to know." His jaw ached from holding his emotions in check. "There's no excuse. I should have known. I should have paid more attention. I should have done a lot of things."

He paced around. He had too much keyed-up energy and nowhere to put it. Piper watched him like he was an animal that couldn't be trusted.

She was probably right about that.

"Look, I know you hate me. I'm the last one you'd do a favor for."

"You got that right." She crossed her arms.

"Could you please just tell her not to give up? I might have screwed up any chance I ever had to be with her, but that doesn't mean she shouldn't try again. Some things *do* last forever. Her songs will. Maybe the next guy will too. She deserves that. She deserves to be happy." He took in a tortured breath. "Can you tell her that?"

Piper hesitated. Some small measure of consideration flitted across her face, like maybe he wasn't the biggest scumbag ever to walk the earth after all. He forced himself to wait in silence for her decision.

He'd spilled his guts and ripped his heart open. If it wasn't enough he'd have to try something else. He had to make sure Mattie knew that what they had was real, no matter how things had started and no matter how they ended.

Piper pressed her lips together, then finally met his gaze. "Yeah. I can tell her that."

It was like a judge had just granted him parole. He closed his eyes and breathed a sigh of relief. "Thank you."

Chapter Twenty-Seven

Mattie spent the first three days after she arrived at the hideaway house being fussed over and coddled. It was an overwhelming amount of attention, but she had to admit that she was starting to feel a little better about life in general. She hadn't cried once today, mostly because she didn't have her phone. Piper refused to give it back until things settled down, claiming that doom-surfing tweets about herself wasn't healthy.

She had a feeling it was to keep her from seeing any messages Adam might have sent, but she didn't argue.

When Kat arrived at the driveway gates, it was a welcome distraction.

"Got a special delivery here," Kat shouted at the intercom. "Open up."

Mattie dutifully pressed the button to open the gates, and everyone wandered outside with her to watch Kat lead three delivery vans down the driveway.

"He threatened to keep sending these to my office if I

didn't let them deliver to you." Kat scowled at the vans. "My office isn't that big."

Three men carried vase after vase filled with pink and white hibiscus into the house.

"How many more?" Mattie asked one in a red delivery cap.

He jerked his chin toward the van. "On the last van now. Probably 'bout fifty left. Whatever he did must have been epic. This delivery paid my rent for the next three months."

Mattie looked questioningly at Kat. "Adam sent a hundred and fifty vases of flowers?"

Delivery man number two tipped his hat as he passed her on the way out. "More than that. There's a hundred in each van."

Della whistled. "I've never had anybody send me more than two dozen roses before. Not even the crazy rabid fans. That's some serious guilt right there."

Lizzie poked Renic in the arm. "You're going to have to up your game next time."

Renic looked affronted. "Who says there'll be a next time?"

Piper and Lizzie both gave him the patented Bellamy stare.

Renic grinned in the face of their obvious disbelief.

"I say you should throw these flowers out," Kat muttered. "He's trying to weaken your resolve."

Della took a vase from one of the delivery guys. "No way. These are way too pretty to waste. Besides, after what he did this is the least he can do."

"If you don't want them, we can have them sent to the children's hospital," Lizzie suggested.

"I still don't see why you sent the Jet Skis back," Della said. "If the man wants to grovel, let him grovel. *Then* kick him to the curb."

Mattie sighed. "Because I didn't want him thinking he can

buy my forgiveness. Besides, we don't need Jet Skis. You live in a city, I don't go to the beach, and Piper's too busy."

"Shame," Della said. "I loved that cute turtle decal on them."

"We should have taken them," Lizzie said. "We could have offered them up for guests to use on the lake, like the kayaks."

"We would have had to ship them cross country. We can buy new ones ourselves," Renic said. "That way we can have the Belhurst Castle logo instead of turtles."

The man with the red hat stopped in front of her and handed Mattie a vase filled with all pink flowers. "I'm s'posed to point out the note on this one."

Mattie took the vase from him and stared at the small red card tied to one of the flower stems. Her name was scrawled across it in familiar handwriting.

"Have a good day." The man tipped his red cap, and the three drivers went back to their vans.

Mattie carried the vase into the house. She'd have known the flowers were from Adam with or without the note because it was such an insane amount. Who else would send her this many flowers? "How did Adam even find this many hibiscus in LA? It's not like we're in the tropics."

"Crazy as he is, he probably had them flown in." Kat flicked her hand toward the back of the house. "Is there a smoking section out there?"

"You're supposed to be quitting." Mattie carried the vase to the kitchen.

"I'm not going to light it," Kat assured her. "I'm just going to suck on it and dream of lighting it."

Every surface inside the house, including some of the floor, had been transformed into a forest of pink and white.

"It looks like a flower shop in here," Lizzie said.

"Or a funeral home," Renic commented.

Lizzie hit his arm. "Stop that."

"You have to admit as apologies go this puts the over in overkill," Renic said. "It makes the rest of us look bad. And here I thought he outdid himself with the Jet Skis."

Mattie hugged the vase in her arms. The red card jiggled every time she took a step, taunting her. The past three days had been filled with overtures of guilt from Adam. It was getting hard to ignore.

Piper peered at the card. "Wonder what he wrote."

Mattie glanced at her. "Thought you'd rather I burned it. That's what you said about the notebook."

Three days ago, Piper had arrived with an armload of mail from Mattie's house, along with a beautiful hand-bound leather notebook and a sealed envelope. Mattie had thrown the envelope in the trash, but she couldn't bring herself to toss the notebook, so she'd buried it in the bottom of her suitcase. Its presence unnerved her so much that she shoved the suitcase into the back of the closet and piled her dirty laundry on top of it.

"Yeah, well. I might have been a little extreme about that."

"Somebody's a drama queen," Della sing-songed. "I mean, did he have to send so many flowers? Weren't his first two presents enough of a message?"

Mattie buried her nose in a flower. "One notebook and a Jet Ski wouldn't be enough, especially after I sent the Jet Ski back. Adam moments are over the top and in your face."

"He sure knows how to escalate, I'll give him that," Renic said. "I wonder what he'll send next."

Mattie *hmmed*. If she had to guess, he might resort to skywriting or commercials on the radio and TV.

"Are you going to read the card?" Piper asked quietly.

"I don't know." Mattie looked at her with curiosity. Her sister had been withdrawn and thoughtful for the past couple of days. It was so unlike her that Mattie had asked her if she was sick. The response had been a scathing retort on busy workloads.

It had been easy to throw away the first card. She hadn't wanted to read the second, but she hadn't been able to bring herself to get rid of it either. The initial anger and hurt she'd felt when she first arrived had faded, thanks to her sisters' efforts. Maybe she should find out what he'd written this time. But did it even matter? Was there anything he could say that would make her forgive him?

A little whisper in the back of her mind said, *Give him a chance to explain.*

Mattie carried her vase of flowers onto the back porch and sat down in one of the cushioned chairs around the outdoor dining table. "I really do love hibiscus."

They reminded her of Syer Island, which reminded her of Adam, which reminded her of why she was hiding out in the first place.

Lizzie sniffed one of the flowers before she sat down next to Mattie. "They don't really smell like anything."

"Good thing, otherwise the house would be unbearable," Renic said.

"They remind me of the ocean." Mattie liberated the card from the flower stem and held it in her hand like a grenade that might go off any second.

"You going to read that, or should I toss it in the pool?" Della asked.

Mattie brushed the envelope with her thumb. "He does know how to make a statement, doesn't he?"

Kat snorted. "He knows how to make a complete ass out of himself. Don't tell me you're softening on this guy."

Mattie stared down at the envelope and didn't answer.

"Oh come on, Mattie. It's just another way to manipulate

you to get what he wants." Kat liberated an envelope from her bag and slapped it on the table. "That's a revised contract release. He drafted his own, but he's refusing to sign unless you agree to meet with him first."

Renic picked up the contract. "Huh. He left a note on every page."

"What's it say?" Lizzie asked.

Renic flipped through the pages, then handed them to Mattie. "Take a look."

There were sticky notes on every page of the contract. Mattie pulled them off one by one as she read them out loud.

I didn't mean to lie to you.

I know you can't forgive me.

Please give me a chance to explain.

Just one meeting. Kat has the address. You set the day.

After that, I'll sign.

The songs are yours, either way.

Mattie put the notes down next to the flowers. They had a rhythm and flow that sparked her imagination. There was a song buried in those lines, somewhere.

"He rewrote the contract?" Piper asked.

"I didn't read the whole thing," Renic said.

"There's only one change," Kat said. She flicked her cigarette with one finger even though it wasn't lit. "Second page, third paragraph. It gives all rights to any song produced as a result of the retreat to Mattie. Not just the two they finished, but any other song as well. Delusions of Glory may perform them, but Mattie retains the copyright and gets full royalties."

"Wow." Piper sat back in her chair looking stunned.

Della picked up the notes and shuffled through them. "I don't get it. Why not just sign the original contract? He's giving her more than she asked for."

Renic nodded with appreciation. "It's quite the gesture, I'll give him that."

Kat snorted. "It's just another con."

"I'm not so sure about that," Lizzie said. "It seems pretty sincere to me."

Mattie stared at the unopened red card. Adam had seemed sincere on the island too.

"You're not going to meet with him, are you Mattie?" Kat asked. "Want me to tell him to get lost?"

Mattie looked at the field of pink and white inside the house. "Tell him I'll think about it."

LATER THAT NIGHT, after everyone had gone to bed, Mattie carried the unopened card up to her room. She pushed the dirty clothes aside and pulled the suitcase out of the closet. She took the notebook and card to bed with her and curled up next to them with a pillow.

Curiosity drove her to open the envelope. A simple fold-over note was inside.

MATTIE,

I'm sorry.

I lied to you because I couldn't think of any other way to get to know you.

But being with you was never a PR stunt. It was a teenage dream. An adult fantasy.

The reality was better than I ever imagined.

I let you down. I should have been the kind of man who would tell you the truth from the start.

The truth is, I love you.

I want you to be happy, even if it isn't with me.

Please talk to me. Meet with me one last time, so you can look in my eyes and see that what I say is true.

You are everything that makes songs worth singing.

Adam

MATTIE REREAD the card until the words blurred together.

* * *

TWO DAYS LATER, Mattie still hadn't made up her mind about meeting with Adam. Her internal arguments for and against were muddy, and at the bottom of them was one simple fact that was becoming impossible to ignore.

She missed him.

When Lizzie suggested they should get out of the house, Mattie at first refused.

"They're probably still looking for me," Mattie told her.

"You're not the juicy topic anymore. Larissa Thompson just filed for her tenth divorce," Piper said. "Come on. Nobody will know we're there. You need to get out."

Della nodded her head in agreement. "We'll take the SUV. People will think we're FBI or something. Nobody will see you."

With all three sisters ganging up on her like that, she finally relented. They piled into the SUV, leaving Renic behind.

"It's a girls' trip," he said firmly. "Besides, I have some phone calls to make. Have fun."

Mattie had no idea where they were going until Della pulled up outside The Flower Pot.

Mattie couldn't make herself open the car door. The last

time she was here, she'd left so angry she couldn't see. Her stomach tied up in knots just thinking about it.

Della jumped out and handed the keys to the valet.

Piper climbed out, then poked her head back in. "Quit stalling. It's just brunch. I promise no fighting. Best behavior. I swear."

Lizzie squeezed Mattie's hand. "Come on, Mattie Cake. This will be good for you. For all of us."

Mattie sighed and got out of the car.

It was eleven-thirty, but the restaurant was empty except for the waitstaff, who didn't act like they remembered her.

"Did you buy out the place?" Mattie asked as she followed Della through the restaurant to the hidden patio.

"Maybe." Della strode across the patio to the table and flounced down into a chair. "It was hard enough getting you out of the house. I wasn't about to let a few customers chase you away."

"Worried I'll start shouting again?" Mattie sat down. "I'm not mad at you anymore."

Della cast a cautious glance in Piper's direction. "That's not what this is about."

Piper frowned at Della, then gestured at Lizzie. "Might as well get this over with before we get derailed."

Mattie looked at her eldest sister. "What's going on?"

Lizzie cleared her throat. "We thought a family meeting was in order. You have a decision to make, and you aren't making it."

Mattie glanced around at the other two, who looked at her with eager but cautious expressions. "Which decision is that?"

"The kick-Adam-to-the-curb decision," Della said. "It's time to put him out of his misery and move on. Kat agrees with me."

"But Renic and I don't," Lizzie said. "We think you should hear him out. It'll give you closure."

"I say he's had enough of your time," Della said.

Mattie looked at Piper. "And you?"

"I think..." Piper looked like she was wrestling with some internal conflict.

"You think I should walk away," Mattie supplied.

Piper had been firmly anti-Adam when the photo landed on the internet, but the past week she'd been quiet, like she was trying to stay out of it.

"No." Piper shook her head. "No I don't."

"Tell her, Piper," Lizzie said gently. "She deserves to know. She can't make a decision without all the facts."

Mattie frowned. "What facts?"

Piper gestured for the server. "Bring us a round of mimosas, please?"

The server nodded and hurried off.

"Piper?" Mattie hugged herself, worried by Piper's reluctance to explain.

Piper saw her face and relented. "A couple of days after you got back, Adam came to see me at the studio. He told me a few things."

"Like what?" Mattie couldn't imagine what Adam had said to get on Piper's good side after everything that had happened.

"He said he fired his manager."

Mattie sat back. "Really. They've been with that guy forever."

Piper nodded. "Yeah. It's a pretty big statement to ditch a relationship like that."

"So what?" Della said. "I don't see how that makes up for what he did."

"Maybe it doesn't," Piper conceded, "but Adam bought out the rest of the photos that guy took and had the ones that were posted pulled off the site. That won't stop it from spreading, because it had been tweeted and retweeted, but still. That's why you aren't on the home page anymore. Adam paid to have it removed."

The mimosas arrived, and Mattie took a long sip.

Piper studied hers without drinking. "That's not all he said."

"Oh?" Mattie watched her sister over the rim of the glass.

Piper exchanged glances with Lizzie, who nodded encouragingly. "He told me he loves you. Shouted it, actually."

Mattie put the glass down. Condensation dripped down the sides onto the table while tears bubbled in her eyes. *I'm not sorry I got the chance to love you.* She remembered the exact words Adam had shouted at her because she'd replayed them over and over in her mind. She'd thought he meant he wasn't sorry he slept with her, which she'd taken a step further to mean he wasn't sorry he got that award-winning shot of her naked. But maybe he'd meant something else. Something more.

Della snorted. "Like that means anything."

"It means something, Della," Piper snapped. "It means a lot."

"Please. He's probably lying," Della scoffed. "It's just pretty words to soften you up so you give him what he wants."

"Really?" Mattie sniffed. There was unacknowledged pain behind those words. "Has that happened to you?"

"Sure, lots of times." Della shrugged. "Everybody says stuff like that at parties so they don't have to spend the night alone. Then they all head out in the morning, on to the next gig and the next bed. Adam's no different."

Mattie's instincts rejected that idea. Adam wasn't the type to go around saying I love you as a party favor. He was the type to save it for someone who really mattered.

"What the hell kind of parties do you go to?" Piper's face twisted up with confusion.

"Ladies," Lizzie interrupted, "we're not here to talk about Della's social life. Piper, tell her the rest of it."

Mattie looked at Piper. "There's more?"

"He told me to tell you that you shouldn't give up on forever, and that you deserve to be happy even if it's not with him."

Mattie blinked at the tears in her eyes, but they fell anyway. This time, though, they were tears of hope.

"Mattie," Lizzie said softly. She put her hand over Mattie's and squeezed. "I know this isn't the same thing, but I know what it's like to have a misunderstanding screw up a relationship. Learn from my mistakes. Talk to him. Just talk. If you still want to walk away after that, then do it. We'll help you. But at least get the full story first."

Della put a soft hand on Mattie's arm. "What do *you* want, Mattie? I'll back whatever you say."

Mattie's heart was full of the love her sisters shared with her. This moment was everything she'd lost, everything she'd missed from that horrible day in the greenroom until now. Della was putting Mattie's needs first, Piper had Mattie's best interests at heart, and Lizzie made sure they never lost sight of each other.

"I love you. All of you."

Piper pulled out Mattie's phone and handed it to her. "Guess it's time to give this back to you."

Mattie brushed tears away while she waited for the phone to start up. There were three hundred thirty-three unread text messages from Adam. She skipped past them to Kat's message string and typed, *Tell Adam I'll be there Saturday.*

Chapter Twenty-Eight

"Dad," Adam said with exasperation. "Would you get away from the window?"

His dad grunted, but he kept the curtain pulled back so he could see out anyway. "Just checking to be sure. You don't want to leave Mattie Bellamy hanging out on the front lawn, do ya?"

"John, come help me with the tea," his mother said.

His dad snorted. "We ain't tea people."

"Mattie is." His mom said. "She's Southern."

"Dad. You're killing me." Adam thought seriously about texting Mattie to change the location of their meeting.

His dad finally turned and gave him a look of smug superiority. "Aren't you glad we haven't moved, son? If we'd done what you wanted, all that so-called evidence you got stashed up there in that room would be gone."

His dad tapped the side of his head. "That should teach ya to use what you got upstairs for something besides playing around in that band."

"Yeah, but if you'd taken me up on my idea I wouldn't have

had to bring her here. I would have all that stuff in a box some-where less embarrassing."

"It's not embarrassing." His mom patted his cheek. "It's a piece of history that I bet you anything she'll appreciate. A girl likes to know where her man comes from. Gives her insight she'll need in the future."

His dad barked a laugh. "Better set fire to it now, son."

Adam couldn't believe he was having this conversation. "I don't need to set it on fire. This house is going to fall down around your ears soon. Why won't you let me make your life a little more comfortable? Name the place, I'll get it for you. Anywhere. You pick."

His mother gave him a kind smile. "Honey, your dad and I don't want to move. We've spent longer than you've been alive in this house. We built a life together here. We loved each other, we made memories, we had you and Brandon. This is home."

Adam started to protest, but she held up a hand to stop him.

"We love this house because everywhere we look reminds us of you and Brandon. If we moved...well, it would be new, which I admit would be wonderful, but it would feel empty. Do you understand?"

Adam remembered that Mattie had said close to the same thing. She'd understood his parents far better than he did. He heaved a sigh and nodded. "Okay. I get it. You don't want things to change."

"You kidding me?" Dad said. "I'd love the back porch to change. I want one of those outdoor kitchens, with a big TV and a cushy couch."

Adam grinned at that. "I can make that happen, but are you sure you want my filthy music money to pay for it?"

His dad let the curtain drop. "I got no problem spending

your money, son. I know you worked hard for it. I just don't want to spend it on some fancy new house."

"Are you trying to say you're finally proud of me?" Adam exchanged looks with his mother. Her eyes glistened with unshed tears. "You told me it wasn't a real job. Remember all those fights we had?"

"Yeah, well. You've grown since then." His dad gave him a pat on the arm. "It might not be a real job, but it pays pretty darn good, so I guess it's okay You done good, kiddo. Brandon too."

Adam pulled his Dad in for a hug. "Thanks, Dad. That means a lot."

"Yeah, well. Truth's truth." His dad cleared his throat. "Now what about that tea?"

Adam followed his parents down the hall to the kitchen. "Want a pool too?"

His dad snorted. "Now what would we do with a thing like that?"

ADAM WAITED on the front porch of his childhood home feeling more nervous than he'd ever felt in his entire life. He'd been so anxious the first time he sang in front of a sold-out stadium that he threw up three times, including once during the middle of the first song, but it didn't even come close to how he felt right now.

A black SUV pulled onto their street and slowed to a stop in front of his house.

Sweat trickled down the back of his neck. He stood up as Mattie got out of the car and forced himself to saunter, rather than race, down the sidewalk to the curb.

Mattie came around the front and stopped a few feet away from him.

Time stopped while she looked at him with those enormous hazel eyes that saw straight past his bullshit, and his insides quivered.

She played with the keys, jiggling them back and forth. Creases appeared between her eyebrows. "Hi."

"I'm sorry," he blurted out. "I didn't know what was going on, but I should have. I never should have lied to you. I didn't mean to hurt you, I just wanted to get to know you, but that's no excuse. I was a blind fool."

"Adam...," Mattie said.

He held out his hand. "I know you probably don't want to be here, but I need to show you something. If you'll let me. Then you can leave and never see me again if that's what you want."

Her gaze shifted to the window then back to him. "Is this your parents' house?"

"They promised to stay out of our way."

Her lips twitched a little. "Your dad is peeking through the curtains."

Adam glanced back at the window. Curtains swung a little as if someone had just dropped them back into place. "Yeah, he's a little anxious."

"He's not the only one," she murmured.

The light in her eyes wasn't anger, he didn't think. He gestured to the door. "Come in?"

She nodded and followed him up the steps.

It might have been his imagination, but he thought he heard his parents' pounding footsteps as they hurried away from the front window. By the time he opened the door, they were nowhere in sight.

He pointed up. "What I have to show you is upstairs."

Mattie looked where he pointed, then glanced around with a frown. "Where'd they go?"

"They didn't want to intrude." He took the first couple of steps, then realized Mattie wasn't following.

She peeked into the front living room, then went down the hall.

He stood where he was, frozen by possibilities. If she wanted to meet his parents, did that mean she'd forgiven him? Or did it mean she was about to tell them how horrible their son was? He felt like a teenager caught sneaking in past curfew.

He shook himself and followed her into the kitchen in time to hear his mother cry out, "Mattie! Come in, come in. We've been dying to meet you. I made sweet tea."

His mother had folded Mattie into a tight hug that Mattie appeared to return. His mother was taller than Mattie, especially in her heels with her hair up in a neat bun. She looked like she'd just stepped out of the classroom, even though it was Saturday.

His dad stood awkwardly nearby. His gray hair was slicked back, and he had on the good shirt he usually wore to dinner or church. He looked pointedly at Adam.

"Well, introduce us, son." His dad's gruff voice caught his mother's attention.

"Now, John, you know perfectly well who this is. Don't mind him, Mattie, he's a little starstruck."

Mattie surreptitiously wiped a tear away and held out a hand to his father. "Nice to meet you, Mr. Brooks, Mrs. Brooks."

"Now you call me John, Miss Bellamy." He shook her hand.

"And I'm Barbara, or Barb, or Babs." His mother patted Mattie's arm.

"Only if you call me Mattie." She smiled. "It's a pleasure to meet you both. Adam talks about you quite a bit."

"Well I'm sure most of it's exaggerated. He likes to make it sound like I was the stubborn one." His dad gestured to one of the chairs. "Care to sit?"

"John, I think they need a little time to themselves right now," his mother chided. "Adam, why don't you and Mattie go on up."

He gave his mother a grateful smile and led Mattie out of the kitchen and up the stairs to his childhood bedroom. He opened the door and ushered her inside, then stood back and waited for her reaction.

The room hadn't changed since the day he'd left. The same navy-blue comforter was still on the bed, the surfboard lamp still sat on the table, and the walls remained covered with posters, flyers, and album covers of all the musicians, bands, and songs he'd found inspirational during his high school years. The Bellamy Sisters were featured a little too often for him to be a mere fan.

In the empty spaces, teenage handwriting filled colored scraps of paper with bits and pieces of ideas that had turned into songs.

The most incriminating part of the room was the giant poster of Mattie Bellamy in a gossamer purple dress glued to the ceiling over the bed. She was turned to the side, with her hair in loose curls that kissed her bare shoulders. Her eyes sparkled, and her smile radiated private amusement.

He knew what it looked like. Every teenage boy knew what it looked like.

He tried to see the room through her eyes, and cringed.

Mattie took it all in without saying a word, though her eyes widened when she looked up at the ceiling.

It was a teenage fantasy to have Mattie standing in his

bedroom. His fifteen-year-old self would have passed out from excitement. His current self was a little out of breath and unsure as he waited for her to say something.

She spun slowly in place, her gaze moving from poster to poster, until she finally faced him and stopped.

He winced, then shrugged. "This is what I was lying to you about. I didn't think you'd work with me if you'd known about all this."

He gestured to the walls.

"I probably wouldn't have," Mattie said faintly. "It's very...you."

She moved slowly toward the largest wall. "I think you have every concert poster we ever had made."

"Probably."

She glanced over her shoulder at him. "Did you go to any?"

"Oh yeah."

"Do I want to know how many?"

"Probably not."

A trace of a smile lifted the corners of her lips. "I haven't been to any of yours. Yet."

She turned back to the wall. "I like Aerosmith too. They're fun. Who's this?" She pointed to a small, rough-around-the-edges flyer of the Blues Avenue Boys. Five whiskered, gray-haired men were posed with their instruments on a small stage. They all had the typical tough blues stare, but he knew from experience that was just for show.

He smiled fondly at it. "The one with the drums is Pop. My mom's dad. He's jammed with the Blues Avenue Boys for over fifty years now."

Mattie touched the flyer with a delicate finger. "Do they still play?"

"Every Saturday night." Adam pulled out his phone and tapped on the music player app. His grandfather's voice filled the room with "Got My Mojo Working" by Muddy Waters. "He loves the standards. They cover all the greats."

Mattie tapped her foot in time to the music and bobbed her head. She smiled at him. "That's fun. I see where you get your edge."

He pressed Stop and tucked the phone back into his pocket. "He's slowing down, now. But he's still got it."

Mattie drifted along the wall, calling out names as she went. "Eagles. Not surprised you have that. Bon Jovi. Bruce Springsteen. Night Ranger?"

She flashed him an amused smile.

"Hey, 'Sister Christian' is a classic."

"It's a good song, it's just..." She shook her head. "Unexpected."

She returned to her examination of his childhood. "Billy Joel. Marvin Gaye. Creed. Journey. The Bellamy Sisters. You were all over the place." She paused at a small piece of paper tucked between Soundgarden and Stone Temple Pilots. "This is the bridge from your first hit, isn't it?"

"Most of our songs are in here, in one way or another." He stared around at the room. "So that's the big secret. You've been my inspiration for a long, long time."

She shook her head. "The Bellamy Sisters, maybe. But your sound is nothing like ours."

"Not the group. You."

She blinked at him. "Me."

"Some of it wasn't even you, it was the *idea* of you."

He looked into her eyes and felt the connection they'd shared on the island take hold. "You're a hell of a lot more than some teenage fantasy, Mattie. You're so talented it makes my head spin, and I can't live with the fact that I had any part in making you doubt yourself. You're not a backup to anyone or anything. Your words touch millions of hearts all over the world, including mine. Please, don't ever doubt yourself. Especially because of me."

She turned her attention to the largest poster of The Bellamy Sisters. "I don't mind being the backup."

It was a live shot of their Daydreams tour. Della was larger than life, front and center, all sequins and sparkle. Piper was leather and rock. Mattie was on keyboards to the side, but the light behind her framed her hair like a halo. She had a dreamy, ethereal quality that made her look like an angel.

She stared at the poster.

"Do you miss it?" he asked quietly. "The stage I mean."

"No." She sighed. "Maybe a little. I miss them. I miss the music we made together. I liked it when we sang for Dad in the living room or put on a show in the backyard. It doesn't matter where, you know?"

He thought about the garage sessions he'd had with the guys and knew exactly what she meant. He loved the crowd, the bigger the better, but if he couldn't have that he'd be just like Pop, singing in a corner of whatever bar would have him, because it was the music that filled him, not the applause.

"Why haven't you gone solo?"

She hugged herself like it was suddenly cold in the room. "It just didn't feel right. Would you?"

"Hell no," he said immediately. "I'm no good on my own. Just ask Brandon."

He was rewarded with a soft chuckle.

"So now you know all the dirty secrets. My parents keep a room-sized scrapbook of my teen years, and I have a giant poster of you on my ceiling because I had a huge crush on you in high school. But you don't have to worry about it, because I don't have a crush on you anymore."

Mattie breathed out a choked laugh. "You don't?"

"Nah." He grinned. "Now I'm in love with you."

She blinked.

He wasn't sure what that meant. He hoped it was a good thing. "I love you for so many reasons. The way you watch the sunrise with that dreamy look in your eyes. The way you light up the room with your smile. I love the way you include all the guys when you're writing songs. Me and Johnny J didn't do that, but we should have. It's added a depth that we've been missing."

Her hand fluttered up to her chest. "Adam..."

He held up his hands. "I know I'm a lot to take. I'm almost done, I swear. The reason I brought you here was to make sure you knew that the way you put heart into lyrics is what convinced me to chase after my own dream back then. You're the inspiration for so many people out there. Don't ever stop writing. Don't ever stop making music. No matter what the next asshole says or does."

"The next..." She swallowed. "What if I don't want there to be a next?"

He held very still.

She took a small step forward, then another, until she was so close there was practically no space between them. "What if what I want is right here in front of me?"

His heart skipped several beats. "Are you saying you forgive me?"

Her lips quirked. "I'm saying I love you."

His pulse raced with all the implications that came along with those three little words. "You do?"

She put her arms around his neck. "I love the way you give whoever you're talking to your undivided attention. I love the way you go all in on whatever it is you're trying to do. I love the way you look at me when you think I don't see. I'm a little overwhelmed by your Adam moments, but I love them too."

She brushed his lips with a soft, sweet kiss. "I love you. How could I not forgive you?"

He crushed her against him and kissed her until the room spun and they were out of breath. Years of waiting, fantasizing, and hoping were finally living and breathing reality.

He pulled away slightly and saw desire in her eyes. "I can't believe you're here. I used to dream about this, you know."

"You did?" She looked a little uncertain at that news. "Was I...never mind. I don't want to know."

"Not like that." He brushed his lips against hers. "Every night I'd go to sleep staring at your face, fantasizing about you standing right here, looking at me just like this."

"Oh." She tilted her head. "What happened then?"

"I woke up disappointed." He looked around at all the things his teenage self found important and realized this was the last place on earth he wanted to be right now. "Thing is, now that I have you here, I'd really like to take you somewhere else."

"Why?"

"Because there's no way I'm making love to you in this room." He shuddered. "My parents are in the house."

Her eyes sparkled. "I'm sure they think we're already doing it. They were young once too, you know."

"No." He laughed. "Just no. I refuse to picture that."

She giggled.

"Well now that's settled, want to go back downstairs? I'm sure Mom has snacks out by now, and Dad's dying to play twenty questions."

"They're sweet. They must be. They made you and Brandon." Her gaze shifted to the poster on the wall behind him that advertised The Bellamy Sisters first world tour. The three of them formed a triangle in blue sequins with Della in front, Piper slightly behind to the right and Mattie further back on the left. He'd gone to three shows that summer. "You think we should get back together."

It sounded more like a statement than a question.

"I think you should do whatever puts the joy back in your eyes. But you're not the backup, Mattie. You've never been the backup. You're the soul. Don't ever forget that."

"The soul," she repeated, softly. Her gaze shifted back to him, and she had the dreamy look on her face that she always got when a song lyric popped into her head. "You're the soul."

"I think there's paper on the desk." He crossed to it and started to shuffle through the drawers. "Or I can go get your bag if you want."

Mattie touched his arm, and he stilled.

"I think I can remember this one," she said.

"You don't want to write it down?"

She shook her head. "Do you still have a setup in the garage?"

A slow grin spread across his face. "Oh yeah. Got a whole studio in there now."

"Show me." She smiled, and his heart sang.

Chapter Twenty-Nine

EIGHT MONTHS LATER

Mattie took Adam's hand and squeezed it as she stepped onto the red carpet at the Grammy Awards.

"Ready for this?" His crooked grin was just for her.

She smiled and nodded. "Definitely."

Cameras flashed on both sides as she showed off the dress Della had picked for her. It was a simple A-line silhouette covered in three-dimensional flowers that flowed from the waist to the ground. She was Alice walking through Wonderland in this dress. She held out her arms and twirled so the dress billowed out around her and was rewarded with *oohs* and *ahhs* from those watching.

"How does it feel to be up for two awards?" one of the reporters asked.

She beamed. "It's a dream come true."

She and Adam, as well as Delusions of Glory, were up for three awards tonight, including Song of the Year, Best Rock Performance, and Album of the Year. Their Syer Island retreat had resulted in three new songs that finished out the *Truth Is I Love You* album.

They were all great songs, but it was the third, "Truth Is I Love You," that really stood out. It had taken them two months to write the song they'd started in Adam's garage. She thought it not only captured the entire beginning of their relationship, but it also showed how she felt about the entire band. It was edgier than her usual pop sound, but softer than Adam's typical rock vibe. Kat had been right. The blend of their two sounds made magic.

It was one of the best songs she'd ever written.

When Delusions of Glory had opened their new tour two months ago, she'd joined them on stage to sing it with them. The rush of being on stage had been intense and exciting, and it made her think seriously about Della's idea to get back together.

"Mattie," one reporter shouted, "when will we hear wedding bells?"

"Are The Bellamy Sisters getting back together?"

"Who are you wearing?"

She smiled and posed and ignored their questions. Rumors had been flying for months about her sisters, but so far that's all they were. Rumors. They weren't ready. Not yet. But the idea had gone from a solid no to a hopeful maybe.

They bombarded Adam with questions when he stepped up to escort her into the Staples Center.

"Is Mattie joining Delusions of Glory?"

"Will you tour together?"

"How's it feel to be here with your high school crush?"

Adam flipped a casual wave in their direction, and he and Mattie walked down the red carpet toward the doors. He whispered in her ear. "It feels fantastic to be here with my high school crush. It will feel even better when we get out of here and out of these clothes."

She laughed and poked him in the ribs. "Don't start that now. We have a long night ahead of us."

"Why not? Nobody will notice if we sneak off to a quiet corner for a little bit. Especially at the after-party."

"They're hunting for photos exactly like that. Remember?"

"They're never getting another photo exactly like that. If they do, my new manager will be put on a spit and roasted."

"Your new manager is much more likely to put you over her knee and spank you. If Jordanna can handle Della, she can make mincemeat of you."

"She's a marshmallow." He gave her a toothy grin. "Besides, she thinks I'm adorable."

"She thinks everyone's adorable at first." She saw Della waiting up ahead and waved at her. "Della!"

Della grinned at the cameras while she waited for them to catch up. "We're almost fashionably late. Everybody else is already sitting down."

Mattie gave her sister a quick hug, then the three of them went inside.

MATTIE WAITED through award after award with her stomach slowly tying itself into tiny macramé knots. She'd never realized before just how long it took them to go through the list of nominees, plus the commercial breaks, plus all the performances. Sitting on literal pins and needles would have felt more comfortable.

During one commercial break, Mattie, her sisters, and Delusions of Glory all clustered into a huddle in the aisle next to their seats. Mattie and Adam stood in the middle of a circle that included everyone they cared most about in the world. Cameras pointed at them, and heads turned occasionally in their direction. Every now and then, someone waved. She wasn't sure how much of the buzz was for her and how much for Delusions of Glory since they were both up for a major award, but the tension in the air only ratcheted up her own nerves to the point where she could hardly sit still.

She felt like a kid waiting for Santa, the Easter Bunny, and the Tooth Fairy all at once. She flexed her hands to use the pent-up energy, but it didn't help.

Piper grabbed her hands. "If you don't stop that, you'll be a meme by the time the show ends. Now smile and laugh like I just said something funny."

Mattie pursed her lips but resisted the urge to stick her tongue out.

"Only a couple more to go," Lizzie said with a calm smile. "Almost there."

"This is taking forever," Flynn muttered.

"Yeah, can't we skip ahead?" Brandon hissed.

"Patience, gentlemen," Adam admonished. He exchanged exasperated grins with Cooper and LT.

Mattie let out a nervous giggle. "I'm with Flynn, this really *is* taking forever. I think they're deliberately going slow to torture us."

"If you don't win, I'm boycotting these awards for the rest of my life," Della muttered.

The music queued them to get back in their seats, but since everyone had taken the opportunity to crawl out of their seats, it took several minutes to get settled.

Finally, the Song of the Year presenter stepped on stage. Sarah Nash was not only a great lyricist, she was last year's winner. Mattie loved her style because the folksy song reminded her of her dad.

Sarah read the list of nominees with a smile and comment for each one. Mattie envied the cool, laid-back composure

Adam held on to in the face of all this stress. She had trouble keeping the frozen smile planted on her face with the camera pointed directly at them.

"And Song of the Year goes to..." Sarah fumbled with the envelope. "Ouch, paper cut. Hold on. Almost have it."

Mattie squirmed in her seat.

Adam gripped her hand.

"'Truth Is I Love You,' by Mattie Bellamy and Adam Brooks, Brandon Brooks, Cooper Peady, Flynn Mackie, and LT Sullivan," she called out.

Everyone sitting around Mattie jumped up and shouted.

"I knew you'd win!" Della beamed. "You write the best songs and now you have proof!"

Mattie hugged everyone she could reach on her way out of the row and down the aisle whether she knew them or not. When she stepped up on stage clutching Adam's hand, the applause grew louder, and included a few catcalls. She clutched the award statue they pressed into her hands and peered out at her sisters.

Lizzie looked so proud it made Mattie tear up. Piper shot her a thumbs-up. Della hopped up and down and pumped her fist in the air.

"This is your moment," Adam told her as he gave her a little push toward the microphone. "You talk. We'll back you up."

It was surreal to finally be living the dream she'd had for so long. She glanced back at Adam. "You sure?"

He nodded encouragingly at her.

"It's funny," she said to the crowd. "I usually have so many words to say but right now..."

She shrugged helplessly.

The crowd laughed.

"First, I want to thank the guys on stage with me. I

couldn't have found the right words without Flynn, Brandon, LT, Cooper, and of course Adam."

She turned to give them all a sunny smile. "I'm so grateful I got the chance to know you and work with all of you.

"I also want to thank my family—my sisters—Lizzie, Piper, and Della." She pointed at her sisters. One of the big cameras swung around to get a shot of the three of them and Renic, all nodding and smiling back at her. "You've supported me, encouraged me, picked me up when I was down, and loved me through everything. You've backed me my whole life, and I wouldn't be standing here without you. I love you."

Lizzie blew her a kiss. Piper pumped a fist in the air, and Della shouted, "I love you, Mattie!"

Mattie brushed a tear off her cheeks and held her hand out to Adam.

Adam leaned toward the microphone and grinned. "She's the words, we're just the melody. This song has soul and the album has heart because Mattie Bellamy agreed to work with us. To the fans who put us here, you know who you are... thanks for listening."

"Thanks for singing," Cooper said into the mic. He moved out the way, and LT stepped up.

"Thanks for having our back," LT said. He stepped to the side.

"Thanks for coming," Brandon waved.

Flynn pushed him out the way. "And thanks for buying!" He gave the audience a toothy grin and waved a drumstick.

Adam waved a salute, and they followed the presenter off stage.

Mattie was floating so high on adrenaline-fueled euphoria that she couldn't stop laughing.

Adam picked her up and swung her around. If his smile

grew any broader, it might crack his face in half. "You did it! I told you it would win."

"*We* did it," she insisted. "You and me. The guys too. All of us. I can't believe it. I really can't believe it. Did that just happen? It didn't, did it. I'm dreaming. This is a dream and I don't want to wake up."

"It's real, fantasy girl. It's all real." Adam gave her a fierce kiss.

"Dude, they're announcing Best Album," Flynn said.

It was too late to get back to their seats, so they all crowded together behind the curtain at the side of the stage and anxiously waited.

"And Album of the Year goes to"—the presenter grinned at the audience—"no surprise here because these guys are my personal favorite, Delusions of Glory!"

Mattie slapped her hands over her mouth to contain the squeal. There had been rumors that the album might win, but she hadn't wanted to get her hopes up.

"Yes!" Flynn pumped the air with both fists.

"That's right!" Brandon pointed at Flynn. "I called it!"

"Get back out there," Adam gave his brother a playful shove.

The announcer stepped back as Flynn and Brandon ran back out on stage. LT and Cooper followed at a more sedate pace.

Mattie felt like turning somersaults. Her heart was so full she didn't think she'd be able to capture everything she felt in this moment, even if she spent a lifetime trying. She gave Adam her biggest, proudest smile and gestured for him to follow the others.

"Go on. I'll be right here waiting."

Adam grabbed her hand. "Oh no, I'm not letting you sit in

the background ever again. You are as much a part of this as we are. Come on."

She beamed at him, and they ran out to take another bow. Together.

* * *

BY THE TIME the show was over and they'd changed into more comfortable clothes, the after-party was in full swing. The group that managed a dozen labels, including Adam's, took over one of LA Center's largest sound stages and transformed it into a one-of-a-kind nightclub complete with live music, plenty of food and drink, and a see-and-be-seen atmosphere.

Twenty thousand feet of space was filled with musicians, their managers, producers, record label executives, and anybody and everybody who was connected in any way with Jupiter Music Group. They were all there to celebrate the stars of the night and to start campaigning for the next award show.

Mattie and Adam were reluctantly separated soon after they arrived. Delusions of Glory's new manager, Jordanna, hustled them off for interviews and meet and greets, while Kat ushered Mattie to a different corner for more of the same.

Mattie shook hands, hugged, and air kissed so many people she lost track. Her sisters stayed within range, but it was Mattie everybody wanted to see. She wasn't used to being the center of attention, and she wasn't sure she liked it. She'd rather Della and Piper handle the schmoozing while she and Lizzie stood behind them making sure nobody got too grabby.

Mattie caught sight of Devon Morales on the far side of the room. He scowled at her, then flipped her off. She offered him her sweetest Southern smile in return, the one that looked polite but really meant *bless your heart.* The phrase could mean any number of things, from *I feel so sorry for you* to *I hope you die in a fire*. Let him sort out exactly what she meant.

The song he'd stolen from her didn't win. Neither did his album. His next tweet would say he was robbed, she supposed.

Della noticed her watching him and shouted into her ear, "Serves him right. Loser."

Mattie had mixed feelings about it. The words were hers, even if he'd stolen credit. If he lost, she did too. It was an odd kind of twist to think she'd both lost and won tonight. "You know, I should thank him."

Della looked at her like she'd grown another eyeball. "Why? He made your life miserable."

Mattie wiggled her fingers at Devon. "Because of him, I went on that retreat with Adam. I came back with three great songs and a man I love. I ended up with exactly what Devon's trying to find. Shame he's going about it all wrong."

Mattie saw Adam near one of the bars and smiled to herself. "Devon can have the song. I found something a hell of a lot better."

Della squeezed her arm. "I'm going for a drink. Want anything?"

"Wait." Mattie grabbed her sister's hand before she could dart away. "I need to tell you something."

Della looked at her with curiosity.

"If Piper's in, so am I."

"You're..." Della's eyes widened. "You sure?"

Mattie put her lips to Della's ear so she could hear her over the noise of the crowd. "I've given this a lot of thought. I want to perform again, but not by myself. I don't want to go solo. If I'm going on stage, I want it to be with my sisters."

"You'd be great at it. You know that, right?" Della looked cautiously hopeful. "You never give yourself enough credit.

And I guess I never wanted to notice that. But you would own the stage all by yourself."

"I want to be on stage with you and Piper, or not at all," Mattie told her firmly. "So if you can convince Piper, I'm in. But it's not going to be an easy sell."

Della looked relieved. "With you on board, it'll be a lot easier. Don't worry. I've been thinking about how to make up with her. I just needed to know that you were ready. We can't do this without you."

Della threw her arms around Mattie and squeezed so tight she couldn't breathe.

"And I won't do it without you and Piper. I love you Dell Bell."

"Love you more, Mattie Cake!" Della's smile could have melted a million hearts. "I'm going to tell Lizzie!"

She darted into the crowd.

Adam made his way back to her, carrying much-needed water for her and a beer for him. He gestured at Della's receding back. "I take it you told her?"

Mattie nodded. "Yes."

"How long will it take her to convince Piper?" Adam asked.

"Not sure. Piper's been building up walls for this moment for years, but Della's a special kind of force."

It was late, and the crowd had started to thin a little. Most would move on to other parties, but Mattie had a different kind of celebration in mind.

She took Adam's free hand in hers and pulled him close. "Let's get out of here."

"Where to?" His eyes sparked with interest.

Mattie put all the desire and love she felt into the look she gave him. "Is there a waterfall around here?"

"If there isn't, I'll make one."

His wicked grin set her insides on fire.

"Silly. A shower will work fine." She flashed him a not-so-innocent smile.

He growled under his breath. "Let's go."

"Thought you'd never ask." She let him pull her through the crowd, out the door, and into the night.

They wound up detouring into the first dark corner they found for a kiss that lasted a long, long time.

The shower, when they got to it, lasted even longer.

Mattie relished the sensations that tingled through her body as his hands caressed her wet skin. "You know what?"

Adam smoothed her hair back out of her eyes. "What?"

"I was wrong. I think love lasts forever. Love, and music."

"And us."

They sealed the declaration with a very thorough, very long, kiss.

* * *

Want more Mattie and Adam?
Tap here to find out how they get engaged!

* * *

**If you're having any trouble tapping on the extra scene,
please type
https://melindavan.com/bonus-material-2
into your phone or computer browser.**

* * *

KEEP READING FOR A PREVIEW OF *HE'S THE REASON WHY...*

PIPER BELLAMY, one-third of the former pop sensation The Bellamy Sisters, leaned toward the camera in her formal living room turned recording studio and beamed at her 150 million streaming followers.

"Good morning! First, I'm so sorry I won't be able to stick around for the comments today. I know, I know. It's your favorite part. Mine too. But wait until you hear why."

She cherished these *Wednesday Morning Coffee Chats.* Connecting with her fans kept her grounded and sane, especially after her little sister, Della, had turned all their lives upside down by going solo. The people who stuck with her after that weren't just fans of The Bellamy Sisters, they were Piper Bellamy super fans.

"Today is finally the table read for *Scorched*. Can you believe it?" She put her coffee cup down because her wild gestures were putting it in serious danger of spilling over. "I can't believe we're finally moving forward on this. When they cast me, what, almost two years ago now? Wow, time flies. Anyway, I was so excited to get started. That was all thanks to you, by the way. I've mentioned it a thousand times but one more can't hurt...if you hadn't put up that Twitter campaign, I'd never have been cast. So thank you, thank you, thank you, a million times.

"Then, as you know, there was the writer's strike, and a problem finding the right leading man. But now, finally, *finally* we're getting started. Today is the first read-through, where we go through the whole script with everybody at one time. Some of us have also spent the past six months practicing some of the big songs, and you know I've put some quality time in the studio, but everyone will be there today, from the director, Tamar Shurer, to Paul Lester, the producer, to...wait, am I allowed to say this? I hope so because I'm going to...Blake Ryan!"

She almost squealed his name, she was so excited.

"He just signed on to play Prince Jesse a couple of weeks ago. They probably haven't even announced that yet."

She put a finger to her lips. "Shh don't tell anybody, okay? Can you say fourth time's a charm? I can't believe they didn't pick him first because I can't imagine anyone else being so perfect for this part. Sexiest Man of the Year, hello! Plus, I get to meet Gina Paige, Jeremy Graham, and Rachel Morris. Seriously, it's a huge, *huge* day for me. A giant step forward into something new and different. Can't wait to see what working on an animated movie is like."

Piper gave her audience a wave and a big smile. "I promise I'll check in on the comments later and let you know how the day went. Bye for now, and remember...you *rock*! Wish me luck!"

She clicked the Stop button, checked to make sure the video uploaded to all of her streaming platforms, then carried her coffee to the kitchen.

Call time was eleven a.m., which left her forty-five minutes to get to the studio. While it gave her plenty of time, she didn't want to be late. Not today. She needed to get going.

She was halfway to the kitchen when she heard the code being entered into the front door security lock. Romi Mizrahi, her friend, bodyguard, and head of security, probably just wanted to check in before Piper left for the day.

The door opened, and a tall, lanky blonde wearing strategically ripped denim shorts, a white crop top, and red-stitched ankle boots bopped through the door like she owned the place.

"Della!" Piper did a double take, then narrowed her eyes at her youngest sister. "What are you doing here?"

"Good morning to you too," Della said, looking offended.

She dropped her red handbag onto the entry table and held her arms out wide. "I want to give you a hug."

Piper submitted to her sister's over-enthusiastic greeting, then led the way to the kitchen. "You should have called first. I can't stay, I have a meeting."

"I know, silly, that's why I came." Della looked around the kitchen like she'd never seen one before, then meandered far too casually toward the coffee bar.

Piper watched her sister over the edge of her coffee cup and did her best to hide her irritation. Della had shown up this morning with a too-sunny smile that Piper didn't trust for one second.

"Explain to me again why you need so many coffee makers?" Della poked a button on the drip coffee maker, then quickly poked it again when it started to gurgle.

"Explain to me again why you're here," Piper countered. She tapped her phone to double-check the time. "I have to leave in fifteen minutes, okay?"

Della flicked the espresso maker on. "You said today was the run-through. That's huge, right? I just wanted to wish you luck. Is that a bad thing?"

"Not exactly, no." Piper watched her sister wrestle with the machine for a few amusing seconds before helping her sort out a shot of espresso for her latte. "But you could have done that over the phone or by text. Showing up in person this early feels like there's strings attached."

"That's just mean." Della pushed her lips out in a fake pout.

"Not if it's true." Piper added frothed milk and vanilla flavoring to the coffee before she handed it to Della. "Is it?"

"Of course not." Della pointed at the large family photo on the wall.

It had been taken at Belhurst Castle, the inn their oldest

sister, Lizzie, operated, just after Lizzie's wedding two months ago. Lizzie glowed in the center next to her new husband, Jackson Renic, and surrounded by her sisters.

"That picture came out great. Usually, bridesmaids' dresses look so hideous, but I actually wore mine again to that dinner thing last month. What did you do with yours?"

Piper stared at the photo. "I shoved it in the back of my closet with all the other costumes."

Lizzie's wedding had been classy and elegant and filled with love. For the first time in a long time, they'd felt like a family again. It made her smile every time she looked at that picture.

Della studied her cup as if something might leap out of it. "This doesn't look right."

"Why are you really here, Dell?"

She sniffed the coffee. "I want some sister time. Let me give you a ride to the studios."

"I have a car, and I know how to drive."

Her sister was up to something, and Piper had a feeling she knew what. It was no secret that Della wanted to get their group back together. She'd already talked their other two sisters into it.

Della hadn't asked Piper directly since the disastrous brunch five months ago when Mattie had had a meltdown. The topic still hung in the air between Della and Piper every time they got together, but neither one of them mentioned it out loud.

Della rolled her eyes. "I'm just trying to be nice. I have to go that way anyway. I'm heading to an open house in Beverly Hills."

"You're house hunting here?" Piper considered having her baby sister as a next-door neighbor and shuddered. Where Della went, crowds followed, and they had eyes only for their star. Della cast a long, long shadow, but LA was far enough away from NYC that Piper had gotten used to being in the sun for a change.

Della carried her coffee to the table and sat down. "Maybe. I don't know. I mean, you're here, and Mattie's here. It would be cool to be closer to you guys. It's a long way from Lizzie, though. Hey, maybe she'll move out here someday."

"There's no way Lizzie is ever leaving upstate New York on any kind of permanent basis. She loves that inn. I don't blame her. It's so peaceful." Piper drained the rest of her now cold coffee. "And Beverly Hills is nowhere near Day Dreams Studios."

"Can't I do something nice for you without you thinking I'm up to something? Come on." Della sounded hurt, but it was a lie. They both knew it.

"You could, but not this early in the morning. You haven't seen a sunrise since you were twelve. Why are you really here?" She needed to push this along. Traffic on the 10 was murder this time of day.

"I just wanted to talk to you." Della sounded unsure now, which was a sign they were getting close to the actual point of the conversation.

"About?" Piper leaned against the counter and gave her little sister her full attention.

Della took a sip of her coffee, grimaced, and set it down. "Nasty. We should get Starbucks on the way."

"We should get to the point," Piper said with what she hoped sounded like patience.

Della bit her lip, then nodded. "Okay. You're right. I do want to ask you something. Just please, *please* listen to the whole thing before you say anything?"

"Okay, I'll try my best."

"Really? Because you don't look like you mean that. You

look like you're about to say no and you don't even know what I'm going to say."

Piper hated the way her stomach tightened into knots whenever this subject was brought up. She'd worked hard over the years to let it go, but her body apparently hadn't gotten the memo. "I know what you want, Della. Hell, people on the space station know what you want because you're as subtle as the Great Wall of China if it was set on fire. So go ahead. Ask and get it over with. This hemming and hawing is painful for both of us, and I have to get going."

Della huffed an impatient sound. "You're not even going to listen."

"I'm listening. Believe me." Piper couldn't stop the growl of irritation. Della could trigger her every nerve despite Piper's best efforts to stay calm. "It's pretty hard to avoid this particular topic, actually, because the rumor is all over Twitter and Facebook and every gossip rag from here to Hong Kong. You really shouldn't use social media to manipulate me. You know it just makes me mad."

Della looked genuinely confused. "What do you mean by that? I haven't posted anything on social media about this."

"You haven't?" Piper frowned. She'd seen a ton of posts about The Bellamy Sisters getting back together. She'd assumed they were started by Della, but she had to admit she hadn't examined them too closely.

"Nope. Not me." Della stared out the back window.

Was she looking for inspiration or escape? It was hard to tell.

"Oh." After a few awkward seconds of silence, Piper added, "Sorry."

Della shrugged. "It's okay. It sounds like something I would have done. You know, before."

"Della—"

"Okay, here it is." Della faced her. "I came here to tell you I'm sorry. What I did was self-centered, and selfish, and unbelievably naive. I thought I was a victim when I was the luckiest girl who ever lived. I hurt the people who mean the most to me, and by the time I figured that out, I was too ashamed to undo it."

Piper swallowed hard.

She hadn't expected to hear the words I'm sorry from Della and have her actually mean them.

She'd expected Della to leap right over the past and on to the future by asking Piper to go along with her scheme to reform The Bellamy Sisters. It was all Della had talked about for the last year—to everyone except Piper.

"If I were you, I'd never forgive me for it either." Tears glistened in Della's eyes. "But I hope you can. Someday. Because I really miss my best friend."

Piper's chest squeezed so tight she almost couldn't breathe. Tears poked at her eyes, and prickles of heat filled her belly. She'd imagined a dozen different scenarios and how she'd respond, but she hadn't planned on this.

Things between her and Della had eased a lot since they'd all come together to help Mattie after nude photos of her had surfaced online. Della had arranged the private jet that brought Mattie home, along with a hideout to keep her away from the media. She'd shown a maturity Piper hadn't known she possessed, and it impressed her so much she couldn't help but soften her own attitude. Maybe her little sister was finally growing up.

They'd met for lunch several times since then, and Della called or texted every other day to check in. The fact that Della was still here on the West Coast instead of at her home in New York City seemed more than a little strange in hindsight.

Della loved the nightlife and the crowds, and she craved

constant attention. Things in LA were a lot more laid-back on a day-to-day basis. There were so many famous people here that it was easier to go unnoticed if you didn't stumble onto a tourist spot by accident. Della hadn't trended on Twitter or Instagram once since she'd brought Mattie back from Seychelles. Five months of silence from the media had to be driving her nuts.

So why hadn't she gone home?

The simple truth was staring Piper in the face with giant, tear-filled eyes.

Piper's planned responses all evaporated, and she let her heart speak. "I'm not mad at you. Not anymore, anyway."

"Really?" Della looked like she didn't believe her.

Piper sat down and took Della's hands in hers. "Look. You'll always be my baby sister. I love you, and I forgive you."

At the look of doubt on Della's face, she shrugged in acknowledgment. "Oh, I admit I was furious at the time. I was hurt that you didn't trust me enough to even talk to me about it first. I thought we told each other everything. So finding out that you could talk to Renic, and not me." Piper swallowed the lump in her throat. "That kind of thing takes a long time to heal. But I'm over it now. I've moved on. You should too. Okay?"

Della sniffed and squeezed Piper's hands. "I'm really, *really* sorry. You're right. I should have had the guts to talk about it with you. It won't ever happen again. From now on, we share everything, even the painful bits. I swear."

Piper swiped away a rogue tear and held out her pinkie. "Pinkie swear?"

Della wrapped her pinkie around Piper's, and they shook. "Pinkie swear."

"Good." Piper's heart felt lighter than it had in a long time. She held her arms out for a hug.

Della dove into her, and they squeezed each other. "I've missed this so much."

"Me too, DellBell. Me too."

"I can't wait for the next tour. It'll be just like old times."

Piper froze. "What did you say?"

Della pulled back so that she could look Piper in the face. Her smile was so bright it would light up the Vegas Strip. "I can't wait to be back on stage with you and Mattie. She's working on new songs for us, and Renic says he can put together an epic world reunion tour."

Piper jerked her head back in disbelief. Della's vision for the future...*her* future...might as well have been a slap to her face.

Dammit, she'd been expecting this question, but not like this. Not after Della had softened her up by saying sorry.

The apology had been heartfelt and sincere, and not a damn thing had changed. Della still wanted what she wanted, and she'd only apologized as a means to an end.

"You're unbelievable." Piper pushed away from her.

"What?" Della's smile faltered. "Worried about a tour? We won't do it until your project is done. I know how important that movie is to you."

"I'm not worried about a damn world tour." Piper's building irritation festered as her sister scrambled to backtrack. "Guess why that is."

"I just thought...I mean, you said...I..." Della shook her hands out. "Come on. I said I was sorry. I *am* sorry."

"You have to actually ask the question, Della. You can't just assume you know the answer." Piper picked up Della's abandoned coffee cup and tossed the contents into the sink with a little more force than necessary. Liquid splashed all over the side of the sink and onto her shirt. She swore and lunged for a paper towel.

"I asked." Della sounded defensive. "You said we should move on."

"No. You didn't ask anything." Piper dabbed at her shirt, but the stain had already soaked into her white shirt. "You apologized for ripping our family apart, and I said I forgive you. I thought for a minute there that's actually what you came here to do, but I should have known better."

"That *is* why I came here. I came to tell you I'm sorry, and I meant it, dammit." Della's voice got louder and higher, just like it used to do when they'd squabbled over a toy as kids.

"I know you meant it." Piper's voice rose to match.

"Then why are you so mad at me?"

"I thought you'd finally figured things out. But you haven't figured out a damn thing." Piper thrust the dirty paper towel into the trash. She sucked in a calming breath and deliberately lowered her tone. "I have to go."

"Wait." Della held out a hand to stop her. "You said you'd let me finish."

"Finish what, Della?"

"You said I have to ask then you don't let me." Della glared at her. "I want all of us together again. No more solo. Mattie already said yes. Lizzie thinks it will work. But you're right. I haven't asked you. So now I'm asking straight out. Will you come back with us? Will you be part of The Bellamy Sisters?"

There it was.

The question Piper had planned on hearing for almost six months was finally out in the open.

Funny, it didn't feel anything like she thought it would. She'd expected a dozen different scenarios. In some of them, she'd actually been tempted to say yes.

She missed performing with her sisters. Sometimes, when she was on stage at the small VIP concerts she held for her fans, she missed her sisters so much she ached with longing. If Della had asked her then, she might have said yes.

But now she realized with absolute clarity what her answer had to be. "No."

Della's mouth dropped open. "No?"

Piper shook her head. "No."

"But...why?"

"Think about it. I'm sure the answer will slap you upside the head eventually." Piper stared down at her coffee-stained shirt, then stalked out of the kitchen toward her bedroom.

Della chased after her, hot on her heels. "You said you missed us. You haven't even put out an album since. I thought—"

Piper threw open the door to her closet and stormed inside. "How did you see this playing out? When you pictured us all together again on that reunion tour, who did you see singing the lead on the new songs?"

Della stilled. The look of astonished confusion on her face would have been funny if the whole thing wasn't so irritating. It hadn't even occurred to her sister that anyone other than her would *ever* be center stage.

"That's what I thought." Piper tugged off her ruined shirt and snatched a replacement off a hanger.

"I don't get what you're saying," Della said.

She backed out of the way as Piper pushed past her out of the bedroom.

"You aren't capable of sharing the spotlight."

"Yes, I am," Della protested. "I share it all the time. I have a whole orchestra on stage with me, plus the backup singers and the dancers. It's not like I'm ever alone out there."

"Backup is the key word here, Della. You don't share. Never have, never will. It's who you are. I thought maybe you would change. You know, grow up. Mature. But I was wrong."

Piper grabbed her bag from the side table near the door but didn't see her keys.

"Oh yeah, you're being real mature right now. You can't even look me in the eye and give me a real reason why you won't say yes."

Piper turned to stare Della down. "I can't—won't—share a stage with you because I'm done coming in second. I want more than that, and you aren't capable of giving it. If we got back together, you'd be front and center while Mattie and I would sit in the backseat like we're part of the crew, and it would just cause more resentment and more fights. I won't do that to Mattie, or us."

She spotted her keys on the floor and swept them up in one fist.

"It wouldn't be like that," Della said. "We wouldn't fight."

"Yes, we would." Piper shook her head. "You never saw how hard it was because all that time on stage you never once looked back."

"I did too. I *had* to check positioning, and I always sang the chorus with you on your mic. Especially that last tour."

"Yeah, I rushed up to wherever you'd decided to stand so we could sing ten words together and then you twirled off in another direction and left me standing there. That's not shar-ing. That's using me as a mic stand."

"That's not fair." Della's shoulders fell. "It was just a show. I didn't mean to make you feel...I didn't do it on purpose."

"I know." Piper put a hand on Della's shoulder. "Since you were four years old, we all made you the belle of the ball. You don't know any different. I get that. Hell, I was a huge part of making that possible. You're the baby of the family, and after Mom died, we all made you the center of attention because we didn't want you to miss out. But you don't need us for that anymore. You have a thriving solo career, and you get to have that limelight all to yourself."

"Dammit, I don't want it by myself. I want my sisters with me. I want *you* with me. Come on, Piper. Let's get back together. Please?"

Piper's will almost buckled at the look of pleading in her sister's tear-filled eyes.

Almost.

She squeezed Della's shoulder and then let go. "Look, I meant what I said. The past is the past. I'm your sister and your friend, and that's enough."

"Enough?"

Piper gave her little sister a half hug. "Love you, but the answer is no."

"Piper—"

She cut off whatever Della had been going to say.

"See you later. Stay as long as you want. I'll have Romi lock up after you leave."

Piper rushed out the door and shut it before Della could say anything else. The last thing she saw was Della's stunned face.

When she pulled onto the freeway, she glanced at the time. Ten forty-five. She was supposed to be there at eleven.

She swore at the clock, the traffic, and herself, and sped up.

"WOULD you stop hassling me and just play?" Blake Ryan, child star turned teen heartthrob turned Hollywood's Hottest Leading Man, according to the magazines, bounced the basketball once, then passed it to his best friend, Marshall, with a little more force than he intended.

"Ouch. I strike a nerve?" Marshall spun the ball in his hand, then threw it back to Blake.

Marshall's blond hair was already matted to his forehead, and sweat poured down the side of his angular face. Marshall had been number three on the Hottest Men list the year Blake hit number one. "All I said was it seems like you're avoiding something. Or some*one*. Maybe both."

"I'm not avoiding anything." Blake dribbled the ball and edged to the right. "I'm getting mentally prepared for an important project with a little court time."

"Give me a break." Marshall shifted to the right to keep himself between Blake and the basket. "We wouldn't be out here in hell's furnace if you weren't bent out of shape about something. I mean, your backyard is great, don't get me wrong, but I'd rather be in the pool, not sweating on the court just as the sun starts to boil. So what're we doing here? Don't you have somewhere to be?"

Blake grimaced. He was trying not to think about it, which was exactly why he'd called Marshall over for a little one on one.

Damn the man for knowing him so well.

Time to change the subject. "How'd it go with Kellie last night?"

He lunged to the left, but Marshall was too quick and blocked him before he could edge closer to the basket.

"Nice try, man," Marshall teased. "I'm not that easy. You can't fake me."

Marshall whipped his hand around to steal the ball.

Blake blocked with his shoulder, twisted around to the right, and took the shot. The ball swished through the net, then bounced off the court and rolled to a stop near the twelve-foot-high stone fence.

"You're absolutely that easy." Blake ran after it.

Marshall bent over with his hands on his knees to catch his

breath while he waited. "Yeah, I really am. Still, last night was a bust. She had to go to the hospital."

Blake grabbed the ball and carried it back to the court. "You get her tangled in that sex swing again?"

"It's not a sex swing, you pervert, it's a hammock, and no. Her sister went into labor. She wanted me to go to the hospital with her to see the baby." His friend shuddered.

"How'd you wriggle out of that?" Blake asked.

They switched places so Marshall could be on offense.

"Told her I had to finish edits on the screenplay so you could have them this morning." Marshall winked. "For the meeting."

"That meeting was two weeks ago. I know because that's when I signed my life away." Blake tossed the ball to Marshall. "What edits?"

"Stop being such a drama queen. It takes a lot less time to do voice work than it does a location shoot. You don't even have to leave town. Easy peasy." Marshall dribbled and faked right, then left, looking for a hole. "I reworked the bar scene. The dialogue needed more snap."

Blake kept pace with him, arms outstretched to block. "You gotta give that scene a rest, man. If you keep harping on the bromance it'll turn our cool caper into a sappy rom-com or something. Besides, the fake-out scene that happens before the con needs the most work."

"Minor detail," Marshall said. "The con is brilliant. That's what everybody will remember."

Marshall dashed right, spun around, and shot. The ball brushed Blakes's fingertips and veered off past the net to bounce down his driveway.

"Shit," Marshall muttered.

They both took off after it because if someone didn't stop the ball, it would roll all the way down to the gate. His house was on a hill, and the run would be more of a workout than either of them wanted right now, especially in this heat.

A few feet down the drive, Marshall stopped running, leaving Blake to retrieve the ball on his own. By the time he managed to get the ball and jog back, Marshall had sprawled on one of the lounge chairs by the pool.

"You realize if you quit now you can't win the fifty bucks I promised," Blake told him. "You have to actually play to win."

"I didn't have a shot anyway. You're already up fifteen points." Marshall squinted at him. "Besides, don't you have to get going? The read-through is in, what, thirty minutes?"

Blake pulled a couple of bottles of water out of the mini-fridge in the outdoor kitchen and checked the time. "Two hours. Man, I'm not looking forward to this. The script doesn't feel tight. I bet you anything they aren't finished."

His friend gave him a suspicious look and took the offered bottle. "You get to be a cartoon. What's not to like?"

For one thing, he'd never done voice work before and wasn't exactly sure how hard it would be to slip into the role when he wasn't acting it out, and for another, the idea of having to record a song was intimidating, but he wasn't about to admit that to Marshall. The teasing would be relentless.

He gave a nothing-to-see-here shrug. "It's in the way. I have better things to do."

Marshall narrowed his eyes. "No, you don't. You literally got nothing better to do, because if you don't finish playing the prince in *Scorched*, we don't get to start *Conned*, and we've given blood, sweat, and most of our twenties to get that project off the ground."

"I know." Blake stared at the pool that took up a large part of his backyard.

The pool was a gift from his mother for his twenty-first birthday. She'd duplicated the one in his tenth movie, *Jake's*

Day Off, down to the hot tub and simulated lagoon waterfall. He'd hosted one hell of a premiere party around that pool.

He and Marshall had come up with the idea for *Conned* that night. They'd known they had a hit on their hands before they'd even written it.

But that was almost a decade ago, and the movie still hadn't been made. They'd both put a good portion of their own money on the line, but it hadn't been enough. They needed a backer if the script were ever going to see the light of day.

So when the studio offered him a deal, it had felt like serendipity and winning the lottery all rolled into one. Their first, second, and third leading man choices for a new animated feature had all flamed out for various reasons, and now they were two weeks from kickoff with nobody even close to being on the hook to play Prince Jesse.

It was a simple deal. If he did the voice work, they'd provide the rest of the funding—twenty-five million dollars—and studio backing for *Conned*. That meant the marketing might of one of Hollywood's biggest studios would be behind his directorial debut. It had been an easy yes, even if it did feel like a waste of time to play with cartoons.

"It's just annoying. *Scorched* feels cheesy to me. Kind of like how ours was when we started. I just don't think it's finished yet, which isn't a good sign."

"Hey, ours ain't cheesy, it's a future classic." Marshall peered at Blake over his sunglasses. "We're going to make something modern and fun. It'll be a thriller caper with a feel-good ending and franchise potential, and we need that deal you signed to do it. We won't get the funding if you don't play your part. You're not thinking of backing out, are you?"

He wanted to say yes.

He wanted to race right past this stupid animated movie and get on with what he increasingly felt was his life's calling.

"I didn't spend my entire childhood on movie sets to be a cartoon. I want to tell a really great story, not ham it up in a studio. I don't have time to deal with a bunch of people who don't know the first thing about the business."

"I thought you said they got Gina Paige to voice the dragon?" Marshall asked. "She's won like, what, five Tonys? Can't say she's inexperienced."

"Not her. Princess Jewel. Piper Bellamy."

Marshall snorted. "Can't say she's inexperienced either. That girl can *sing*. She can carry your lame ass through all the songs. Can't believe you get to meet her and I don't."

That stung, mostly because he'd been thinking the exact same thing himself ever since he'd been coerced into taking on the role in order to secure the funding for their own movie. "I can sing."

He meant to sound confident, but it came out defensive. He *could* sing, but it wasn't something he'd ever trained for or practiced, a fact he was now regretting. His mother always wanted him to take singing lessons, but he'd thought they would be a waste of time. He could sing well enough to kill it at karaoke, but he was an actor and soon-to-be-director, not a singer.

"Oh sure, you have some raw natural talent but you're nothing compared to *her*. She'll run circles around you."

Blake flipped him off.

"Aww," Marshall drawled in a baby voice, "is it going to be difficult for you, Mr. I Won an Oscar When I Was Ten Years Old? Are we feeling intimidated because we're finally going to be the amateur in the room?"

"Shut up."

Marshall, who could always tell when he got to Blake, grinned. "Gee, is someone feeling a little sensitive? Come on, it'll do you good to have to face something you're not already an expert at. You'll get to feel what the rest of us feel every time you walk on set for a change."

"I'm not worried about the singing, okay? It's not a big deal."

"Well, I know you're not worried about the acting, so if it's really not the singing, and it's not the acting, then what...oh. *Oh!*" Marshall's grin widened. "I got it. It's not a what, it's a *who*. It's a full table read, right? That means Rachel the Leech will be there today."

Blake closed his eyes and shuddered. "Don't remind me."

Marshall hooted a laugh. "Blake and Rachel, together again. Come on, it's animated. It's not like you have to show up at the same time as her in the studio."

"Yeah, but first I have to get through today." Every time he thought of Rachel Morris, his pulse raced, and not in a good way. More like in a buried-alive sort of way. "I can't believe they cast her. Seriously, what are the odds?"

"Come on, man, she wasn't that bad." The broad grin on Marshall's face said he knew exactly how bad it really was, and he was delighted about it.

Blake stared at him. "You do remember the day she sent five hundred and thirty-two text messages because I went to a screening with my mother instead of that wrap party, right? And the way she wormed her way into that dance scene? Oh, and the time she reamed whats-her-name"—he snapped his fingers twice, wracking his brain for the name—"Winslow... remember, the short redhead? Rachel cornered her in the makeup trailer and ripped into her about flirting with me. She couldn't even say her lines after that. It delayed the shoot three whole days."

Marshall held up his hands in mock surrender. "Okay, sure, Rachel's a little high maintenance and a bit psycho, but she's definitely doable. I get why they picked her. She has a great voice, and she's a pretty good actress, too. So what if she was a little clingy. It's been years, I'm sure she's over you by now."

"She makes me claustrophobic." He'd been seventeen when Rachel Morris had planted a kiss on him. She was two years older and a lot more mature, and at first, he'd been *very* interested in her.

She had fascinating lips that had mesmerized and enticed from across the room. He'd fantasized about those lips for weeks until he'd finally experienced them firsthand.

After the kiss, she'd attached herself to him like superglue, and he'd realized that some things were much better when experienced from a distance—and that his mother had been right. Work relationships could be a bad, bad, *bad* thing.

"You know, she would probably work for the girlfriend in *Conned*. Want to ask her while you're there today?" Marshall's eyes flashed with barely contained amusement.

"You can be a real ass sometimes, you know that?"

"I do. It's a God-given gift." His friend's shit-eating grin was proud and unashamed.

"If you were really a good friend you wouldn't sound quite so gleeful."

"I'm not just a good friend, I'm your *best* friend." Marshall bared his teeth. "I have to put up with all your shit and help you hide the bodies, and in exchange, I get to enjoy your suffering. It's in the contract."

"I don't remember signing anything."

"It's verbal and completely binding." Marshall stood and pulled off his shirt. "Forget about Rachel. You get to record in your own clothes in an air-conditioned studio next to a Bellamy Babe. What's so bad about that?"

"Your fixation on the AC is not helping."

"I had a total crush on her in high school, remember? She was smokin' hot. That dark hair and those eyes...damn. I'm a sucker deep brown puppy dog eyes." Marshall tossed his shirt on the lounge chair, then sat down to pry off his shoes and socks.

"It's an animated movie, it doesn't matter what she looks like." Blake drained the rest of the water in his bottle and tossed it into the trash. "The point is she's never done anything like this before. We'll spend more time teaching her how to act than actually recording. It'll slow the whole project down, which means ours will be stuck in development hell."

Marshall snapped his fingers. "Hey. You can introduce me to her. Take me with you to the reading."

"Hell no."

"Come on." Marshall kicked his shoes out of the way.

"It's a closed set. Besides, the last thing we need is you trying to charm the room. You'll disrupt everything and then we won't get the reading done."

"Me, disruptive?" Marshall put a hand on his chest and blinked with wide-eyed, complete bullshit innocence. "Never."

"Be serious, man. The faster this movie gets done, the faster we get the green light on *Conned*." Blake drained the bottle of water and stood up. "Enjoy your swim. I have to get cleaned up."

"Yeah, well, be sure to practice your songs in there," Marshall called out.

"You know it creeps me out that you still listen to me singing in the shower," Blake shouted over his shoulder.

* * *

HE LIVED ONLY ten miles from Day Dreams Studios headquarters, a sprawling campus in Glendale where the core animation work was done, which meant it took him almost an hour to get there in the cursed LA traffic.

The read-through was being held in Building Two, which contained several large studio spaces for recording motion, voice-overs, and action sequences, along with three theaters and several floors filled with offices and editing suites.

Five ivy-covered buildings surrounded a central courtyard that featured a large three-tiered fountain, a basketball court, park benches, and lush, carefully tended gardens. Artists had crafted tributes to all the legendary Day Dreams animated characters out of the greenery to greet visitors, and small sculptures waited among the vegetation to surprise and delight.

It felt like walking into a theme park, without the tourists.

Once he was past security inside Building Two, he followed the signs to a large studio space with black walls and a black ceiling with tracks running across it in a grid pattern. The floor in the center of the room was painted black, and along the edges ran with the type of exit indicator lights used on airplanes.

Tables formed a square big enough to serve dinner at Hogwarts on the black portion of the floor with chairs that indicated at least ten people per side. Each place featured a name tag, a copy of the script, a box of pens, bottles of water, and a bowl of M&Ms.

More chairs formed a gallery of sorts along the walls.

They'd gone out of their way to make this a special occasion, he noticed. There was an ice sculpture of a dragon at one end of the table and another of a compass at the other. In between was enough food to keep an army full for a month.

Several tables huddled along one side held computers he thought were probably used for animation. He pictured what they might do in a space this large and realized this must be where they did their live-motion capture.

"Blake!" Paul Lester, the producer, rushed toward him beaming a smile that could power a fleet of electric cars.

He was a gray-haired man with enormous sideburns who wore an untucked turquoise shirt with neon-pink flamingos all over it.

He grabbed Blake's outstretched hand in both of his. "I'm so glad you're here! When they told me you said yes I about fell off my chair. I'm a huge, huge fan. It's great, you coming on board like this at the last minute. Thought we never were going to break ground, especially after Charlie bailed like he did. Thought the whole deal was cursed."

Paul pumped Blake's hand up and down with enthusiasm. "Can't wait to see what you do with our rogue prince. Diane's worried you'll try to play it too cool, but I told her no way. You'll do right by her baby."

Paul paused, hands still clutching Blake's, momentarily distracted by something in the distance.

Blake pulled his hand back before Paul could start up again. "Diane's the writer?"

Paul waved at someone in the distance. "Good morning! Be sure to check the table. I made sure there was plain yogurt just for you." He turned back to Blake and leaned in to whisper, "Not sure why she wanted that because she just loads it with fruit. Why not buy the kind that has it already in there, I say. Anyway, where were we? Oh yes. Diane. She's an amazing writer. Fantastic. Fresh. A go-getter. The story has spirit, you know? She's captured a real swashbuckling fearlessness. Reminds me of when I was a kid watching *The Princess Bride*, except not quite so campy. More modern, with a kick-ass couple to really add punch. Not that *The Princess Bride* didn't have that. But this has more edge, you know? Can't believe this is her first production. Wait until you meet her. She's going to *adore* you and Piper. Where's Piper? What time is it?" Paul checked his watch. "Dammit, I swore we'd start this on time. We're already fifteen minutes late."

Paul hurried off, gesturing to the now quite substantial group clustered around the catering table. "Gather 'round, friends. It's time to officially kick this baby through the gate, so to speak."

Blake watched him go, stunned. It was like being run over by an information freight train.

There was a shuffle to determine who was supposed to sit where, then negotiations on who *wanted* to sit in their assigned space, followed by deals for seat switching and general discussions of the latest projects. Nobody actually sat down.

Blake stood behind his assigned seat. The director, Tamar Shurer, a legend who'd worked with his mother back in the day, was supposed to sit to his left, with Piper Bellamy in between them, but so far, he hadn't seen either woman.

He spotted Rachel Morris headed in his direction with grace and determination and suppressed the urge to run. The last time he'd been this close to her, she'd worn tattered jeans and flip-flops, and her hair had been chestnut brown. Now, she was a platinum blonde in a designer dress that fit so tight she probably couldn't breathe and sky-high heels.

She had the same imperious tilt to her chin that she'd had at nineteen, and her lips were still enticing, only now he knew exactly what those lips promised. A gorgeous but oppressive prison of affection with no chance of parole.

There was a reason he'd changed his phone number when that project, and their relationship, wrapped.

He gripped the back of his chair and wished like hell the read-through would get started in the next two seconds.

"Hi, handsome. Long time no text." Rachel held her arms out wide, obviously expecting a hug.

"Hey, Rachel." Blake gave her the Hollywood hug, which basically let him keep her at arm's length and relegated her to air kisses instead of the real thing.

"You're not still worried about me texting you, are you?" Rachel winked. "I promise it was just a phase. You don't have to hide."

His smile was plastered on so tight it started to ache. "Nah, texts are yesterday's news. I'm sure you've moved on to the next big thing."

She blinked, then giggled. "Can't tell you how excited I was when I heard you would be lead. It's a perfect choice. Just wish I could sing that duet with you. Then again, I don't see Piper Bellamy anywhere. If she doesn't show, I'll fill in for her during the read, so maybe we'll get to sing together after all."

He hoped like hell that Piper Bellamy showed up soon and that she had a backbone of steel. Rachel would sweep in and take over if she didn't, which was the last thing he wanted. Rachel had a way of slowing production to a standstill while simultaneously making sure nobody was able to relax. If she wasn't so damn talented, she'd never be hired for anything because she was so difficult to work with.

"Good morning, everyone," a gravelly smoker's voice shouted behind him.

Tamar Shurer, infamous for being a taskmaster with a heart of steel and a will of stone, clanged a bell back and forth with vigor. "Get to your seats, please."

She was a small woman, barely over five feet, and thin enough that a strong wind would probably blow her away. But her ability to project her voice made up for that. Her hair looked like she'd been swimming in the ocean and hadn't bothered to brush it after.

He knew from past experience and stories his mother told him that Tamar was like the tide, able to grind a boulder down to a pebble and then make a sandcastle out of it. She did more than craft a story; she created an experience.

She put her hand on Blake's shoulder to steady herself

while she climbed onto a chair. "Good morning, everyone, and welcome to *Scorched*! Please take your seats. Now, please. We have a lot to sort out and we're already a year behind. Sit, sit, sit."

Rachel patted Blake's back and winked at him. "We'll continue our little chat later."

Some moved to their seats at the table, while a whole group dressed in workout clothes filed in from the hallway to take the chairs along the walls.

Tamar stepped from the chair onto the table, then released his shoulder. "Thank you for the assist, Mr. Ryan. You can take a seat."

"My pleasure." He sat and looked around the room. At some point, it had filled with people, most of whom he didn't recognize. He'd never seen so many at a simple table read before. He hadn't realized there were that many speaking roles.

Tamar cleared her throat. "Okay, quiet, please. Quiet. Yes, even you, Paul."

It took a few seconds for the message to travel through the room and for people to give her their attention. She waited with the air of someone who knew she would be obeyed.

Once quiet settled, she smiled. "Thank you. As you can see, we're a little crowded this morning so keep the chatter to a minimum. I want to make a few personal remarks and then we'll get to it. For those who haven't figured it out or who are trying to forget, I am Tamar Shurer, and I am your director."

The audience applauded, and a few whistles permeated the air.

Tamar waved the applause away. "Let's see if you still like me at the wrap party, shall we?"

A smattering of giggles filled the room.

Tamar pointed to a woman on the far side of the room. "The lovely lady with the notebooks is the woman who wrote this magnificent tale. When Diane showed me this script five years ago, I knew it was something special and I jumped at the chance to be a part of it. Unfortunately, we hit several speed bumps along the way. Timing was bad, economy was bad, the cast was bad...no, I'm kidding on that part. Mostly."

The audience groaned, and chatter broke out here and there as stories were exchanged.

Blake knew they'd had trouble casting his role, but he wondered what else they'd had issues with. He glanced at the empty chair next to him. Why wasn't Piper Bellamy here? Missing the table read would leave a bad taste in everyone's mouth. He wasn't the only one who'd noticed her absence, either. He saw several people keep checking it as if she would magically appear.

"Finally, we are here," Tamar said. "We have the best people, the *right* people, and we will tell a great story. Enough with the pep talk. Now for the bad news. It's August, and the promos have already gone out for a Christmas release. That leaves us three months and change to get the voices and final animation in place."

Groans traveled around the room as that news sank in.

"I thought it was launching next summer," a high-pitched voice asked from somewhere to the left.

"I heard *next* Christmas," a man on the right said.

Tamar shook her head. "No. This project is already over budget, and next year's release is already scheduled. It goes now, or not at all. Much work has already been done, so it's not impossible. I wouldn't be here if it was. Paul will be pushing the schedule so be sure to check in with him before you go anywhere."

"Better yet, don't go anywhere," Paul said. "There's cots in the storeroom if you want to move in. It's only the next three months of your life. No big deal."

Nervous laughter skittered around the room. Most probably thought he was kidding, but Blake had heard the rumors about Paul's work ethic. He was ruthless when it came to deadlines and an absolute perfectionist when it came to the final product.

"Right. So let's get to it." Tamar clapped her hands together once to get attention. "To make sure we have a firm foundation, we will go around the table. Introduce yourself, your character, and read the paragraph on page one."

Tamar eyed her chair dubiously. Apparently, it was easier to get up on the table than to get back down.

Blake stood and held out a hand to help her. "Madam Director, allow me."

"Thank you." Tamar took his hand. "And this, ladies and gentlemen, is why Blake Ryan is our prince."

"Piper!" Paul exclaimed.

Everyone turned to see Piper Bellamy standing just inside the doorway. She didn't look anything like what he'd expected. She was tiny to start with, barely taller than Tamar. He had vague memories of her in concert videos and social media. On stage, she'd seemed taller, somehow. She was drama and edge, with studs on her clothes and attitude. She brought the rock to her sisters' pop, but he was more of a Rat Pack blues fan, so that was all he really knew about her.

Today, she looked like a woman running late for a yoga session, with her hair up in a simple ponytail and downplayed makeup. For the first time, he could see what Marshall found so attractive about her. She was effortlessly cool and surprisingly feminine in basic black.

He'd always had a weakness for girl-next-door types, probably because they were so hard to find in Los Angeles, but it didn't change the fact that waltzing through the door over thirty minutes late was completely unprofessional.

There were a lot of divas in Hollywood who thought it was okay to waste people's time. He'd never liked those people much, no matter how great they looked in yoga pants.

"My dear girl, I hope everything is all right." Tamar hurried to Piper with her arms outstretched. "Was there an accident? I knew something must be wrong, you're never late."

Chatter broke out around the room as everyone lost interest in the drama of a late arrival and went back to entertaining themselves.

Piper's cheeks were red, and she was breathing a little fast, like she'd been running. "Nothing's wrong. I'm so sorry I'm late, Tamar. I had a little family drama this morning but everything's fine."

Paul followed Tamar, his shirt flapping in the breeze in his rush to get to their late-arriving star. "We're just getting started. Do you need anything?"

Someone let out a long, drawn-out sigh. Blake would bet anything it was Rachel. Like him, she usually showed up early and had even less tolerance than he did for those she thought unprofessional.

"No, thanks," Piper said in a firm tone. "I'm interrupting. Please, continue."

Tamar gestured for Piper to sit and addressed the room. "As I was saying, it's time for introductions. Piper, you're up first."

Piper dropped her bag next to the chair and sat down.

Blake stifled his irritation. She might be late but she was here now and it was time to get things moving. He leaned toward his new costar and whispered, "Name, character, and read the paragraph on page one."

"Right. Thanks." Piper nodded and flipped the script in front of her to the first page. "I'm Piper Bellamy, also known as Princess Jewel of Tiranell. My family has a magic map that leads to a stone rumored to provide protection to whoever owns it. The evil sorcerer Malignon has kidnapped my sister, Elaine, to force me into using the map to find the stone, which I will exchange for my sister's life. I'll do anything to save my sister. I'm loyal and fiercely determined, but my map is difficult to read, and I have no idea how to defeat the dragon who guards the stone."

She turned to Blake. "And you are?"

He smiled at her, then addressed the room. "I'm Blake Ryan, but feel free to call me Jesse. My kingdom of Carenth has suffered from attacks by strange flying beasts who have been eating all of our crops and killing our animals. I'm also on a quest to locate the protection stone. I have no idea where the dragon hides, or what I'll have to do to get the stone, but I do have a handy talking compass that always points true to help me out."

His paragraph ended there, but he felt like it wasn't finished so he ad-libbed a little bit. "I'll do whatever it takes to save my family and my kingdom, and I can't wait to slay the evil beast."

"Hey, if anything, it'll be me doing the slaying, you insignificant royal worm of a man," Gina Paige, the woman cast to play the dragon, said in her thick British accent.

She sat opposite him and looked like a queen on her throne as she surveyed the room.

Everyone laughed.

The introductions moved from him to Jeremy Graham, the evil sorcerer, to Rachel Morris, the kidnapped sister, Elaine, and on around the room.

It took over an hour, after which they launched right into the actual read.

The first few minutes of the movie focused on setting up the relationship between the sisters. Rachel, who'd been doing table reads since she was a teenager, threw herself into her character so well that it might have been the actual voice-over.

Piper sounded like she was reciting a dissertation out loud. There was no personality behind her words, no warmth or heart.

Didn't she know that she was supposed to be getting a feel for the character?

She glanced at him as if sensing his scrutiny. He realized he was frowning at her and looked away. If this was her idea of a performance, they were in serious trouble. She had no feel for the character, no acting skill at all.

There was no way this movie was going to be finished on time.

He slumped into his chair and stared at the script without really seeing it. This had to be the most painful table read he'd ever experienced, and that included the one when he was eight years old and had been forced to listen to adults debate the many different ways to say the word endless.

When Piper reached the last line before the break where a song would be inserted, the atmosphere around him changed. Her voice shifted to something suddenly real.

"Elaine." Piper drew out the name as she stood up. She shoved her chair out of the way like the frustrated young woman she was supposed to be playing, completely in character. "I don't *want* to stay here forever. I want to see the world!"

Blake jerked his head up, startled.

All the longing for adventure was in Piper's voice and on her face as she reached out to her sister. Suddenly, he could feel the castle walls closing in around them, and he saw Princess Jewel, trapped by a society that demanded she fill a role she wasn't ready for while denying her everything she truly wanted.

The group sitting along the wall quickly moved into positions around the room, their faces bright with anticipation.

Music started up from speakers in the corners.

Piper sang, "I want adventure and danger and daring. I want heroes and monsters galore. I want to *live* before I reach twenty. It's not fair that I'm trapped behind these doors!"

Piper's voice was filled with all the emotion she'd left out of her spoken dialogue. When she sang, she became that frustrated young woman she was supposed to be.

Blake watched her, stunned, as she danced toward Rachel, took her hands, then whirled away toward a group of background singers. Their voices filled the room as they tried to convince Princess Jewel that duty and family were more important than adventure and excitement.

"Excellent!" Tamar hummed under her breath and tapped her foot.

To Blake's surprise, it was.

They'd obviously rehearsed this many times. It was pitch-perfect and full of energy, and he couldn't help but clap along to the beat.

Rachel rushed around the room to intercept Piper. "They can't make us stay, they can't turn us away. Together we'll take on the world!"

Her voice soared through the room. There was a reason Rachel's career had started on Broadway. She didn't need microphones to make herself heard, which was why she usually sang solo. Other voices disappeared when Rachel Morris belted out a song.

Piper and Rachel launched into the chorus, but instead of disappearing, Piper's voice rose into a harmony that wrapped around Rachel's contralto and merged until the two formed one uplifted sound that brought the room to their feet.

When the song finished, everyone cheered like they were at opening night. It was a feel-good, take-on-the-world kind of song, and they'd nailed it.

If they could get her to act half as well as she could sing, maybe this movie would not only get done on time, it would be a hit.

* * *

Click here to find out what happens next for Piper and Blake in *He's The Reason Why*

Free Stuff!

Carrie Collins didn't know she was craving something sweet until Dr. Ben showed up on the menu.

Sign up for my no-spam newsletter, and get *Seasoned With Love* absolutely free! You'll also get a weekly letter from me containing exclusive content, advance notice of new books and sneak peaks, the chance to win free stuff, plus you'll get to see the inner workings of my mind. What are you waiting for?

CLICK HERE TO SIGN UP NOW!

The Bellamy Sisters

Seasoned With Love

Trouble Walked In

Places I've Never Been

He's The Reason Why

You Found Me - Coming Summer 2022

* * *

The House of Xannon

Stronger Than Magic

Finding Flame

Promise of Magic

Taking Earth

Elements of Magic

About the Author

Melinda VanLone writes romance and urban fantasy, designs book covers, and dabbles in photography. She currently lives in Florida with her husband and furbabies. When she's not playing with her imaginary friends you can find her wandering aimlessly through the streets taking photos, or hovered over coffee in Starbucks.

You can find Melinda haunting these spots on the interwebs:
www.melindavan.com
melinda.van@gmail.com

facebook.com/MelindaVanLone
twitter.com/melindavan
instagram.com/mvanlone

Made in the USA
Columbia, SC
12 July 2022

63180666R00202